...rs are saying about
...ngs of the Asylum...

'Captivating, unsettling, atmospheric, and unnerving,
this story of one woman's fight to forge her own path and
escape the binds of society in life is not to be missed!'

'I was completely engrossed in the action, reading
the book in mainly just one sitting – once started,
I could not put it down. It is a compelling read but
not one to be read alone in an old house!'

'This story became so much more than I expected...
The author takes us deep inside Violet's psyche
and I felt like I was right there alongside her'

'Fast pacing, sharp prose, mysteries of the mind between reality
and deceit – I was as mesmerized as horrified by the story!'

'Love it! Amazing read! Amazing storytelling! Amazing story!'

'Noel O'Reilly can spin such a gripping and
fascinating narrative. I was there, in the story, at all
times!... Oh and then that ending... it took me by
surprise and what a gorgeous surprise that was!'

'A dark, chilling and gothic novel. Perfect for fans of historical
fiction and asylum settings. I definitely recommend it'

Noel O'Reilly was a student on the New Writing South Advanced writing course. He has worked as a journalist and editor at the international business media company RBI, and is now a freelance writer. His first novel is *Wrecker* and *The Darlings of the Asylum* is his second. He lives in Sheffield.

Also by Noel O'Reilly

Wrecker

The Darlings of the Asylum

Noel O'Reilly

ONE PLACE. MANY STORIES

HQ
An imprint of HarperCollins*Publishers* Ltd
1 London Bridge Street
London SE1 9GF

www.harpercollins.co.uk

HarperCollins*Publishers*
Macken House, 39/40 Mayor Street Upper,
Dublin 1, D01 C9W8, Ireland

This edition 2023

1
First published in Great Britain by
HQ, an imprint of HarperCollins*Publishers* Ltd 2022

ISBN: PB: 978-0-00-827530-3

This book is produced from independently certified FSC™ paper
to ensure responsible forest management.

For more information visit: www.harpercollins.co.uk/green

This book is set in 11.2/15.5 pt. Bembo by Type-it AS, Norway

Printed and Bound in the UK using 100% Renewable Electricity at
CPI Group (UK) Ltd, Croydon, CR0 4YY

To Georgia

'My devil had long been caged, he came out roaring.'
—STRANGE CASE OF DR JEKYLL AND MR HYDE
by Robert Louis Stevenson

'Of all the theories current concerning women, none is more curious
than the theory that it is needful to make a theory about them.'
—'The Final Cause of Woman' by Frances Power Cobbe,
in WOMAN'S WORK AND WOMAN'S CULTURE:
A SERIES OF ESSAYS, edited by Josephine E. Butler

PROLOGUE

We file down a broad staircase, most of us in the uniform dress of vertical stripes. Our skirts rustle, our boots thunder on bare wood. Some are mumbling, others mute. Morbidity hangs about us like a cloud. The attendants descend alongside us in their white nurses' dresses and caps, some helping women too infirm or demented to make their way down alone. Others keep a watchful eye on the disorderly. The staircase turns back on itself, and I glance over the rail down into the murky hall far below, a floor of square black and white tiles like a chessboard. The sheer drop makes me light-headed, so I grip the sinuous wooden handrail more firmly.

We shuffle down to the next landing, trail past the wooden dado carved in an ornate antique pattern, endlessly repeated, hypnotic. The panels are scuffed, the varnish faded, the wood splintered and crudely repaired. But it was grand once, this building. Listen carefully and you will hear faint echoes of laughter, high-spirited banter, ghosts of long-forgotten balls.

A sudden violent flurry, a rhythmic snapping inside my skull, then something bursts out of my ear. It's outside me now, a fluttering sound, high above. I look up and see a frantic blur circling under the ceiling. It soars into the round atrium with its broken panes, the glass so grimy that only the dimmest light seeps through. The other women have seen

I

it now, and they too are gazing upwards, crying out. The bird swoops down into the stairwell and entangles itself in the hair of an old lady, then tears itself free. Shrill voices bounce off the hard walls of the stairwell, deafening. Attendants cry for order. This way and that the bird flies. The line of women is disordered; we huddle, we clutch one another, here on the landing and there on the stairs below, ducking and cowering and holding our heads in our hands. One devil laughs hysterically.

I see the bird, just as it flies headlong into the wall, hitting it with a soft thump, then flopping to the floor. It is a blackbird, a female with drab brown plumage. The bird nuzzles the wall with her head as if hoping to bore her way to safety. One wing pumps vigorously. The other scrapes back and forth feebly. There is blood on the yellow beak. Feathers float in the air, like soiled snow. The women step back in horror from the wounded creature, raising a din with their cries.

'Order, get back in line, come along now, ladies.' Gradually, we are subdued and coaxed into an orderly queue. Then we continue our descent. The clomping of our boots fills the stairwell once more. I look back only once. The blackbird is still feebly pushing her wings back and forth, a drowning swimmer at the end of her strength.

BRIGHTON, 1886

1

Perhaps it all began when Felix Skipp-Borlase appeared unannounced at the archery meeting. An April shower had sent the lady contestants running for shelter under the colonnade of the old pumphouse. Conversation soon turned to which couples had been seen walking out together and who'd been jilted, the marriages to be announced in the coming weeks – and the latest scandalous divorces. I found myself distracted. Sudden showers, changes in the weather, atmospheric disturbances and the like, have always jolted my senses into life. And I wanted to escape. Large gatherings of young women always made me nervous. So I slipped away and stood alone under a canopy of dripping ivy that trailed between the columns. A few feet away a cluster of white and yellow daffodils shivered and swayed in the gusts as if entranced, their heads bowed under the weight of the raindrops. My attention was often diverted by the world around me in this way. While other young women used their eyes for flirting, I would gaze about me, longing to render the scene as a painting or a sketch.

But my reverie was disturbed by Felix's familiar voice. I turned to find him escorting both his mother and mine through the gathering. It was a surprise to see him there. Normally, only a very select set took part in the archery meetings. Felix risked being cut by the stuffier types present. Some would no doubt consider his family *de trop*, and that made me feel protective towards him. He was a dear old friend of mine, after all.

Mama was projecting the full force of her charm at Felix's mother, a tall, narrow creature, stiff with self-regard, her cold gaze flitting about the gathering as Mama wittered on. Felix walked along beside them, his hand on his mother's elbow. It was a pity he had chosen to come in a Norfolk jacket, as though he were a duke's son on a shooting range. He ought to have been more at ease among the snobs at the archery contest; he was more than their equal, having achieved his place in the world through his own efforts. When he caught my eye, he bowed theatrically, attracting attention to himself. He gazed up at the heavens, holding out his hands, palms up, shaking his head at the elements for interrupting our sport. I smiled and nodded, then reached for my bow, picking it up and pretending to look it over so I wouldn't be obliged to speak to him – not just yet.

Mama had been trying to marry me off for years and she had fixed on Felix as the perfect solution. She missed no opportunity to remind me that I was approaching the grand old age of twenty-four, when I would become an official old maid. During Felix's visits to our home, she would discreetly withdraw, leaving us alone together in the drawing room, and she always encouraged us to walk out unchaperoned along the seafront.

I had known Felix since I was twelve and he fourteen. He was a boarder at Eton College along with my oldest brother Lance and our families became acquainted as both resided in Brighton. The Skipp-Borlase family lived in a grand house facing the sea and as children my three brothers and I were allowed to play with Felix on their private lawn. My family were minor landed gentry, but down at heel, whereas they were rolling in money – new money. Felix could buy almost anything that took his fancy. *Almost* anything, I stress – for he couldn't buy breeding, only attain its veneer through marriage. And there was no question of Felix marrying me. Our long friendship meant I could be at ease with him, without my affection being misconstrued. I was always fond of him, and at one time my feelings amounted to something more than fondness. I'd been dazzled by him, I suppose.

I saw him glancing at me, awaiting my approach as he spoke to our two mothers. As luck would have it, the bell sounded, the call for the ladies to return to the archery targets. As I followed the other women across the lawn, anticipation stirred in me, the excitement of competing in a sport at which one knows one might excel. My closest friend Lottie Hamilton-Rainey caught up with me. We were a perfect contrast, her fair and me dark. I sometimes feared she had befriended me to enjoy a sense of superiority, knowing her family was far better off than mine. For my part, I linked up with Lottie because she was popular with the girls from the day school. I had never been allowed to attend.

'Violet, I do believe Mr Skipp-Borlase has come expressly to see you,' she said. 'What a deep creature you are with your intrigues.'

'Nonsense. I have no intrigues.' I quickened my pace and looked away.

'Really? Then why the scarlet countenance?' Lottie glanced over her shoulder at Felix. 'He does have polish, I must say.'

'Are you trying to rattle me, so you can beat my score?' I said, as we took our places side by side in the line of archers preparing to take aim.

The man officiating called the ladies to attention. Lottie went first. She drew the string of her bow backwards in her elegant way, fully aware of the effect she was producing as she peered out from under the brim of her straw hat with its pink linen flower and single white feather. Her perfect profile and dainty retroussé nose were presented to good advantage, while her pose invited all present to admire her pinched little waist. Her first arrow landed in the blue circle and vibrated there for a moment. Then she shot her remaining five, achieving a rather low score, but nobody was concerned with the score when they were watching Lottie.

Next it was my turn. As Lottie went to retrieve her arrows, I pulled on my glove with a shaking hand. 'Cupid's arrows, by any chance?' said the lady alongside me, glancing at Felix and sniggering with her gloved hand over her mouth. This was precisely what I'd feared. I raised up my bow and arrow, my shoulders tense and stiff, and pulled the string back until I was at full stretch and the riser vibrated in my grip. I was utterly out of sorts and painfully self-conscious with so many eyes fixed on me. To make matters worse, the sleeves of my dress were still damp after the rain, and restricted my movement. As the taut string quivered, I imagined Mama scolding me later for grimacing in an unladylike way. Distracted, I let go before I was ready. It was a poor shot. My second was a little better, but well below my usual standard. I heard Felix cry 'Bravo!' and gritted my teeth.

He stood not far behind me and I couldn't put his presence

out of mind as I took aim. He had a new affectation, which was uttering silly upper-class expressions like 'Haw!' and 'By Jove!'. He called for the servants to refresh his glass. Soon he was heard boasting about his recent weekend at an old school friend's country estate and how he'd shot at least two hundred game birds, 'enough to keep the town's milliners in feathers for months, don't you know?' He was trying to hold his own and was probably relieved to have found people who weren't too grand to converse with him.

Every one of my arrows missed the bullseye. When the ladies' round was over, Felix approached me.

'Felix, an unexpected surprise,' I said.

'Your mother's idea entirely, I assure you.'

'I thought that might be the case.'

'She wanted to go in the carriage and it would have been churlish of me to refuse. She's very persuasive.'

'She most certainly is. Well, I apologize on her behalf. Apart from anything else, she's succeeded in completely putting me off my game. That was a terrible display.'

'Was it now? Not to my eyes. Although, now I recall it, your mother did say you carried away the ladies' second prize last year. But I shan't pretend I regret coming when I have the pleasure of seeing you look so radiant.' His gaze swept over me. He lowered his voice: 'I know what these people think. That I'm a vulgar parvenu. But I'm afraid I don't care. All this emphasis on breeding, it's old hat, if you don't mind my saying.' He gazed about at the forbidding huddles of chattering toffs. 'Most of this lot don't have two pennies to rub together. The world is changing. The country needs more men like me – men who know how to make money as well as spend it.'

'Take care, or you'll sound chippy.'

'If that's the case, you really ought to approve. After all, you're the one who goes about quoting Eleanor Marx.'

A servant passed and I reached for a glass of murky water from the gardens' famed natural spring. It smelt of bog water and had a sour metallic taste. Felix helped himself to claret.

'To your good health,' he said, raising his glass before downing half its contents in one gulp. His face was flushed. I saw how nervous he was, and felt guilty about being cross with him earlier.

Just then Lottie appeared, trailing fragrance in her wake. 'Mr Skipp-Borlase, how delightful to see you,' she said. 'I didn't know you were a toxophilite.'

'I'm not, I'm afraid.' He looked vexed at Lottie's presence, and seemed immune to her fetching blonde curls. 'Horses are more my thing. Matter of fact, I've just broken in one splendid specimen, and I intend to keep her at my new home in Brixton.'

'A house in Brixton? My word!' said Lottie, glancing at me. 'Well, I hope you enjoyed watching Violet, at least. It's a pity you didn't come last time and see her at her best.'

'I'm afraid there'll be no trophies for me this afternoon,' I said.

'If you'll excuse me, my mother wants me,' said Felix, slipping away.

'No trophy for Mr Skipp-Borlase either, it appears – at least not today,' said Lottie. She leant towards me in confidence. 'The way he was making up to you! The two of you were really clicking.'

'Hardly!'

'Oh, Violet, why are you so perverse? The family are the richest in town, everyone knows that. And just think of it:

a house in Brixton too. How many houses do these people need? Such luxury, such dash.'

As Lottie went on in a similar vein, I could not forget her reputation for gossip. It was quite normal for young gentlemen and ladies to chatter at such events, but the manner of Felix's arrival, escorting both of our mothers, implied our acquaintance had gone beyond mere friendship. And with Lottie's help, the rumour would spread throughout Brighton society that Felix and I were all but formally attached.

*

The morning after the archery match, I joined Mama in the morning room. She was humming tunelessly, while buttering a slice of toast. She was clearly in high spirits, which in Mama meant constant gay laughter at nothing in particular and a general flirtatiousness towards the world at large, even when her audience was only me. She'd got the maid to take out the best tea set, which was another worrying sign. One had to tread carefully when Mama was in this humour as there was always a risk her excitement would boil over into mania.

'How kind of Felix to take me to the archery in his carriage yesterday,' she said. 'And so lovely to see Octavia.' I winced at the mention of Octavia, Felix's stand-offish mother. 'He's a dear boy, charm itself. I really don't know why you haven't invited him along before.'

'I didn't invite him yesterday, either. You did. And you made it difficult for him to refuse.'

She burst into her tinkling laugh. 'Come along now, you must admit Felix fitted in perfectly – even among those dreadful snobs.' Those 'dreadful snobs' were the society types she had been assiduously cultivating since we'd moved to Brighton a decade previously.

'He looked like a character in a stage farce,' I said. 'That jacket, for heaven's sake!'

'I thought he rather cut a dash.'

'And he was drunk too.'

Mama put her teacup down, primly. 'What is wrong with you this morning? Do you have one of your headaches?'

'As a matter of fact, I do.'

'I suppose you think I should have consulted with you before arriving with Felix and Octavia yesterday. But it was all on the spur of the moment.'

There was a moment of thick silence. We both knew she didn't do things on the spur of the moment.

'Aren't you going to have any breakfast?' she asked. She looked at the miserable pots of home-made jam and cold poached eggs laid out on the table. 'You're cross with me, aren't you?'

'Yes, I'm cross. You should have forewarned me, at least. Apart from anything else it put me off, Felix turning up like that. My score was hopeless.'

'Oh, listen to you. Your priorities are a mystery to me. There are more important things in life than pleasure-seeking and winning trophies. And if Felix isn't welcome to come and watch you play, then who on earth is? I'm thinking of inviting Gerald and Octavia to the next contest.'

'I'd rather give up archery altogether than suffer that.'

'To hear you speak, anyone might take you for a frightful snob.'

'That's utterly unfair. I deplore snobbery.'

'Of course you do, with your socialist pretensions. Your convictions are all wafer-thin if you're embarrassed when a dear friend rises above his station.'

'I wasn't embarrassed, at least not for that reason.'

'It's not as if Felix failed to hold his own. The gilt wore off most of those families a long time ago. It's all show.' She paused, and looked out of the window. The unforgiving sunlight exposed the lines in her forehead. She sniffed and dabbed her nose with a napkin, then frowned as her gaze lingered on a corner of the bay window. When she spoke again, she sounded fretful. 'If only your father would get that casement repaired. The timber will rot if it's left like that. Must I attend to everything in this house? And with only three servants to assist me. The eggs were cold again, this morning. Oh, when I think of the house in Hurstpierpoint and our huge garden, and the orchard – and how I once commanded a staff of twelve.' She turned to me, her gaze misty. 'I rather thought Felix might . . . *say something* to you yesterday – if you'd only given him the chance.'

'Say something?' I said, my face aflame. 'Say what? Did he imply he had something to tell me?'

'Of course not. He's far too discreet. And he would need a signal from you first.'

'Mama!' I choked on a crust of cold toast. 'What an idea! Felix and his parents are family friends, nothing more and nothing less. We haven't the least thing in common. He's a dear friend, but I hardly think we could ever . . . It's unthinkable. You must bring this scheming to an end. All it will do is drive a wedge between myself and Felix. As it so happens, I've been thinking I should write to him and suggest that we should spend some time apart in case people get the wrong idea.'

'But you can't possibly do that. Have you forgotten the tennis match next month?'

The tennis match! Mixed doubles with Felix as my partner. I had been looking forward to it immensely. But now Mama seemed to be attaching a special significance to the event. Surely Felix wouldn't think it fit to 'say something' to me at the tennis match, with all our family and friends present? My head throbbed. I would have to bring my mind to bear on the matter another time.

2

As a young girl, I rather looked forward to my encounters with Felix. We met mostly during his school holidays. He was invariably chivalrous, which was a welcome contrast to my three brothers, who were caught up in boyish chasing and tumbling and took little notice of me. Little Archie, my fourth brother, came along later. Felix was an only child and always had new toys to show off: a spinning top, hobby horse or model railway engine. He took riding lessons, which made me envious, for like all young girls I adored horses. It was about that time my father was forced to sell our brougham, and the horses with it, so purchasing a horse simply for my amusement was out of the question. Regardless of Felix's family's exceeding wealth, I could never take him altogether seriously, especially his precocious attempts to impersonate a full-grown man. And I resented him in spite of his gallantry, sensing his presumption and conde-scension, and all on account of his family's money. His father had made a fortune overseas, whereas Papa had only a modest annuity from his family's estate, together with various small stipends, and Mama had no inheritance at all to speak of. Papa did at least have expectations for when his oldest brother passed away, but there was no saying when that might be. Felix was in awe of his own father, who liked to boast that he had raised himself up from nothing. He would often repeat comments the great man had made at the breakfast table whilst perusing *The Times,* on the empire, trade, the Irish Question or some other dismal topic. After I'd spent time with Felix, I would amuse my brothers by doing impressions of him.

Our friendship endured into adulthood. He joined his father's bank in London and spent much of his time there. I looked forward to his regular weekend visits. There was so little to vary the tone of my existence between my precious weekly art classes and the occasional sporting fixture to work off my pent-up energies. My pastimes stretched the meagre household finances, but Mama was convinced that sporting activities and ladylike accomplishments like painting would help bring me to the notice of eligible young men.

When I came of age, Mama paraded me before possible suitors. It was wretched to be scrutinized while attempting to exhibit the social graces. I received just two proposals. Mama rejected the first as it was from a young gentleman with older brothers and thus without expectations. The second was from a man a good fifteen years older than me who was endowed with a considerable fortune, but, to my great relief, he withdrew when he discovered my maternal grandfather had been confined to a lunatic asylum. He feared the hereditary taint might be passed down the line.

★

One morning, soon after the archery contest, I was awoken by the cooing of pigeons on the window sill of my room. Their heads rubbed together as if they were trying to kiss but their beaks were in the way. At a certain point, the larger bird, the male, jumped on top of the female, flapping its wings to balance as his feet slid around on the smooth feathers of its mate's rounded back. Shortly, there was a frenzied rubbing together of tails and then a brief shiver of desire and it was all over and they were side by side again on the ledge, uttering deep throaty croaks. Another clutch of eggs was on the way.

I sat up in bed and must have surprised the birds, because I heard the clatter of wings as they flew away. Since my childhood, I had enjoyed drawing birds, and would idly sketch them in the margins of storybooks or any scrap of paper to hand. I would try to capture the shapes they made in flight, the sensation of movement. Papa once showed me how to create the impression of bird flight by drawing birds in progressive stages of flight in the corner of a notebook. When the pages were flipped there was an effect like that of a zoetrope. I showed my brothers the trick and, for once, I succeeded in holding their attention for a few minutes. I tried again later with galloping horses, but the novelty had worn off.

I got out of bed, keen to sketch the pigeons I had just spied upon. I looked around my cluttered room, my kingdom stuffed with treasures. There were piles of sketchbooks on the chest, the floor, on chairs and over every other available surface. My pictures were everywhere, on top of the wardrobe, under my bed, stuffed into drawers in my chest. My easel was placed against the wall. I had persuaded Papa to buy it years before for a shilling at an auction of the property of a recently deceased lady, an amateur painter. I got up and went to the wardrobe and got my watercolours and brushes and put them on my table. I began to draw the mating pigeons.

I had drawn ever since my French governess had put a crayon in my hand when I was small. Later, when a little older, at the time we lived in our grand house in Hurstpierpoint, I painted portraits of members of my family – and drew the servants too, if they would let me. Later still, when I was obliged to accompany Mama on her social visits, I secretly drew caricatures of her friends on any slip of paper that came to hand, the back of an envelope, the margin of a newspaper. And as a young lady, I drew portraits of my closest friend, Lottie. She loved posing. I told her not to pose stiffly or stare out at the viewer. I would get her to turn her head to one side as if I'd caught her unawares, or suggest she looked out of the picture, as though she was about to get up and leave.

I was never one of those swotty girls to be found in the park making accurate botanical drawings. And I had little sympathy with Mr Ruskin's instruction to draw from nature. I had once attempted to read a volume of his *Modern Painters* and found myself dozing. Why should I follow his edicts? I was part of nature, not a mere observer. I wanted to convey my response, my feelings. And to use my imagination. And my imagination knew no bounds. I hid my most revealing productions in the linen chest or the bottom of the wardrobe, out of sight of prying eyes. But I could never quite bring myself to throw them away. In my watercolour sketch the pigeons became doves and were joined by satyrs, and sirens of the bird variety sitting on a heap of human bones, and nymphs whose limbs were covered in fur, and all of them circling in an other-worldly ritual, a dance. When my sketch was finished, I realized I'd been at work for almost three hours.

I sat at my desk, breathing heavily. My head began to throb.

I sensed that I'd been in flight from some uncomfortable truth since the moment I had awoken. I had thrown myself into painting to escape it. The courting pigeons represented something which I had hidden from my conscious thoughts while I drew: my supposed courtship with Felix. I left my sketch to dry and reached for a pen and ink.

Dear Felix,

I must apologize for my rudeness at the archery meeting. I was taken by surprise. The last thing I want you to think is that I don't value your friendship. Of course I do. How could I not, after all the happy hours we've spent together – and when I think back it seems to me both of us in our different ways had an awkward time of it with our respective parents – but I digress. What am I trying to say? Oh, only that there are differences in our mutual dispositions, or do you not agree?

You see, my problem is that I'm a singular creature and I experience the deepest urges to escape the humdrum, everyday world. I have violent emotions that I struggle to contain. I'm not remotely sensible or dependable. It is not too much to say that I long for another kind of life altogether. If my desires are frustrated or allowed to wither on the vine then it could lead to unhappiness, or worse. You, I would say, are quite the opposite. You're cheerful, diligent, highly competent, practical, masterful – that's your nature. And it seems to me that is precisely what makes us tick as friends – that we complement each other so well.

And, as a dear old friend, I'm sure you won't mind me poking my nose into your private affairs. At some point you will turn your mind to affairs of the heart, and you won't want to make a dreadful mistake that you will rue to the end of your days. It seems to me that what you need is a young lady with common sense – someone robust, someone able and willing to manage a large household, someone who shares your interests, your political affiliations, and your other interests. You will need a lady with social graces, someone who would excel at entertaining foreign dignitaries at stuffy events. This wouldn't suit everyone. It might be disastrous if you married someone, only to discover she found the endless round of formal engagements very trying indeed. You are attractive and highly eligible, and you should have little trouble finding the right person.

I would never wish to do anything that might jeopardize what we have between us, but I have recently woken up to the realization – oh dear, how can I put it? – that some of those close to us might be harbouring certain expectations and are even making manoeuvres behind our backs. Neither of us would want to be pushed into something, especially a decision of such importance. Whatever we choose to do it must be our own choice freely made. It might be prudent for us to spend some time apart. So what I propose is this: the tennis doubles match with Lottie and Richard is arranged for three weeks' time – I say that we don't meet or communicate before then.

Please take my concern as proof of my esteem for you. I only want what's best for both of us.

Yours affectionately,
Violet

Posting the letter put my mind at rest. I had taken a decisive step towards resolving a misunderstanding I had carelessly allowed to develop while my mind was on other things. Three weeks should be sufficient to put a distance between Felix and myself. However, I received a response from Felix in the next post which did little to reassure me.

My Dearest Violet,

First, the manner of our parting at the archery contest. Heavens, I took no offence at all. Although I must admit I was in a stinking mood afterwards and the dog was well advised to give me a wide berth. But one of my annoying traits is that I always bounce back from these things after a good night's sleep.

The truth is I don't quite see eye to eye with you on all the points you make. First, this idea of me not knowing what you're like. Balderdash! Nobody knows you better than I do. You think I haven't noticed you're apt to fly off the handle when you're riled, that you've got a mind of your own and a sharp temper, that you're not remotely an 'Angel of the House'. God forbid that you were. You remind me of my own dear Mama in a lot of ways. She's no pushover, I promise you. You won't find Mama bent over her embroidery in the evening. She can be a cold fish and she likes to get her own way – and heaven help anyone who keeps her waiting. But she's all the better for that, to my way of thinking. As for your own mama, she's the sweetest creature on God's earth. With regard to your idea that I should marry a hearty down-to-earth no-nonsense girl – you don't understand me at all. I am determined that my future wife – whomsoever that might be! – will be brainy and able to hold her own in any company. My household will be sophisticated and high-tone – not the home of a vulgar arriviste.

Now, to address your qualms about our different interests and predilections. I can't help thinking you're rather missing the point. My view is that in a friendship, and equally in something more serious, it is better that two people complement each other, not match one another in every way like Tweedledum and Tweedledee. It occurs to me that your concerns might derive from a certain lack of confidence in your own eligibility – in which case your hesitancy is wholly unwarranted. By the same token, I understand how you might feel. For my own part, I am absolutely determined to improve myself. Of necessity, my efforts so far have been to ensure my future prosperity, but I intend to be far more than a vulgar money man. I aim to hold my own in the arts, in music and literature. This is where my parents aren't entirely up to scratch. The last musical performance they took me to was the Great MacDermott at the Empire Theatre. Don't panic. I wouldn't dream of taking you to such a place. The pavements outside were overrun by the lowest sort of women. A disgrace. In London I intend to get a box in the best theatres and hear the greatest orchestras in the world.

And as for painting and sculpture and the like – which I know are your most abiding passions – I've reached the conclusion that my parents' taste is somewhat wanting. Their house is full of huge items of forbidding furniture and bric-a-brac and clutter. I fear their snobbish acquaintances are sneering behind their backs. I won't stand for that. The house in Brixton will be in the latest style, all in the most impeccable taste, and no expense will be spared. With your artist's eye, you can help me achieve that. I intend to fill the rooms to bursting with art, so we must go to London and visit some galleries. I'm determined to buy some excellent pictures that will hold their value, but I don't always know the good from the bad. My own taste would be for rousing battle scenes, blood and gore, naval battles where you can almost taste the salt water and smell the cannon smoke. But I don't think many ladies would want that hanging in the dining room. So, I'm in your hands. I'm determined to educate myself in the arts in the same way I have in political economy, finance, horsemanship and firearms. I have the capacity, you know. I don't like to brag, but, as you know, I'm the director of several companies so I am a man of considerable substance. But I'm determined that my achievements will amount to more than a paper empire. I want to build a solid legacy, to play my part in pushing back the frontiers of free trade. Only last night, I fell asleep with my nose in Ricardo's work on economic principles.

But that's all for another time. On your chief point, I couldn't agree more — there's been far too much interference from our respective parents. They only want what's best for us, but we need to take a firm hold of the reins, of course we do. Let's go into purdah for a short while, as you suggest. That should keep them off our backs. I'll arrive prepared to reopen diplomatic channels. Until then, I bid you adieu.

With love,
Felix

3

It was a warm day in May when the tennis doubles match was held, and we played in the glare of the low afternoon sun. I was pent up, my concentration hindered by qualms about what Felix might do when the match was over. I hardly looked him in the eye throughout. He had complied with my wish that we avoid each other's company in the intervening weeks, but I couldn't forget his intention of coming 'prepared to reopen diplomatic channels'. Despite such tensions, we found ourselves three points from victory over Lottie and Richard Andrews, her fiancé.

The sight of Lottie simpering and waving her racket about girlishly on the other side of the net inspired a murderous instinct in me. I had a score to settle with her as her enthusiastic gossiping hadn't helped matters with Felix one bit. I looked across the net at her in her new tennis dress and jacket of plain white flannel. She looked fresh, even after an afternoon of play. Such a contrast to myself, in my everyday dress with the skirts gathered at the rear, and a plain tennis apron before. I'd taken in my dress during the recent fashion for exceedingly narrow skirts, which created an additional hindrance.

I bounced the ball, readying myself for my serve, before thwacking it over the net. Lottie succeeded in lobbing it back, but I pounced on it as it bounced, returning it with an unladylike grunt and at such force that Lottie had to duck to avoid losing her head. There was a collective gasp from the chaperones who sat alongside us under their parasols in a row of wicker chairs. A smattering of applause followed. Lottie waved her finger at me in mock anger. Felix put his racket under his arm so he could applaud.

'Keep up the good work,' he said. 'I'd give a hundred to kick Dougie Andrews into a cocked hat.' There were big sweat patches under his arms. He crouched ready for the next service, and I struck the ball at Lottie. As I lunged, my hair broke free of its pins and began to unravel. The ball hit the net and I went to pick it up.

Dougie smiled at me over the net. 'Bad luck,' he said, tipping his straw boater. 'You have a very strong service for a lady, I must say.'

'Better luck next time, partner,' said Felix, as I passed him on my way to the back of the court. I got into position, stretched upwards to swing at the ball, and felt a sudden stab in my side as if a knife had been thrust between my ribs. I fell forward, almost bent double, clutching my side, as Felix rushed over and put his hand on my shoulder.

'Pulled a muscle, have you? Rotten luck. We were almost home and dry.'

'It's my corset, damn it,' I hissed. The beastly thing had a rip in it where the point of the whalebone poked through, but the family finances hadn't stretched to purchasing a replacement. For a moment, I stood there wincing with my eyes shut.

'I say!' Felix said, uncertainly.

The rector, who was officiating, was on his way over. 'Don't you think it would be wise to call it a draw . . . ?' he lisped.

'Certainly not!' I said.

Lottie broke in: 'If Violet's game to play on, then so am I. We don't want everyone to say the match was abandoned on account of a couple of feeble women.'

It was settled then. I returned to my position at the rear of the court. When I lifted my arm, my ribs smarted awfully, but I threw up the ball and struck it. My service was feeble, but even so Lottie was unable to return it.

''Vantage, Miss Pring!' called the rector.

Lottie chose this moment to trip over the hem of her skirt and stagger, her straw hat falling off as she dropped in a decorous heap. She reached under the hem of her skirt to grasp her delicate little ankle in its lilac stocking. 'Drat! Oh, heavens!' she cried. Dougie rushed over and squatted down beside her. Felix ran up to the net. The chaperones jumped to their feet. A young gentleman, a friend of Dougie's who was a qualified physician, came to attend to Lottie's injury. All attention was now on her, and I was forgotten.

Dougie called over: 'Perhaps we should agree on a draw? Poor Lottie's ready to drop.'

'Oh, don't let's make a fuss,' said Lottie. 'I've only turned my ankle. That's hardly an excuse to deny Violet a well-earned victory.' She rose to her feet and limped back to her position to a round of applause from the chaperones.

I had to close my eyes tight to recover my concentration. Then I took a deep breath, threw the ball into the air and struck it hard. It spun towards Lottie who made only a half-hearted effort to return it. I waited for a burst of applause, but instead the chaperones stared at me in silence. For several heartbeats, I stood there panting, a bead of sweat rolling down my forehead. Finally,

26

the spectators stirred, glancing at each other with raised eyebrows. Their applause, when it came, was polite, rather than enthusiastic.

I was in dangerously high spirits after my victory over Lottie. My throat was parched, so I went to the large refreshments table. Spread across the white cloth was the usual assortment of pastries and cress-and-cucumber sandwiches. Servants circulated offering ices, teas and claret cups on trays. I gulped back two lemonades one after the other, the juice rolling down my chin, the cold water numbing my nose and throat. I was breathless and my ribs stung fearfully where the whalebone had cut into my flesh.

'You'll make yourself sick,' said my brother Archie, who was gobbling a pastry.

'Don't speak with your mouth full,' I said.

'You looked awfully silly while you were playing, by the way.' He pranced about in imitation of me.

I shook the racket at him. 'Shove off or I'll wallop you with this.'

A little distance away, I saw Lottie sitting in a chair, her ankle raised on a cushion with an ice pack bandaged over it. She was surrounded by a group of admirers. I picked up a glass of claret and marched over, hoping Felix wouldn't feel able to press his attentions on me if we were among a group of friends. I watched as her head swivelled on her long slender neck as she entranced each young gentleman in turn. They were all far too gallant to peek at that exposed ankle. Dougie Andrews, her fiancé, stood with his hands in his pockets.

'Hail, the conquering heroes! To us!' said Felix, raising his glass as I approached. 'Felix and Violet forever!' This was an expression we often used when younger, in the days when we romped about the lawn pretending to be cavaliers on horseback.

27

'It seems I owe you that hundred pounds, Violet.' He turned to the others and cried, 'Three cheers for the losing pair!'

'And three cheers for the winners,' said Dougie, his glass aloft. After the cries of hooray subsided, Dougie said, 'By Jove, you're a demon with a racket, Violet. I feared for my life.'

'We ladies would be a match for you gentleman if we could move freely about the court,' I said. 'I propose that in future we're allowed to wear trousers.'

There was moment of uneasy silence, then laughter.

'I say, now there's a thought,' said one chap, with a lewd snigger.

'This is what I love about Violet,' said Lottie. 'She's so shameless.' Lottie was the mistress of the backhanded compliment.

'Will we see you at the Empire, like Vesta Tilley?' said one of the other gentlemen, with a chortle.

With irritation, I saw that Felix was sidling towards me. 'You should see Violet with a bow and arrow,' he said as he took his place alongside me. I suppressed a shudder at his proprietary tone.

'Yes, I can picture that,' said Dougie, gazing at me. 'I bet you're a jolly good shot.'

'I invariably hit the target,' I said. The wine had gone straight to my head and I was muzzy and feeling reckless. The young men had formed a circle around me. For once, Lottie had to make do with her coterie of lady friends. Having established herself as an invalid, she couldn't very well get up and reassert her prominence.

'I've never known a girl with such a ferocious service,' said one of the other young gentlemen.

'I've been practising with my brother. He never makes allowances for the fairer sex.'

'Good for him.'

'I like a girl with a bit of pep,' said Dougie.

'Violet, you do know your hair is down, don't you?' called Lottie.

I felt a tap on my shoulder, and turned to find Mama beaming at me.

'Look at you, pink in the face,' she said. 'Let me tidy up that hair of yours.' She took me by the arm and led me away. When we were a safe distance, she put a hairpin in her mouth and stepped behind me. I felt her tug at my hair.

'What do think, Mama? Wasn't I sensational?'

'In my day it was thought indecorous for a woman to run about like that,' she said. She gave my hair a pat. 'There, that's better. Now, let's have a look at you.' She took a step back, looking me up and down. 'You're easily Lottie's equal. Perhaps you'd even surpass her, if you mended your ways.' Her voice became pensive. 'But Lottie is unassailable. She's already won three proposals. Perhaps you would have too, if you didn't go striding about with your arms swinging.'

'Times are changing. A lady isn't expected to mince about the way they did in your day. And Lottie's looks and deportment aren't her only attributes,' I said. I was alluding to the Hamilton-Rainey family fortune, so unlike our own straitened circumstances.

'Shush now.'

'I don't suppose any of them suspect that comb in Lottie's hair is a hairpiece,' I said to Mama.

'Dear me, keep your voice down,' she replied, then smiled as she saw Felix making his way over.

'Would you mind if I borrowed your daughter for a short time, Mrs Pring?' Felix asked Mama.

'Oh, you're more than welcome to her,' she said, with a laugh.

I had no option but to let Felix lead me away with all eyes upon us. It was late afternoon and the trees sent dark spidery shadows all down the length of the plush green lawns. I glanced at him and he smiled. He was theoretically personable, and well groomed, as always, with an upright manly bearing.

'We made a fine team, don't you think? Completely in tune with one another. And you certainly threw yourself into it!'

'Yes, Mama's told me off about that.'

'Has she now? Well, I rather approve.'

His voice seemed strained, his self-possession forced. The sun was sinking, projecting dazzling orange flares through the tree trunks. He glanced over his shoulder, nervously.

My head throbbed and all my powers drained from me. I simply couldn't face a conversation about our relationship, and decided I must somehow put Felix off for today.

'Shouldn't we get back to the others?' I asked. 'They'll be getting ready to pack up.'

Felix was gazing at me intensely. I realized he hadn't taken in what I'd just said. Without warning, he took a firm grip of my arm and pulled me behind the thick trunk of a tree, out of sight of our party. There was a queer glint in his eye, as his hands encircled my waist and he kissed me full on the lips. His kiss had a bruising intensity. My blood failed to warm in response, my senses didn't tingle, the way they did when I read romantic novels. My pulse accelerated in his embrace, but not with passion, only panic. He was suffocating me. I had the feeling that my tepid response was only serving to stoke the flames of his passion.

He broke off, breathless and red in the face.

'My God, you're beautiful,' he said, hoarsely. 'I almost can't bear it.'

'Stop this. Stop it now. This isn't the time or the place, and besides—'

'Listen to me, please, Violet,' he said, recovering his composure with an effort. 'There's something I have to say.'

'It will have to wait for another day,' I said, quickly. 'I'm not feeling well.'

'But it can't wait. You know that.' He smiled uncertainly.

'We must talk, of course we must, but not this minute. Not with everyone here watching. So, if you wouldn't mind . . . '

'It won't wait, I'm afraid.' He took a deep breath. 'You and I, my dearest, we complement each other perfectly. We're something new – we're not like that stuffy lot over there . . . '

This was a prepared speech and it was clear where it was heading. I had to act quickly. 'Felix, I must interrupt you. I have something important to say.'

'Just allow me to finish first. I expect you've got the jitters. I have too.' His voice had become urgent. 'Damn it, we have to think of our families' expectations!' Then his speech became more measured as he returned to his script. 'In all sincerity, I'm offering you a chance to be all that you could be. I have the means. And I won't stand in your way, whatever you wish for. I'm not putting it well, I know, but my feelings are utterly genuine. I think about you day and night, Violet. Your very name brings me out in goosebumps.'

'Please, Felix!' I cried.

He looked back towards the others, his face rigid, then took a deep breath and looked into my eyes. I averted my gaze. His hand slipped into his pocket. 'I am deeply in love with you and—'

'Listen to me, Felix!' I cried. 'I've given this a great deal of thought and . . . ' I choked on the words, acidic lemonade bubbles rising in my throat.

'Just let me finish, please,' he said.

He spoke on, but I was distracted. Under the trees, midges whirled in a manic dervish in a shaft of hazy amber light. High above, a red balloon was suspended in a sky of soft blue and I dearly wished I could have been up there in the basket, floating away.

'You will never want for anything, I can assure you of that,' Felix was saying. 'And I can say with all my heart that I'll always treat you decently, you can depend on it.'

He began to draw his hand out of his pocket, and I glimpsed the corner of an envelope. Did it contain a formal proposal of marriage?

'Stop!' I cried. I slapped the back of my neck where a midge had just bitten me. 'I'm a little overwhelmed. And exhausted after all that running around. We'll have to continue this conversation later.'

Felix withdrew his hand from his pocket – empty. For a moment he glared at me, pale and thin-lipped. When he spoke, his tone was cold and formal, with a hint of threat. 'I shan't pretend I'm satisfied with this outcome. But, of course, I'll wait. I'm determined on it.'

We were silent on the long walk back to the gathering. Having evidently noted my demeanour, Mama took me to one side. 'Well?' she said, still smiling.

'Well, nothing.'

Her smile remained fixed in place, but a nerve twitched under her eye. Her gaze sought out Felix where he stood, close to his mother and apart from the others, his head inclined as he spoke into her ear. 'What on earth did you say to him?' she asked.

'I told him I needed a little time to consider.'

'You said that? Imagine how he must feel after all he's done to recommend himself to you.'

'Imagine how *he* must feel! What about my feelings? You must have known of his intentions. How could you let me come here today without informing me?'

'I assumed you had understood. Everyone else was expecting Felix to make his move. But not you, it transpires. You live in a world of your own. And now you may have ruined your chances.'

'I don't care. If I marry it will be for love, not just to gain an establishment.'

Mama glared at me. 'Mind your tongue, for heaven's sake. Suppose they should overhear you?' She closed her eyes and began massaging her temples with her fingertips, a warning one of her headaches was imminent. 'Tell Susan to call a cab immediately. I've been in the sun too long.'

I wandered off, advancing into blinding golden light with no sense of where I was going or why, the sights and sounds of the afternoon happening in a far-off place in which I played no part. I was burning with anger, with the world, with Felix, and, most of all, with Mama.

4

In the days after the tennis match, Mama retired to her room most afternoons complaining of headaches. Social engagements were cancelled, proof that her condition was critical. She was a virtuoso at creating moods and atmospheres and the household was run with the intention of soothing her nerves and avoiding upsetting her. It didn't help matters that my older brother Lance, Mama's favourite, had recently left Cambridge without a degree, having begun his studies late after years of idling in Brighton. He now spent his days loafing about the house, when not frequenting neighbourhood hostelries. The details of his failure were known only to Papa and Mama.

Everyone blamed me for Mama's fragile condition. But trying to reason with her would solve nothing. As far as she was concerned, I had perversely put an advantageous marriage at risk, and there was nothing to be said on the matter. The only way to end the impasse was to write to Felix and profusely apologize, claiming my behaviour was the result of reckless physical exertion on the day of the tennis match, and hinting I would be receptive to a second approach. And I did in fact compose such a letter, but at the last moment I simply couldn't bring myself to post it.

After several days during which Mama was too fragile to come down for dinner, Susan, the housemaid, announced one afternoon that Mama would be joining us.

There was a definite drop in the temperature when she made her entrance in the dining room. Papa broke the silence.

'I'm glad to see you're feeling a little better, my dear.'

'We shall see,' she replied in a wispy voice. 'Have we heard from the boys?' My two middle brothers, Roger and Edward, were boarders at Lancing College. Due to our reduced circumstances, the boys had been unable to follow Lance to Eton. Mama blamed Papa for this, as he had refused to take advantage of his connections to gain salaried employment. It was curious that Mama should want to raise such a fraught topic when in so weakened a state, but also typical of her.

'We had a letter from Roger,' said Papa. 'It's sketchy on detail, as usual, but he did mention that the new chapel is finally taking shape. And, oh yes, he's joined the debating society, which is encouraging. Interestingly, his first debate was on the Oxford Movement. Now it just so happens, I read a very interesting article recently . . . '

Lance yawned audibly at this, only covering his mouth at the last moment.

Susan entered with a covered tureen and placed it on the table. Papa lifted the lid, releasing a whiff of asparagus. Little Archie made a face. We passed our plates to Papa and he served. The asparagus was undercooked and impossible to pierce with a fork. Lance picked up a spear with his fingers and chewed on it. Mama sat rigidly, picking at the scrawny green shoots. Archie attempted to slice a stalk in two and sent it flying across the table. Mama closed her eyes and winced. Then there was silence but for the clinking of knives on china. I tolerated this situation for a few more minutes before my patience was exhausted.

'How long must we go on like this?' I said, putting down my knife and fork in the correct manner, which Mama always insisted upon.

At the sound of my voice, she recoiled, looking about her with a startled expression, but said nothing.

'I'm speaking to you, Mama.'

'What is it you are saying?' she replied.

'I'm asking how long you intend to carry on like this.'

'I've no idea what you mean.'

'This chilly silence, this death by a thousand cuts – when will it stop?'

'I think you should remember that your mother hasn't been at all well,' said Papa.

'Mama, I understand that you're cross with me,' I said.

'Cross? Did I say I was cross?'

'Yes, cross because I haven't agreed to become engaged.'

'I've nothing to say about it. You're almost twenty-four – old enough to know your own mind.'

'But it's clear you're not pleased.'

'Naturally, I'm not *pleased* to see my daughter throw away the best chance she will ever have. But this is not the time or place to discuss it.'

'I never see you at other times. You're always in your room.'

'I am unwell!' she cried, pitifully.

'Dear God in Heaven,' muttered Lance.

'Am I to be driven from my own table?' said Mama.

'Oh, come along, that's not what I'm suggesting at all,' I said.

'Oh, Lord, must we have all this again?' said Lance, with a sigh.

'I'm afraid we must,' I said. 'Mama's cross about Felix, as you all know very well. Mama, you know I've no intention of upsetting you.'

'This isn't a matter for the dinner table, as your mother pointed out,' said Papa to me, with a nod towards little Archie.

'Isn't it better to clear the air rather than leave the whole house on tenterhooks?' I asked.

'Enough!' said Mama. There was silence as Susan entered and cleared away the plates.

When she'd withdrawn, I said: 'Mama, a marriage proposal is supposed to be the most romantic moment in a woman's life, not the most miserable.'

'Miserable, you say? Miserable that a fine upstanding young gentleman, one whose family have close connections with our own, one who allows you a greater latitude than you could ever expect, who is loyal and has tremendous prospects, should ask you to marry him? You're impossible. All you ever do is look for defects in that young man.'

I imagined phrases like these had incessantly run through her head in the days she had lain in her sick bed, seething.

'If you don't mind, I shall excuse myself,' said Lance, standing up and leaving the table without pushing his chair back into place.

'Now, look here, young fellow . . . ' said Papa, but Lance had already left the room. A moment later, the side door out into the yard slammed. Lance was in the habit of smoking at the side of the house.

'Mama, I realize I have made a great error in allowing my friendship with Felix to become so intimate and to last for so long,' I said. 'The last thing I want to do is hurt his feelings . . . '

'Not hurt his feelings? You are prepared to break his heart!' she cried. 'How do you expect me to respond, when you threaten to throw your life away? And his too. If you let Felix go, you'll never get over it.'

'I'm afraid I shall. It's you who'll never get over it.'

'Come along now, Violet,' said Papa. 'There's no call to speak to your mother in that way, especially when she's unwell.'

Mama rounded on him. 'You're the one who's to blame for all of this, allowing her to read your appalling books when her young female intellect was ill-equipped to negotiate the hazards. It turned her mind.'

'That's most unfair,' said Papa. 'I saw no harm in encouraging her to gain an understanding of the world.'

'And this is the result — these feather-headed notions, this lack of any common sense. All you've done is furnish her with sensational opinions with which to pepper her conversation and outrage my acquaintances.'

'I don't see why I should refrain from giving my opinion out of politeness to your friends,' I said. 'And if you were concerned about me being feather-headed you should have let me go to the girls' day school like Lottie and the other girls of our acquaintance.'

'We hadn't the money to send you to school.'

'But the boys went . . . '

'Of course, the boys went. They have to make their way in the world. But you — you at least could have found a husband. But not any longer . . . ' With that, she groaned, threw down her napkin, rose to her feet and fled the room. The side door slammed a second time.

Little Archie piped up: 'Please may I leave the table?'

'Finish your dinner first, my lad,' said Papa, but Archie was already bolting out and a moment later his footsteps were heard stomping up the stairs.

'Well, then, it's full-blown anarchy, is it?' said Papa, severely ruffled.

I knew from past experience that Mama was quite capable of running up and down the street wailing in broad daylight, so I excused myself and followed her out.

I found her in the yard standing alongside Lance, both of them leaning against the wall. Lance was smoking a cigarette.

'Let me have one of those,' said Mama.

'I'm not sure that's a good idea,' said Lance.

'Do as you're told, for heaven's sake.'

'Whatever next?' said Lance, opening his silver cigarette case and handing her one. She put the cigarette in her mouth as he struck a match and lit it for her, cupping his hand around the flame. I looked across the street at the fine villas opposite, wondering what the neighbours would think if they saw my mother smoking outdoors like a common prostitute.

'Please, Mama, can't we put a stop to this?' I pleaded. 'I can't make up my mind if you go on forcing the issue in this way.'

She stared at me in fury, her face grey after inhaling the tobacco. 'How did I succeed in raising such a cold-hearted egoist? Not a trace of affection or constancy in you. All I have ever wanted is what's best for you children. And Felix, though still young, is a man of means.'

'You're not suggesting the family could gain financially from my marriage?'

'Not at all! How could you suggest such a thing? We might accept advice on our investments, but your father would never countenance asking for support in that way. But good breeding will only get us so far, and the world is changing. I'm determined the boys will enter a respectable profession and that you – well, that you will marry well. We must all be prepared to compromise. We can't have everything we want in life. That's a lesson every woman must learn.'

'All this concern with social standing,' I said. 'Perhaps what really worries you is how it will reflect on you if I refuse to marry Felix.'

Mama rushed up the iron steps to the side door. On the threshold, she turned to me and wailed: 'How dare you! What a heartless creature you are.'

I saw there was no use trying to persuade her to abandon her scheme. There was only one person to whom I could possibly turn for help.

5

Papa used to call me 'Honeysop' when I was a child. I alone among his children was allowed to visit his study, and his books provided me with the nearest thing I had to a proper schooling. But I knew I must tread carefully. There was only so far Papa could be persuaded, and I was always anxious about retaining his regard for me, not to mention his love. Above all, it was important not to disrupt his habits, as habit was everything to Papa. His life was dedicated to maintaining his own peace of mind, which entailed constantly appeasing Mama.

As soon as I entered his study, I was in thrall to the strange enchantment of that place. The room and all the furnishings smelt of cigar smoke, as did Papa himself. Black bookcases with gilt edging lined the walls, filled with leather volumes on every imaginable subject. The room was a cocoon, sealed from all the irksome fuss and noise of the world beyond. Throughout my childhood I had gone there to bathe in Papa's affection, which I valued more than almost anything.

'Such a relief to be back here – the only sane room in this house!' I said, as I dropped into one of his sumptuously uphol-stered armchairs.

'Long may it remain so,' he replied, looking up over the top of his reading glasses. The *Westminster Review* lay open before him on his desk.

'Mama has me at my wits' end. How long before she has us pushing her about in the bath chair with a blanket over her knees?'

'I should think the anaesthesia in her lower limbs will cease –' he lowered his voice '– as soon as she gets what she wants.'

This was Papa and me at our old game, furtively laughing at Mama behind her back and letting off steam by sharing our mutual complaints.

'We'll have no peace unless I agree to marry Felix. Of course, my own preferences are of no importance,' I said.

Papa turned to gaze out of the window for a moment, then cleared his throat. 'I understood you were fond of the chap?'

'Fond, maybe, but no more than that.'

'Well, I dare say he's sincere. He always seemed quite level-headed.'

'He is sensible, as a rule, which is why his sudden urgency has come as a surprise. Perhaps Mama has mesmerized him?'

'Oh, she's capable of that.' He turned a page of his periodical, then peered at me. 'You look very well, my dear. You're in full form. I should say this young chap's feelings towards you have, shall we say, matured.'

I blushed and couldn't meet his gaze. 'Well, whatever he might be feeling, it's not mutual. Surely, in the circumstances, it would be prudent to postpone any hasty move towards engagement.'

He mused on this for a moment. 'You seem pretty compatible on the face of it. It might be sensible to accept a good offer now it's on the table. Just remind me, how old are you, now? Twenty-two, is it?

'Twenty-three, almost twenty-four.'

'Well, there you have it. There's a glut of unmarried women of your age out there, huge competition. And Felix is very amenable, given your temperament.'

'What's wrong with my temperament?'

'Oh dear, I seem to have put that rather clumsily. This sort of thing is all very much your mother's province, you know.'

'The point is I don't wish to marry a dull financier merely for his money.'

'I wouldn't suggest that you marry him just for his money. Although money does guarantee happiness and, believe me, the lack of it certainly brings misery.'

'But I don't love Felix. If you have any advice about how to endure such a marriage, then I sincerely wish you'd offer it.'

Papa took pause, staring into space. In the past, when I had raised any matter of a personal nature, or otherwise entreated him to intervene in any decisive way at all, he would acquire a sudden deafness. On this occasion, however, he frowned, and appeared to deliberate.

'In my experience, a good marriage requires compromise on both sides. As for your mother, I have tried to accommodate myself to her wishes,' he said, loosening his cravat a little and rolling his head on his shoulders. 'I didn't stand in her way when she chose to go into Society, and I've permitted her to receive whatever friends she chooses, even those whom I find uncongenial. All of which has come at some cost, financial and otherwise.

'But you must remember that I did take the upper hand when it came to sending the boys away to school, much against your mother's wishes. The quid quo pro is that I have surrendered control of the feminine realm to her. As for your own expectations of marriage, all I can say is that times have changed since our days. There was less sentimentality in the past. I would suggest that your generation have unreasonable expectations. A young lady, such as yourself, should be thinking above all about getting a good home, yet I suspect you value romantic infatuation far above companionship and as a result you're prepared to cast off prudence and restraint. My advice is that the absence of love should not be seen as an obstruction to an advantageous marriage and, more to the point, there is little money in our family.'

Was this the best Papa could do? Previous experience suggested it might be. And I was frightened of anything coming between us. I'd come to depend on his affection and respect to maintain my own equilibrium. Even so, circumstances were such that I knew I must push him further. It took an effort of will.

'Could you not speak to Mama on my behalf?' I asked.

'I'm afraid your mother will not be moved.'

'And no doubt she'll make life intolerable for you if you cross her.'

'Now, look here, young lady,' he said, his voice sharp, at least by his standards. 'The truth is that your mother is at heart a practical woman, and I am an overindulgent father. But, as you seek my advice, I might point out that one should consider one's duty.'

'My duty? Surely it is understood these days that love is the cornerstone of a good marriage?'

'Love?' he mused. 'When one thinks about it, what do we actually mean by the word? What is this curious notion? Little more than a convenient soubriquet for all sorts of uncivilized compulsions, I would wager. We must temper sentiment with common sense and propriety. This, now I come to think of it, was my intention in letting you read my books. To awaken your reason and sense of moral duty. After all, we can't go through life doing just as we please, can we?'

'But isn't that exactly what *you* do?' I cried.

'I most certainly do not! Let me remind you, I have considerable responsibilities to fulfil.'

By which he meant various little chores, such as occasionally sitting on the Royal Commission or undertaking vestry duties.

'Papa,' I said, 'is my future happiness of no consequence at all?'

'My dear girl, I take the view that there are far more interesting things to think about than whether one is happy or otherwise.' At which, he looked down at his periodical, a clear signal that our interview was at an end.

★

The following Wednesday, I attended Miss Fanshaw's class at Brighton Museum as usual. I loved the building, but in my sour mood the Moorish arched doors and painted tiles seemed drab and bogus. I took my place at my easel and waited in silence while the other students chattered amidst the clutter. Tables were covered in a chaotic array of paint pots and brushes, with tubes left lying about and paint oozing out of their nozzles like worms of various colours. The students stood in lively groups around the more popular girls' easels. We had all learned our craft by drawing marble busts, had studied form, composition, perspective, and engaged in endless technical studies. In particular,

Miss Fanshaw had insisted on us doing line drawings over and over again. All of this was complemented by lectures given by visiting artists and day trips to London galleries. Around the room were pictures: landscapes, portraits of favourite cats and dogs, flower arrangements and seascapes – rows of moored boats were particularly popular. My choice of subject and approach was rather different to the other ladies. Some were snippy about my compositions. I had the audacity to paint from my imagination. I had ideas and a tendency to get above myself.

There was an especially heightened atmosphere that day as we had a visitor: the artist Mr Wilfred Lilley, who had agreed to offer us instruction. He was conversing with Miss Fanshaw, the drawing mistress, at the front of the room. His languid demeanour contrasted with Miss Fanshaw's. She was a spinster in her thirties with a good height and robust figure. Her face was animated, her bearing erect and her manner forthright.

Lottie sat at my side gossiping, as was her wont. 'Would you say he was dashing, at all? He's certainly not as handsome as Dougie.'

I peered at Mr Lilley, without turning in his direction. He had raven-black hair, flecked here and there with grey, which was looped around his ears and almost reached his collar. He had a full beard.

'Some would say so,' I said. 'He's a certain type.'

'Don't you think his face is gaunt, though? He looks like he needs a good feed.'

'Gaunt? Perhaps. But in a wolfish way that's rather attractive.'

Lottie raised her eyebrows. 'Well, I expect his bohemian existence is the explanation. The *Brighton Gazette* ran a column on him. Apparently –' she leaned closer to me and lowered her voice '— he fled London recently for undisclosed reasons and has taken up rooms near the family home. One of his early paintings caused quite a scandal, and,' she continued in a near whisper, 'he was rumoured to have formed an attachment with one of his models.'

I took another look at the gentleman artist let loose among Miss Fanshaw's students. He appeared well made and was certainly handsome. As Miss Fanshaw held forth, I watched as he glanced about him, peering at the young lady artists through lowered eyelids with long dark lashes, a hand resting on his loosely knotted purple necktie. His fingers were long and fine, I noticed, almost feminine.

Miss Fanshaw called for silence. 'Now, ladies, if I may have your attention. I am delighted to be able to introduce you all to Mr Wilfred Lilley, whose reputation you will all be familiar with.' One or two ladies glanced at each other and smirked. 'Mr Lilley is my most esteemed friend and peer and, if there is any justice in this world, he will one day take his place among the greats.' Mr Lilley dismissed this notion with a shake of his head. 'I haven't time to mention all of his famous artistic associates, but he is acquainted with Mr Burne-Jones and his circle.' Murmurs were exchanged among the young ladies. 'His early career showed great promise and we await the world's judgement on his more recent pictures. Before he offers his critique of your work, he has generously agreed to say a few words about his recent sojourn in Paris and his experiences with French painters.'

'Good afternoon, ladies,' said Mr Lilley. 'And thank you, Miss Fanshaw, for your invitation.' His voice was deep and rounded. 'As for my opinions, I can't pretend to speak for anyone but myself, I'm afraid. But I would venture to suggest that artists in England find themselves at a crossroads – if not a dead end.' He looked down at a sheet of notes in his hand, then stuffed it into his suit pocket.

'What should be our direction of travel, you might well ask. We hear much about the Glasgow and Newlyn schools, the impressionist influence. No doubt you will have seen Mr Whistler's paintings, little more than tonal abstraction, attempts to capture the essence of light, suitable for wealthy households to provide a contrast to Mr Morris's patterned wallpaper. Interior decoration run riot, in other words.'

One or two of the brighter young ladies chuckled at this.

'The problem is we've missed the boat. In Paris, impressionism is no longer *de rigueur*. Younger men must look elsewhere for direction. The question is, what does one do when the Royal Academy shows no leadership? Leighton continues ad nauseum with his grandiose Hellenic fantasies. His models, with all their classical grace, are lifeless as antique statues, his settings stale dreams of a world that never was. Leighton says he wishes to elevate rather than deprave. Personally, I'd rather be depraved than bored. Where's the passion? Where is any authentic feeling whatsoever? The merchant classes stand before these works and see themselves reflected. As if this hypocritical vulgar money-grasping country could be compared to classical Greece or Rome. As for Alma-Tadema, his Roman bath scenes are an invitation to ogle suburban housewives cavorting in fancy dress, their modesty preserved by a discreetly placed peacock feather here or there.'

The ladies turned to each other to express their surprise at such rudeness about other artists, and the inference that some of the nation's most popular works might be indecent. Some felt Mr Lilley's attitude was uncalled for in a gentleman yet to forge an artistic reputation of his own.

'We must decide which direction to face,' Mr Lilley continued. 'Will it be aestheticism and art for art's sake, or should we attach ourselves to the Symbolist movement? And who knows what new schools will emerge next week? How can one move with the times when faced with so many possible futures?'

It was all very well for this gentleman to talk of 'so many possible futures'. For me, it appeared there was only one possibility: to be the ornament of a rich man's home, entertaining businessmen and diplomats to support my future husband's efforts to finance railways in South America. I glanced at the ladies around me. Some were rapt, while others slumped in boredom or frowned in confusion. What were any of our endeavours compared to those of a true artist, like Mr Lilley? We were mere women with no cause to take on a heroic struggle with destiny. Was I alone among them in craving the freedom that men enjoyed?

'Perhaps the culprit is photography,' he was saying. 'The dogma of "truth to nature" has in our times been degraded to "truth to photography". Any picture with a realistic semblance to what the eye can see is elevated to the highest art, though the subject is no more than trite anecdote or mawkish moralizing. Social pictures of striking miners, for heaven's sake! Leave that to newspaper journalists, here today and gone tomorrow. True art should live for all time.'

Did he not realize the ladies in his audience were fond of painting anecdotal and sentimental subjects? He had reached the end of his talk, and, at Miss Fanshaw's request, he took questions.

'Don't you think photographs can be a useful reference, especially when one is drawing indoors?' asked Miss Fanshaw.

'I suppose so, Gwen. But the principle use for photography is to make a journalistic record,' said Mr Lilley.

Lottie's hand shot up. 'Is there any harm in pretty and well-painted pictures?' she asked, smiling brilliantly. As ever, Lottie's sole intention in addressing a man was to make him fall in love with her.

'Are you suggesting we pander to public taste?' asked Mr Lilley.

'Well, as you put it that way, perhaps not,' said Lottie, lowering her gaze.

'I'm pleased to hear it,' said Mr Lilley. 'I despise those painters who alter their pictures at the request of rich bourgeois collectors. I, for one, will never compromise. I leave that to Millais, who was made a baronet last year, a traitor to his early ideals.' His head jerked backwards as he shook his fringe from his face. 'These gentlemen are, to coin a phrase, fanners of the soul's sleep. True Art should serve higher forces.'

I felt excited and emboldened by Mr Lilley's defiance, even if his argument somewhat eluded me. As the tumult subsided, I called out: 'Please, Mr Lilley, just one more question if I may? You mention higher forces – could you be more specific about what these forces might be?'

For a second or two, he simply stared fixedly at me. Then he cleared his throat, and responded. 'I would suggest that artists disregard bourgeois taste, that we break with stultifying convention. We must express a personal vision, and follow fearlessly wherever that may lead.'

At this juncture, Miss Fanshaw brought this stage of the

proceedings to an end. We resumed our work and Mr Lilley passed among the lady artists doling out his guidance. I turned my attention to the self-portrait I was working on, in which I had portrayed myself as an archer in ancient times, Diana or Artemis or perhaps Boadicea. The portrait was in the half-length format and was based on drawings of my own reflection in the bedroom mirror, while the body was modelled on sketches of the naked figures in white marble which I had made on an excursion to the South Kensington Museum. I'd attempted a sfumato effect which gave the picture a hallucinatory quality. My black hair flared out wildly and around my head was a halo of light, or an electrical aura that flowed from within me. I had the pelt of a hare around my neck. Folds of clinging diaphanous cloth were gathered below my hips. The contours of the torso could just be discerned. It was precisely the kind of overreaching and attention-seeking that raised eyebrows among the other lady artists. Now that my work was about to come under Lilley's scrutiny, I wished I'd chosen a more prim and proper subject. As I daubed more paint onto the outlines of a limb too clearly visible through filmy cloth, Lottie leant towards me.

'Rather charmless, isn't he?' she said.

'Haughty and self-opiniated.'

'Not your type then. Nor mine either. There's something raffish about him too, wouldn't you say?'

'Bohemian, rather than raffish, surely?'

'Bohemian? Yes. Well, that's better, no doubt. But hardly more respectable. Did you notice his scuffed shoes? And it's well known all artists have loose morals.'

'The looser the better, as far as I'm concerned.'

Lottie turned to me in shock, then snorted with laughter.

'For a moment I thought you were serious! I never know what you'll say next, Violet. It's what I find most endearing about you. But whatever would Felix have thought, if he'd just heard you?'

'Why do I never meet men like Mr Lilley?' I asked.

'Violet, really! Are you serious?'

'Of course I'm not. It's hopeless to even think about it.'

A moment later I became distracted when Mr Lilley's cologne alerted me to his proximity. I had the distinct impression his glance was straying every so often in my direction. But then again, why shouldn't it? I was sitting next to Lottie Hamilton-Rainey, Brighton's most celebrated belle. Glancing over my shoulder, I saw him, his head nodding slowly at some remark of Miss Fanshaw's, his eyes glazed as he looked at a student's work. His hand moved to his mouth to cover a yawn, then he muttered something in his low timbre, pointing out some fault in his victim's composition as she turned puce.

A moment later I heard him right behind me. Lottie must have instinctively sensed his approach as she had begun applying her paintbrush with a passion without precedent. She paused, leaned back from the canvas, holding her head at an angle and pouting with concentration as she judged her own efforts. Her picture was a bucolic landscape featuring two lovers in a cornfield. The female figure had rosy cheeks and the male had a blade of straw protruding from his lips. Her work had advanced more in the last ten minutes than it had in the previous ten weeks.

Mr Lilley's deep tones were heard right behind us: 'Now this . . . *this* is good. Exceptionally so.'

Lottie started, recovered herself, then turned to beam at him.

'May I ask the artist's name?' Mr Lilley asked. He was looking at *me*, and it was *my* painting to which he referred.

'This is Miss Pring,' said Miss Fanshaw. 'She's one of our brightest prospects.'

'Miss *Pring*,' he repeated, as if savouring my name on his tongue. He began to study my picture avidly, his gaze passing slowly over the surface and into each nook and cranny, scrutinizing every fault where I'd exceeded my level of technical accomplishment.

'Violet has a gift, but is yet to find her own style,' said Miss Fanshaw. 'I should point out this is her first attempt with tempera.'

Mr Lilley nodded his head and frowned. 'I thought so,' he muttered.

'She has caught her own likeness well, wouldn't you agree? As for the way she's depicted herself staring out of the canvas and straight at the viewer – isn't it audacious?'

Mr Lilley turned from the picture and looked at me. 'Would you mind explaining what you intended to achieve here?'

I had a choking sensation and had to swallow before I could answer. 'I'm not sure I can explain. I want to express my feelings, my own ideas, I suppose. Words can't explain it. Why bother painting at all if you can express something in words.'

Lottie raised her eyebrows at me.

'Violet is dedicated to her work,' said Miss Fanshaw. 'I have asked her about the figure in the painting. Is it Diana and if not, who? And what is the context? Are we to guess at whom she is firing the arrow? How are we to interpret the picture with no recognizable symbols or allegorical context?'

'But this is precisely what fascinates me,' said Mr Lilley. 'The subjectivity of it. Quite fitting for what is essentially a romantic self-portrait. A courageous decision to reject traditional allegory and symbol, with all its literalism and simple-mindedness.'

The room had grown quiet and I could sense my classmates' attention settling on me.

'Does that mean you like it then?' I asked.

'Well, there is no consistency of handling and your subject matter is eccentric. But yes, I like it a great deal. I applaud you.'

'Oh, I so hoped you would!' said Miss Fanshaw. 'I've encouraged Violet's experimentation, but of course one worries she'll stray too far from public taste. If I had half her talent, I'd stop teaching and spend every hour in my studio.'

I glanced at Lottie and saw she had turned a sickly colour.

'Remarkable eyes,' said Mr Lilley, staring at the picture. 'Haunting. With something predatory in the gaze, quite fitting for the subject of the huntress. And a remarkable sense of rhythm in the composition. There is room for improvement. The figure is a little boneless under the drapery, perhaps due to a lack of training in anatomy, and the foreshortening of the arm isn't well done. But overall an arresting effect has been achieved. This dreamlike quality is unique. I rarely see such a well-developed personal style in a young artist's work. I should like to see more. You've exhibited, I assume?'

My senses were raised to such a pitch I was incapable of speech. I shook my head.

'Well, then you must!'

'Violet did receive a payment from *The Young Ladies' Journal* for a pencil and wash drawing last month,' said Miss Fanshaw. 'I had to badger her to submit it for publication.'

'Is that so?' Mr Lilley asked, looking at me.

'The princely sum of three pounds, eleven shillings and sixpence,' I said.

He smiled. 'Not nearly enough, I'm sure. And what was your subject?'

'A scene from Christina Rossetti's "Goblin Market".'

'A splendid choice. I see from the work in front of me that you are more than capable of capturing the peculiar qualities of that lady's poetry.'

He took a card from his pocket and handed it to me. At the top it read 'Mr Wilfred Lilley Esq.' and underneath there was an address in Kemp Town.

'If you feel I can offer any further guidance, I should be delighted to receive you – and, of course, Miss Fanshaw – for tea at a time convenient to yourselves.'

'Thank you. I'm greatly obliged.'

'The privilege is all mine.'

I nodded and smiled as demurely as could, but inside I was beside myself with excitement.

6

Most of that night I lay awake, reliving the encounter with Mr Lilley over and over, the details embellished on each imagining. At first light, I fetched my box of pencils, inks, watercolours, paintbrushes and jars from the bottom of the wardrobe. Tying an apron over my dress, I sat down at my desk under the window and removed the cap from a tube of paint. The odour acted on me like a drug.

That first day, I produced several chalk sketches with a fervour bordering on mania. Hours seemed to pass in an instant. I painted from memory or drew any object to hand – a pine cone, hairbrush or apple core. If I couldn't find a chalk of the right colour, I'd use a crayon of a similar colour instead, and create an interesting effect. Then I turned to watercolour. All manner of bloated slithering and squirming forms slid out of my mind as if out of a primeval pond, serpents, eels and so on, as well as flowers with gaping ravenous mouths and upright poking stamens like probing tongues. My absorption was such that I became weightless, as if I'd lost all bodily form, the stem of the brush as fine as a hair between my fingers. I focused intensely on each dab or caress of the paintbrush, and when I found a perfect hue and placed it against another, the entire surface of my skin rippled as if under a caress. My fingers, my apron and dress, even my hair, were all stained with colours.

The next day, I persuaded Susan, the housemaid, to sit for me. I overcame her initial reticence about neglecting the polishing in the living room by paying her tuppence out of my meagre allowance. I fancied I could later use my sketches of her face for pictures of saints and fallen women and the like. As my confidence grew, I took Wilfred Lilley's endorsement as a licence to embrace the unthinkable. I decided to paint a mermaid. I remembered Miss Fanshaw's plein air class earlier that year on the beach. The sea had been choppy. How was I to capture the waves rolling in one after another and collapsing hypnotically before my eyes? It was like trying to paint the passing of time. I dabbed flecks of paint, pure white, greens, blues, depicting my own sensations. Now, weeks later, in my room, I imagined the tide in a waking dream. Without consciously intending to, I painted a watercolour of an inverted mermaid lying on a beach, the top half a fish's head and body and the bottom a woman's legs. I decided I must do a version in oils.

I couldn't afford a new canvas so I scraped down one I'd painted on before. I did a rough preparatory sketch in crayon. For the mermaid's limbs I first underpainted in white, then painted over it in luscious flesh tones. Her sexual parts were human, and I left no detail of her anatomy to the imagination. Perhaps this was a revolt against Mama's squeamishness, but I didn't stop to think about it. Impatience drove me, a desire for immediacy, to express my feelings directly without stopping to think. I loved the physical experience of painting, breaking into a sweat, letting my hand, my body, my mind take charge. My shoulders ached, my neck ached, the arm that held the palette ached, my feet were sore from stamping about in front of my easel. When it came to the sky I scumbled, dragging a dry brush over wet paint, a technique I'd learned from Miss Fanshaw. I stood back to look, then made a new assault, raking the surface violently with a palette knife until I got the texture and depth I wanted.

Afterwards, I hid my mermaid behind the wardrobe. Later, when the paint was dry, I would put it in the bottom of the linen chest away from Mama's prying eyes, along with other similarly questionable pictures. All my powers spent, I lay on my bed, my neck and shoulders burning, my heart palpitating. A new weather front arrived that evening, bringing warm cloying air that made it hard to breathe as I lay sleepless in my bed. I was forced to throw off the bed covers. Deep into the night, lightning lit my window in flash after flash, faster than thought, followed by mountainous rumbles. The air was left charged and expectant in the storm's wake, with a lingering odour of singed metal.

I awoke early, exhausted yet tingling with energy. A lattice of pale light from the window frame rippled on the wall over my bed. Gulls screeched on the rooftops. It was four in the morning and already light. The new day struck me with the power of revelation. I got up and put on my painting clothes, then immediately began working again. Mr Lilley's address to the art class came back to me. I thought of how the times were making machines of us, constraining our senses, binding and constricting us in our clothes, tying us up in regulations and paper records and contracts – in unwanted marriages. It seemed to me that art had become enslaved to this project, little more than a box of conjuring tricks, to create the illusion of depth and form on a flat plane, to calculate perspective with mathematical precision. The imagery in a picture was no more than a code, perhaps to suggest other sensory experiences, such as music for example, shown through a row of maidens silently blowing long slender antique golden trumpets. Or else the picture's meaning was a kind of puzzle, and the viewer only needed to know the key to its symbolism, allegory, metaphor or implied story. I was impatient with these rules, this technique and trickery, this literalness. I wanted to express my sensations and emotions directly as I painted, in answer to a mysterious inner compulsion, to convey experiences that could never be expressed in words. I painted and drew for myself alone, although I longed to show Mr Lilley what I'd done, to hear his opinion again – his *praise*. During that long airless summer day, I was in a state of euphoria, entranced by colour, form, texture, pattern, the play of light. I wanted to look at the world until my eyes burned with the intensity of it. The armpits of my dress were wet with perspiration.

That afternoon, hunched over a drawing, aching and stiff, I was distracted by a fly that had trapped itself between the panes of the sash window. It buzzed furiously and attempted to batter its brains out repeatedly between the glass. I leapt up to set it free, but it was too stupid to find its way out of the open window, so I swatted it with a cloth I'd been using to mop up spilt paint. All that remained was a red smear on the glass and the vividness of the colour brought me back to another afternoon, many years before, when I was a child in the nursery and for the first time the paint pots were brought out for my amusement. I'd clutched the brush in my pudgy little fingers, dipped the tip into a pot of gooey red pigment, and found myself beguiled by the lurid scarlet stain that had spread over a sheet of virgin white paper.

I'd been so excited that I'd upset the pot and sent a crimson puddle spreading over the table and dripping onto the floor. The nurse had carried me away, kicking and howling in protest. After that, I was forever demanding the paint box be brought out, especially when the alternative was learning any lesson by rote. I lost myself entirely in filling sheets of paper with splodges of colour and there were often tantrums when it was time to stop. Mama came to refer to exuberant episodes of this sort as my 'vibrant' moods. Now, as a grown woman, I was in peril of becoming *vibrant* once more, intoxicated by Mr Lilley's praise.

My enhanced state was sustained for several days, during which I scarcely left my room and ate next to nothing. As I laboured, I seethed about Mama. I recalled my adolescence and her strictures on feminine etiquette: *Look at you swinging your parasol, you gawky thing!* I remembered long afternoons cooped up in airless rooms, suffocating in layers of skirts and petticoats, while listening politely to the dull conversation of my mother's society acquaintants. I recalled tedious Sunday strolls along Lady's Mile with other well-bred girls and their mothers, when I longed to romp around on the South Downs 'half savage and hardy' like Catherine in *Wuthering Heights*. There was the occasional treat of a paddle in the sea, weighed down by my skirts and restricted to the crowded water just in front of the bathing machines, while young gentlemen were permitted to swim from the beach in plain view. But now, as I approached my twenty-fifth year, a great rock had fallen into the stagnant pond of my existence.

Compared to Wilfred Lilley, Mama, Papa, my brothers and I were the very model of the stolid bourgeoisie. All was dull pretence. Mama with her shallow friendships and affectations.

Papa hiding in his room, living through his books, forever worshipping at the feet of Great Men yet never for a single moment daring to follow in their footsteps. So unlike Mr Lilley, who was intent on pursuing a higher goal, on setting his own standards in the face of ignorance and conformity. But what had any of this to do with me? I knew the type of woman who acquainted herself with artists: work girls, fallen daughters from respectable homes, ladies of the night. But I had also heard that some had deigned to pick up the paintbrush themselves.

All the while I laboured, I felt the oppressive silence out on the landing beyond the closed door of my room, and Mama's inexorable will coercing me to give in to her wishes. Every brushstroke or pencil mark I made was an effort to resist her.

In the midst of all this, I received an invitation to have tea with Felix in the Grand Hotel the following day. For an hour or so, I persisted with painting, but Felix constantly intruded on my thoughts. The world that he lived in, the Grand Hotel, the past history we shared – it seemed a phantasm. I should simply write and say I was unable to see him. Or better still, send him a telegraph. It would send a clear signal I had no intention of ever becoming his wife. Beset by all these thoughts, I couldn't concentrate on my work. I grew uneasy. I owed Felix an explanation – and perhaps also an apology. I cleared a space on my desk and wrote to him.

Dear Felix,

Please excuse the brevity of this letter. I have received your invitation, but I'm afraid I'm unable to meet you for tea. When we last met, I believe you were about to make a formal proposal of marriage, but the truth is that I've developed grave doubts about whether it would be wise for me to accept such an offer.

I must tell you that while I hold you in the highest regard and have the greatest affection for you as a longstanding friend, I do not feel certain that my feelings for you are those you would wish for in a future wife. And I am increasingly concerned about our compatibility of character.

I'm sure neither of us would be happy with a marriage of convenience, whatever our parents might think. And it would be a dreadful state of affairs if we discovered, after we were married, that we were unsuited to each other. We would find ourselves condemned to forever present a false front to the world – or, worse still, proceed to the divorce court.

I know this will be desperately disappointing for you, and I can assure you it is distressing for me too. But I hope that after a period of reflection you will see this is all for the best.

I'm deeply sorry for not addressing this matter sooner.

Yours with affection,
Violet

I sealed the envelope, and sat before the mirror to tidy up my appearance before rushing off to post the letter. But I got an awful fright when I saw the woman staring back at me. Her hair was bedraggled and greasy, her complexion sallow, her face drawn and, worst of all, her bloodshot eyes loured at me with an intense and wild expression. There was a deep groove between the eyes and dark rings beneath. I looked unwell.

I began to muse on how Felix might respond on reading the missive I was about to send him. He would be incensed. He would have every right to point out my failings towards him. I felt a kind of grief for our past and the people we'd been, and I had a dreadful feeling that I had betrayed my most loyal friend. It would be callous to send him a short note dismissing all that had passed between us. The honourable thing was to meet with him, however appalling the prospect might be. I tore up the letter, and sent him a telegram accepting his invitation.

*

And so, I found myself sitting opposite Felix at a table by a window overlooking the seafront. He wasn't his usual self at all. He looked grim and Felix was never grim. His face was pale and his posture rigid. His hands rested on the table before him, the fingers linked with the thumbs raised and constantly tapping each other. I couldn't bear to look at him, and was fearful of meeting his gaze. I looked down at a slice of sponge which I hadn't touched. The table was covered by at least three pristine white tablecloths, neatly spread one on top of another at right angles. Somewhere, someone was tinkling on a piano, playing a sugary Strauss waltz. Overhead, a wreath of stucco rose branches framed the room's high ceiling, as white as snow or icing sugar. It reminded me of a wedding cake – a sickening thought. A waiter in a smart uniform skirted our table, carrying a tray aloft, his nose in the air.

'Look at that fellow,' said Felix, when he had passed. 'I've never seen such a snot-nosed waiter.' He raised his hand and snapped his fingers. 'I say, old chap, over here, if you wouldn't mind.' The waiter turned abruptly, approached and waited on our table with a scornful demeanour. 'Two more teas. No, wait, on second thoughts, forget that. Two champagnes. The oldest Pommery you have.'

The waiter raised an eyebrow. 'Pommery, sir?'

'Yes, that's right.'

'Very well, sir.'

'Not for me,' I said.

'Don't be a bore, old girl.' He turned to the waiter. 'That's *two* glasses.'

The waiter bowed, and turned on his heels. It was entirely unlike Felix to behave in this high-handed way, and it made me more nervous still. 'It was no more than he deserved,' he said. 'Insolent fellow. Working in a place like this gives some chaps ideas above their station.'

'Felix, there's something I want to say,' I said.

He put up his hand to stop me.

'Let me have my say first. I think that's fair in the circumstances. It's time we had a frank exchange. I need hardly explain how I felt after our last meeting. Papa, in particular, was furious . . . ' He made a choking sound, as if his words were trapped in his throat. He stared out of the window for a moment, recovering his composure. 'Perhaps I've taken leave of my senses meeting you after that, but my heart demands I give you the opportunity to explain yourself. However, first, so that there's no misunderstanding, let me make it plain that I wouldn't expect you to be a glorified housekeeper. You wouldn't have to give up any of your passions, your art, your archery or any other blessed pastime you wanted to take up. I wouldn't stand in your way even if you began agitating for women's suffrage. I might even make a donation to the cause,' he said, snorting contemptuously. 'I understand you've been spending all day painting. You can carry on like that for all eternity, as far as I'm concerned.'

This threw me. I was sure I hadn't mentioned that I'd been painting, so how did he know? Were the lines of communication between the families still open, despite Mama lying sick in bed?

Felix was still speaking. 'But I would strongly suggest that if you want to paint glorious pictures, you must escape from this dark little island with its chimneys and fog and smuts. Look at it out there, for God's sake.'

I gazed out at a row of bathing machines abandoned to the elements. The end of the pier had evaporated in a thick sea fret, the ghosts of its gaudy oriental domes suspended in thin air. Further out, the masts and rigging of fishing boats appeared here and there like so many broken charcoal lines. The lonely seafront was deserted, and the sea and the land mingled as one mysterious element. Under the shelter of the pier, a young couple canoodled, the chap trying to steal a kiss while the girl pushed him away, laughing.

'I've always loved the rain,' I muttered, almost to myself.

'Why must you be so perverse? Let me take you to Bolivia with me. Show you colours you've never imagined. Exotic birds, butterflies, old painted Spanish cathedrals beyond your wildest imagination. What are the drizzly humps of the South Downs compared to vast mountain ranges and rainforests? Just picture us in the Plaza Murillo, promenading – a couple of swells. If only you'd look beyond the idea of me as a businessman. You ought to see me as an explorer. There'll be time enough for leisure, trust me. A clever chap these days lives off dividends rather than spending his life bent over a desk. He follows where the best investments lead – crosses new frontiers, brings the benefits of civilization to people everywhere. Africa is next.'

'Felix, you're almost shouting.'

'I don't give a damn!'

The waiter arrived with the champagne. I picked up my glass and took a large gulp. Felix sat with his arms folded, glaring through the window at the drizzle. I tried to recall the words I'd memorized.

'Listen to me for a moment, Felix,' I said. 'Don't you think you should make absolutely sure we're making the right decision? There must be a hundred girls with titles you could approach.'

'I don't consider myself beneath anyone just because she happens to have a title.'

'Sorry, I'm expressing myself very poorly. I wasn't for a moment suggesting you should look up to people for such reasons. It's just that I've been thinking about . . . ' There was a rush of blood to my head and I was forced to take a breath or two, before continuing. Somehow, I couldn't find an appropriate way to say what I meant – that I didn't love Felix and had no desire to be his wife. 'After so many years you must surely be aware of my temperament. I'm wilful and moody and selfish and bad-tempered and hopelessly messy and untidy, an utter slattern.'

'Oh, you needn't trouble yourself about that. I'll hire additional staff to compensate.' This was said with heavy sarcasm.

'You'd change your mind if you saw me in one of my moods.'

'I think I'd rather enjoy it,' he said, turning to me. 'You'd be magnificent. I know you're high-spirited, damn it. I'm not looking for someone to put in a gilded cage just to enhance my prestige. I want you. I *love* you, Violet!' Other diners turned to gawp at us. The waiters got into a huddle to converse. Felix lowered his voice. 'I love you just as you are. I can't imagine myself with anyone else. And we've got more in common than you think. I want the world and I believe you do too. What a team we'd make. If you'd only come to your senses.'

'But think, Felix,' I said, throwing my napkin down on the table. 'Don't you see this has all come about because we became friends when you were young and impressionable, and also because I was always a cut above you, if you'll forgive the expression. I suspect that I came to represent something, a standard, I suppose. A false standard, actually. But surely you see that marrying me will only prove that you've never really overcome your sense of inferiority. I'm sorry to put it this way, Felix, but I fear it might to be the case.'

He was silent for a short while, staring across the room, his brow knotted.

'You don't seem to know me at all,' he said. 'You think I only want you to prove my worth – by marrying above my caste. As if my sole ambition was to raise myself up to the level of every chinless wonder with a title and a hundred hereditary defects.' He looked around at the well-heeled people on the tables around us, as he said this. 'And you're usually so brainy. Don't you see I could never settle for a dull conventional girl after you? There's nothing that would give me more satisfaction than to have you sit at the dinner table, scandalizing my acquaintances with your opinions.'

A wave of light-headedness overcame me, and I clutched the table. 'I can't breathe. I need some air.'

'You're a funny colour. We'd better get you outside.' He reached across the table and took my hand before I could withdraw it. 'Forgive me.'

67

I couldn't bring myself to speak.

'I'll bring the carriage round,' he said. He rose to his feet, and called over the waiter he'd earlier insulted. 'I say, old boy, would you mind bringing the bill over quick as you can. And our coats. And if I could trouble you to have my carriage come around to the front.'

I stood up unsteadily, and he escorted me to the exit. I felt I might pass out at any moment.

He took my arm, but didn't look me in the eyes, just stared ahead intently. 'I must apologize. No doubt you think a true gentleman would never behave in such a way. My heart is breaking, I suppose.' His carriage drew to a noisy juddering halt outside. 'Here we are. I'll get you home right away.'

Felix and I sat opposite each other in silence on the way home – he looked out of one window of the carriage and I looked out the other, as raindrops rolled diagonally across the panes. As soon as I alighted, I burst into tears, and had to wait outside the house until I'd mastered myself.

INTERLUDE

Red-brick walls tower over me on four sides. About me, women amble around a circular gravel path, either alone or in pairs or groups. A narrow bar of weak light stretches across this side of the yard; the other side is cast in shadow. I pass a stone bench where country women with ruddy complexions huddle in their tartan shawls, murmuring conspiratorially. Puffs of pipe smoke rise from them. Guards pass among us, marching slowly in pairs, watching our every move, whistles attached to strings around their necks. A lady in late middle age shambles towards me. She wears a straw hat, a shawl over her shoulders, a scarf tied at the neck. Her face is strained, her colourless eyes wide open but gazing inward. I step out of her path just before she can collide with me.

Glancing up, I see the sky framed by the rectangle of the walls. Busy clouds rush over, anxious to find a more salubrious place to cast their shadows. Down here, at the foot of the walls, there are flower beds, or rather an impenetrable tangle of gnarled shrubs, ivy and bramble and roses bristling with sharp thorns. Only the hardiest and most stubborn bush could survive such smothering darkness and dankness, those whose roots can reach deep into the earth. Here and there a plant has pushed up a pallid bloom whose petals will have dropped by nightfall.

Out of the corner of my eye, I see some devil push a frail old lady into a prickly bush. The offender hurries away, losing herself among the other women. Her victim cries for help as she tries to remove herself from the thorny branches. Two burly guards are weaving through the women. They soon identify the culprit, skulking among her sisters. A shock of black hair, a face that is all points: chin, cheekbones, nose. She looks shocked at her own devilment, but affects a demeanour of innocence. Seeing the guards, she suddenly dashes, pushing other women out of her way. But she is quickly cornered, then dragged, kicking and screaming, to a bench, and forced down onto it. There is a frenzy of hair-pulling, scratching and attempted biting. The two attendants each raise a leg and bring their thighs down over hers, one on either side, clamping her down between them. Each then seizes a wrist, so that all the woman can do is wriggle her shoulders and yell. Shrill women's voices fill the air as we all gather around the bench.

'Fetch chloral!' shouts the woman who is in charge.

'Take your filthy hands off me, you monsters!' cries the culprit, spitting at her two assailants. A moment later, a third attendant arrives, forcing herself through the melee. She drops out of sight, reappearing shortly after.

'Order!' she yells. This is enough to subdue the patients. 'Line up before the door. Right this minute, every single one of you.' She points to the door that leads back to the ward. We comply, shuffling into a queue.

As we await further orders, I turn my head. The two guards have relinquished their hold on their charge. They are panting, dabbing their sweating faces with their aprons. The madwoman's head lolls in her lap and a thread of spittle hangs from her bottom lip. Her hair is scraped back to reveal a very high forehead. Under her eyes there are dark bags, deeply scored. She snarls in a broad Sussex dialect: 'Let go of me drackly, you hear. If you dursn't, I'll cut your heads off. You got no call to treat me so, nohows. Naun but madbrains, the lot of you.' Her chin falls to her chest. 'I mun go now. Policeman be a-waiting outside for me.'

On the other side of the wall a wren bursts into luminous song.

7

After my meeting with Felix, I arrived home to find an oppressive hush had descended over the house. The drapes were closed, muffling all sound and casting the rooms and passages into shadow. In the hallway, Susan told me Mama had suffered a seizure and the doctor had come. I went straight to Papa's room and found him slumped over his desk, scratching his head as he pored over an untidy pile of papers covered in dense rows of figures. He looked haggard and sickly in the light of the oil lamp, and seemed irritated by the interruption.

'The doctor's been called for – is Mama worse?' I asked.

'Awful news, I'm afraid,' he said, taking off his spectacles and rubbing his eyes. 'It's the family finances. Your mother's taken it badly. I'm just now assessing the full implications.'

'Oh dear. Perhaps I should go to her.'

'I wouldn't trouble yourself. The doctor's with her. He has her under heavy sedation.' At which, he shook the creases out of a sheet of paper on his desk and returned to his calculations. I left, closing the door softly behind me.

Despite the family's straitened circumstances, Mama had always insisted that a certain mad-doctor should attend her during her intervals of nervous prostration. Dr Harold Rastrick was a physician of the highest repute, a leader in his field, the head of a lunatic asylum called Hillwood Grange. There was something unnerving about the man, a quality of pure malevolence. On previous visits, he had taken the liberty of interviewing me and asking all manner of impertinent questions as if I was his patient, rather than Mama. At times I almost believed Mama was feigning her neurasthenia so that she and her vile doctor could conspire against me. At any rate, he exerted an undue influence over her. In my weakened state, he was the last person I wanted to see. So I remained in my room and waited for him to leave. I picked up a book from my chest of drawers, *Lady Audley's Secret*, sat in my armchair, and opened it. The words swam before me and I could take none of it in. Dr Rastrick's mere proximity filled me with horrible unease. Although I suspected he was no more than a quack, he had a quality of intensity about him, of stern and unyielding concentration, and once his gaze was fixed on mine, I felt it almost impossible to look away. And I feared his 'examinations', not least because I had only the haziest recollections of them afterwards, as if he had syphoned off my thoughts and memories and carried them away in his case. His alliance with Mama was quite abhorrent, and I had no doubt that each fed the other with untruths about me.

I heard voices down in the hall, Papa and Dr Rastrick. I sat and waited, rigid with tension, the novel open in my lap. Footsteps sounded on the stairs and then on the landing outside my room. I heard two firm raps on my door and jumped.

'You may enter,' I said, trying to modulate my voice.

Dr Rastrick stepped into the room, his countenance stern and reproving. He had a gift for putting one at a disadvantage. He couldn't be described as handsome, but he was manly and

72

certainly had presence. He was in his mid-thirties, with a stocky build. His suit was well-tailored, as always, his beard neatly trimmed.

'Good evening, Miss Pring. I need to examine you,' he said, brusquely. He put his case down on the bed, opened it and took out his stethoscope.

'It's not a convenient moment, I'm afraid.'

'Your mother's asked me to take a look at you.' He put the stethoscope around his neck.

'There's no need.'

'Your general demeanour indicates otherwise. So, if you wouldn't mind, undo the top buttons of your dress for me.'

'I told you, I'm not ill.'

'I'll be the judge of that. I've taken an interest in your case for some years. There was an incident when you were fifteen, you may recall, which was the cause of your mother's first bout of neurasthenia.'

'I'm not a child any longer.'

'Then stop behaving like one.' He approached me and took hold of my wrist, lifting it to take my pulse.

'This is an affront,' I said, under my breath. He affected not to notice, so I rose to my feet and tried to wrest his hand from my wrist.

'Stop this nonsense immediately, or I'll call for the maids and have them hold you down,' he said under his breath. We stood glaring at one another for a long moment. Dr Rastrick maintained his composure, but there was a cruel glint in his eye. Close to, there was something sinister, even evil in the man. I was sure he took a perverse satisfaction in showing his power over me. My urge was to fight him, but I feared he had been in earnest when he threatened to call for the staff to hold me down. What choice had I but to sit down and undo my dress? I turned to face away from him, and felt the cold touch of his stethoscope on my skin.

'Your heartbeat is faster than I'd like it to be.'

'Of course it is – after the outrageous way you've treated me.' I spat out the words.

He stepped away, removing the stethoscope from his neck. He put it back in its case, and took out a black notebook. 'I shall need the answer to some questions. Have you experienced nervous sensations recently?'

'No more than any other normal person.'

'Palpitations?'

'Not especially.'

'Disturbed sleep?'

'On occasion.'

'Numbness?'

'Not at all.'

'Have your menses been regular in recent months?'

'How many more questions are you going to ask me?'

'How you had any violent outbursts recently?'

'No, I have not!' I snapped.

He paused, the ghost of a smile on his face. 'I ask you once more: have your menses been regular?'

'It's none of your business.'

'It's very much my business. I'm aware you've thrown yourself into painting in recent weeks. This excessive behaviour may well have damaged your nervous system. Bodily energy isn't inexhaustible, and women are especially vulnerable during the monthly periods.'

'So you want to bar me from painting because I'm a woman and it's in my nature to be feeble? Has it occurred to you that women might be unhappy for other reasons than their bodily functions? You'll never understand how insupportably dull the life of a young woman can be, with so little to occupy her mind. And if you had any perception at all, you'd know my behaviour was in response to the marriage arrangements I've been obliged to accept in spite of my own hopes and desires.'

'Considering anecdotal detail of that sort is fruitless. My business is to examine physiological causes. In the circumstances it would be wise to do an internal examination.'

At first, I had no idea what he meant. When I realized, I shook my head vigorously. After a long pause, he rose to his feet.

'Very well, we'll leave that for a later date. My priority now is to ensure you are fit and able when your wedding day arrives.'

'Wedding day? No such arrangement has been agreed. And in any case, that's no concern of yours.'

'Anything affecting your health is my concern. You must desist from painting and drawing and abstain from all strenuous physical exercise.' He glanced at the book I'd been reading, which now lay open on the floor. 'I would further advise that you stop reading. You're to stay at home and avoid all social engagements, other than those necessary for the . . . ' He paused. 'For the forthcoming arrangements. I'm prescribing laudanum in the first instance. I'll leave instructions about the dosage and frequency with your father.'

'Why with my father, pray? I'm not a child.'

'Be that as it may, I want to ensure your compliance. I'll look in on you on my visits.'

'That won't be necessary,' I cried, but he had already turned his back on me. Without another word, he left.

Afterwards, I had such a violent headache that all I could do was lie on my bed in my day clothes. As I lay there, I tried to untangle my thoughts, but the effort only made me feel sick, so I waited, all rational thought suspended, as waves of nausea came and went. At some untold hour, I awoke from a sleep as thick and black as treacle. The room was dark, but my mind was suddenly luminous and clear, frighteningly so. Mama's supposed nervous prostration was a ploy to use the crisis in the family fortunes to exert the utmost pressure on me to marry Felix. If there was to be any hope of my having another sort of life, I would have to act quickly. But what could I do? My options were limited to say the least. The nearest I had come to envisaging another way of living was during my conversation with Mr Lilley. I went to the chest and took out his calling card, the one he had handed me the day he'd visited the art class, and which was now in a drawer of my desk. I got up and wrote to Miss Fanshaw in the moonlight, telling her I wanted to accept Mr Lilley's invitation to visit his studio to receive his opinion on my work, and asking her to be my chaperone.

8

The following week, after the art class, Miss Fanshaw and I set out for Mr Lilley's rooms. The air seemed thrillingly alive that day, lit up with hope and excitement. The stifling world ruled by Mama seemed far away, and the enticing possibility of another life, a world inhabited by men like Mr Lilley, was tantalizingly close. I had my recent work in my basket, along with a small selection of older drawings and watercolours. We left the museum and went along the seafront, assailed by the stench of the fish market. Out on the shingle, fishermen old and young huddled together in a conspiratorial way, some mending their nets amidst a forest of masts, puffs of smoke rising from their pipes. Down below, ragged boys were shouting at the better-off on the higher promenade, urging them to throw down pennies. Walking with Miss Fanshaw was invigorating. She had a long stride and the wind was behind us, speeding us forward, in contrast to my aimless dawdles with Felix. As she paced, she held forth on her favourite topics: the Woman Question and Art. We passed the aquarium clock tower and headed beyond the pier along the seafront. I was waiting for a chance to talk about Mr Lilley, so as soon as she paused, I jumped in.

'You must know Mr Lilley very well?'

'Oh, indeed, although I wouldn't say he was in the inner circle of the group in St John's Wood. At one time both Mr Lilley and myself were seldom out of Rossetti's studio, you know. But in the end, I tired of the schoolboy larks. I'd have found it more amusing if they weren't so dismissive of women's painting. The trouble we've had getting Evelyn De Morgan exhibited! Yet she's the equal of any male painter. There's a reason why I moved to Brighton and set up my academy.'

She stopped talking long enough to blow her nose, so I leapt in again. 'Do you have any idea why Mr Lilley left London in such a hurry?'

'I'm afraid not. But he is a mercurial character. His parents live down here and perhaps he needed to fall back on their support,' she said, tucking her handkerchief into her sleeve. 'And he'd fallen out with everyone in London. Which is hardly surprising, the way he goes about disparaging Millais and others with higher reputations than his own.'

'And wasn't there something about an attachment, a young lady?'

She didn't answer immediately and her expression turned pensive. She removed a glove and raised her hand to her face, touching her eye with a forefinger, perhaps to remove a fleck of grit. 'Yes, there was someone: Fanny Kerrich. A delicate girl, thin as a reed. She did his laundry. She was serious about her art, mind.'

'She's an artist, herself?'

'Oh yes, and a talented one. She married Charles Eldridge when his career was taking off.' Again, she was quiet for a period, seeming to lose herself in her recollections. 'Eldridge is a baronet now, you know? Fanny wasn't the first young lady from humble origins to marry up and she won't be the last. But I remember when—'

I broke in impatiently, keen to hear more about Lilley's relationship with Fanny. 'I suppose Mr Lilley was awfully fond of Fanny?'

Miss Fanshaw frowned. 'Fond is putting it politely. You know that she modelled for his *Pygmalion*? It caused a sensation: poor Fanny's ribs poking out like those of a consumptive, the bluish tinge in her cheeks as she emerged as flesh and blood out of that cold demure white marble. She looked all too human, as if you'd just peeked into a public bathhouse and seen a skinny work-girl in nothing but her slippers. There was a tremendous poignancy about the picture, for anyone who knew her. The details were so particular it was assumed she'd modelled undressed. The critics gave it a mauling, of course, complaining about the picture's crude realism and distasteful morbidity. But it launched Mr Lilley's career – he even rivalled Ned Burne-Jones for a brief period.'

'And how did he feel when he learned Fanny was married?'

'He took it to heart. And not long after – I shouldn't reveal this, but it's well known in the art world – he put himself up for a series of large pictures illustrating Briar Rose, the old fairy tale, for a country house in Oxfordshire. He spent months on compositional sketches of recumbent sleeping beauties, only for the commission to go to Burne-Jones. Wilf tried to recover some pride by entering a picture for the RA's summer show, but it got a dreadful press reception and was rejected.'

'So, he moved to Brighton to lick his wounds.'

'Quite possibly. Male pride is a delicate flower; the slightest touch of frost and it wilts. The tragedy is he has a genuine talent, but it's not allied with worldliness.'

She went on, but a noisy conveyance passed, drowning her out. When it was gone, I asked her the question uppermost in my mind. 'I imagine it's a rare thing for a female painter to secure the support of an established artist?'

She gave me an arch look. 'A word of advice, my dear. Keep your feet firmly on the ground. Now, when I was your age—'

'I've heard that more women are being apprenticed to painters and some work in their studios?'

'A privileged few, perhaps. But, for most, art will never be more than a pastime – although a rewarding one, if you make the time for it. That's not to say it's impossible to be a female artist. You should come to an exhibition of Miss Zambaco's work next year. I'm planning a class trip. As regards my own career, my early successes were resented by the men, you know . . . But look, here we are.' We turned into Sussex Square.

We passed a landscaped garden embraced by a crescent of grand houses with iron balcony railings and stone pillars at the front. I looked through the windows at rooms stuffed with handsome standing clocks, sideboards ornamented with marquetry, marble busts on pedestals, peacock feathers and the like. Miss Fanshaw led me out of the square and through a cobbled mews towards an old house with black flint-cobbled walls at the far end. She rapped on the door with her parasol and shortly afterwards footsteps sounded inside the house. The door opened and Mr Lilley stood before us. He seemed to bristle with energy.

'Miss Fanshaw! And Miss Pring. Good afternoon to you both,' he said. 'Won't you come this way.' He wasn't overly tall, I noticed, perhaps a couple of inches taller than me. He stepped aside and whisked us down a narrow hallway and up a staircase with a threadbare runner, and then into his living room. It was light and airy, just as I'd imagined an artist's rooms should be. There was an odour of cigar smoke. He invited us to sit on a divan of faded green velvet while he went to fetch a cane chair from a corner, then sat opposite us, crossing his legs. He wore a black lounge suit which fitted him well, but the cuffs were a little worn. We were separated by a small occasional table on which stood three glasses and a bottle of wine. I moved a cushion with an arabesque pattern out of the way and saw it had been positioned to hide a small tear in the divan's upholstery where feathers poked through.

'Now, I have a bone to pick with you,' said Miss Fanshaw. 'I was very disappointed you were unable to join the planning committee for Maria Zambaco's exhibition next year. She modelled for you, after all.'

'Maria? Yes, of course. Dark-red hair. A terrible fidget. And argumentative. Didn't she have an affair with, remind me now . . . ?'

'With Ned, yes. More than once.'

'I might have guessed. But has Miss Zambaco really produced a body of work large enough for an exhibition? She was making medals, the last I heard of her. Curious little portraits, like those on coins. Where does that fit in? Of course, she has her own money. No doubt that helps.'

'I suppose you gentlemen prefer girls from humble origins – far easier to persuade them to do your bidding.'

They continued in the same vein, talking about mutual acquaintances among the London artists, the rival schools, dropping the names of various famous artists. I felt out of my depth, with little to contribute, which made me nervous. My gaze was drawn to a large canvas leaning against the wall. In the foreground was a mermaid whose raised tail ended in a majestic double fluke. She lay in a kind of swoon on rocks under a full moon, while another of her kind sat in a shadowy recess strumming an antique harp. They might have been twins as their faces were identical. I had often noticed how artists tended to populate their paintings with the same woman's face. Light from a large south-facing window fell directly onto the picture, highlighting a diagonal seam across the mermaid's face, like a scar, as if the canvas had been scored with a knife and then repaired. But most striking was the starkly lifelike rendering of the languishing mermaid's body, or at least the human part of it. She was apparently modelled on a thin girl with sallow skin, prominent ribs and large red calloused hands. Her flesh appeared mottled, goose pimpled perhaps, the finish of the painting lumpy. I was shocked by Mr Lilley's depiction of the female figure. This was far from the idealized presentation of women I had seen in other paintings. Was this a quest for truth, or a descent into decadence? The mermaid's fishy half had been left unfinished, all but the large tail, and had been sketched out in charcoal, waiting to be painted over. Propped against the wall beside the painting was a preliminary sketch of a female nude in the pose of the mermaid.

Mr Lilley saw me looking at his picture. 'I thought it too smooth, so I'm trying different kinds of execution,' he said. 'But I can't make up my mind on the finish. It's painted from nature, of course.'

'Did you carry your mermaid up from the beach then?' I asked.

'I most certainly did – dripping wet. The trouble I had persuading the conductor to allow her on the omnibus!'

The thought of a girl coming to this room and removing every stitch of her clothing both appalled and excited me. I felt emboldened. In other words, I was in that vibrant state my mother so deplored. In such moods I felt capable of almost any shocking thing. I saw there were other pictures in the room, scattered here and there. Most were half-finished canvases of reclining drowsing women: saints, Arthurian princesses, ladies sporting antique chignons and so forth.

'You know why men like Mr Lilley paint rows and rows of sleeping damsels, don't you?' said Miss Fanshaw. She was addressing me, but she was looking at him. 'It's to silence women's tongues, so we won't say anything to challenge them or hurt their pride.'

'Please, go ahead and hurt my feelings, Gwen, if you think you can,' he said.

I broke in before she had the chance. 'It looks as though you've drawn your model's hands just as they are. Did she mind?' I was conscious, as I said it, of my own rather large hands.

He looked wistful for a moment. 'I've painted all of her just as she is. Truth is what I'm after. Would you say the picture is obscene because I refuse to idealize her?'

A frisson hung in the air, enough to momentarily silence even Miss Fanshaw.

Then she laughed and said: 'If your intention is to seek truth, it seems odd you've chosen to depict an imaginary creature such as a mermaid.'

'Truth in your eyes must be dreadfully mundane, Gwen,' he responded.

'No doubt your picture's full of symbols, but what use is that when only *you* can interpret them?' she said.

'Would it be more helpful if I painted in morse code so everyone got the message?' He tossed his hair out of his eyes with a jerk of his head, a mannerism I remembered from our earlier encounter. I found it boyish and charming.

Mr Lilley and Miss Fanshaw continued fencing in this manner as I took in the rest of his habitation: a black-stained cabinet, a Japanese screen, various fans and lamps. Clothes were hung on pegs by the door. There was a tower of books against the wall and the names on the spines were familiar from Papa's study: Gautier, Baudelaire, Pater, Swinburne.

I looked more closely at his pictures of reclining dozing damsels. Every surface was draped in the richest fabrics, all rendered in fine detail. One group of drowsing women sat in a row, resting their heads on each other's shoulders. Others lay about on a marble floor lost in a general torpor, petals scattered around them. They were attended by women plucking lyres or scraping violins, instruments presumably chosen because they were unlikely to disturb anyone's sleep. Those figures yet to fall into a state of incurable lassitude wandered about making obscure gestures to one another, or moved in sinuous rhythmic formations as if under a spell or performing a ritual dance. Again, I saw Mr Lilley's women all had the same handsome, if lugubrious, face, with necks as white as swans' and almost as long. Surrounded by all these drowsing beauties, I found myself stifling a yawn, as if I too might be absorbed into Mr Lilley's silent world of lounging unconscious women.

Miss Fanshaw was still holding forth. 'We've seen little improvement since Mrs Barrett Browning published her poem.

It remains well-nigh impossible for a woman to be an independent female artist—'

Mr Lilley interrupted. 'The only real freedom a woman needs is sexual freedom.'

'Well, that's very convenient for you, isn't it? I take a very different view.'

'I don't doubt it. But don't you think it's time we looked at Miss Pring's work?'

Now that the moment had come, I began to tremble. I picked up my basket and took out my own pictures, placing them on the low table. At the last moment I lost my nerve, so I took out only the more conventional and finished work, and left my recent more audacious productions in the basket. I couldn't bring myself to reveal pictures that had created such mental disturbance while I was painting them. I feared Mr Lilley might laugh at them or consider me affected. He went to fetch an oil lamp and put it down on the table to better illuminate the flaws in my work, then took a cigarette case from his pocket and lit a cigar. Without asking first, he poured wine into the three tumblers on the table. He leant over the table and gazed down at my first picture, a pen-and-wash drawing, exhaling streams of thick smoke from his nostrils. Quickly, he turned to the next, a watercolour, and soon he had worked his way through all my work.

'Your drawings are well done and show dexterity of hand,' he concluded.

I was speechless. This was far fainter praise than I'd hoped for. To hide my feelings, I took a sip of the wine. My father's claret was much smoother than this rough vintage, but at least it soothed my nerves. Mr Lilley pointed at the picture at the top of the pile and studied it, frowning.

'You have a good technical facility. This watercolour has a certain delicacy and pureness of feeling. You might improve by training your eye a little more. I could help you with that.'

I was utterly crushed and could think of nothing to say. I had come to Mr Lilley's rooms full of foolish hopes and had overreached myself.

'Well, there we have it,' said Miss Fanshaw. 'Most encouraging. And Mr Lilley has offered to give you instruction, which is a rare privilege.'

I sensed Mr Lilley's gaze upon me, and my eyes filled with tears. I clenched my fists, trying to control my emotions.

'Your archer . . . ' said Mr Lilley. He had adopted a softer tone. 'The picture I saw at the museum. The painting made a deep impression on me. I was surprised by its vigour and muscularity, the sheer defiance, which is not what I generally expect from a lady artist. It was a glimpse of what you might achieve. Perhaps you should come again when you've attempted more in that vein.'

'I have attempted more, sir, but I don't feel ready to show you.' I took a large gulp of wine.

'A pity you didn't bring your new work along.'

I paused for a moment, my heart thudding rapidly. 'Oh, but I did.'

His stirred in his chair, drawing himself more upright. 'You did? Then you must let me see.'

The warmth of the alcohol had spread through me. I took out the pictures and put them on the table, then waited, arms folded in a show of false nonchalance. As Mr Lilley scrutinized my work, he rocked forwards and backwards, his cane chair creaking underneath him. He took his time, waving away wreathes of cigar smoke with his hand, his attention so absorbed that ash fell onto whatever picture he was viewing. Finally, he leaned back in his chair, looking bewildered. Before him lay my unfinished watercolour of a back-to-front mermaid. 'I didn't expect this,' he said, frowning.

'Violet's imagination knows no bounds, which is admirable, but I do wonder whether she would improve her prospects if she reined herself in somewhat,' said Miss Fanshaw.

Mr Lilley seemed oblivious. He was peering at me in so penetrating a way I couldn't hold his gaze. 'We both feel the lure of mermaids, Miss Pring, but you've been drawn into deeper and more treacherous waters than I ever have.' He sat surrounded by plumes of coiling smoke, as if he was smouldering from within. 'I admire the sheer imaginative daring, the vigour, the genius of your conception, the way you've embraced this ungodly paradox, your disregard for taste or conventional morality. I'm inclined to say what we have here is something new in English art. No! More than that. In all of European art.'

'It feels like something new, certainly,' said Miss Fanshaw. 'Although it makes me think of photographic superimpositions. However, I wonder where work like this could ever be exhibited? Even Paris might baulk at it. But it is good.'

'It's not good. Words like good or bad could never do it justice. It's remarkable. You have other work, I suppose.'

'I do,' I said, breathlessly. 'And I've every intention of producing more.'

'Then you must bring it and show it to me.' He turned to Miss Fanshaw. 'Let's arrange another visit. And soon.'

'Why ever not?' She looked at her fob watch. 'But look at the time. I'll refresh myself, if I may, and after that we had better leave.' She crossed the room to the privy and closed the door behind her.

I put the pictures into my basket and stood up. Mr Lilley leapt to his feet and took both my hands in his own, looking searchingly into my eyes.

'You have outstanding promise, I have no doubt of it. Tell me you will never surrender your ambitions.'

'That's very generous, but I couldn't possibly pursue an artistic career in my circumstances. At least not in any professional way.'

'Then you must escape your circumstances. If you leave your card with me, I'll try to arrange introductions. I know of one or two women who have their own studios. It's not impossible. And they have exhibited too – or at least they did so before they were married.'

'Oh, I see – before they were married.'

'Marriage should never be a barrier to a talent like yours. You must never give up. You must pursue an artistic career at all costs.'

I was reeling in the face of such praise, too overwhelmed to offer a response. Could this really be happening to me?

Ten minutes later Miss Fanshaw and I were walking back along the seafront, this time with the wind in our faces. Miss Fanshaw forged ahead, holding forth as usual, but I took little of it in. I was lost in a reverie about days spent in artists' studios making clever conversation and drinking wine and smoking cigarettes at three in the afternoon. I imagined myself as Mr Lilley's muse inspiring him to greatness.

'Well, you have come away with some encouragement about your work,' said Miss Fanshaw.

'I certainly have. But what use is it when my fate is to be to be married off?'

'Married off? Is that how you view the marriage sacrament? Don't sound so glum about it. There's no prohibition on married women going to art exhibitions, or of going on outings with other ladies to do *plein air* paintings.'

'I don't want to be that sort of artist, someone who exhibits inoffensive pictures in the local church hall.'

Miss Fanshaw drew to a sudden halt and peered at me, frowning. 'My dear girl, in some ways you remind me of myself at your age. Like you, I dreamed of establishing myself as an artist. I found it nigh on impossible without a wealthy husband or other benefactor. So I became a skivvy in the studios of gentleman painters, managing their diaries, finding costumes for them. Some of them made advances on me, and hinted it would be detrimental to my career if I refused to surrender. But I did refuse, and found myself dropped, and without connections it is impossible to succeed in the close-knit world of artists' cliques. I was a rather plain girl, so imagine how it would be for someone with your looks. I advise you to keep your feet firmly on the ground. Gentlemen of Mr Lilley's kind may talk about sexual freedom for women, but as long as women remain financially dependent on men it's freedom of a very perilous sort.'

'I assure you I've no interest in Mr Lilley.'

'Which is as it should be.' She resumed her quick-march and we found ourselves moving through a crowd of tourists who had just disembarked from a pleasure boat at the pier, and were now scattered about the pavement. 'I have a strong belief that women should be educated in the dangers of sex and the degenerate nature of men,' said Miss Fanshaw in her usual strident voice, oblivious to the outrage of the respectable ladies with small children sharing the pavement with her. 'Sex before marriage is an abomination. How on earth will we win our civic rights if we allow gentlemen to treat us like ladies of the night?'

'Do you mind?' cried one of the respectable mothers surrounding us. 'I suggest you continue your conversation elsewhere.'

We walked on in silence for a moment.

'Suppose I chose not to marry,' I said. 'How would you say an unmarried woman with no proper education might go about making a living? Would she be reduced to taking in laundry like Mr Lilley's model, for example?'

'Not if her hands were as soft as yours. She might consider something less colourful and more worthwhile, such as becoming a Poor Law Guardian. And if her lack of education proved a barrier then she could try being a governess or telegraphist. In the meantime, I would advise you to join our women's association and take part in its activities.'

'You mean I should take up good causes, I suppose – ragged schools and mothers' meetings – and attend long public talks?'

'Why ever not?'

We had arrived at Castle Square where we were to go our separate ways. Miss Fanshaw fixed me with a certain look, and said: 'As you're no doubt aware, young lady, you're a handsome woman. Exceptionally so. You have a look of the gypsy about you. That could take you a long way – perhaps too far. I feel I must warn you that Mr Lilley is a man with a naturally enthusiastic temperament. He takes up ideas, and people, with great conviction, and while his own constancy might waver, he demands others remain faithful to the last. I mention this as a friend who wishes you well. Good day to you, Violet.'

Once free of her and left to my own thoughts, I was in no great rush to get home. It seemed the world had fallen under a spell and everything was lit through with a wondrous light. Dazzling late-afternoon sunlight streamed down North Street making silhouettes of the crowds rushing along the pavement or weaving their way through the jumble of cabs and omnibuses. Queasy music from an organ grinder lent a dream-like atmosphere with its cheerful mechanical pooping and trilling and lurching shifts of tempo. The music churned in sympathy with my own emotional state and increased the sense of a world tilted subtly out of balance. A long line of plucked chickens hung by their feet outside the Godwin Foster and Brown store. Outside an inn, a woman with blackened teeth and periodicals under her arm was shouting over and over: 'Tit-Bits – all the latest news!' The doorman outside the Clarence House Hotel tipped his hat at me as I passed. I caught my reflection in the window of a shop and almost didn't recognize myself, so ecstatic was the smile on my face. I pondered Miss Fanshaw's word of warning, and I wondered if it might be worth risking all, even for just a few weeks' fulfilment – especially when the alternative might be a lifetime's disappointment.

9

When I got home, I found my brother Lance skulking in his usual spot, leaning against the wall in the back yard.

'What's wrong with you?' he said. 'You look strange. In one of your moods, I suppose?'

'I should like to stay in this mood for the rest of my life.'

'Where have you been to get you into this state?'

This was exciting as Lance usually made a point of showing no interest in my affairs. I assumed the ironical tone we sometimes used with each other. 'I went to the rooms of a notorious artist and spent the whole afternoon there drinking.'

'Not alone, surely?'

'No, of course not. With Miss Fanshaw, my art teacher. But don't mention it to Mama or Papa. Things are bad enough as they are.'

He blew out a stream of cigarette smoke. 'You should marry Felix. He's rich, for God's sake.'

'But I don't love him. Oh, Lance, what would you do, if you were me? You've never worried about behaving properly, so perhaps you have some advice.'

'You'll have to marry someone sooner or later – or end up an old maid. You need to start producing children. What else would you ever do? And if you're bored, you can always take up with another man. I'm told the lives of women in the top one thousand are a constant stream of sordid affairs.'

'How sweet of you to worry about my future happiness. And what about your future? What will you do now you've failed at Cambridge?'

'I didn't fail. Didn't Papa tell you? I was sent down.'

I was shocked. 'Sent down? But why?'

He shook his head, and tapped some ash from his cigarette.

'Come on, I've shared my secret,' I said. 'Tell me.'

'Over a trifle. Smashed up the room of an insufferable prig.'

'What! You're not serious? How could you?'

'We were all very drunk. And he deserved it, at any rate.'

I took a step away from him. 'What will you do now?'

'Well, as Papa has refused to pay off my debts, I intend to join the Guards.'

'I suppose that's not surprising, given that killing is the only thing you've ever taken much interest in.'

He glared at me briefly, then resumed his demeanour of sullen indifference. 'I wish I could go off and fight right now, quite frankly. It's what this country needs – a proper war, on a grand stage. It's what I need, anyhow.'

'Really, Lance! What's become of you?'

I entered the house and went straight into Papa's study, which was cloudy with cigar smoke. The room was in shade apart from the glow around his desk lamp. He was bent over a chaotic pile of papers and didn't raise his head to greet me.

'May I speak to you?' I asked.

'It's not altogether convenient, I'm afraid.'

'I wouldn't prevail upon you were it not a matter of the utmost importance.'

'It can't possibly be more important than my current business.'

'My life might depend on it.'

He removed his spectacles, closed his eyes and rubbed them with his hands, then turned to face me. 'Good Lord, what on earth is going on? Very well then, what is the matter?'

I sat down in an armchair and announced: 'I have been awakened to the possibility of another kind of life.'

'Indeed?'

'I have decided to pursue a career as an artist.'

Papa's shoulders drooped and he sank deeper into his chair with a groan. 'What on earth has brought this on?'

'This afternoon I met an artist, Mr Wilfred Lilley, and he praised my work in the highest possible terms. He has offered to set me up as an apprentice in a respectable art studio. When I last spoke with you, I confided my misgivings about my compatibility with Felix—'

'May I stop you there, young lady? You said you met this fellow, Lilley. You're not suggesting you met him alone?'

'Of course not. I went with Miss Fanshaw. As I was saying, Mr Lilley commended my work and in the course of our conversation I developed a strong conviction that I will only ever be happy in life if I answer my chosen calling. As a lover of the arts and literature, I hope you will understand my feelings.'

'I understand only that you're in a very dangerous state.' He lowered his voice. 'I hope this doesn't portend a recurrence of your unfortunate condition, Violet. I've seen you in this heightened state before.'

'This is not the same thing at all.'

'Remember how your mother suffered. I feared she'd lose her mind.'

'That's entirely unfair. You and I have often talked over the years about how Mama keeps all of us in thrall to her hysterical outbursts. It happens whenever she doesn't get her way. She has schemed endlessly to bring about the marriage to Felix. I'm asking you to support me in choosing another path in life.'

Papa began to bluster. 'If you don't wish to marry Felix, then so be it. But why must you dally with a louche artist and ruin your chances of ever getting a respectable man to marry you? Must I remind you that everyone in this family has a duty to fulfil?'

He stared at me furiously. Where was his usual equable good humour or his affection? 'If my fate is only to marry a rich man and grace his house, then why did you ever encourage me to read your books?'

'There's a great gulf between the life of the mind and how one must conduct oneself in reality.'

'But shouldn't ideas have some bearing on how we lead our lives?'

'Only if we are prudent.'

'Then surely prudence is only another word for cowardice? I believe there are men left in this world who still try to live their lives according to a higher standard, regardless of public reputation. I'm convinced Mr Lilley is one of them.'

He replied in a low rasp, almost spitting out his words: 'Not another word about this Lilley fellow, do you hear me? And under no circumstances mention this to your mother.'

For a moment, I was shaken and silenced. Papa sat at the table staring ahead of him rather than looking at me.

'Well, then,' I said, eventually. 'I have no intention of being a burden to the family. All I request is a small allowance until I'm able to gain employment. I propose to find work and live alone.'

He turned to glare at me. 'Work? What sort of work could you ever do?'

'I shall find employment as a telegraphist or a governess.'

'Hah! I shan't be advancing you any funds. There's none to be had.'

'None?'

'Not a penny. The family's financial circumstances are even worse than I'd thought. I had hoped to inherit an annuity, but it emerged that your uncle's gambling debts necessitated the sale of the family estate which has swallowed up all of the inheritance on which I was depending. The shock brought about your mother's recent seizure. So, now you see – the world doesn't revolve around you alone.'

10

I had trouble sleeping that night. I began to see myself in a new and unflattering light, as someone intent on pursuing my selfish desires and utterly unaware of the troubles besetting my family. While I'd been painting and dreaming of becoming Mr Lilley's muse, Mama had been beside herself with worry over the family finances. I felt like a spoilt child, and my artistic ambitions seemed like a monstrous self-indulgence. I fell asleep, chastened and ready to discard my wild longings and false romantic notions.

In the morning I received a note from Mr Lilley, inviting me to tea. Included was a small sketch he'd made of me. He had caught my likeness, but had subtly changed some features so they conformed to a general ideal of beauty. On the back he had written: 'I'm not sure I've entirely captured you.'

I tore up the invitation and threw it in the grate.

Once I had dressed, I went to Mama's sick room and found Lance sitting at her bedside. They were hand in hand. He kissed her forehead, stood up, and left, closing the door quietly behind him.

'Cheerio, my dear,' said Mama, with a little wave. She looked tiny under the bed covers, as if she'd shrunk. There were blue marks under her eyes, like bruises.

'I've been so worried about you, my love,' she said, tremulously, as I sat down beside her.

'I'm sorry, Mama. I've been very selfish. I didn't mean to be. I got carried away with my painting and – well, with other things.'

'Oh yes, your enthusiasms. I've always done my best to protect you. You've always been a wilful creature.'

'I realize how unacceptable my behaviour has been. I didn't know about Uncle Jonathan and the money from the estate. Not until Papa told me last night. I've been completely wrapped up in myself. Oh, Mama!'

'My dear, you mustn't upset yourself. Your father and I will find a way to manage the situation. We always have in the past. It's you that I'm worried about . . . you and Lance and the other boys. I've always done what I thought was best for you – for all of you.'

'I know you have.'

'You never told me how your meeting with Felix went. Not well, I expect.'

I shook my head.

'Mama. I've come to my senses. I'm going to write to Felix and apologize for the way I've treated him.'

'Only if you think it's for the best. Never mind me.'

I nodded, and broke into tears.

'Oh, my dearest child!' she said, drawing my forehead down onto her breast.

Dear Felix,

First, I must apologize for what happened between us at the tennis match. I genuinely hadn't known your intentions and I suppose I was overcome by panic. It all seemed so momentous and there had been all the excitement of the day, and perhaps I'd been in the hot sun for too long. I know some time has elapsed since that afternoon, but I wanted to take time to reflect on my feelings, and ensure that I was absolutely ready before communicating with you. I will perfectly understand if your feelings have changed after my behaviour on that day, and later at the hotel. However, if you are willing to make a second approach, then rest assured you will receive a very different response. Forgive the brevity of this letter, but I'm rushing to get it in the post.

With all my love,
Violet

There was no reply from Felix that day or the next. I could settle at nothing, and waited nervously for each arrival of the post. At last, in the final delivery of the second day, a letter arrived addressed to me in Felix's handwriting. How confused my feelings were as I opened the envelope.

My dearest angel,

I have just received your letter and I can hardly believe my luck. Of course I'll still have you as my wife. It's a blessed relief you've finally come to your senses. I won't deny I've been under a cloud these last weeks.

I apologize for the delayed response, but my letter had to be forwarded to London where I'm currently residing. Things are frenzied at the bank, due to major developments in Bolivia. I'll tell you all about it when we next meet. I'm going to be signing contracts and meeting officials in London — there's so much detail to be thrashed out and then we must entertain our South American visitors late into the evening.

All of which means I won't be in Brighton for at least a fort-night. Naturally, I'd far rather spend every day there with you. Perhaps we could squeeze in a visit to our future residence in Brixton at some point? I need your advice on soft furnishings and other dark arts beyond the ken of the male imagination. I assume that the future Mrs Skipp-Borlase has overcome her qualms at the prospect of being filthy rich and having a staff of ten at her command.

With immense love — and relief,
Your Felix

My engagement to Felix was announced in the *Brighton Gazette*. A short engagement was agreed: we were to be married in two months' time. After the announcement, relatives arrived from distant shires to shower Mama with compliments and to admire me, the blushing bride-to-be. Refreshments were served and the best tea service brought out. Great-aunts I didn't know existed made an appearance. They looked as though they might have been born in the last century. Great-aunt Idalia gazed pitifully on me and lamented: 'Oh, my dear, I so wish I had never married!' Great-aunt Marjorie was of the same mind. 'The best one could hope for in our day was a companionable marriage and a good social alliance.' The ladies spent the rest of their visit talking about people in their circle who had passed away.

A dressmaker came to take my measurements and I requested a claret wedding dress, but Mama insisted on white satin. A compromise was reached: I would wear a simple cream-coloured dress that I could wear again on later occasions. I refused outright to wear a veil or train. There was also a new travelling dress for the journey to Brixton, the prospect of which made me feel faint.

There was a trying afternoon when Mama entertained Felix's mother at home. It was stiflingly warm so the window was open and navvies could be heard outside, swearing at each other as they built new houses nearby. When Mrs Skipp-Borlase first arrived, I got the impression she was still piqued about my delayed response to her son's proposal of marriage. But then her general habit over the years had always been to wait grandly until she was addressed before deigning to speak, which made conversation strained. The imminent marriage did nothing to alter this. It was always painfully apparent when Mama and Felix's mother were together that the camaraderie between our respective families depended largely on my father's affability and Mr Skipp-Borlase's talkative and forthright personality. When Mrs Skipp-Borlase did speak, she mostly complained about the difficulty of getting good service in certain stores only frequented by people with extreme wealth. Or else to boast about Felix, for example how he had learnt to speak Spanish in a single month or how he had taken command of the bank's Bolivian investment portfolio when he was only twenty-three. Mama blanched at the mention of Felix's achievements – the contrast with Lance couldn't have been more pronounced – but Mrs Skipp-Borlase continued to boast, regardless, oblivious to the mood of those in her company. Mama's condition was still fragile and her efforts to sustain conversation bordered on mania as she wittered about the next church bazaar or the proposal to build a clock tower at the crossroads in town. Even so, she gave me a sour look if she caught me fidgeting or stifling a yawn. Bored to distraction, I tried to appear as if I was paying attention by making occasional remarks, such as 'Oh really, how very interesting!' or 'Is that so?'

At a certain point, Susan entered to say that Mrs Runniforde had just called. Ordinarily, this announcement would have grieved me as Mrs Runniforde was a great hypocrite and the most notorious gossip in the neighbourhood, but on this occasion I felt she would be a welcome respite from Mrs Skipp-Borlase's cold reserve.

'Oh, Mrs Skipp-Borlase, how pleasant to see you again,' said Mrs Runniforde as she entered the parlour. Mrs Skipp-Borlase offered no reply, staring through the new arrival as if she wasn't there. But Mrs Runniforde was unabashed. 'I wondered whose carriage that was outside,' she said, as she took a seat on the couch opposite the fine lady. They made quite a contrast, Mrs Runniforde comfortably rotund and expansive, and Mrs Skipp-Borlase narrow and sitting on the edge of the seat, rigidly erect.

'Did you have far to come?' asked Mrs Runniforde.

'Octavia lives in Brunswick Terrace,' said Mama. 'Overlooking the lawns, with a fine vista of the sea.'

'Is that so?' said Mrs Runniforde. 'And you brought your carriage? You might easily have walked from there. But why not show it off when you have the chance. Brunswick Terrace, is it? A town house then. You have another residence, I suppose? A country seat, perhaps?'

Mrs Skipp-Borlase stiffened even more, her lips pursed, her nostrils flaring like a thoroughbred horse.

Mama tried to rescue the situation. 'Octavia was just telling us about a charity walk at Lady's Mile. It's organized by St Michael's.'

A sour expression formed on Mrs Runniforde's rosy face. 'As you know, my dear, I don't care for that church. Far too "High" for my liking, a very strong whiff of popery. Of course, I'll make an exception for Violet's nuptials.'

She turned her gaze on me. 'You've succeeded in snatching a husband in the nick of time, you clever thing,' she said with a laugh, the rolls of fat on her chin wobbling. 'Don't mind me, Mrs Skipp-Borlase. I jest, of course. Violet's head would never be turned by such considerations.'

Mrs Skipp-Borlase retained her silence and frigid countenance, all but for a slight tremor in her finely chiselled cheek. Meanwhile, Mama's face had become ashen.

'We're among friends, are we not?' said Mrs Runniforde. 'No airs and graces. May I say it's a great relief to me to be here and not be forced to listen to that tittle-tattle about Mr and Mrs Winslow.'

So, this was why Mrs Runniforde had come – to gossip with Mama about a local scandal.

'I'm not sure Octavia wants to hear about that,' Mama said, quickly.

'No more than I did, when I was told,' said Mrs Runniforde. 'I'm sure there's not a vestige of truth in it. You know who I mean – the ones who live in the end house on Montpelier Terrace. He takes the train up to London every morning.'

'My dear, wouldn't you rather . . . ' began Mama, but Mrs Runniforde seemed not to hear.

'Well then, as you know, I hate to pry into other people's affairs, but it appears this lady has taken a fall, if you follow me,' said Mrs Runniforde. 'She fell in love with a younger man – of dubious character, as I understand it – and the rotten swine jilted her. She'd taken to drink, you see, and lost her way. Her poor husband might never have found out if a concerned neighbour hadn't given him the wink. Well, he confronted her and it all came out. If ever there was a lesson on the need for temperance, then this is it.'

'I think that's quite enough, my dear,' said Mama.

'I refuse to listen to tittle-tattle, but it's believed the couple live separate lives under the same roof,' continued Mrs Runniforde. 'And yet there they were in their private pew on Sunday. Keeping up appearances, no doubt. You never know what goes on behind closed doors, do you?' she said, looking at Mrs Skipp-Borlase.

'What business is this of ours?' I cried, unable to restrain myself.

'That's just what I said when I was told about it,' says Mrs Runniforde.

'And yet you repeat it here, and heaven knows where else,' I said. 'Why is it women are always punished in these situations, when a blind eye is turned to men's indiscretions? I expect that if her husband had gone astray then his wife would be expected to forgive and forget, as if it was perfectly natural for men to cheat on their wives.'

'What on earth is she saying?' said Mrs Skipp-Borlase, looking at Mama.

'Violet! Have you forgotten yourself?' cried Mama.

'Did I say something amiss?' said Mrs Runniforde.

'I'm sorry. Forgive me, if I've spoken out of turn,' I said.

The women sipped their tea quietly for a moment. I glanced at Mrs Skipp–Borlase and found she was studying me narrowly.

'What do you think to this artist chap who's come down from London, recently?' asked Mrs Runniforde. 'A Mr Lilley. It was in the *Brighton Gazette*. None of these gentlemen are to be trusted, you know. They lead the most scandalous lives, taking up with their models and so on. It's fortunate that you're spoken for, Violet.'

'Do you simply believe every word you read in the popular press?' I asked.

'Charming!' said Mrs Runniforde, with a sour expression of her face.

'Violet, really!' said Mama.

'Are you quite well?' asked Mrs Skipp–Borlase.

'Actually, no,' I said, rising to my feet. 'I'm feeling rather faint. Please would you excuse me? I expect it's all the excitement. I dearly hope to see you again soon, Mrs Skipp–Borlase.'

The woman nodded imperiously and with that I left the room.

INTERLUDE

Rushing, rushing, breathless, down a long corridor, chased by my own echoing footsteps. I pass a gaslight and my shadow races ahead of me, leaping high on the walls. I clutch my skirts, hoist them, so I won't trip over the hems. The passage grows narrower and more airless, sucking me into its depths as a snake swallows its prey. The walls are scored along their length. I reach the double doors and wait, struggling to catch my breath. A brass nameplate announces NEUROANATOMICAL LABORATORY. I rap on the doors, and wait, my heart thumping against my breastbone. Cold sweat rolls down my brow.

Keys rattle and the doors swing apart. I slip past a young man blocking my entrance, into glaring white light. A room takes shape, pivoting queasily about me like a macabre carousel. On an operating table, a white sheet moulds the outline of a human frame, two dainty feet protruding from one end, the toes fallen outward. At the other end is the head. Familiar delicate features, closed eyes, prominent cheekbones and sunken cheeks, skin white as a marble saint under the harsh light. In life, she was forever plaiting and unplaiting her fair locks, but now there are no curls to frame her face. A neat incision has been made around her hairline. The top of her head removed.

I look away, my stomach heaving, and my gaze is drawn to a bench, on top of which is a bone saw with bloodied teeth, alongside it a claw-ended hammer. On another table something that looks like a slimy sliced cauliflower is set out in two neat rows, each part labelled with a small card. It is only now that I see him: that devil, in a blood-smeared apron. He stands by a set of hefty weighing scales. In one tray are the weights, on the opposite lies a specimen of human offal, still bleeding. It is the woman's heart.

11

A day or two following Mrs Skipp–Borlase's visit, Mama summoned me to the morning room shortly after breakfast. It was oppressively warm – a fire burning in the grate although it was midsummer. The light was subdued, the far corners of the room in shadow. Rain pattered outside, as if it would never let up. Mama appeared to be in the midst of her correspondence, which was spread over the occasional table in front of her. But something in her demeanour struck a false note. She was opening an envelope in such a distracted way that she cut her thumb on the paper knife, then put it in her mouth to suck it. I sat down in the armchair opposite her. She avoided meeting my gaze. Having opened the envelope, she didn't so much as glance at the letter but put it on the table with a shaking hand.

'What is it, Mama? What do you wish to say?'

'I'm concerned that you will ruin your chances of happiness.'

'Why? What have I done?'

'I asked Susan to air all the rooms before the summer party. She found certain pictures of yours when she was clearing out your linen chest. The girl took such fright I had to fetch the smelling salts.'

My mind reeled. At first, I couldn't recall what pictures

these might be. Then I remembered that recent intense period when I produced several pictures that seemed somehow to have painted themselves. Afterwards, I had only the vaguest recollection of working on them. There was the inverted mermaid, where in the lower half I'd omitted no detail of the female anatomy. I had blanched at showing it to Mr Lilley. There were other paintings too, produced in the same fever of imagination. I had used Susan's likeness in a painting of Eros and Psyche in an embrace. And there was a degree of nudity and a certain voluptuous licence in the picture that went beyond what I'd allowed myself before. Now, I grew hot under my clothing as I imagined Mama looking at this. I had trespassed beyond what Mama would consider decent. And how would I ever look Susan in the face? I remembered other pictures I'd made that were in a similar vein. Only gradually did my awareness return to the present moment, the insistent rhythmic drip of rainwater onto the window sill outside and the crackling and hissing of logs on the fire. I couldn't bring myself to look at Mama, but I found my voice.

'You pried into my personal belongings,' I said.

'I did no such thing.'

'The pictures weren't meant for Susan's eyes – or yours. Others would view them differently. The world is changing – all too slowly, but it is. Why should I live in fear of my own imagination?'

Mama glared at me. 'Selfish child. You think only of yourself. When have you ever thought of me?'

'I never meant to offend you—'

'Offend me! It's you I fear for . . . ' She let out a long bellow like an animal in pain.

'Mama, stop this, for God's sake, please,' I said, shocked and in panic. I got down on my knees beside her and tried to embrace her.

'Don't touch me,' she cried. 'Get away.' She collapsed into mournful sobbing.

I had seen her this way many times before. I returned to my own chair and waited for the storm to pass. In time she became calmer. She sat sniffling and dabbing her eyes with a handkerchief. Every so often a great shudder passed through her.

'Forgive me, Mama,' I said quietly.

'I should have suspected something like this would happen,' she said. 'I should have intervened. Dr Rastrick—'

'Please, not Dr Rastrick.'

'Well, something must be done,' she snapped. 'It's not as if this is the sole cause of concern. Your behaviour when Octavia came to visit was most odd. You withdraw to your room for hours on end and now I discover how you've been occupying yourself. This isn't how a normal bride-to-be behaves during her engagement.'

'What else am I to do? I've been measured for my dress.'

'Listen to me very carefully, young lady,' she said, adopting a new more forceful tone, 'we're going to put this episode behind us. Nobody but you and I need ever know of it. I'll talk to Susan and make sure this goes no further. But I fear for you. I've always feared for you. Even as a child – those tempers of yours, the waywardness. My only aim is to rescue you from your own worst excesses. Felix is a decent young man, and I know he loves you with all his heart. Just think how he would react if he were to see these pictures?'

'Felix has encouraged me to paint after we're married.'

'After you're married, you'll be his responsibility.'

I rose to my feet. 'Very well. I agree to do whatever you wish. Now, please return my pictures to me.'

She looked off across the room. 'When you produced those pictures you weren't yourself; you were possessed, in an unbalanced state.'

'Please give them back.'

She turned pale and trembled. 'I can't. They're gone.' As she spoke, she glanced at the fireplace.

I walked over to the grate and looked down at the smouldering coals. I imagined my life's aspirations writhing in the flames, collapsing in on themselves, releasing thick smoke as they were sucked up the chimney. Then I rushed out of the room, slamming the door behind me.

*

The dreadful confrontation with Mama was too much to bear and I developed a fever. I lay in bed, drenched in perspiration, for two days, listless and incapacitated. But when I began to recover, I had time to reflect on my predicament. My fury abated, to be replaced by a new determination to thwart Mama. When I felt strong enough, I wrote to Miss Fanshaw to request that she act as my chaperone on a second visit to Mr Lilley. I told her I had experienced a crisis in my work and urgently desired his professional advice. I received a reply in the final post. Miss Fanshaw told me that she would accompany me, if only to prevent me being tempted to make the visit alone. As chance would have it, she was going to tea with Mr Lilley after the art class the following day, and I could join her if I so wished.

The next morning, I was still weakened from my fever and my mind was somewhat muzzy. I spent considerably more time than usual on my appearance, tying back my naturally wild black hair. My complexion was pale, so I covered my face in powder. I put on my favourite dress. It was silk and cornflower blue, the colour only a little faded by age. Like all my dresses, it had been mended here and there where the moths had got at it, but the repairs were hardly noticeable. It was tailored in the loose fit and simple style Mama so objected to, without a bustle, belted at the waist and free of swags, ribbons or other feminine frippery. Over the dress I wore a matching basque. I appraised myself in the mirror and was quite satisfied with the effect. My figure was trimmer than usual after three days on nothing but water.

Rather than walk to the art class with Lottie, as I usually did, I set off alone. I was in an agitated state of mind and in no mood to make idle conversation, especially not with Lottie. I set off down the hill to the high street and walked towards the museum. Conscious of being a lone woman, I adopted a confident and purposeful gait, looking directly ahead. I reached the museum without incident. Then – catastrophe! At the entrance there was a notice to say the art class had been cancelled as Miss Fanshaw had been taken ill. I began to trudge homeward. The traffic had come to a standstill at the crossroads in the town centre. I was forced to weave a precarious path through hansom cabs, broughams and omnibuses, the road sticky with damp clay from building works nearby which clogged the wheels of the conveyances. I was startled by deafening sounds, the shouts of irate cabmen, jangling harnesses, whinnies and snorts. As I slipped nervously past twitching horses and carriage wheels, which threatened to lurch forward at any moment, I remembered a child had been crushed to death in this very spot a few weeks previously. I suffered a residual faintness from my illness and did an about-turn, deciding to walk downhill and go home along the seafront. When I reached King's Road, I looked west towards my home, towards safety, towards resignation, and then I turned the opposite way to gaze into a blinding haze of white light in which I could just discern the chain pier stretching into oblivion. I dabbed my brow with my handkerchief. The heat was intense and cloying, and a storm was in the air. I began to trudge homeward. But after perhaps a dozen steps my feet, of their own accord, turned about and took me in the opposite direction. I proceeded east with no clear intention in mind. Perhaps I would simply take a stroll around Sussex Square and then return. The lonely road stretched before me and I became intensely alert to my unchaperoned status. I turned my head only once, as I passed the pier, and saw two shabby men loitering, leaning against the cables suspended between the toll booth and the first platform. They leered at me as I passed. I remembered seeing prostitutes working this strip in the past, but that was generally after dark or on public holidays when there was always custom to be had. Beyond the seafront railing, mouldering wooden groynes strewn with dark tangled seaweed stretched into the sea, which was a dirty beige mirroring the shimmering headache-glow of the sky. I had a sickening sense I was being followed, but when I glanced behind me the path was clear. By the time I reached my destination, I was perspiring quite heavily. After a moment's hesitation, I knocked on Mr Lilley's front door.

The door opened, with a puff of strong cologne. Mr Lilley looked startled to see me standing there all by myself. 'Miss

Pring! I had a telegram from Miss Fanshaw to say she was indisposed, so I hadn't expected . . . '

'Please forgive me. I shouldn't have come. I shan't trouble you . . . ' I turned to leave.

'Oh, but I insist. Come up.'

As I followed him up the stairs, he glanced over his shoulder. 'You must excuse me. I expected to be alone, so I told the char not to bother. I'm afraid you're about to see a bachelor's lodgings in a wholly unadorned state.' We entered the room, and he told me to take a seat on the green divan while he opened the window and rushed about removing clutter to an ante-room in the corner. 'One moment,' he said, slipping behind a curtain in the wall, which I hadn't noticed on my previous visit. I heard his footsteps thumping faintly as he ascended a staircase, and again as he descended. He reappeared, a key in his hand which he deposited in a drawer, before coming to sit down opposite me.

'I have my studio in the attic. There's a marvellous skylight – that's why I took the rooms. I'm superstitious about anybody seeing my work before it's finished, otherwise I'd take you up.'

'I've interrupted you. I should leave you in peace to get on with your work.'

'Not at all. I'm delighted to see you. Last time, with Gwen here, we hardly had a chance to chat, God bless her. You've brought some more work, I hope?'

I began to tell him what had happened, but burst into tears.

'Heavens above. You poor thing. Has something terrible occurred?' He went to fetch a handkerchief and handed it to me. It was clean and crisply ironed with his initials stitched in a corner.

'I wanted to fool you into believing me a sophisticated woman and I've made an utter fool of myself instead,' I said.

'Don't be silly. Personally, I'm in floods of tears at the slightest setback. Just sit there and compose yourself while I make tea.' He went over to the anteroom and bustled away, whistling a popular tune. He called from the doorway with a tea caddy in each hand: 'What's it to be – Gunpowder or Bohea?'

'Gunpowder, please. I'll stop this silly snivelling soon, I promise.'

When the tea was poured, he asked me to explain why I was in such an emotional state. I told him about Mama destroying my art.

'Never! Outrageous. The most appalling act of vandalism. This atrocity must be avenged. Let me think. You must make new versions. Is there a studio you could hire?'

'It's too late for that. I'm to be married in a few weeks.'

'Oh, rotten luck! But we can't let something as trivial as marriage hold you back. If your husband's a remotely sensible fellow, he won't object to you producing art. Otherwise I shall challenge him to a duel. Of course, you'll need materials. I can help you with that, and I can offer free tuition if you think it worthwhile. I've been thinking a great deal about those pictures of yours. I forbid you to throw away your talent. I haven't seen such natural ability in years, not since Evelyn De Morgan first showed me her work.'

'Thank you, you're too kind. But I'd better leave. Just imagine how it would appear if my family discovered I'd come here alone. Worse still, if my fiancé's family found out.'

'It must have taken tremendous courage to come here. Don't spoil it now by running away. Your secret's safe with me. I mean what I say about your work. You have a pure and unspoilt talent and that's exceedingly rare, believe me.'

'I hardly know what I'm about.'

'Your technique is somewhat naive, of course it is, and you have produced little work so far, but what you lack in finesse you make up for in vigour and expression. In my view, imaginative audacity and intensity of feeling trump draughtsmanship every time. You need to work on composition, flesh-modelling, handling of colour and other techniques. But your work has virtues it takes most artists a lifetime to acquire – the simple handling, the lack of theatricality of attitude that mars so many of our best painters' work, the wonderfully loose and expressive brush work. Of course, you will need opportunity to succeed and, more importantly, discipline. But, my gosh, you express your feelings. Your work is natural, impulsive. I wish I could say the same for my own. I'm afraid I've allowed myself to get completely hamstrung by self-consciousness.' He pointed at the mermaid picture I'd seen on my previous visit. I saw he'd done more work, without necessarily improving it. 'Tell me, should I paint over this canvas, remove any semblance of a subject, cover it in impressionistic daubs? I would sincerely like to know. But let's not waste time saving my career, when we should be launching yours. How are we going to make an artist of you?'

'What you describe is all rather daunting. I'm sure Miss Fanshaw thinks I should accept that I'll never be more than an amateur watercolourist.'

'There are trained professional women artists these days and some have achieved a public platform, but you need drive and determination to get your work sold at Agnews. The tide is turning though, with the Woman Question on everyone's lips. But Brighton's such a backwater. And you can forget London. The art scene's too crowded and dominated by men. Go to Liverpool if you want to come to notice. You could sit to some fashionable artists without harming your reputation, and worm your way into their studios that way. Women of breeding are prized in those circles. And, of course, painters are always on the lookout for a special kind of beauty such as yours.'

Naturally, my face grew hot, hearing this.

'If I were poor, it would be much easier,' I said. 'I could work in the studio of a male artist. But for a genteel lady that would be scandalous. I'm sure that's what Miss Fanshaw would say. And Mama would never recover from the shock.'

'Notoriety can sometimes help establish a career, of course. And I advise you to paint on a large canvas if you want to be taken seriously. I mean that literally. But what it all comes down to in the end is money. Once you're married, you might persuade your husband to support you. It would help if he became a collector.'

'Oh, he's very keen on that. He thinks my being an amateur artist will raise the tone of the household and add a charming feminine touch.'

He took a cigarette case out of his pocket, opened it and held it towards me. I took one and put it between my lips as nonchalantly as I could. He struck a match and I took a puff, then let myself down by coughing. I watched Mr Lilley's eyelids droop as he drew on his cigarette. When he blew out the smoke, his lips formed the shape of a kiss. I followed his example. With each puff I felt a surge of dizzying excitement, and by the time the cigarette was smoked, I was languishing in a state of sensual lassitude that was altogether new to me. Perhaps I had finally found the means to soothe my fraught nerves.

Mr Lilley studied me as he exhaled a stream of smoke. 'Forgive my candour, but you don't sound terribly fond of your fiancé.'

'I'm not.'

'That's rum. But this chap must have some redeeming features?'

'He really does love me. I should have put a stop to it, I know. I've been a fool.'

Mr Lilley uncorked a bottle of wine and poured it into tumblers. We talked and talked and talked. He told me about the disappointing reception his recent work had received, his struggle to decide which school to follow. How he would never compromise, never lower his standards to meet the demands of a fickle market. How he feared failure and obscurity and longed for recognition. How he felt weighed down by expectation, and was constantly looking over his shoulder at younger artists.

He listened intently when I told him about Mama's hysterics, Papa's ineffectual disposition, about the joys of being the only daughter in a family of boys. About how as a child I had admired my eldest brother Lance, even though he was always vile to me, and about my being jealous of Lance's friendships.

I made him tell me all about Paris. I told him I'd longed to go there ever since my governess Mademoiselle Dufort had told me about her adventures. He promised to take me there one day, by hook or by crook. We drank more wine, all the wine in fact, then he opened a second bottle, and we became more recklessly open. I shared secrets I'd never shared with anyone else. We talked about the temper of the times, the new movements, socialism and feminism. He said he despised the grandeur and complacency of the age. We agreed that art should be free of moral purpose, sufficient in its own ends. I told him of my dislike of rules, laws and hierarchies. He told me he loathed English common sense. Then we turned to fashionable gossip. And then we talked about ourselves again.

'My fiancé doesn't understand that I'm not a proper woman at all,' I said. 'I have no love for my mother, and I'm selfish and wilful, without any of the feminine virtues, of constancy, modesty, reticence and . . . to be perfectly honest I can't even recall the others.'

'I think chastity might be among them.'

'At the top of the list, I should say. Just like a man, to remember that one. Anyhow, in short, I'm as far from being a model wife as can be.'

'I'm shocked. This Skipp–Borlase chap needs to be informed before it's too late,' he said. 'I shall write to him tonight and save his skin. I'll inform him that his fiancée lacks obedience and sympathy, and is about as domesticated as a stray cat. No, on consideration, I shan't write. It's too urgent for that. This wedding must be stopped pronto. I'll send him a telegram instead. Or go and knock on his door. Hang it if I don't. Why don't we both go? What a jape that would be.'

'Let's do it. Right away. We'll explain that I have none of the qualities a sensible man is looking for in a wife.'

'But I disagree. From what you've told me you have deep affection and fidelity – for your father, at least. And for that awful brother of yours – although why that should be, I cannot imagine. But look here.' He picked up the wine bottle, which was empty. 'Better bring out the cognac, I'd say.'

He went into the anteroom and was gone for a few minutes. I sat and waited. Outside, horses' hooves scudded on the cobbles. Stale air poured through the open window, warm and thick. The tide had an exceptionally ripe smell that afternoon, and I could taste the sea's salty essence on my lips. In the distance the waves crashed in and out, dragging clattering shingle in their wake. Through the open door of the anteroom, I watched Mr Lilley, bent over the sink with his back to me, and the sight of him and his lithe sinuous movements made me grow hot under the layers of my clothing, which constrained and suffocated me. I was dizzy and befuddled, and my throat was dry. I knew I should leave – and the sooner the better.

Just then, amber light flooded the room, turning a streak of seagull dropping on the window pane into a mysterious dark hieroglyphic and directing a dusty shaft of light into the darkest recess where it alighted on a large iron bed, illuminating it like a theatre set under stage lights. The bed linen was piled in disarray. The sheets looked pristine – and I thought about Mr Lilley's model, the laundry girl, Fanny, and I had the ridiculous thought that clean sheets must be a benefit of being acquainted with washerwomen. On the other side of the room, Mr Lilley's mermaid glared intently at me. A deep shadow had fallen over the painting, accentuating its atmosphere of mystery, peril and doom. The model was well cast as a siren, with an uneasy gaze and gaunt frame, the very type of the unattainable femme fatale so fashionable in pictures then.

He went to a dresser and returned with a bottle and two clean glasses. 'This is the cure for just about everything, in my experience. I brought it back from Paris, where it cost me practically nothing. A little drop will steady you.' He swilled the brandy in his own glass and sipped, and I followed his example.

'I don't mean to be forward, but why do you always give the women in your pictures the same face? Is she your famous laundry girl, by any chance?'

'Famous, you say?' He frowned. 'I suppose she is. Yes, it's Fanny's face.' He squirmed in his seat, and took a large gulp of brandy. 'When you chance upon a good face you might as well use it.'

'Sorry. It was rude to pry.'

'Not at all. She was a good helpmeet to me, and a talented artist in her own right.'

'She worked in your studio?'

'No, I kept her out of the studio. Mostly, she used to book models for me, and costumes for the subject pictures I was commissioned to do in those days. She even kept the books. She was a quick learner in every respect. I helped her get an education. Now she spends her time with earls and shipowners and the likes of Ned Burne-Jones. Good luck to her, I say.'

His last remark sounded sour and his demeanour hinted there might have been something between him and Fanny, and that it hadn't ended happily. I was intrigued and jealous, but I sensed he didn't want me to enquire further.

A moment later, he seemed to have shrugged off his momentary gloom. 'I promise that I'll do all in my power to help you escape from this mess your family have got you into,' he said. 'You deserve better.'

It had grown dark. There was a rumble of thunder and several seconds later the window was lit for a split second with intense light. Rain began to drum on the roof, and clatter down from the guttering. I walked unsteadily to the window and closed it, wiping away condensation to peer out. Down below, a puddle was already forming in the yard.

'I should have left an hour ago, at least,' I said.

'You can't go out in this. Why don't you tell your mother you were caught in the downpour and decided to stay overnight with a friend?'

'But I couldn't possibly stay here,' I said, rising to my feet.

Mr Lilley got up too. We found ourselves face to face. He reached out, took my hands in his and stepped towards me until we were toe to toe. His face advanced towards me, his lips slightly open. I was suddenly overcome with dizziness.

'Excuse me,' I said, freeing my hands and turning from him. Fearing I would faint, I made my way unsteadily towards the bed and sat on it. The excitement of the earlier afternoon had dissipated and I felt dreadfully tired. I couldn't keep my eyes open a moment longer.

12

In the grey light of dawn, I sat on the edge of the bed and waited for a wave of nausea to pass. I was light-headed, clammy, trembling with cold and feverish at the same time. I felt a soreness in my very core and was depleted, my limbs aching. The room reeked of alcohol. Mr Lilley was dozing on the divan. I placed my stockinged feet down on the cold floor and walked unsteadily about, looking for my boots. When I'd laced them up, I went to the window, stepping as lightly as I could, and opened the curtains a little to look out – only to find the world had disappeared behind a thick sea fret. I opened the window-catch to let in some air, then crossed to the anteroom to splash my face with water. When I returned, Mr Lilley was on his feet, looking out of the window and rubbing his back.

'I have to get home. I'd better leave,' I said.

He turned to face me. 'I'm most awfully sorry. I should never have kept you so long yesterday, and well . . . Please forgive me.'

'Don't apologize. It was nice to get to know you. But I need to somehow explain my absence to my mother – and as soon as possible.'

'How far have you to go?'

'A couple of miles.'

'Not on foot?'

I nodded.

'I can't allow that. Not in this weather.'

A moment later he had rushed out onto the streets in pursuit of a cab. In his absence the stillness of the room was a physical presence, the silence hissing in my eardrums. I sat on the divan and fought off a wave of nausea by taking a series of deep breaths. Inside, I felt hollowed out. My gaze fell on an alcove where there was a tall wardrobe of honey-coloured walnut. The dim morning light had thrown a faint sheen on the wood. I crossed the room, treading softly across the creaking floorboards. The wardrobe doors grated as I opened them. A masculine smell was released, of cologne, laundry soap, mothballs and the subtle essence of Mr Lilley himself. His clothes hung in a line before me on ornate brass hangers, some of the material threadbare, some good as new, various dark coats, suits, tartan waistcoats, silk shirts, some white and others purple or scarlet. Some residue of sensuality stirred in me from the night before. I felt faint and had to catch my breath. But I couldn't resist letting my fingers caress the row of sleeves. I reached for a shirt, a white dress shirt, and took it off the hanger. It had fancy pleating down its front. I held it against myself, looking at my reflection in the mirror on the inside of the door. Then I held the material to my face and neck, feeling the soft silk and a rasp of static electricity as if a residue of Mr Lilley's soul still lingered in the fabric. I passed the material over my mouth and my own moist warm breath was blown back over my cheeks. A shiver passed through me. In some obscure fashion, I felt as if our souls could fuse, that we could become one and the same. It was too much. I grew faint. My throat was parched. Then I heard the keys turn in the door below. I put the shirt back in its place, clumsily, and pushed the door shut, hearing its guilty scrape. Footsteps stomped up the stairs, and a moment later Mr Lilley was there in the room, and I was sitting on the divan.

'Your carriage awaits you – at the end of the mews,' he said.

'I have no money.'

He took out his wallet and shook its entire contents into my open hand, only a few coins but just enough to cover the fare. 'It's been the greatest pleasure to meet you again,' he said. 'A privilege. And don't hesitate to get in touch if you need any help. You must pursue your calling. You have genuine talent. I mean that sincerely.'

He shook my hand firmly. Then he saw me to the door, where the cab was waiting.

A moment later the cab was trundling in thick fog through the streets of Kemp Town, which were otherwise deserted apart from a ghostly milk cart doing its rounds. In the cab I felt more alone than I could ever remember and was hideously nauseous. My nerves were stimulated to an almost unbearable degree as if every fibre of my being thrilled and resonated like a tuning fork. The onward motion and rhythmic rocking of the vehicle jogged my mind into wild fancies. In my mind I held intense conversations with Mr Lilley. We wondered what might have been had we met sooner, and what he would have achieved with me as his muse and handmaiden, two souls knit together, two bodies . . . Perhaps he would have been feted as a great artist. His wealth and prestige might in time have assisted my family in their financial difficulties. The thought that I was fated to spend my life with Felix Skipp-Borlase when it might have been Mr Lilley pained me almost beyond endurance.

I realized I was close to home and asked the cab driver to draw up around the corner out of sight of my house. With a feeling of dread, I climbed the iron staircase to the side entrance and entered the passage that led to the kitchen. There was a deathly hush inside. I tiptoed up the stairs. Entering my room, I closed the door behind me as softly as I could. I poured water into a tumbler from the vase on my chest of drawers, flannelled my face and neck, then closed the curtains and sat on my bed.

Right away, there was a knock on the door. I opened it to find Susan outside.

'Mrs Pring says she wants you in the morning room, miss.'

'At this hour? Could you tell her I'm unwell?'

'She was very firm about it, miss.'

'Very well then, let her know I'll be down in a few minutes.'

I looked at myself in the mirror. My hair was dishevelled and my dress full of creases. The silk smelled of stale cigarette smoke. I took it off and threw it into the laundry basket. Then I washed my face again, tidied my hair as best I could and changed into a sober grey dress. Taking a last glance at myself in the looking glass, I made my way downstairs.

The morning room was in heavy shadow. As my eyes adjusted to the gloom, I perceived Mama's dark shape sitting on the couch in silence, her posture rigid, a white handkerchief clenched in her hand. When I opened the drapes to let some grey morning light into the room, she shielded her eyes with her hand.

I broke the silence. 'Mama, what was it you wanted to speak to me about?'

'Would you like to explain where you were last night?'

'I was caught in a deluge and stayed at Lottie's house.'

'Liar! When you didn't return, I sent a telegram to Miss

Fanshaw. She sent this letter in reply.' She pointed at a folded letter on the table in front of her. I went to pick it up, then sat in an armchair facing her to read it. The paper trembled in my hand.

Dear Mrs Pring,

You ask if I know of your daughter's whereabouts. For reasons which I hope will soon become apparent, I must first explain that I recently accompanied Violet on a visit to the rooms of the artist Mr Wilfred Lilley in Kemp Town. I assumed that Violet had informed you of this. The intention was that Violet should receive advice on her work from Mr Lilley. You may recall that last month Mr Lilley gave my students instruction at the Wednesday class in the museum, and his comments were very well received.

Subsequently, Violet asked me to accompany her on a second visit which was to have taken place yesterday after the class. In the event, I was taken ill and unable to go. I'm not for a moment suggesting Violet would have visited Mr Lilley alone, but I thought it prudent to let you know about the arrangement. Of course, it is more likely she went to visit a friend, perhaps one of the young ladies she is friendly with in the art class. As I'm sure you're aware, I have always maintained the highest standards of moral probity in relation to the activities of my academy, and I have had no complaints.

Yours most sincerely,
Miss Gwendoline Fanshaw

My thoughts were thrown into disarray. How was I to explain myself? The room was spinning around me.

'You stink of tobacco and there's alcohol on your breath,' said Mama. 'That tells me all I need to know. To think my own daughter is leading an immoral life.'

'That isn't so, Mama, I promise you. Please let me explain what happened. I went to talk with Mr Lilley about my work. We talked for some time and then, as you'll recall, there was a dreadful storm and I found myself marooned. Mr Lilley's behaviour was perfectly gentlemanly.'

'You spent the night with that man. You're ruined. A woman's virtue is her most precious commodity.'

'My virtue is intact, believe me. I admit that what I did might look questionable from a conventional point of view, but there was no impropriety.'

'No impropriety? No impropriety when you're engaged to be married in a few short weeks? Are you mad?'

'We did nothing but converse. Mr Lilley was most helpful. He has inspired me to consider new possibilities – in art and perhaps also in how I might live my life.'

'If you could only hear yourself – so puffed up with self-opinion when you know nothing of the world. You can't afford these grand notions.' She put her handkerchief to her nose and blew into it, then loured at me. 'Do you understand how fortunate you are to have had an offer from Felix? You are risking *everything*.'

'I didn't intend to spend the night . . . But what does it matter? Felix need never know of it. I accept that I must marry him.'

'To think how you've conducted yourself with regard to that young gentleman. And you care nothing for my feelings, or for the family's standing. You're a wanton, faithless and disloyal devil.' She turned a shade paler and put her hand over her mouth. 'Suppose you were seen entering or leaving that man's house. And in this state! You will ruin us.'

She got to her feet and staggered towards the door, pausing with her hand on the doorknob. With her back turned, she said: 'It's my fault. I must have somehow failed you as a mother.'

Then she fell to the floor in a dead faint.

HILLWOOD GRANGE LUNATIC ASYLUM, SUSSEX

1886

13

I awoke to muffled sounds, altogether strange to me: wails, urgent shouts, metallic jangles and creaking and slamming on all sides that reverberated inside me. Where on earth was I? Was I not in my own room? No, I was in a cramped little bed in a narrow cell. I tried to rise, but was pinioned by bed sheets wrapped around me with severe tightness. High yellowed walls closed in on me. Over the bed a small wooden crucifix looked down. A narrow stained-glass window let in a meagre light, tinted with watery green and gold. There were iron bars over the window.

Wild with panic, I set about wresting myself free of the sheets, then sat on the bedside, breathless, stiff and groggy. Black mist threatened to overwhelm me, but I forced myself to think, to search for an explanation for my plight. I remembered Mama collapsing after we had argued. But other fragments of memory confounded me. A row of carriages. Sleek coachman standing in a group, smoking and talking. The sound of the distant tide, and me, stumbling on the shingle in a flimsy evening dress at sunset, my shoes in my hands. Murky scenes with the quality of dreams – or of nightmares.

I'd been sedated, I was sure of it. A great heaviness oppressed me and there was a stickiness behind my eyelids. I was wearing a nightdress altogether unfamiliar to me, a drab over-washed rag that chafed my skin. I was sore all over, with tender spots on my arms and ribs. What on earth had happened to me? I saw faces, a crowd. Women in silk dresses and feathered hats. Mama and I quarrelling. What then? Try as I might, I could remember no more, and the effort left me with stars floating before my eyes.

Below the window there was a small desk with a chair under it. I got up on the chair so I could peer out. In the distance, soft green slopes floated in the heavens, with two windmills, their sails stilled. Far down below there was a rectangular yard with flower beds, surrounded by high walls. My head reeled at the drop. Beyond the walls there were pastures with cows grazing, and further out parkland, with lawns leading up a steep incline to a dark, dense and tangled wood. It was all a dream, surely, and I would soon wake up.

I jumped as I heard a key rattle in the lock of the door. The chair wobbled and I almost fell. A squat sullen-looking creature entered, with a bellicose stare and jutting lower lip. She wore a white pinafore and nurse's cap.

'Now then, my lady, what have we here?' she said, moving stealthily towards me. 'We can't have you doing yourself a mischief.'

'Who are you? What is this place?'

'This place? Why it's . . . ' She paused, biting her lip. 'This is a hospital, miss. You've been taken here so we can look after you. Until you're better, that is.'

'What is it you're saying? I don't understand. I'm not ill. What hospital, pray?'

'Get down first, then I'll tell you.'

134

I stepped down from the chair. I saw she had a bunch of keys hanging from a belt around her waist. I felt my chest rise and fall rapidly.

'It was all made clear last night, but no doubt you've lost your bearings. It's often the way with new arrivals. This is Hillwood Grange.'

I gripped the chair to steady myself. Any effort at thinking made me light-headed. The woman went to the table, and poured water from a jug into a basin, constantly glancing over her shoulder at me.

'We need to get you down to the dining hall for breakfast. Once you've put on your day dress and given yourself a wash, you must come out and get in the queue. And don't forget to bring out your bedpan for emptying. You'll get used to the routine soon enough.'

'I assure you that I won't be having breakfast here or emptying any bedpans,' I said. 'There has been a terrible mistake. Tell whoever's in charge here that I must speak with him immediately.'

'You must wait your turn, miss. Dr Rastrick's a busy man and much in demand.'

I had a fearful start at the mention of Dr Rastrick's name.

She went to the door and began smoothing out creases in a garment hanging on a hook. She turned to me. 'Hurry up, now. You need to get a move on, if it's not too much trouble. Here's a dress ready for you, freshly laundered.'

When she was gone, I took deep breaths and told myself to keep my head. Someone had made a terrible mistake. I would get to the bottom of it and secure my immediate release. I took off my nightdress and was shocked to find livid bruises on my arms, yellowing around the edges. I slipped on the vest that was provided. It was faded and darned in several places and I shuddered at the thought that other women had worn it before me. Then I took the dress from the hook on the door and held it before me at arm's length. It smelled of carbolic soap and another sour odour, like mildew. The cloth around the collar and armpits was brown and sweat-stained. On the inner collar were the words 'PROPERTY OF HILLWOOD GRANGE LUNATIC ASYLUM' – as if anyone would ever want to steal such a rag. The material was coarse, a thick calico, and it chafed my skin. The garment was grey with vertical maroon stripes. It looked like a prison uniform in a newspaper illustration. I put it over my head, and buttoned it at the front with shaking fingers. The sleeves were too short. Then I washed my face in the bowl on the table by the door. There was no mirror for me to dress my hair. Finally, I put on the pair of clumpy boots left for me on the floor. They pinched my toes, and for some reason that was what finally undid me – I burst into tears. But I knew I must pull myself together. I had to find Dr Rastrick and demand my immediate release. My stomach knotted at the prospect, but I knew I was perfectly sane and that he must see reason.

When I was dressed, I took a deep breath and opened the door to brave whatever awaited me. I found myself in a narrow corridor with three doors on each side. At one end was a deserted dormitory with rows of beds on either side, packed close together, and with cupboards down the centre. All was still and quiet. At the other end of the short corridor there was a door. Beyond it I could hear a hideous tumult. Slowly, I pushed the door open and stepped into a wide high-ceilinged echoing chamber, and was assailed by jarring women's shouts, gushing water, slamming doors. There were women everywhere, old and young, healthy and malformed, in ragged queues or staggering about alone and dazed, some in the same striped dress that I wore, others in a state of near-undress, a few in what must have been their own dresses from home. There was an overwhelming stench of ordure. I backed into the wall, frozen to the spot. Nobody came to my assistance, or instructed me about what I should do. The walls were covered in brown tiles to above head-height and lime-washed above. There appeared to be only three sinks for perhaps two dozen women. A whining simpleton was having her face roughly flannelled by an orderly in a white apron. Some crazed creature was being dragged across the floor by another staff member who held her under the armpits. A crone wandered about in a state of total nudity, all skin and bone and bruised hips, gazing ahead of her on some obscure quest. Most of the women had the appearance of paupers, but there were women of the middling classes too, and a few who appeared quite refined, like the fey skeletal young woman leaning against a wall opposite me who wore her own pretty dress. Her gaze was abstracted. She wore a chain of withered daisies and dandelions in her hair. When she moved to join a queue, she seemed to float just above the floor.

My arm was seized. I was thrust forward. 'Come along now!' I was taken to the far end of the chamber where there were three WCs, with women waiting in line outside them. I took my place behind an old lady of genteel appearance, albeit bedraggled. She cradled a full bedpan under her arm. 'Awfully pleased to meet you,' she said, graciously offering her hand, and inadvertently tipping the bedpan so that its contents spilled over her dress. 'Will you be dining with us, my dear? The food's rather good.' At which, she put her bedpan to her lips and supped at it, before giving me a toothless smile.

'Don't mind her, she's quite mad,' said the woman in front of her. She too was getting on in years, with softly curling silver hair, delicate features and a rather grand bearing. 'One can't blame her for drinking her own slops, mind. It's no worse than the food here. New lady, are you?'

It seemed wise to humour these women; they might be dangerous. 'Yes, I am, as a matter of fact. Although I shan't be staying.'

'Nor I, my dear. Very well spoken, aren't you?' she said. 'It's always hard at first for the likes of us. Watch your step with that devil – Nettleship.' She nodded towards a woman. It was the one who had come to my room earlier.

'Is it always as bad as this?'

'Oh, this is quite usual. What brings you here, if you don't mind my asking?'

'I wish I knew.'

'I see,' she said, nodding sagely. 'One of those. It'll all come back to you.'

'And yourself?'

She leaned towards me with a confidential air, and lowered her voice. 'There are so few here from my walk of life. Can your discretion be relied upon?'

I nodded.

She lowered her voice. 'I am the Queen's own older sister and rightful heir to the throne, which she herself has acknowledged by secret message. My husband is Admiral of the Fleet. Preparations are being made so I can live in Windsor Castle once Victoria has removed herself. However, the Prince of Wales opposes it. Of course he does. He has sent witches into my room to kill me and, when that failed, he entered into a plot to have me shot. The worst insult is that I'm detained here, in spite of giving thousands of pounds to the hospital. I have reason to believe my letters to my sister, the false queen, are being intercepted.'

I had reached the front of the queue so I dashed into a privy. Once inside, the door safely bolted, I had a brief moment of respite to collect myself. I realized I wouldn't be able to withstand this ordeal for long, and must find someone who could point me towards Dr Rastrick. Afterwards, as I washed my hands and face at the sink, a woman in staff uniform appeared at my side. She looked amenable, with watery eyes and a red nose and a general demeanour suggesting a soft and mawkish nature.

'Who's in charge here?' I asked.

'I am, I suppose.'

'Thank heavens. I need to speak to Dr Rastrick immediately. Can you tell me where I might find him?'

'You're new here, aren't you? You can't go and speak to Dr Rastrick, not just like that. Be patient. He'll see to you soon enough. And if he can't put you right then nobody can. You won't find a man more stiff with learning than our Dr Rastrick. In the meantime, do get into the queue over there, if you wouldn't mind. We must get on. I'm due to take you ladies down for breakfast in a few minutes.'

'Is there someone with more authority with whom I can speak?'

'Oh, heavens. I can see you're going to be trouble.'

'I must insist. It's urgent. I . . . ' I realized it was hopeless pleading sanity. 'I'm not well. That is, I have a fearful pain.' I clutched my stomach, and winced.

'The housekeeper, Mrs Tuckwell, is in charge of the women's wards. You'd better speak to her. Here she comes now.'

Brisk footsteps sounded behind me and I turned just as a tall woman swept past, a look of grim determination on her face.

'Miss Tuckwell, may I speak with you? I'm Violet Pring.'

'It's *Mrs* Tuckwell,' she said, without looking me in the face. 'And I know who you are, Miss Pring. I'm afraid this isn't a convenient moment, so if you wouldn't mind . . . '

'This is urgent. I wish to make a formal complaint.'

She came to a sudden halt, and turned to glare at me. 'You haven't been here ten minutes – what can you possibly have to complain about?'

'Well . . . ' I floundered, 'I think there's been a mistake. I shouldn't be here. And I'd like to know how I've come to be covered in bruises.'

She reared, raising her eyebrows. 'If you have a genuine complaint, speak to one of the attendants after breakfast.'

'In that case, I demand to see Dr Rastrick – as soon as possible.'

She took a wooden board out from under her arm which had a sheet of paper clipped onto it, and began perusing a long list of items. Then she marched off. I caught up with her and paced alongside her.

'Didn't you hear me?' I asked.

'The physician superintendent has a lot of other ladies to worry about besides your good self. And it's not his practice to consult with patients until they've settled in.'

'Settled in? What do you mean? I'm not staying here.'

'The aim is to take your mind off your troubles through rest and employment.'

'Employment? Surely, you're not in earnest?' I was breathless, trying to keep pace with her.

'I'm very much in earnest. Perhaps the laundry would suit. It might do you some good.' Her gaze swept over me. 'You're strong enough, by the look of you.'

'Will you at least explain to me the grounds on which you're holding me here? I'm no more insane than you are.'

She came to an abrupt halt and swung around, fixing me with a fearful glare. She was taller than me so I had to look up into her face. 'What did you say just then, madam?' she said in a low tone, bringing her face close to mine.

'I only meant to say . . . Well, look around you. You can see I'm not like these other poor creatures.'

'You've been admitted. All the paperwork is in order. Now, are you finished?'

Without waiting for a response, she marched away.

14

The women in charge, the 'attendants', ordered the rest of us into a queue and then we left the washroom and marched down a broad staircase. A meagre light reached the stairwell from above, giving the staircase a gloomy and forbidding aspect. The stairs circled down three floors into a hall far below, lit by a murky light.

On reaching the next landing, the women formed a queue leading to a pair of large doors and waited. There was a smell of freshly baked bread. The doors opened and another group of women shuffled out and were herded upstairs as we took their place in the dining hall. I found myself waiting in a queue at a counter in a high-ceilinged room large enough to be a ballroom. The floorboards were bare and sudden harsh noises constantly tried my nerves: scraping chair legs, clattering trays, women's jabbering voices, boots clamping over creaking floorboards. As I waited, clutching my metal tray, I kept my gaze lowered, fearful of being accosted by a deranged woman. I felt the same sense of nightmarish unreality I'd felt on the stairs. The chamber was lit by two large chandeliers high above, most of the lamps unlit, so there was scarce light enough to illuminate the ceiling and the higher parts of the walls. As it was a fine morning, daylight seeped in from three floor-length windows, the shutters open to allow a dim dusty light to hover over tables set out in long rows. The windows overlooked the well-kept lawns and woods I had seen from my cell. I reached the front of the queue, and a woman put a thick slice of buttered bread on my metal tray, along with a tin bowl of thick porridge and a tin mug of tea. I chose a table apart from the other women and sat down. I wasn't left alone for long. A woman of startling appearance immediately sat next to me. Her hair stood on end in bristles that fanned out around her head and seemed to vibrate at any disturbance in the air. She had a lined, fleshy face and small sad eyes.

'You should eat up,' she said, spooning her porridge into her mouth. 'New here or transferred from another ward?'

'New, but I shan't be staying.'

She leant closer to me. 'I'm Ada. Ada Meggett. While it's just the two of us, a word of advice. You've got to watch yourself with all of them here. That one over there, she's a devil.' She indicated who she meant with a nod. It was Mrs Tuckwell, the tall woman who had given me short shrift earlier. She stood by the wall near the doors, arms folded, surveying all before her. 'I suppose you're wondering why they've got me here. There was a gas explosion. Several of my neighbours were planning to kill me. I told everyone, but no one believed me. Ceiling cornice came down on my head, it did. You can't be too careful.'

As she spoke, an assortment of other women of frightful appearance took their place at the table around us, among them the legitimate heir to the throne, who I'd met earlier, and a woman who was spectacularly wall-eyed.

'And what about you, my dear?' Ada asked me. 'What brings you here?'

'I've no idea why I'm here. There's been a mistake.'

'God bless you,' she said, with a look of pity. 'You have your own room, I suppose? The better sort usually do.'

Across the table was a woman with a bloated face and sickly pallor. A few tufts of hair were all that remained on her scalp which was raised and blistered. The muscles of her forehead were drawn tightly together in a scowl. She scratched her neck and face continually, and her skin was covered in sores. Ada saw me looking at her.

'Childbed – that's what Peggy's in for,' Ada confided to me. She leant closer and lowered her voice. 'They found her wet-nursing her own dead child and suspected the worse. Poor little thing's in heaven now, safe from harm, being looked after by the angels.'

Any appetite I'd had quickly deserted me, even though my stomach growled. I realized one of the staff was standing behind me. It was the mawkish attendant I'd spoken to earlier, rather than Miss Nettleship, the vicious one who had come to my room. 'You must try and eat. You've a long day ahead of you,' she said. To be rid of her, I sipped the tea, and picked up the hunk of bread and bit off a corner.

'Good butter that is, fresh from the dairy,' said Ada. She looked across at the child-murderer. 'Are you finished with that, Peg?' The woman stared sullenly into space, oblivious, so Ada took her bowl of porridge and made short work of it then turned to me, her mouth full. 'Voices keep me awake at night. They get in through the keyhole. Read my thoughts and repeat them to others. I've been sent here because I did something wrong. I was very wicked and didn't want to tell anyone what I'd done.'

The table was soon fully seated on both sides. Next to Peggy, the child-killer, was the painfully thin young lady I'd seen earlier in the washroom. Her grey eyes appeared huge in her cadaverous skull, her fair hair was wispy, her scalp showing through it. Although the room was warm, she had a black velvet cape over her shoulders. Even so, she was shivering. Her long neck rose out of the folds of her hood, a slender stem that seemed too slight to bear the weight of her head. She gazed out of the window, expressionless. Her head was turned, so I could see the nape of her neck and a thick growth of soft down on the prominent bone at the top of her spine. I was aware of a sour odour and felt sure it was coming from her. A scarlet drop fell from one of her nostrils. It left a red stain under her nose. She seemed wholly unaware of this. Another fell, falling on her pretty dress. There were several red spots on it already.

'Poor Edna May,' muttered Ada in my ear. 'She had the feeding tube this morning, God help her.'

'She's been fed by tube? How shocking. Surely she's too frail for that?'

'That's what happens to naughty girls who don't eat their meals. It's a lesson for you.'

I began spooning cold porridge into my mouth and forcing it down.

'They're harder on us, I should think,' said Ada. 'As we're on the secure ward.'

'The secure ward?' I asked, horrified. 'What do you mean by that?'

'Didn't they say? Surely, you must have noticed. Just look around you.'

'What does that mean – the "secure ward"?'

'It's where they put the incurables, the freaks of nature, the imbeciles, the epileptics –' as she spoke, she looked about, her gaze alighting on examples of each type '– the ones on suicide watch, the vicious ones who should be locked up in prison by rights. Didn't you see how the ladies from the sitting before us kept their distance when we changed over?'

'This can't be right,' I said. 'My parents wouldn't agree to it.'

'Well, perhaps it's just for the time being,' said Ada, taking hold of my arm gently. 'Maybe the other wards are full and you'll be moved when there's a bed for you.'

There was a burst of loud cackling laughter. It was the wall-eyed woman on the other side of the table. She spoke in a broad country dialect, as did the women alongside her. 'You dursn't think you'll get out of here anywhen soon, lady,' she cried. 'The gate's always locked and the gatekeeper's dog will have your leg off, soon as look at you. The walls is fifteen foot and the woods is full of gin traps.'

'Oh, ain't she prissy holdin' her cup of tea,' said the woman next to her.

'A lady of account, I reckon,' said Wall-Eye, nodding. She fixed her less wayward eye on me. 'You'll catch hurt if you try to flee the crazy house, I'm a-warnin' you. One took to 'er 'eels t'other-day evening but she soon heard the keeper a-coming. Let out a scritch to raise the dead.'

'There be stink pits in them woods!' cried her neighbour.

'And snares!' shouted another still. 'And a knucker hole where a water demon lives!'

'Barrow wights have been seen after dark, and witch hounds,' said the wall-eyed woman. 'And a black hound, big as a calf, with eyes like flaming coals.'

'Oh, but there was one lady who did get away,' said the true queen of England. 'Before my time, but the older patients still talk about her. Jessie, her name was. She hid in a coal cart and was never seen again.'

A reverential hush descended on the table at this memory. Heads nodded and knowing looks were exchanged.

'Since Jessie's time they've taken to searching every dray and dog cart that comes or goes,' said the rightful heir, in her dignified way. 'The night watch patrols the building after dark. One's only means of escape is to be discharged by the physician superintendent.'

'Or to depart to the hereafter,' said Ada.

15

Alone in my narrow little room, I was assailed by echoes beyond its walls, disembodied shouts, boots stomping back and forth maddeningly on the floor above, slamming doors, jangling keys, trolleys scuffing walls and doors as they passed through, wheels grinding, and underneath all of it the mechanical cranking and screeching of a great machine, with no care for the unlucky creatures locked inside it. I still had no memory of what had occurred between my quarrel with Mama and awaking distraught in the asylum. Perhaps if I had been allowed some of my belongings around me, they would have prompted associations, and I might have been able to remember. But I had nothing: no pictures, no clothes, not one of the baubles and gewgaws I had bought in church bazaars. I had no freedom to come and go, and was forbidden from approaching my family, even by letter.

During the day, I insisted on keeping to my cell. I refused to take up 'employment'. There would be no going among the madwomen and allowing myself to be treated as if I was one of their kind. I would stay in my room until I was permitted to discuss my discharge with Dr Rastrick. For the time being, all I could do was pace up and down. Every half hour or so, an attendant put her head around the door to ensure I wasn't doing myself any harm. I would have given anything to be at home, gazing out of my window at the rear of the tall houses opposite, with iron fire escapes zigzagging down to the ground. What I missed most was simple everyday things – even Cook's lukewarm, over-boiled eggs. And buried in the empty quiet of the countryside, I longed for the sounds of Brighton, the rumble of the carriages on Western Road, the cries of street sellers, the organ grinder's jaunty melodies, the shrieks of gulls, the rhythmic tap of cables on the masts of moored boats and, above it all, a general hum, as if the town itself lived and breathed.

The thought of Dr Rastrick made me tremble. Outside this place, I could fend him off, but here I was at his mercy. It was quite possible, even likely, he had a hand in my incarceration. If only I could remember those last days in Brighton. I had little trouble recalling his visits to the house in the past, the fear he inspired, the sense that he had dark designs on me, and would seize on any opportunity to take me under his control.

Who could I turn to? Papa perhaps. But he had consented to my removal to the asylum. Felix? The very thought of him and his family was unnerving. Whatever the reason for my incarceration, appealing to them could not be anything but humiliating. My older brother Lance? Hopeless! The only person in whom I had any faith was Miss Fanshaw. If I was able to paint, I'd have some vestige of my former life. More than anything else, I wanted to be taken seriously as an artist. I asked the attendants to enquire if my portable paintbox and my sketch book could be sent from home. They told me any stimulus of this sort was forbidden by Dr Rastrick. I asked for a book to distract myself. This was refused on the same grounds.

Several days passed and my loathing for that little room intensified. Yet I dreaded even more the times when I was forced to go among the other patients, whether to perform my ablutions or to endure the nightmare of the dining hall. The staff flatly refused to let me eat alone in my cell. And there was the daily excursion to the 'airing court', a dismal yard with flower beds around the perimeter where the patients paced around in circles in desultory fashion. The first time, I stood in a corner so I could keep my distance from the rest. I watched swifts high overhead, darting and tumbling tirelessly under shifting clouds in a blue sky. I wasn't to be left in peace for long, however. Miss Nettleship approached me and said I must exercise, or I wouldn't get better. So I had no choice but to tramp around the yard.

My mood worsened. A heaviness, a desolate feeling over-whelmed me. My eyes felt swollen and sore. I could barely keep them open. Even when outdoors, trudging around in the airing court, I felt numb, cut off from my fellow prisoners. Not even nature could stir my spirits. Coherent thought was impossible.

One afternoon I was sitting hunched over my little desk facing the blank wall, leaning on my elbows, head in hands, when I was startled by two firm raps on the door of my cell. A moment later, the door opened with its usual jarring creak.

Then I heard a male voice, one I knew well: 'That hinge needs oiling. I'll speak to Mrs Tuckwell about it.'

It was Dr Rastrick! I leapt to my feet.

'Please, sit down,' he said. He was looking at my hands. I realized I was wringing them, and stopped. I turned the chair so I could face him and sat down, trying to compose myself.

'The housekeeper tells me you wish to speak with me,' he said. 'I have a moment if you'd like to tell me what's on your mind.'

What was on my mind? Rather than asking that, he should have been providing me with an explanation for this outrageous treatment. I was thrown by his attitude, and I sensed his malevolence as he stood with his back to the door in his impeccable suit, fixing me with his steady gaze.

I found my voice: 'I have been here over a week and nobody has given me the least indication of why I'm being held here, or what treatment I'm to receive or when I might be discharged. I've been refused pen and paper. I'm not allowed to read so I must sit and mope for hours on end with nothing to occupy my mind.'

'I assure you we're doing everything possible to restore you to health. For example, by moving you from the ill-effects of the family home—'

'But I'm not unwell. I'm entirely in my right mind. And I'd far rather be in my family home than shut away here. I demand that you let me speak to my father.'

'Your father doesn't have the eye of an experienced alienist, which is why he's put you in my care. But if I might finish explaining, the hospital environment with its regular hours and routines is organized to distract you from dwelling on the morbid thoughts that have led to your confinement here.'

I interrupted before he could go on. 'As if it wasn't enough to abduct me and imprison me here without explanation, I have since discovered I'm on the ward with the most dangerous women, the incurably insane.'

'You have a most colourful imagination. The decision to—'

'I demand that while I'm waiting for my parents to remove me from here, that I'm at least put in a safer ward.'

'I'm afraid that's out of the question.'

'This is monstrous. Any rational person would judge me completely sane.'

'I'm afraid a good many of our patients declare themselves sane.' His tone was level, measured, his outward manner considerate, in contrast to my shrill petulance. Yet I was sure I detected a glint in his eye. He enjoys this, I thought. He revels in this power over me. 'Only yesterday one of the male patients, an engineer with severe delusions, wrote to the Lunacy Commission accusing me of wrongful arrest. We have to take great care when discharging patients. Many misjudgements have been made in the past concerning patients who successfully ape the behaviour of sane and rational persons but reveal themselves to be criminally insane as soon as they are at large—'

'Criminally insane! What are you suggesting?'

'I must remind you not to interrupt me when I'm speaking. Since I entered this room, I've observed many alarming indications of your state of mind. I put it to you that your perception of your own conduct is somewhat at odds with the impression you make on others.'

I saw I must moderate my voice and demeanour. Any show of emotion would be used as proof against me. I realized I had been fidgeting the whole time, fiddling with my hair, crossing and re-crossing my arms, even stamping my foot. I tried to compose myself.

'To answer your question about reading and drawing and the like, I can't allow you to exert yourself mentally in any way. However, some physical work would be beneficial.'

'Isn't that exertion too?'

'Moderate physical exertion will stop you dwelling on morbid thoughts.' He sighed. 'I doubt that cleaning would suit you, but perhaps you'd consider helping out in the kitchen garden? I hadn't intended to mention this today, but, as you press me, you have been brought here to be treated for a grave disorder. In the course of treatment over many years, I've been able to observe the gradual progression of your illness, and I've also gleaned anecdotal information from your mother to confirm my opinion. For example—'

'What is this nonsense? I've never been your patient. I agreed to your wearisome examinations merely to humour Mama. She is your patient, not me.'

'I repeat: do not interrupt me.' As before, his tone was mild, but with a subtle hint of menace. 'Your mother and I have always had an understanding that you were my patient, and this was reflected in my fee, as your father will testify. And I can assure you that, far from neglecting you, I will be paying special attention to your case. It might reassure you to know that I consider your disorder to be of some scientific importance.'

'Pray, do explain why I should find that reassuring?'

'It would help if you tried to mend your tone.'

'Heaven help us! Tell me, what must I do to prove I am sane? Just explain it to me and I'll do whatever you wish.'

'To begin with, an acknowledgement of the seriousness of your condition.'

'What are you saying? That I must agree to be as mad as you say I am, or you'll never let me out – is that it? And suppose I did so, wouldn't that simply entitle you to keep me here for as long as you wished? I demand that my father is sent for immediately.

Had he known of these conditions, he would never have agreed to them.'

'I must inform you that your father signed the admission forms himself, and has agreed to pay the fees for your admission as a private patient.'

'Papa! That is impossible.'

'He is acting with the best intentions, anxious to help you in any way he can.'

'I must speak to him!'

He sighed. After a pause, he said, 'Miss Pring, do you have any recollection of what happened to you in the days before your arrival here?'

I felt a sharp pain in my head, and my mind was suddenly dark, as if the lights had been put out. I lost all awareness of my surroundings. When I came to, I was slumped in my chair, and Dr Rastrick was on one knee at my side, holding my wrist in his hand.

He rose to his feet. 'My visit has been a strain for you, as I feared it might. You must rest now. Mrs Tuckwell will make the necessary arrangements. Good day, Miss Pring.'

After he had left, I struggled to collect my thoughts. Why had Papa signed the papers admitting me to such a place? Normally, Mama would do anything to avoid a scandal. But perhaps – and this was a frightful thought – perhaps that *was* the explanation. I was sent here to *prevent* a scandal. And what was the 'grave disorder' Dr Rastrick referred to? Had he persuaded Mama and Papa that I was suffering a form of derangement? I saw a new and sinister explanation for Dr Rastrick's visits to my room in the past. But these troubled thoughts didn't preoccupy me for long. The attendant arrived, and I was put under sedation.

16

The following day, two dresses arrived from home. They were wrapped in soft paper and when I tore it off I found the dresses had been freshly sponged and pressed. I looked for a note, but there was nothing. I put one of them to my face to inhale its fragrance, and was transported back to Brighton and to our airy drawing room with its round bay window. I burst into tears. When a little recovered, I laid the dresses on the narrow bed, still sniffling and shuddering. One of them was my favourite blue silk dress. I myself had sewn on the lace trimming at the neckline and cuffs, with help from Susan. The thought of the two of us sitting side by side stitching almost undid me again – even though I'd always hated needlework. The dress was the one that I'd worn on my visit to Mr Lilley. That thought made me unsteady, shaky. I held the dress under my chin and wished I had a looking glass in which to view myself. Then, with trembling fingers, I put it on. I ran my hands over the bodice, and shook out the creases in the skirt. The softness of the fabric was divine after the rough calico of the striped uniform. I was no longer an anonymous lunatic, but my former self. In this armour I felt ready to finally brave the recreation hour. I had made up my mind that I must comply with Dr Rastrick's rules or I would never persuade him to let me write to my parents and secure my release.

But as I stepped into the main ward room that first time, my nerves threatened to get the better of me. My first impression was of a large corridor that resembled a suburban drawing room, but in a strange and disturbing dream. There were windows on both sides of the room, so it was well lit. I sensed many gazes turning on me, and immediately regretted wearing my lovely dress, contrasting as it did with the drab striped uniform most of the other ladies wore. About thirty women of different ages sat about on benches along the walls or at tables where they were occupied in reading periodicals or playing board games, while others sat in armchairs, lost in their own musings. I kept to the sides of the room, moving towards some chairs by a row of windows looking out over well-kept lawns. I passed women who stood alone, apparently lost in distressing thoughts, or else talking to an imaginary friend. Others paced up and down to no apparent end. Somewhere a woman was scraping a violin, its tuning slightly out, the strains barely audible above the muted babble of voices and the twittering of birds in a row of cages hanging along one wall. The scraping bow set my nerves aquiver. The only member of staff I could see was the feeble attendant, Mrs Clinch.

With relief, I spotted Ada Meggett, who had befriended me in the dining hall on my first day. I went over and sat next to her on a seat not far from the windows, a little apart from the bulk of the women. It was apparent Ada was not having a good day. Her eyebrows were drawn upwards, giving her a startled expression, and her hair was more upright and electrified than ever. Ada glanced about her nervously. 'They're watching me.

Don't think I don't know it. I hear them at night, whispering, calling me a prostitute. I'm to be punished.'

Just then, I heard a piercing shriek and almost jumped out of my skin. It had issued from a tiny creature on the floor not three yards away. It was little more than two feet in height. At first, I thought it was a grotesque bird, dressed for some bizarre reason in the asylum's regulation striped dress. Its arms were disproportionately long, its trunk round and humped, and two large bare feet poked out from under the hem of a skirt. The creature waddled underneath a table, its head bobbing back and forward with each step just like that of a pigeon. It had a very small head and was nearly bald, the eyes widely spaced. It began flapping its long arms up and down as if it would take flight and swoop down on me. I tried to avoid its gaze as it hissed and stamped its foot, its bony head cocked and one of its round eyes gazing at me.

'Keep back now or she'll have your hand off,' said Ada. 'They say her mother is a local witch who did the deed with a raven and this was the outcome.'

At that moment Mrs Clinch appeared, flushed and snivelling. She bent down to take the creature by the end of one of its upper limbs. I saw it had a form of rudimentary human hand. 'Strangers bother her, I'm afraid,' Mrs Clinch told me. 'She'll get used to you, won't you, my pet?' She looked down and smiled at her charge. 'She came out of the womb like this, poor child. They call her the Bird-Girl, but her name's Jemima. She knows few words, but attends you if you call her name. You'll know if she's cross because she hisses or stamps her foot. And when she's happy she cackles like a goose. Whatever you do, don't ever touch her when she's not expecting it, or she might nip you. But she's harmless enough, aren't you, my dear?' She looked down at the creature again. 'You know not to wander off like that.' She turned to me. 'There's something in the air today. The women are skittish. It's the change in the weather, I think. Did you hear the wind last night? Blew seven different colours of hell out of the sky. And –' she lowered her voice '– a headless white horse was seen running through the woods – and not for the first time.'

I looked about, and saw no sign of Miss Nettleship. 'Surely, you're not completely alone, Mrs Clinch? Miss Nettleship is somewhere about, I suppose?'

'She's off today. A lot of us have gone down with the contagion. Mrs Brewer's on her way in from the village on short notice. But they say a tree's blown down on the road. Mrs Tuckwell will drop in soon to keep an eye on things. At least, I do hope so.' She looked about her, nervously.

I saw that this hopeless woman was all that stood between me and a roomful of lunatics. There was a loud shriek. Nervously, I looked about me to discover the cause. Eliza Feldwicke was pestering another patient. I had recently seen her in the airing court, causing mayhem by attacking other patients until she was subdued by two attendants. Since then, she had exposed herself indecently to a gardener. When they locked her in the strong room, she tore off some of the padding from the wall. Eliza was an alarming sight, with her wild black hair, wide-open eyes and thin-lipped mouth turned down at the corners.

She scowled at her victim. 'Do that again and you'll catch hurt,' she said. 'I'll slit your throat from ear to ear.' She pushed the woman so that she almost fell. 'Reckon you better than I, do 'ee?'

Mrs Clinch called from across the room: 'Eliza, stop that moiling right now or we'll put you in the side-arm dress.'

'Only give her a liddle pook. I seed her give me dirty looks,' cried Eliza.

'Leave the lady alone. That's your final warning.'

'Bugger off!' muttered Eliza under her breath.

It was quiet for a few minutes. I sat next to Ada as she gabbled away incoherently. I took none of it in – I was increasingly nervous about the proximity of Eliza. I glanced and saw her stalking a lone woman, a white-haired old lady who was standing at the side of the room talking earnestly to herself. She spat on the old lady and pulled her hair, then moved away.

The women were on edge. Nobody wanted to catch Eliza's eye. I sorely wanted to slip out of the ward and return to my room, but feared attracting her attention. I knew she was close because she was filthy in her habits and I could smell urine and stale sweat. A moment later she stood toe to toe with another lady, looking up into her eyes. Her victim this time was Rosabel Crimwood, the lady who considered herself the rightful heir to the English throne. She returned Eliza's gaze imperiously.

'That's my shawl. Give it back,' said Eliza. 'Or I'll cut your heart out.' She seized Rosabel's shawl and tried to pull it from her shoulders, without success.

My nerves couldn't withstand another minute of this. I rose to my feet and made my way towards the door which was on the opposite side of the room. After I'd taken a few steps, I heard Eliza's voice.

'Why, who has we here?' she called. 'Lady Muck's showed her face today. Ain't seen her do no work, eh, ladies? Proud as Satan, I reckon.'

I knew she was referring to me, but I continued to pace towards the door without looking in her direction. Suddenly she was standing before me, blocking my path and leering. With a sudden lunge she grasped my skirt and held onto it.

'Feel the quality of this riggin',' she said. 'Think yourself too good for us, princess? Pride comes before a fall.'

'I'd like to return to my room,' I said. 'I'm not feeling well.'

She kept hold of my skirt. 'Hark at her. All tip-tongued and giving herself airs. Don't get miffy with me, mistress, or I'll cut off both your ears.'

Ada appeared at my side. 'Leave her be, Liza,' she said coaxingly. She took me by the hand. 'She's the Mary Magdalen, aren't you, my dear?'

'Aye, and I'm the Emperor of China,' said Eliza. 'I'll learn this one not to look down on me.'

I heard the voice of Mrs Clinch, the attendant. 'Oh, Mrs Brewer!' she cried. 'Thank the Lord, you're here.'

In a trice, Mrs Clinch and Mrs Brewer appeared behind Eliza and seized her by the arms. She let go of my skirt.

'Away you come,' said the strapping Mrs Brewer.

'You shouldn't ought to do this,' yelled Eliza, struggling to throw them off. 'I'll stop the butter churning, you'll see. There'll be wilting and withering hereabouts. Churn owl stole my hairbrush. Go and fetch it. Churn owl hid it in the orchard.'

My dearest Papa,

Finally, after more than a fortnight at Hillwood Grange, I have been given permission to write to you. Up until now, Dr Rastrick forbade it, maintaining quite reasonably that any reminder of my home and family might worsen my condition. This prohibition has now been lifted, in part because I have agreed to take up employment. I was at first reluctant to cooperate with the methods of the hospital, due to my distress at being separated from those I love and all that is dear to me. But I have learned the error of my ways. I heartily endorse Dr Rastrick's philosophy and, as his methods are based on the most advanced science, I expect to make a full recovery and to return home very soon. I already feel far removed from the distressed and confused state I was in when I arrived here.

You will perhaps be surprised to hear that I have agreed to work in the kitchen garden. Here on my desk before me I have a jar of pink dahlias that I was permitted to pick as a reward for my labours. They are a reminder of life beyond the locked doors of this institution. I have got quite used to having soil under my nails. And, as you know, I have never been the sort of woman who squeals at the sight of a wriggling earthworm.

Oh, how I long to see you and to hear all the news about the family! Please write to Dr Rastrick URGENTLY and ask when I might be allowed to receive visitors. I think of Mama constantly. Send her all my love. I hope she is not worrying overmuch about how I am faring here. I would love to hear from her if she felt able to write to me. I can't recall the summer party, but I sense that something happened there. From this vantage point, I appreciate how concerning and disturbing my behaviour must have been throughout those last weeks. I simply wasn't myself. But having had time to reflect, I can assure you that I have come to my senses. Tell Mama I will write to her as soon as Dr Rastrick allows. And send my love to the boys.

I'm uncertain if you're aware of this, but I have been placed on

161

a wing they call 'the secure ward'. This where the most dangerous women are held, those in advanced states of derangement, with incurable conditions and distressing physical abnormalities. I am becoming more used to it, but it was a tremendous shock to me at first, as you might imagine. Naturally, I have asked Dr Rastrick if I can be removed to another ward – one more appropriate for someone who has, after all, only suffered a minor episode of nervous prostration, and who is now rapidly recovering. While I would never challenge Dr Rastrick's methods, and I bow to his superior knowledge, I wonder if you could support my plea to be removed to a ward where the women's conditions are less chronic and of a more temporary nature.

As you may have been informed, the hospital routinely edits patients' letters and removes lines that might cause distress to their loved ones. If this is the case, you will be able to see where my words have been concealed. So, I reiterate that it would be much easier for you to judge how well I have recovered if you were able to visit me here and see with your own eyes.

With all the love in my heart,
Violet

P.S. I have only the vaguest recollection of what happened in the days immediately prior to being removed here. If there is anything important I should know, do please enlighten me.

My dear Violet,

I was greatly heartened to hear from you. I saw no evidence that your letter had been edited in any way. At any rate, you will be reassured to know that Dr Rastrick has promised to keep us informed of your progress once a month. Your mother and I understand that this has been a greatly distressing experience for you, and we think of you constantly. We entered into this course of action with the most profound regret and only after great deliberation – both between ourselves and with Dr Rastrick, who has proved a pillar of strength throughout.

I'm afraid that I won't be able to visit you in the hospital for the time being. Dr Rastrick insists that your recovery depends on your being removed from all of associations with your former life and from all of your daily habits and enthusiasms. As I understand it, he means to separate you from unhealthy associations that might provoke the excessive emotions that have upset the balance of your mind and led to your confinement. I would urge you follow his instructions to the letter if you wish to make a satisfactory recovery.

I note that in your missive you chose not to ask after Felix, no doubt because you are still in shock due to your change of circumstances. He has behaved with all the decorum one would expect of him, and is currently on an extended sojourn in South America to pursue his business interests there. We have not seen his parents since the episode at the summer party, which is hardly surprising.

You asked for news of your brothers. Archie is preparing for his first term at prep school and is making a tremendous fuss about it, as you can well imagine. Roger is looking forward to returning to Lancing College, whereas Edward, true to form, has the dreads. As for Lance, he is still kicking about the house. He has announced his intention to join the Guards, and I hope and pray he succeeds.

As regards your mother, it must be said that she is doing her best to adapt to her new and trying circumstances. We have been obliged to let another servant go, which has added to her difficulties. She sends her love, and prays for you nightly. She wishes you to know that everything she has ever done in relation to yourself was designed to ensure you had a happy and fulfilled life. She will write to you when Dr Rastrick deems it appropriate.

To turn to your complaint about the 'secure ward'. Dr Rastrick has informed us of this circumstance, and I bow to his superior knowledge in these matters. God willing, in time you will be moved to more congenial surroundings. I'm encouraged – and admittedly quite surprised – to hear that you have agreed to do some gardening. This can only be for the good. I would further advise you to put your trust in the scientifically proven methods of the hospital. In your solitary moments, try not to let your thoughts turn in on themselves and please do make the most of this chance for rest and respite.

As for your last few days here, I'm advised by Dr Rastrick not to discuss this with you until you are better. It's for the best, I'm sure.

With all my love,
Papa

Papa's letter was a bitter disappointment to me. It was clear that Dr Rastrick had briefed him not to discuss anything of importance, and that he would resist any future intervention by Papa on my behalf. Learning of Felix's adventures in South America inspired the most confused feelings. I was happy that he was thriving without me, but the idea of life continuing as normal made me feel as if I was already half-forgotten. I was overwhelmed with loneliness and the sense of having been abandoned. And I still had no insight into the circumstances that led to my confinement to the asylum.

17

From the windows of the ward, I sometimes saw convalescing patients down on the raised lawns, walking along the pathway or resting a moment on the benches. I prayed I would soon be among them. I had discovered that my only hope was to be removed to another ward, and thence to a halfway house in Burgess Hill, before returning to my home. To achieve this, I must become the very model of placid feminine compliance. I even chose to attend the Sunday Divine Service in the draughty little chapel in the grounds. I laboured in the kitchen garden without complaint, even if my back ached and my hands became raw and calloused. My obedience won me a concession from Dr Rastrick. I was given access to books from the chaplain's library. Apart from Tennyson and the Bible, I was restricted to battered old children's books, with split spines and pages that gave off a mouldy odour: *The Water-Babies* and *Alice's Adventures in Wonderland*. There was also an old French grammar book, battered and with missing pages. It reminded me of Mr Lilley, and his promise to take me to Paris. I pored over this book avidly, and by degrees the French I'd learned from my governess, Mademoiselle Dufort, when a child, came back to me. As for Mr Lilley, it seemed unlikely I would ever set eyes on him again, so what harm was there in the occasional daydream about what might have been? But I yearned far more intensely just to be free, to be in my own home surrounded by my precious belongings, of being able to go wherever I pleased. It would be worth paying any price for that.

★

One warm day in late July, I was working side by side in the garden with Ada Meggett. Her electrical hair was hidden underneath one of the straw hats we all wore while we worked. The hats had a flap at the back to keep the sun off our necks. The straw made my head itch on those warm summer days. There were various vegetables in terraces, and an orchard beyond. Much of the food eaten in the asylum was grown in the garden, and fifteen to twenty women laboured there daily with three attendants keeping watch. The garden was walled on two sides; the other two walls had presumably tumbled down long since. There was a glasshouse where tomatoes, cucumbers, French beans and the like were grown. At the far end there was a large thatched barn where fruit was kept after it was picked until ready to eat, and a hut where we put the tools, the staff watching carefully to make sure nobody went off with something they could do mischief with.

We were at work sowing for the winter harvest: runner beans, pumpkins, carrots, beetroot. The garden seemed to calm Ada. Perhaps it was the soothing hum of the bees, which the country women called 'dumbledores'. We were relieved by a cool breeze and Ada took her hat off to fan her face which was pink with exertion. She was no more used to such work than I was, having lived in Brighton all her life. A bell rang and we walked over to sit on the shady side of the fruit barn to eat our crust of bread and cheese and drink a mug of beer.

'I'm beat, I am,' said Ada, fanning her face with her hat. 'Worked hard for others all my life, don't deserve this. Listen to that pair over there. What are they saying about me?'

'They're not talking about you.'

She looked at me askance. 'Can you be so sure? I've heard them. Calling me dreadful names. Saying I'm a prostitute. Everyone knows I'm the worst sinner on earth, without hope of forgiveness. I'll be arrested before long.'

'Nonsense. Don't you think the police have enough to do without chasing after you?' I wondered what might distract her from her delusions. 'Why don't you tell me about yourself, your life before you were sent here?'

'You wouldn't want to hear about an ordinary woman like me and all my dreary comings and goings. I've let everyone down, my parents, my children . . . '

'I should like to hear your story. Tell me about your childhood.'

She looked this way and that, scuffing her boot heel on the dry earth. She turned over a large stone with the toe of her boot and dozens of pale woodlice scurried for safety.

'You tell me about your life and then I'll tell you about mine,' I said. 'What were your parents like?'

'Good people,' she said, firmly. 'Father only wanted what was best for us. Mother was a virtuous woman, godly and clean in her ways, hardworking to a fault. We were poor as poor. No money for clothes, but we were never dirty or ragged. Money was always tight. Dad was the only one who got to have an egg – in a glass of milk . . . '

I thought about my own house, and Cook's boiled eggs every morning.

'There was no free schooling in my day so I never went. Dad taught me to read, and he was stern as any schoolmaster. You'd get a rap across your knuckles if you didn't pay attention.'

I didn't go to school either, I thought.

'I was the oldest,' continued Ada. 'So I did the general run of housework, running errands, carrying coal, cleaning grates, dusting, cleaning, looking after the little ones, pummelling the beds every morning. I used to dream of getting a job in the dyers and cleaners shop, or even Hanningtons store, where a girl could earn one and six a week. I'd have my own money then. But I was wanted at home. The only way out was to get a husband. There was this young man, Jim, a few years older than me. I always seemed to bump into him when I was doing errands. He was the opposite to Dad. Always joking and singing. He liked a drink, whereas Dad was a teetotaller. Oh, the stories Jim told! All his escapades. I never knew whether to believe him or not, but he always made me laugh, and laughter was in short supply at home. So I threw in my lot with him. I was pregnant when I went to the altar, God forgive me. My first child was born only a month later, a little boy, but he died in infancy. Then I had three girls one after another. Jim always complained they were no use for bringing money into the house. He was away a lot. He was a tool fitter and spent one week at home and the next in Manchester. He travelled all over with his work, and sometimes I didn't see him for two or three weeks. We got the cottage on Helmont Street through the railway. All the railway workers live in that neighbourhood. I was always house-proud. I kept that house spic and span, the floor sanded, the irons scoured. I wouldn't let anyone know how hard up we were. You have to keep up appearances. We were one of the first streets to get connected up with gas lighting indoors.'

She turned pale and lifted her hand to her cheek, her fingers trembling. 'Gas! The whole house was wrecked and a heavy cornice pole fell right on top of me. When I came round, I saw all the windows were blown out. That's when my hair went crisp, I'm sure of it. And I'll never be able to hear in this ear again. I wish I could go deaf in the other so I couldn't hear the voices.'

'The voices are in your head,' I said. 'And they'll go away, I'm sure.'

Just then, the bell rang, and we rose, rubbing our stiff backs and stretching our limbs before getting back to work. Listening to Ada, I realized how cossetted I had been in my own life. I had read books by Mr Mill and Mr Carlyle in Papa's study, but there seemed little scope for me to improve matters, beyond expressing an opinion which nobody was particularly interested in hearing. The sole project of my existence had been to make myself as marriageable as possible.

I knelt in the soil alongside Ada, sowing row after row of seeds, and covering them in soil with my trowel. I thought about Ada's story. Her life had been so different to my own, and yet at its heart there was a curious parallel. She had been forced to throw in her lot with Jim because it was her only hope of gaining money and of leaving the family home, while I had found myself forced into accepting a proposal from Felix for the same reason. I had a bond with the woman labouring alongside me, but I would never have known it had we not been thrown together in misfortune.

★

A day or two later, Ada and I sat side by side in the ward on our straight-backed chairs – not the most comfortable seats, but a step-up from the benches where the women of lowest status sat, the cretins, epileptics and so on. Dr Rastrick appeared with a young man, his new assistant medical officer, a gangling creature called Dr Binkes, with jug ears and a diffident demeanour. He was young enough to still have pimples on his chin. It was clear Dr Rastrick had Dr Binkes under his wing, and was training him. They passed Annie Weech, a hunchbacked dwarf who sat for hours without moving a muscle, her legs too short to reach the floor. She had a large deformed chin and one shoulder higher than the other. She sat perfectly still in her chair, gazing fixedly from under drooping eyelids. Her demeanour was decidedly sinister. I could picture her suddenly leaping out of her chair and pouncing on someone, like a spring-loaded automaton, and I couldn't get this unsettling notion out of my mind. As Dr Rastrick led Dr Binkes forward, he turned to him and remarked: 'Another congenital idiot.'

They stopped when they got to where Ada and I were sitting. 'There's someone I think you'll be interested in meeting,' Dr Rastrick said. I hoped they were coming to speak with me, but it was Ada they approached. She was having one of her bad days, coherent and delusional by turns. Her upright hair was restless, vibrating constantly. The doctors paused a little distance from her, and put their heads together, the tall young man inclining his head to listen to his chief. 'Now this lady, Mrs Meggett, is a copybook old maid type, prone to religious apparitions or hallucinations about being ravished during the night, symptoms that betray the ovarian and uterine disturbances of the menopause.'

Dr Binkes seemed distracted. He'd spotted the Bird-Girl, Jemima Penty.

'Ah, I see you've spotted our Miss Penty,' said Dr Rastrick. 'Note the large lower jaw. I've measured it. It projects more than an inch beyond the contracted upper jaw and possesses an extraordinary range of anteroposterior, as well as lateral, movement.'

'Like a beak, I suppose,' Dr Binkes stuttered. Jemima cocked her head and uttered one of her alarming squawks, then hissed and stamped her foot. Dr Binkes took a step backwards, almost falling into the lap of Annie Weech.

'A remarkable instance of hereditary degenerative defects, don't you think?' said Dr Rastrick. 'One rarely encounters so pronounced an example.'

Dr Rastrick placed a chair in front of Ada for Dr Binkes to sit upon. I observed them out of the corner of my eye. Both men took their case notebooks out of their pockets. I smelt carbolic soap and was sure it was to do with Dr Binkes. He had a raw scrubbed look about him. His collar must have been very well starched because the skin on his long neck was pink and mottled. Ada stared blankly ahead, her forehead deeply grooved in a frown, her lips mumbling inaudibly. She was afraid of Dr Rastrick, I was sure of it, and anxious to please him.

'And how are we this morning, Mrs Meggett?' asked Dr Rastrick. He turned to Dr Binkes. 'We brought her to this ward after she'd been unable to sleep for two entire weeks and became confused. She's been treated with hyoscine, but as you see is still a little agitated.'

Ada reached forward and took the younger doctor's hand in her own. Why was she playing up this way? It was as if she was afraid to relinquish her delusions. I wanted to shake her back into her senses.

'Mrs Meggett's diagnosis?' asked Dr Binkes.

'Religious melancholia, according to her admission certificate. Will you permit me to touch your hair, Mrs Meggett?' Without waiting for her assent, Dr Rastrick passed his hand over the upright crinkles. 'Ah! A slight electrical charge. Here, feel it.'

Dr Binkes followed suit, with his free hand – Ada still had a firm grip of the other. Judging by his reaction, he wasn't quite so attuned to Ada's electrical hair as his master.

'We shouldn't rule out the possibility she has an electrical condition,' said Dr Rastrick. 'You'll be aware of Caton's work on electrical currents in the brains of dogs and apes?'

'Certainly, I've come across it.'

'Good man. I strongly advise you to keep abreast of developments in this area. What we see here is physiological evidence of abnormal electrical discharges within the body, in all probability a symptom of brain lesions.' Dr Rastrick had taken out his case book and was making notes. 'The religious preoccupation is only an indication that the brain is overloaded and losing mental force.'

He showed Dr Binkes his notebook. 'These are the signs and symptoms I want you to record on your rounds. Build up a complete and accurate picture.' He tapped the page with his pencil. 'Take down all physical evidence. Be diligent about it. As we assess the patient, we observe closely the demeanour. In relation to Mrs Meggett, her heavy and dull expression, for example.'

Ada frowned, hearing these ungallant remarks.

'Women are particularly useful for such purposes, of course,' said Dr Rastrick.

'Are they?' asked Dr Binkes.

'Being closer to nature, the sex is more impressionable to atmospheric stimuli.'

The longer the doctors spoke, the angrier I became. Why wouldn't Dr Rastrick refrain from talking about Ada's hair, and instead encourage her to talk about her life before she suffered the shock that turned her mind?

Ada began to speak in a tiny wisp of a voice, quite unlike the way she spoke to me.

'Tell me, where am I? Where have you put me?'

'Come now, Mrs Meggett, you know where you are,' said Dr Rastrick. 'We've talked about this.'

'Oh yes, I remember where I am now!' Ada cried. 'I'm in Heaven!' She lifted Dr Binkes's hand to her lips, kissing the back of it as she gazed into his eyes. He had a protuberant Adam's apple and it bobbed up and down at that moment. Ada's hair quivered.

'Is this *Him* you've brought with you?' she asked Dr Rastrick. She was suddenly timorous, whispering: 'Is this Our Lord Jesus?'

'This is Dr Binkes, our new assistant medical officer. He'll be coming to help me with my work, and may come to see you when I'm away.'

'What was the cause of Mrs Meggett's illness?' asked Dr Binkes.

'Her admission certificate records it as a gas explosion.'

'And what's your view on recording what patients say in case notes?'

'Mostly of little use. Unless it provides useful information about their bodily functioning.'

'And their delusions, hallucinations, memories of their past life?'

'Environmental information tends to be extraneous, in general. We can't make a diagnosis based on such ravings.'

Unable to endure Dr Rastrick's pomposity and obtuseness a moment longer, I turned away. I watched a demented elderly lady hobble through the room. She spent her days pacing endlessly from end to end on some long-forgotten errand, weaving between tables and chairs. I realized Dr Rastrick's instructive remarks had come to a close.

'I hope you're beginning to see the scope of what we're about here,' Dr Rastrick said to Dr Binkes, giving him a pat on the back. 'I have a particular interest in researching the aetiology of moral insanity in females. There are a number of unfortunate women here in that category.'

And as he made the remark, he turned his head and smiled at me for reasons best known to himself. The muscles tightened at the back of my neck.

18

August had come and I had maintained my compliant behaviour. I'd had no opportunity to speak with Dr Rastrick, so when his summons finally came, I flew from the kitchen garden, dashed through the main building and rushed up the stairs. The attendant Mrs Clinch was hardly able to keep up with me. The consultation was to take place in the housekeeper Mrs Tuckwell's small station on the secure ward. It was my first visit there. My breathlessness seemed out of place in the hushed stillness. Dr Rastrick didn't look up as I entered, but continued to read his notebook which was open on the counter. The room was a narrow galley, and the walls closed in on me. Locked cupboards ranged along one wall, from which drugs were dispensed, I supposed, and opposite there was a worktop and stove with a kettle on it. I noticed a few books on a shelf, dealing with medical matters. There was a vent on the floor and I could hear the gas boilers roaring down in the basement. At last, Dr Rastrick turned and gestured for me to sit on a stool at the counter. His gaze passed over me from head to foot. The look in his eyes was disconcerting, but difficult to read.

'You needn't have run here,' he said.

'I didn't want to waste time,' I replied, perching myself on the stool. 'I rarely see you.'

'I'm sure you're being well looked after. Now, if I could have a look at your eyes.' He moved to stand over me, moving directly into a physical examination, with no enquiry as to how I was feeling. His time was precious, and he didn't want to waste it in idle talk.

'I can see perfectly well, I assure you.'

He brought his face close to mine and parted my eyelids with his thumb and forefinger so he could peer into my soul. 'Just a little bloodshot and cloudy today,' he concluded.

He held my wrist in his hand and took my pulse, staring at his stopwatch. When he had finished, he stepped over to the counter. 'I need to listen to your heart, so open your dress, if you wouldn't mind.' I obliged, at pains to conceal my irritation. As I unbuttoned my dress, I smelled my own perspiration. He took his stethoscope out of his case and put the earplugs into his ears. With each minute that passed, the possibility of making my case was slipping away. He pressed the stethoscope against my exposed skin, close to the breastbone. Somewhere outside I could hear the squeak of a trolley wheel that needed oiling. Dr Rastrick moved the stethoscope to the same position on the other side of my breastbone. He made a humming sound as if he'd heard something untoward. My hands trembled where they rested in my lap and I saw the black soil under my fingernails. A sudden vertiginous sensation swept over me and I shut my eyes, desperate to conceal my symptoms from Dr Rastrick. He took soundings in several places on my back. When he was finished, he put his instrument away and I buttoned myself up. For a long moment he stood at the counter, silently recording his findings in his notebook.

'Everything is all right, I take it?' I asked.

'Both your heartbeat and pulse are higher than I would like.'

'Well, I've just rushed up the stairs from the gardens. On the whole, I've been feeling much better.'

'The wonder of the stethoscope is it allows one to detect irregularities even when there are no visible symptoms. I see in the notes that you experienced some nocturnal palpitations when you first arrived. Has there been any recurrence?'

I hesitated. I was inclined to lie and say there hadn't been, but I'd mentioned it to the attendants. 'A little. But no more than I'd expect after such a wretched change of circumstances.'

He looked down at his notes. 'The records show your menses are irregular, a recognized symptom of want of nervous force. And, just so you know, I've notified Mrs Tuckwell that your stools and urine are to be inspected.'

'As you see fit. But I hope you're also noting down that I'm improving day by day. In fact, there's something I wanted to ask. I wondered if I might be permitted to do some drawing, or ideally painting. It would distract me from morbid thoughts and soothe my nerves. I might draw flowers from the garden, or views of the pleasant hospital grounds perhaps – as you deemed appropriate.'

Dr Rastrick frowned. 'Painting is a harmless enough pastime for someone with robust health. But that's not the case here. And I fear there is a pathological aspect to your drawing and painting. You yourself refer to morbid thoughts.' He paused, studying me intently with his pencil poised. His gaze was cold and searching. 'Tell me, Miss Pring, have you had any disturbing thoughts recently, or visions?'

'I'm not sure I understand what you mean. Thoughts of what nature?'

'Anything that has troubled your conscience. Perhaps at night, when alone.'

'No, I don't think so,' I said, avoiding his gaze.

'You have not found yourself dwelling on your visit to Mr Lilley, for example?'

I experienced a confusion of emotions at this unexpected mention of Mr Lilley, and grew uncomfortably hot under my clothes. My hands were wringing in my lap and it took an effort to compose myself.

'I haven't been constantly thinking about Mr Lilley, I can assure you,' I said. 'And at any rate, what business is that of yours?'

'It is important that I record any disturbing thoughts or other evidence of emotional lability. Anything that might pertain to physical degeneration.'

'Physical degeneration! Can't you see how hard we work in the garden?'

'I was referring to the mind, the likelihood of lesions in the brain. But I think it's best if we leave it there, for now. I recommend that you comply to the letter with our rules, or face the consequences. Rest assured, every effort is being made on your behalf. You may go now, Miss Pring.'

Mrs Clinch escorted me back to the garden. This time she marched ahead while I tarried, all my spirit drained from me. The sun had gone in, and a grey and dreary mood had fallen over all. Mrs Clinch parted with me at the arch in the wall that led into the garden, and hurried back to the ward. My workmates and their guards had left the vegetable plots and were gathered some distance away, outside the shed, putting away the tools for the night. They were too distant for me to hear their voices.

I made my way slowly along the path under the wall towards them. I passed a row of cold frames where cabbages, spinach and radishes were growing under glass. Ahead was a field of chard, ready for picking. After a quick glance around me to make sure I couldn't be seen, I walked through the chard, trampling as much of it underfoot as I could.

19

It was dinner time and, as always, I sat next to Ada Meggett. She was lapping up a plate of Irish stew. I spooned some into my own mouth and forced the greasy broth and gristle down. Poor Peggy Paynter, who had murdered her own infant, sat across the table. She had pulled out all but the few last tufts of her sandy hair. She seemed to be fading away, with her white eyelashes and pale eyes, her puffy complexion and dull expression. Every so often, she sighed heavily. Wall-Eye, whose actual name was Judith Wicks, was next to her, talking intensely to one of her mates, their heads together. She noticed me gazing at her, and turned to me.

'Dr Rastrick has jars of pickled brains in a cupboard, all in a row, all of maids that was locked up here,' she said, with a blast of her demented cackle. 'As soon as they draws their last breath, they be wheeled down to the lab so that he can slice off the top of their noddles and take out their brains.'

'Zactly so!' said one of her friends.

Judith leaned toward me to make herself heard. 'There be doors here that ain't never opened. Secret chambers where wicked things is done to us in the name of learning.'

For a moment all that could be heard was the clinking of

spoons in metal bowls. I nibbled a slice of stoneground bread that had been dipped in lard.

'Rastrick do have his *darlings*, of course,' said Judith.

I put the bread down. 'His darlings? What do you mean?'

'Them ladies his junior men must keep notes on, them he's forever fiddling about with, them he picks on for his tests.' As she spoke, several of the women around her nodded their heads.

'And who are these darlings? Can you name any of them?'

'Well, who can rightly say?' said Wall-Eye. 'But one thing I do know. They'll never leave Hellwood. Not alive, dear me, no.' She cackled again at the thought.

Ada touched my arm. 'Are you going to eat that suet pudding, dear?'

I shook my head. 'You may have it, Ada.'

★

Another day, a number of women were told they were to have their photographic likeness taken. When it was my turn, Miss Nettleship escorted me down the central staircase all the way to the bottom, and into the part of the building where the male wards were situated, an area unfamiliar to me. I had to sit on a bench outside the room for some time. There was a sign on the door: 'Neuroanatomical Laboratory.' From time to time, I heard Dr Rastrick's muffled voice behind the door.

The door opened, and a patient walked out, looking dazed. 'Next, please!' cried Dr Rastrick. I stepped inside and saw Dr Rastrick's laboratory was a large airy room, with windows along one side looking out over pastures where cows grazed, with the woods in the distance. Dr Rastrick was standing beside the new man, Dr Binkes, at the side of the room, their backs to me. Neither of them turned as I entered. They were looking down at a photograph on top of a cabinet.

'The point is we can create a taxonomy of different symptoms, so specimens can be compared across other hospitals and clinics,' said Dr Rastrick. 'I intend to publish some of the photographs in book form, with an accompanying monograph.'

A camera waited on its stand in the centre of the room, the lens facing a grey sheet slung over a line a few yards in front of it.

Dr Rastrick turned. 'Ah, Miss Pring. This way, please.' He directed me to a chair between the camera and the grey sheet. Stooping to pin a square of paper with the number seventeen scrawled upon it to the front of my dress, he said, 'I need you to keep your face as still as possible for the second or two required to make the exposure.' Without another word, he buried his head and shoulders under the black tent behind the camera. I did my best to keep my face motionless, as instructed. Dr Rastrick emerged and slid a glass plate out of the camera.

'You may wait here, Miss Pring,' he said. 'It'll take a few minutes at most.' He rushed into what looked like a storeroom in the corner of the room.

When he was gone, Dr Binkes wandered up and down by the window that looked out over the lawns, his arms folded. Through the glass, I heard the faint rasps of crows. A framed photograph on the wall showed a view of grey rolling hills culminating in a ridge, set against a sky which was cloudless and flat in an unearthly way, as if all the light and hues of nature had been drained from the world. A metal panel on the bottom of the frame stated: 'A View of Firle Beacon, Sussex. Dr Harold

A. Rastrick. Silver Medal in the Landscape Category, 1879. East Sussex Photographic Society.'

I looked about the room. There were gleaming metal cabinets along the walls, with labels on the drawers: 'Dispensary', 'Specimens', 'Electrical', 'Surgical' and so on. Instruments of various sorts were laid out on top in orderly fashion. In a corner there was what appeared to be an operating table, and near it a sink and faucet and weighing scales. It was unnerving. What took place there, when it wasn't in use as a photographic studio? What did Dr Rastrick do on that operating table? What were the specimens in his cupboard? Could they by any chance be the rumoured pickled human brains?

I noticed a large sheet of Bristol board attached to the wall in the far corner. Photographic portraits of female patients were pinned to it in neat rows. They were all patients on the women's secure ward. It gave me a horrible start, a vertiginous sensation. A few of the women wore their own dresses but most were in the striped asylum uniform. Each woman had a large number pinned to her dress, and her name was handwritten on the print at the bottom. The plain background was no doubt the same sheet that was hung behind me when I posed for my own likeness. The effect was to make the ladies anonymous, all of a set. I realized the women in the pictures were all quite young. I saw Peggy Paynter, the young woman who had killed her own infant, and Eliza Feldwicke, the scourge of the ward, but I couldn't see Ada's face among them. There was almost nothing in the pictures to link the women to the lives they'd known before they became ill. I remembered the story about 'Rastrick's darlings'. Is that who these women were? If so, I had been summoned here to be added to their number.

I stared at the photographs with growing unease. The women looked like ghosts of themselves. Grey and washed out. They certainly looked mad. But so too would anyone, if they were photographed in that fashion.

Dr Rastrick emerged from his darkroom carrying a photographic print, still glistening with chemical solution. He showed it to Binkes.

'I'm looking for a more light-sensitive formula,' he said. 'I experimented with a longer exposure this time, and sensitized the paper with silver nitrate. There are still faults though – probably due to fixing.' He seemed to suddenly remember I was present. He crossed the room and stood alongside me, presenting the photograph with a proud smile. 'Well, what's your verdict, Miss Pring?'

I looked at a picture of a doleful woman in a blank grey world, staring into the middle distance. My complexion was sallow and there were dark pits under my eyes. Where was my former healthy glow? Even my dark locks, once so lustrous, now looked dry and lifeless. Apart from that, there was a miasma surrounding me, a wispy veiled light, hovering in the air and trailing across my face.

'I see you're not entirely convinced,' said Dr Rastrick to me. 'Not the best print, I admit, but a perfect likeness, at least. Photography cannot lie.'

'I wish you'd destroy it. What use is it to you?'

He seemed taken aback. 'Well, there are some basic administrative uses, such as identification. But my chief aim is to use these pictures as references – for clinical purposes.'

'References – what do you mean by that?'

He raised his eyebrows. 'A reference is an example of

a symptom. Before long, every hospital of this sort will be using photographs as a standard component of data.'

'But I don't want my photograph passed around like that,' I cried.

Dr Rastrick went to the door and held it open for me. 'Thank you for your cooperation, Miss Pring. Now, who's next?'

A rumour circulated in the ward: a patient had died – and by her own hand. Dr Rastrick appeared and stood in close conference with Mrs Tuckwell, the housekeeper. A deep hush descended as every woman eavesdropped.

'Not an hour ago,' said Mrs Tuckwell. 'We kept a close watch on her. She must have planned it very carefully.'

'Which one was it?' asked Dr Rastrick.

'It was Mrs Paynter.'

'I see. She's in my group. Diagnosed with puerperal fever on admission after infanticide. What were the circumstances?'

Mrs Tuckwell's reply was inaudible.

'I'll have to forward the depositions right away,' said Dr Rastrick. 'There'll be a full inquest. I'll instruct Mr Pockock to look into whether the brackets in all our gas fittings can be re-fitted so they're unable to bear the weight of a patient. Meanwhile, can I leave things in your capable hands?'

'Certainly.'

'You'll offer some reassurance to the patients?'

She nodded. And with that, he hurried out of the ward.

Mrs Tuckwell clapped her hands smartly. 'Ladies, may I have your attention? There's been a tragic incident this morning. One of our patients, Mrs Paynter, has taken her own life. I ask you to join with me in a minute's silence. You might like to say a prayer for Mrs Paynter.' Mrs Tuckwell took out her watch and gazed at it while we sat or stood in silence broken by the occasional sniffle or the inarticulate utterance of an imbecile. Some of the women wiped their eyes with their sleeves. When the minute was up, Mrs Tuckwell spoke again. 'I would ask you to remember Mrs Paynter in your prayers. This is a very upsetting day for us all, but the best course of action is to continue with our work as usual, rather than allow ourselves to be overwhelmed by morbid thoughts.'

I realized how little I knew about Peggy, apart from the fact she had taken the life of her own child. Sending her to this cold and heartless place was cruelty beyond imagining. I couldn't forget what Dr Rastrick had said to Mrs Tuckwell: *She's in my group.* What was he doing with his 'darlings'? I remembered what Wall-Eye had said: 'They'll never leave Hellwood. Not alive.' The idea was preposterous. And yet Dr Rastrick had showed not a jot of compassion for Peggy; anything was possible. And then I had a truly horrific thought. Could it be that at that very moment Dr Rastrick was performing a post-mortem on Peggy? Delving into her brain to see what he could find?

Not far away, Jemima Penty, the Bird-Girl, was standing in a corner, abandoned, her bumpy disfigured head pressed against the wall. She was crying. I clapped my hands, and she turned to look at me. On an impulse, I put out my hand to her, the way you might beckon a small child. She turned away. But a moment later she looked back, so I gestured to her again. She waddled over, and looked up at me warily, cocking her head. I leant forward and lifted her up, putting her on my knees. Instinctively, she rolled into a ball, making a nest of my lap. Her arms were covered in goose bumps resembling the skin of a plucked fowl. I hesitated for a moment, but overcame my squeamishness and gently stroked her misshapen head, with its sparse feathery hair. Her skin was warm. She trembled, her protruding shoulder blades sliding in and out as she eased herself into a comfortable position. Perhaps this was the closest thing to maternal love she had ever experienced. I hummed a lullaby and soon she was fast asleep.

20

Over the following days, the ward was subdued. There was a great deal of talk about Peggy's suicide. The country women believed her death was not due to her illness, but brought about by supernatural forces. I felt remorse. For weeks I had witnessed Peggy's growing distress, and I'd been too fearful to approach her. I never once tried to help her in any way. None of us had. How could I distract myself from such morbid thoughts?

I had settled into a routine of reading the Bible to Judith Wicks, the woman known as Wall-Eye, and the group of her cronies who sat smoking with her during the recreation hour. Whenever I read a particularly gruesome passage, Judith would break into her hysterical cackle. One day, she asked me if there was a favour she could do for me in return. I was reluctant to get into her debt, but there was one thing I wanted desperately, and Judith was always on the lookout for things she could filch and trade; anything left unattended in the ward disappeared instantly. I asked her if she could get me a pencil. By the next afternoon I had my wish. I found a piece of flint in the garden with an edge keen enough to use as a pencil sharpener, and remembered where I'd seen some coarse sheets of paper lining fruit boxes.

I was filled with excitement at the prospect of being able to draw and decided to draw some of the patients: their faces and what they revealed of their character and their former lives, their hopes and fears. They were good subjects for portraits, and the crude materials at my disposal seemed fitting in the circumstances. While working alongside Ada in the garden during the day, I began to study her face and to commit her features to memory: her bone structure, the wrinkles and pouches in her skin and, most importantly, her eyes, the expression that haunted her gaze. When alone in my room, in the last hour of daylight, I sat at my cramped little desk and worked on a picture of her, the pencil scratching quickly over the rough paper. I kept a second piece of paper on the desk, on which I'd copied out some lines of Tennyson. If surprised by one of the attendants, I would put the quotations on top of my picture to hide it.

To begin with, my aim was simply to capture Ada's likeness. But, as I drew, I recalled our chats as we worked, all that she had suffered and lost, the insights into the person she had once been. In the days that followed, I worked my way through two pencils and the third was pared down to a nub. I was truly indebted to Judith Wicks' light fingers now. For how much longer could I depend on her? All day long, I waited for the hour when I could work on my portrait. I wanted to show Ada's soul, to convey her sorrow and longing in her face. We had studied portraiture in Miss Fanshaw's art classes, and she had arranged a trip to the National Portrait Gallery in London. The ladies, giddy with excitement, caused great consternation in that stuffy institution as they paraded through room after room, sniggering at the dark imposing portraits of great men from English history. Why shouldn't Ada's portrait be given the same dignity as those of historical old rogues in galleries?

Of necessity, I had to work on Ada's likeness by comparing my picture daily with the original, and then making adjustments until I was sure I had succeeded. There was never sufficient time, and I worked in a state of febrile intensity in which the minutes flew by. In any given day, I succeeded in completing an area no bigger than an ear or chin.

One evening I had lost myself entirely in my work. At a certain point, I had a strong sense that somebody was standing behind me. There had always been a risk that I became so absorbed that I failed to hear the door opening. Swiftly, I covered my drawing with the list of Tennyson quotations. I turned and, to my great surprise, saw Dr Rastrick's wife staring straight at me. I knew her from her visits to the wards, when she came to help out. She was a plain-featured sturdy woman with a lively and sympathetic countenance.

'Do excuse me intruding, Miss Pring,' she said softly, with her well-bred accent. 'I didn't mean to give you a fright. Is that a drawing you're doing?'

I shook my head.

'I should love to see it.'

What choice did I have? I removed the sheet of paper that covered my picture and revealed it.

'My word, you have a talent. But I haven't introduced myself. How rude of me. Please call me Ellen. I hate stuffiness, don't you? I shouldn't have dared come into your room like this, only Harold, Dr Rastrick that is, well, he's in London until tomorrow. Oh, but you draw beautifully . . . May I?' She picked up the picture and studied it. 'Extraordinary. You've captured her perfectly. I know the patient. Mrs Meggett, isn't it? I took up art myself at one point. I've still got the paint tubes somewhere, watercolours, and crayons and paper. I even bought an easel, would you believe? But you see I don't have the slightest ability. I've no imagination whatsoever, and I've always been ham-fisted. But you – well, what can I say? But you must be wondering what I'm doing here.'

'I suppose you'll tell Dr Rastrick that I've been drawing.'

'Certainly not. You can depend on my discretion in all things. In any case, Harold would be incensed if he knew I'd gone to a patient's room. I'm only supposed to help with correspondence and so on.'

'He forbids me from drawing.'

'Oh dear, is that so?' She sighed. 'I'm afraid my husband is a man of a very original stamp. My policy is to agree with everything he says – and then take no notice of him. But I must get to the point, mustn't I? I get a feeling about certain patients. Is Harold being beastly, at all?'

I was tempted to pour out all my worries, but reined myself in. 'He never listens to me.'

'I see. I'm familiar with his temporary onsets of deafness.'

'He seems intent on proving I'm not in my right mind, when in fact I am perfectly sane.'

She paused to consider this. 'I'm sure he has your best interests at heart, but I understand his methods are rather unusual.'

'Unusual?' My pulse raced. Did I dare mention the 'darlings'?

'One hears little things from the patients. The problem is Harold's dedication knows no bounds; and nor does his ambition,' she said. 'If I'm honest, I can never account for men's behaviour. I much prefer dogs. They're far more loyal. And predictable.'

'Please say nothing of this to Dr Rastrick,' I said. 'He will forbid me from drawing, I'm certain of it.'

'My dear, I assure you I can be trusted. It's been a great pleasure. We'll talk again.' She looked down at my hand. I was still holding the pencil. 'Oh dear, that stub of a pencil won't last you long.'

And then she was gone. The following evening, I returned to my cell at the day's end and found a small parcel on my desk. Inside were ten unused pencils. There was no note attached, but I knew who had sent them.

★

One day, not long after, Dr Binkes came to the ward. It was his first visit unaccompanied by Dr Rastrick. He was making his way around the periphery of the room, his bearing stiff, a frozen smile on his face. Mrs Clinch told me Binkes would be talking to a number of the ladies and I was on his list.

The air was still and cloying that afternoon. There was a storm in the air, late summer's final temper tantrum. The ladies were fanning their faces with whatever was to hand, periodicals or handkerchiefs. Somewhere in the room, I could hear Mrs Clinch saying 'Put out your hand!' to Jemima, the Bird-Girl. I turned and saw her put a biscuit into Jemima's hand. Dr Binkes was keeping his distance from Jemima – and from me too, I felt. I was sitting next to Annie Weech, the doll-like dwarf with the macabre demeanour, a 'cretin' in Dr Rastrick's terminology. I was planning a portrait of her. She sat without moving a muscle. There was a sheen of sweat on her forehead, and for a split second I saw her wince, as if in pain.

I wandered over to the window and stared out. A silent drama unfolded down below on the lawns. Ellen Rastrick was with her maid and their pet black Labrador. They were often seen going into the woods together. But that day the high branches of the trees thrashed angrily. Mrs Rastrick had her hand on her hat, trying to hold it in place. Her coat tails flapped. The dog strained at the end of his leash, looking up at turbulent dark clouds, then wheeling about his mistress, winding the lead around her skirts. The maid was chasing the dog, trying to unravel the lead while the dog cringed behind Mrs Rastrick, his jaw opening and snapping shut, his tail low and wagging. Mrs Rastrick took the dog's snout in her hands and mouthed something to him, but the animal threw his head back and opened his jaws in a soundless howl at the woods.

I was startled by an urgent shout: 'Somebody, quick! It's Annie. Having a seizure!'

I turned to see Annie lying on her back on the floor, her head rolling, her tongue lolling out of her mouth, her tiny black boots kicking wildly. I heard a crack as her skull hit the floorboards and then a low moan in her throat. It was the first utterance I'd ever heard from her. Her mouth was open and her large misshapen jaw contorted. I cowered, my back to the window. Dr Binkes rushed over and dropped onto his knees beside Annie. He seized a cushion from an armchair and put it under her head, laid his hands on her shoulders and then, with the greatest care, rolled her onto her side. Mrs Tuckwell, the housekeeper, rushed to his side and crouched beside him. Annie was foaming at the mouth. Some patients gathered around, the bravest, or most curious.

'She's possessed!' cried Wall-Eye.

'She has the evil breath!' said Eliza Feldwicke, the scourge of the ward. 'Take her away or the spirit will enter us too.'

'Keep back!' cried Dr Binkes, revealing himself to be surprisingly commanding in an emergency. 'I do not wish to hear any more nonsense about possession or evil breath. Miss Weech is simply having a seizure. Mrs Clinch, please go to the dispensary at once and fetch potassium bromide.'

Everyone in the room watched the drama unfold. Mrs Tuckwell ran off to her station and went inside. Hovering on the periphery unseen, I saw the documents that Dr Binkes had been carrying lying on a chair, his case notebook and a bundle of papers clasped by a rubber band. I had an overwhelming urge to make off with these papers and find out what the doctors had written about me. Making sure I wasn't seen, I picked up the documents and slipped through the door into the washroom, then dashed towards the privy, bolting myself inside. I soon discovered that Dr Binkes's case notes were not all that was in the bundle – there were also notes made by Dr Rastrick. With foreboding, I thumbed through the notes written in Dr Rastrick's forward-thrusting hand. They dealt entirely with the women in his research group, his 'darlings'. On Monday, 5 July 1886, Dr Rastrick had written this about me:

Of good appearance – the features without malformation or asymmetry, but marred by bad temper and deprived of their composure. The high forehead is indicative of intelligence and force of character, but the physiognomy may be misleading.

This must have been written during or after his first consultation with me. I looked at his entries on later encounters. There was more scrutiny of my appearance, but I searched in vain through his case notes for a record of anything I'd said. On another day, he had written:

> *Very excitable this afternoon, restless, suggesting mania. Gesticulates constantly, touches hair and mouth compulsively when speaking. A vein in the left temple is pulsating, the left eyebrow quivering. The pitch of the voice is shrill, strident. There are paroxysms of excitement, remonstrances and wild gesticulations and other indications of violent and uncontrolled passion. Stamping of the foot, along with other instances of maladapted behaviour. A predisposition, probably hereditary, to facial tics and other involuntary jerks which bring to mind Gilles de la Tourette's paper of recent years.*

Then I removed the rubber band from the other documents and found they were typewritten records of Dr Rastrick's observations on patients. The typed script gave them a permanence and authority that was unnerving. I leafed through the pages until I found those relating to myself. Here then, was Dr Rastrick's verdict on me.

> There are secure grounds for postulating that the patient has a hereditary predisposition to insanity. Her grandfather in the maternal line was confined to an asylum several times. Interviews I have conducted with the patient's parents convince me that her condition has been exacerbated by two factors: problems during puberty; and unhealthy relationships within the family.

The patient is of the type that reaches sexual maturity with exorbitant expectations of love, while at the same time exhausting her nervous system with intellectual pursuits. Convulsive explosions of violence are characteristic of insane neurosis.

It is tempting to conclude that a pattern of promiscuous behaviour early established has alienated the patient from her natural feminine functions. Overall, environmental information is indicative of a history of sexual capriciousness, nervous debility, volatile temper and transgressive impulses.

Although the patient demonstrates reasonable intelligence, she exhibits definite marks of mental degeneration, which have manifested in a disavowal of natural feminine affect. She has acknowledged her volatile condition, but I judge this more a calculated attempt to gain an early discharge than a genuine acknowledgement of her unstable state of mind. In my judgement, she remains a risk to herself and others.

The patient appears to have no understanding of what led to her confinement. I'm tempted to term this forgetfulness 'moral amnesia'. Early findings from the research suggest her physiological symptoms correspond with those of others in my research group. It is notable, for example, that the uterine functions have been suppressed during her time here.

This is an intriguing case. In the light of the circumstances leading to her confinement, an early release would be manifestly undesirable. We shall have to see what kindness and firmness can achieve to prevent

a further deterioration of the patient's condition. Given
that there are no indications of delusion, my provisional
diagnosis is moral insanity.

I sat on the closed seat of the privy, shivering as a cold draught
flowed under the door. For a long moment I feared I would
be violently sick. I shut my eyes and breathed deeply, as water
dripped incessantly in the cistern overhead, and rain spat-
tered against a window high on the wall behind me. When
I had recovered myself a little, I opened my eyes. Someone had
scratched a message about Mrs Tuckwell onto the back of the
door: 'FUCKWEL IS A HORE'. My thoughts were in violent
disorder. Until this moment, I had been blind to the truth
about Dr Rastrick's objectives. Now I saw he had no intention
of discharging me, not now, possibly not ever. In his clinical
notes he had created a false history of my character, an unfair
and vicious description of my nature. He had brought me here
to entrap me. For what purpose, I dreaded to think. I wanted to
flush his poisonous lies down the lavatory, but had just enough
self-command to resist that impulse, seeing it would only play
into his hands. Then I remembered with a jolt that I'd put myself
in great danger by running off with the notes. Would I be able
to sneak back into the common room without being seen – and
before Binkes realized the notes had gone astray? With a shaking
hand, I put the rubber band around the documents, tearing
a page as I did so. Then I ran through the deserted washroom,
the echo of my boot heels bouncing off the tiled walls. Reaching
the door, I opened it slowly, peered into the room and, seeing the
coast was clear, slipped out, closing the door softly behind me.
The bundle of documents was clutched behind my back. Thank

heavens, nobody was aware of my presence; the women were still preoccupied with Annie's seizure and stood in a circle with their backs to me. There were one or two overturned chairs. I could hear Dr Binkes's lowered voice: 'Shush now.' I dropped the case notes where I'd found them and took my place at the back of the group.

Dr Binkes was down on his knees, cradling Annie Weech's deformed head in the crook of his elbow and stroking her forehead. Mrs Tuckwell was squatting down next to Dr Binkes. She passed him a small bottle, which he put to Annie's lips. She choked and cloudy liquid rolled down her cheeks, but her gullet pulsed as a measure went down her throat. Dr Binkes administered the rest of the dose and Annie grew calmer. Her eyes closed and her body became limp in Dr Binkes's arms.

I tottered towards an armchair, and dropped into it, reeling. Dr Rastrick's voice: *insane neurosis . . . the patient exhibits definite marks of mental degeneration . . . moral amnesia . . .*

What happened after my confrontation with Mama over the night I'd spent in Mr Lilley's rooms? Why could I remember nothing of the days that followed? Until I discovered what happened, I would be at Dr Rastrick's mercy.

An early release would be manifestly undesirable . . . her physiological symptoms correspond with those of others in the group . . .

The darlings! Was it possible he was contriving to keep all of us under lock and key for the rest of our days?

Given that there are no indications of delusion, my preliminary diagnosis is moral insanity.

Was he perversely misdiagnosing me, or had he any grounds for finding me insane? Or could it be that he was intentionally driving me mad? He had chosen to include me among his 'darlings', so it suited his purposes to find my condition was extreme. Yet, I was disoriented and no longer sure I could trust my own judgement. I didn't recognize myself in his description. But perhaps that was how I appeared to others. Whose opinion could I trust if I couldn't be sure of my own?

I started at the sound of a male voice. 'Good grief, Miss Pring.' Dr Binkes was towering over me. I was lying on the hard floor, looking up at him. I must have swooned. He cried: 'Mrs Tuckwell, over here please.'

I tried to speak but my jaws were locked. The demonic spirit that had possessed poor Annie was now inside me. Mrs Tuckwell's features hovered over me, her nostrils and chin. A vile syrup was forced down my throat. I remember nothing more.

21

I awoke the next morning so exhausted and with such heaviness of spirit I could scarcely rouse myself. An attendant entered my cell and exhorted me to get up, so I rose to my feet, light-headed, depleted, my head throbbing. The world around me was veiled and at one remove. The revelations of the previous day returned with the power of a bodily blow. I had to support myself for a long moment by leaning on the desk, looking down at dandelion stalks on the window sill, dangling limply out of the tin mug. The washroom that morning seemed harsher than ever, the ritual humiliation of the morning ablutions almost more than I could bear. When it was over, I was herded into the ward with the rest of the women. My thoughts were interrupted by the strident tones of Mrs Tuckwell.

'Ladies, may I have your attention?' The drone of chatter came to a stop. 'As some of you are probably aware, the annual inspection by the Commissioners in Lunacy will take place next week. The inspectors will be looking at all the facilities here. They will also be taking a tour of the wards and it is likely that they will want to speak to a number of you in person to make sure that your view of the hospital accords with appearances. There is no need to be frightened of these men. They are learned and you may find them stuffy, but they have your interests at heart. An inspector might want to ask you one or two questions about how we're caring for you. Don't be afraid, he only wants to make sure the highest standards are being maintained. And we have no worries on that front, do we, ladies? But should you have any little concerns, you're within your rights to inform the inspectors in confidence and I can assure you they will be addressed.

'In the meantime, however, we have work to do if we're to show ourselves in the best light. I'm sure you'll all want to help us give the inspectors a good impression. The staff are all working very hard to prepare, and I know many of you will want to volunteer to help. Let's get the ward just that little bit more tidy, well-ordered and clean than usual. Speak to Mrs Clinch if you'd like to add your weight. And, lastly, there'll be double helpings of treacle tart for all.'

★

That week the asylum was a hive of industry. Patients roamed the corridors with buckets and mops, not content until they could see their reflections in the floor. The walls were whitewashed, every surface was scrubbed or polished, and freshly cut flowers were put in vases around the ward.

I worked outside with Ada. Our task was to rake the yellow leaves that had begun to gather on the footpath into piles and then put them into sacks for composting. All morning we heard the noise of gardeners mowing the lawns. Once they were finished, we were put to work pushing rollers over the grass, back-breaking work. When it was time to break for lunch, we were permitted to sit on the benches, which were normally out of bounds to patients, other than those convalescing. Ada said it felt like being royalty. Those days, I only saw Ada when we were working in the kitchen garden. Dr Rastrick had approved her transfer to another ward three weeks earlier, saying her health had improved. I watched her take off her straw hat and use it to fan her face. Her electrified hair had settled down and sat naturally around her head. She was shortly to be removed to the halfway house in Burgess Hill.

She had a thoughtful demeanour that day and I sensed there was something she wanted to confide. When she'd eaten her crust and cheese, she began to speak, but without turning to face me. 'I got to thinking about what I told you before, turning it over in my head,' she said. 'My life wasn't quite as I told you, not really. I don't think I mentioned that my father was a strict evangelical. Sundays, we were marched off to the Ebenezer Chapel. You didn't dare to cross him. He had an ugly temper and his word was law. And he was tight-fisted. He never gave Mother enough for the housekeeping. You never saw him or Mother in new clothes. Later on, we found out he'd squirrelled his wages away, hid some about the house, put more in the bank. And yet we had nothing at home. He was a miser, you see. There were terrible rows. I used to lie in bed at nights in terror, listening to the shouting downstairs. There was no kissing and hugging in our family, only tongue lashing. Mother was a hard taskmaster. I got the worst of it, being the eldest. Her and Father always made me feel I was a terrible sinner. Even so I had hopes. I used to walk up to the pleasure gardens in Preston and see the lovely new houses. I thought it would be nice to have my own house one day, and to have a family and be able to take the children to play in the park. Silly notions, really. But the truth is my whole life was a lie.'

'Are you sure you should be dwelling on all of this?' I asked. 'You don't want to upset yourself when you've been so much better.'

'Oh, but it helps to talk.' She put her hand on mine. 'I've kept a lot inside all these years. And since that time you asked me about my childhood, I've thought it all over. My life was a lie and there's no denying it. I found out Jim was leading a double life. He had another wife and family in Manchester. No wonder we saw so little of his money.'

'Heavens!'

'It all came out when the other wife got suspicious and looked into his affairs. She got it out of him, and wrote to me. When I found out, I thought it made sense in a funny way. He was always telling tall stories, boasting about things he'd done. Nothing was real to Jim. He was a bad lot, through and through.'

'What did you do?'

'What could I do? I just carried on as usual. You have to keep up appearances. I lied to the kids and hoped the neighbours never got wind of it. I kept that secret for ten years. Life wasn't much different to before. But I wouldn't let Jim near me, not after finding that out. And it was a relief, if you want to know. No more getting pregnant. And I never liked it anyway, his drunken breath in my face. We got by somehow. It would have stayed that way if it hadn't been for the gas explosion. That set it all off. I got mixed up in my mind. But it wasn't the change of life that drove me mad, as Dr Rastrick likes to think. It was years of living a lie, and feeling I was somehow to blame. And then there was the guilt about getting pregnant out of wedlock.

I never got over that. Father disowned me. He wouldn't even let Mother visit me after I was married. I was cut off from them, my own kin. No wonder it felt like a punishment when my little boy died.'

'Don't think such things, Ada. You're a good and kind person. None of this was your fault.'

'I did my best and that's all any of us can do. If it hadn't been for you, Violet, I might never have faced up to the truth at all.'

We hugged each other there on the bench, as a gust sent a flurry of dead leaves across the footpath. The bell rang and we got back to work. It was a warm humid day and my dress was soon damp with perspiration. My mind was on fire. It was clear that Ada's derangement hadn't been caused by her innate feminine fragility, as Dr Rastrick insisted. If anything, her spirit and backbone were remarkable given her circumstances. I'd never wondered what it might be like to be among the army of downtrodden women, toiling day after day without hope of relief to make the clothes I wore, the soap I washed with, the linen on my bed, the matches I used to light the fire in the grate. I had nothing to compare with their lives, other than a few weeks of toil in the kitchen garden. The staff in our house must have come from similar backgrounds to Ada, and the women who made my dresses too. The densely packed lanes in the middle of Brighton seethed with people in desperate poverty, the railway workers' cottages where Ada lived, or the houses on the hills below Queens Park where the female penitents' home was sited, those insanitary back lanes where laundry women stood in the streets smoking while working men spilled out from the numerous pubs, lawless places where respectable persons set foot at their own risk. I remembered the ladies of the night who haunted the streets around the theatres, cackling as they passed by in their gaudy frocks. I felt an unaccountable qualm as I thought about them. It was all a far cry from my world of tennis and archery, soirees, art lessons and promenades on private lawns. And yet I had forged a bond with Ada. We were both raised in families where love was a finite resource, where we were never sure of our place. Money, or the lack of it, was always a concern for us both. And I sensed there was something else too. That in some profound way, we had both been living false lives.

★

In early September, the inspectors came. Every patient was issued with a uniform dress, freshly laundered and pressed. Even Jemima Penty, the Bird-Girl, was given a clean frock and a ribbon for her hair, such as it was. Those with their own dresses were permitted to wear them provided they were in a respectable condition. Before breakfast, Mrs Tuckwell announced: 'The inspectors are doing a tour of the ward this afternoon during the recreation hour, so you'd all better behave yourselves. Remember now, we're one big happy family here.'

After work was finished in the garden, I rushed to my room and scrubbed my hands and face. I did the best I could with my hair. I put on my blue silk frock. It was frayed and much darned, and the stains on the collar and under the arms hadn't quite come out in the wash. When I'd done my best to smarten up my appearance, I went to wait in the ward. The inspectors arrived, together with Dr Rastrick and members of the asylum's Committee of Visitors, who I'd seen at assemblies in the Great Hall on formal occasions. There were two inspectors from the

Commissioners in Lunacy. All of the gentlemen were laughing and in high spirits. Mrs Tuckwell introduced the inspectors to the patients: Dr Wyon, the younger of the two, who was about my father's age, and Dr Page, an ancient old dodderer. Mrs Tuckwell then took them on a brief tour of the ward, pointing out various details to them, the view from the windows on either side, the rack with the periodicals, the bird cages, the vases with flowers picked from the gardens. The two inspectors nodded and smiled. I studied them. The ancient fellow was constantly yawning. He smelled of liquor and had presumably just enjoyed a large lunch with Dr Rastrick. His sole interest seemed to be in the curiosities: Jemima, the Bird–Girl; Annie Weech, the hunchbacked dwarf who sat as rigid as a doll. He sat down next to poor starved and deluded Edna May and questioned her while she answered in her most coquettish manner. The younger inspector seemed altogether more alert, making his way around the ward methodically, listening intently to individual patients, his bald head shining under the oil lamps. I succeeded in catching his eye.

We sat side by side. His notebook was in his lap. I knew how careful I would need to be about what I told him and what I kept to myself. He sat down and asked me various trivial questions about my living quarters, the facilities, the food, my work. He was pleased to hear I was getting plenty of fresh air and was gainfully employed. Then he asked me if I thought my treatment was helping me recover. He opened his notebook and made a note with his pencil. 'Now, Miss . . . ?'

'Miss Pring. Violet Pring.'

He made a note of my name.

'Do you feel you have been getting better since you arrived here?'

My mind was blank.

'Please, take a little time to compose yourself. Try taking a deep breath.'

'I wonder if I'd fare better in another hospital. Perhaps the methods used here don't suit me.'

'I visit hospitals like this all the time. I can assure you the methods here are very much in line with what I've seen elsewhere.'

'Well then, perhaps the problem is that Dr Rastrick is pushing ahead too quickly with his research. He sees what he wants to see and ignores anything that contradicts his opinion. His mind's made up.'

Dr Wyon shook his head.

'I'm not the only patient who fears this is the case,' I continued. 'At least two of Dr Rastrick's darlings have died since I arrived here.'

He looked up from his notebook. 'Dr Rastrick's "darlings"? What on earth . . . ?'

'It's what everyone calls the women in his research group.'

'Good grief.' He made another note. 'If there is any evidence of malpractice, the Lunacy Commission will take immediate action. Can you recall any specific actions Dr Rastrick has taken which concerned you?'

'He's keeping my father away so he can continue with his experiments. He twists my words when I speak to him. He never writes down what I've said, only makes notes about my demeanour, my gestures.'

He studied me closely.

'He's shown you his notes?'

I shook my head. 'I saw them. They were left unattended. I wouldn't have, but . . . '

'I see,' said Dr Wyon, closing his notebook. 'Now, these are serious accusations. Can you provide any evidence at all?'

What could I tell this man? That Dr Rastrick and Mama had colluded in having me locked away because I had rebelled against Mama's wish that I should marry Felix? That I could remember nothing that happened in the days before I was locked away? I had no evidence against Dr Rastrick at all.

After a moment's silence, Dr Wyon said: 'Very well, Miss Pring. I am aware of Dr Rastrick's research on female patients and I will make sure to speak to a number of the women in that group. If their feelings compare with your own, then rest assured I will look into the matter. In the meantime, I advise you to take as much rest as possible, and resist becoming overwhelmed by morbid thoughts.'

That night I lay sleepless in bed, defeated and wretched. I regretted speaking to the inspector, fearing that the consequences would be a terrible punishment from Dr Rastrick. It was a stuffy evening, so I had my little window open wide. At a certain hour, I became aware of men's voices outside. I stood on my chair to look out of the window. It was a still night and not a leaf stirred, as if the earth had stopped revolving. Sound carried far through the air. Down below, a group of men sat in a circle of chairs outside the room Dr Rastrick referred to as his neuroanatomical laboratory. He was proud of this marvel of modern science and no doubt wanted to impress his guests. The open doors of the laboratory threw a square of light onto the ground where the men were sitting. Moths flitted in and out of the glow, circling and tumbling. Beyond the pool of light, there was profound darkness. Dr Rastrick's guests were the two inspectors who had come to the ward earlier. They sat nursing whisky tumblers in their hands, while Dr Rastrick paced to and fro and regaled them. He was in expansive mood.

'Have you read Maudsley's book yet: *Body and Will*?' he asked his colleagues. 'He makes the case that with defective inhibitory control the individual changes from a higher more complex organization to a lower kind. It's indicative of degeneration.'

'Maudsley, he's a dreadful windbag, don't you think?' said the older of the two inspectors. 'I haven't read his book, nor do I intend to. But, I say, have you chaps read that novel about the doctor with a split personality – *Dr Jekyll and Mr Hyde*? What you just said about degenerates reminded me of it, Rastrick. I read it on the train. Sensational bunkum, but more fun than wading through Maudsley's tosh.'

'Why have you chosen to direct your research at women, Rastrick?' asked Dr Wyon, the inspector who had interviewed me earlier.

'Because, to put it bluntly, the race depends on females for its survival. But the sex lacks rationality and tends towards excessive emotion.'

'Well put,' said the older doctor.

'I'm not sure I agree, old fellow,' said Dr Wyon. 'I'd say that women lack self-control because their minds haven't been trained in the faculties of attention, discrimination, analysis and so forth. Unfortunately, their intellect is squandered on trashy novels and idle pursuits. Education would give women a more sober view of life, and instil better habits suited to their higher calling as mothers.'

'We need to tread carefully when educating women,' said Dr Rastrick. 'They must be prepared for the crises of female biological organization, or they risk succumbing to nervous disorders.'

'And yet women in the labouring classes work through the menstrual cycle all the time,' said Dr Wyon. 'You've only to look at the women in your laundry for evidence.'

'Not to mention the rigours of childbirth!' said the older man.

As I listened, I thought how fortunate women were that such enlightened men had taken charge of the rigours of childbirth and the duties of motherhood. Who else, but a man, properly educated, could shoulder such responsibilities?

'To blame female insanity on biology rather overlooks other possible causes; pauperism, for example,' said Dr Wyon. 'We might more effectively reduce mental disquietude by improving women's pay.'

'Gentlemen, I put it to you that our final aim should be to eradicate over coming generations all hereditary diseased cerebral development,' said Dr Rastrick.

There was a moment's silence.

'Ambitious!' said the older inspector. 'But my view is we must simply do our best for these poor souls, and pray that when we send them off, we don't find them back on our doorstep a few months later.'

'Your idea worries me, Rastrick,' said Dr Wyon. 'As a Christian, I baulk at anything that smacks of usurping God's will. And as a scientist, I should like to see some empirical evidence to justify your theory.'

'The research is underway here and now in my neuroanatomical clinic,' said Dr Rastrick. 'As you've seen, I'm developing a taxonomy of women's insanity using case observation and photography. My ambition is to create a neuroanatomical hospital along the lines of Dr Charcot's facility in Paris. I have visited the hospital myself and met Charcot.'

So, now Dr Rastrick was getting to the point. He was going to tell them about his darlings. I listened intently, as if my life depended on it. Perhaps it did.

'You're an enterprising chap,' said the old fool. 'You speak French?'

'French and German. I have a retentive memory. I've been able to familiarize myself with Dr Morel's ideas on degeneration and many other texts besides. I'm an honorary member of the Medico-Psychological Society of Paris. Soon, one of Charcot's bright young assistants, Dr Serrurier, will be visiting my hospital to further his research. However, my ambition is to go beyond what they are achieving in France. England should lead the world in asylum medicine. My goal is to use our system to prevent the inheritance of madness in future generations, to weed out degenerate stock. Bear with me a moment, while I describe how such an institution might work in practice. Women with hereditary insanity could be sequestered at least until beyond reproductive age – but in many cases for life. Long-term patients would provide captive samples for experiment and categorization. We might, let's say, perform hysterectomies on a sample of women, and compare their symptoms with those who have similar conditions but haven't been operated upon. Enlightened asylum superintendents could share such information. Nothing should be ruled out, not even vivisection, if it could be carried out humanely.'

'Steady on, old chap!' protested Dr Wyon.

'Bear with me, sir. Consider the data at our fingertips and what use we might make of it. Imagine the benefits of such a system for other forms of social pathology, for example in crime prevention. All we need is sufficient backbone to push ahead into the future. Remember that no advance in medicine was ever achieved without a human cost.'

The horror! To Dr Rastrick, the darlings were nothing but laboratory animals to be experimented on at will. Had he forgotten his oath to care for his patients? And how proud he was of his heartless ideas, how enthusiastic, his hands gesturing theatrically.

'Correct me if I'm wrong,' said Dr Wyon, 'but you seem to be suggesting we lock up female mental patients to prevent them from breeding. And as for some of your other ideas . . . '

'Gentlemen, we are speaking theoretically,' said Dr Rastrick. 'We might have to wait decades to get the legal framework in place. But, in the meantime, I propose we work within the bounds of the present asylum system to tackle what is nothing less than a threat to the future of the race. These ideas should be openly discussed in medical circles and in government. Should we abandon the progress of scientific understanding out of fear of censure from the ignorant? I'm already working within the Medico-Psychological Association, but meeting resistance. I'm involved in talks about a new Neurological Society which might fare better. This is an opportunity for our profession to set the agenda. We should be advising at the highest level on mental hygiene in society.'

'What would that entail exactly?' asked Dr Wyon.

'Alienists could advise on bringing up children, how to choose marriage partners, organization of family life and so on.'

'I see what you're about, Rastrick,' said Dr Wyon. 'You're floating these ideas to test our reaction. My view is that individual doctors can alleviate social problems such as overwork, intemperance and vice, and we are free as individuals to campaign for a fairer distribution of the fruits of labour, if we so choose. But it's not within our remit to make decisions on who has the right to be born.'

'Well, perhaps we should leave it there, gentlemen,' said Dr Rastrick. 'It's time we went inside for a nightcap. I have a very old single malt that I only bring out on special occasions. I insist that you join me. At any rate, if we stay out here, we'll wake the patients.'

'We'll wake the dead,' said the old fool.

I trembled violently after hearing Dr Rastrick cold-bloodedly set forth his ambition to imprison forever any woman who he judged to have degenerate blood. And as for his proposal to experiment on women's bodies and minds! But at least Dr Wyon seemed more humane. Was there the faintest hope he would help me to escape?

22

How could I sleep after hearing Dr Rastrick expound his ideas? What he had described wasn't mere theory, it was happening there and then at Hellwood. I had already seen how he defined me in his case notes as someone with a hereditary predisposition to insanity, as suffering from insane neurosis and presenting a risk to myself and others. It was no doubt the same for the other 'darlings'. And now I feared that he never intended to release us.

As I lay there, in horror one moment, in outrage the next, I thought of Peggy Paynter, the patient who'd murdered her infant and then taken her own life. To him, she was nothing more than a case study of the dangers of pregnancy for a woman with hereditary infirmities. Her madness was the result of mysterious lesions in her brain, not a consequence of grinding poverty and squalor and who knows what kind of ill treatment at home. I'd learned more about the lives of these women in two months than Dr Rastrick had learned in years. As far as he was concerned, my derangement, like Mama's neurasthenia, was caused by madness in the maternal line. Yet Dr Rastrick never remarked on my Uncle Jonathan's descent into drunkenness and dissolute behaviour, when there was no family history of madness to explain it.

I saw the sinister reasons behind Dr Rastrick's intrusions into my past life. He had succeeded in inveigling himself into my family from the time of my childhood. Mama had always complained that Papa was too soft-hearted to keep me in hand, so she'd turned to Dr Rastrick. He appeared at times of crisis and assumed the authority of a second father to me. Perhaps he had deliberately kept Mama ill, plying her with sedatives so he could control her affairs. She deferred to him in all things. She even hinted at times that he had advised her about my education, and about the foundations for an orderly family life – despite having no children of his own. He went as far as advising on suitable marriage partners for me. And now, somehow, Dr Rastrick had got what he had always secretly wanted: to lock me away and add me to his list of research specimens.

But what was at the heart of this? Why was he so determined to prove that women were weak vessels, at the mercy of their biology? Did he derive some obscure gratification from controlling us? He used the discipline and order of the asylum to keep us docile, with the help of sedatives when required. He spent as little time with the patients as possible, leaving his minions to do the legwork, while he wrote his clinical papers and met with his peers in London or Paris. We were pawns in his game to achieve prominence in his profession. And he had a greater purpose beyond self-aggrandizement. He planned to build a golden future where the race was rid of all defective people.

I remembered the stories the patients told, about a secret asylum hidden within the building, doors that were never opened, patients heard screaming in the dead of night. There were two asylums, the one seen by visitors and the authorities, and another hidden one. I'd noticed how the atmosphere changed subtly when Dr Rastrick came to the ward to do his rounds. All was calm and ordered, yet at the same time the women performed more the way lunatics are supposed to. There was a theatrical air to it all. Was this the way it was? Or could it all be in my imagination? Was I losing my grip on my sanity?

I was still turning over these thoughts when the first birdsong pierced the darkness. The attendants wouldn't call to wake me for another hour or more. I hadn't slept at all and it was hopeless trying now, so at first light, I got out of bed and crept to my desk. I took out my latest drawing from the drawer and got to work on it, my eyes dry and sore with exhaustion. The portrait was of Eliza Feldwicke, the wild woman who frightened the life out of me when I first arrived, and who was constantly making a nuisance of herself on the ward. I had furtively glanced at Eliza a hundred times until I knew her features by heart, her dark eyes with their defiant glare, the set of her jaw, her nose with its bend at the bridge – a clue to her violent history, the angry curve of her mouth. I sketched her in her uniform dress, without neglecting to show her collar turned up in her characteristic way. As I drew, the fears that had gripped me loosened their hold. I recovered some sense of control. I was determined to make my portraits as unlike Dr Rastrick's photographs as possible. They would show each woman's individual character, capturing her rage or anguish or loneliness, and giving clues to the life she had once led.

It seemed the subjects of my art were changing now I was confined to the asylum. Apart from my self-portrait as an archer in a mythical past, I had not made portraits for some years, not since I'd painted members of my family, and later the ladies in Miss Fanshaw's art class when we sat to each other. I occasionally drew pictures of my friends on scraps of paper, but they were little more than doodles. In the main, my paintings were romantic and poetical dreams in mythical settings, or else drawings from nature. But in the asylum I wanted to draw the women around me, just as they were, each with her own identity and story. I would bear testimony to their lives. In those frightening weeks, I wanted to look at the world around me, rather than withdraw into my imagination. As the pencil scraped on the paper in the quiet of the morning, I lost myself in my work, and I felt I got to know Eliza, that sly wayward creature, in a way I never could have done by talking to her.

If only I could have shown my work to Mr Lilley. Perhaps he would have dismissed my new drawings as 'social' or 'genre' pictures, or even as mere journalism. On the other hand, he may have seen qualities in them to admire. I realized that in my imagination he was often hovering over me as I worked, and I was filled with longing to see him again and to know him better.

All that day, as I went about my duties, I longed to return to my drawing of Eliza. After the attendant left me that evening to settle myself before going to sleep, I got to work. The days were still long enough to allow an hour or two of good light. But to my annoyance I heard a soft, barely audible knock on the door. It might have been a mouse. Quickly, I pulled open the drawer of the desk and put the drawing inside, but the drawer caught and I couldn't close it. I turned to see Mrs Rastrick standing before me, carrying a basket.

'I'm terribly sorry, I didn't mean to intrude. It's just that I've brought something for you.'

She took a box of crayons out of the basket and handed them

to me. I thanked her and opened the box. There was a full set of colours, and most had hardly been used. Next, she took out a pad of drawing paper and handed it to me.

'Now, tell me, quickly, have you done any more drawings?'

I took my sketches out of the drawer. A picture fell on the floor. It was another portrait I'd begun working on – of Jemima Penty, the bird girl. Ellen Rastrick picked it up and held it to the light, studying it. She frowned and turned pale, and put her fingers to her lips. They were shaking.

'It's a rough sketch,' I said, quickly. 'Perhaps it was wrong of me to attempt to depict such disfigurement . . . '

A single tear fell rolled down her cheek.

'I've offended you,' I said, reaching to take the picture out of her hands.

'You haven't! Not at all,' she said, without meeting my gaze. 'It isn't disfigurement I see here. You've brought out her humanity. It's quite beautiful in its way. I'm so glad I brought you the crayons. It's a sin to stop someone with such talent from following their vocation. If only we could persuade Harold to let you work on your art just as you please.'

'Please, don't say anything to him. If you do, he'll stop me drawing, believe me.'

'I suppose he will,' she said, sighing. 'What are we to do with him? I am at a loss. I wish I could help you, but I don't know how.'

'Do you know why he treats us as he does?'

'He is an unhappy man, scarred by his own childhood, but I confess I don't understand him.'

★

The following day, without warning, Mrs Tuckwell informed me Dr Rastrick had permitted me to receive a visitor. I had a surge of hope, assuming it would be Papa come at last. Mrs Clinch took me down to the Committee Room which was in the entrance hall opposite the administrative offices. I had never been there before. The room was a long gallery with windows overlooking the lawns. There was a table down the centre with a fierce sheen, with high-backed chairs along either side. There was a smell of wax and stale cigar smoke. I sat down at the far end of the table, furthest from the door, and Mrs Clinch sat as sentinel at the other end. On the walls were sombre portraits of Dr Rastrick and the four previous incumbents, men with self-regarding countenances in dark suits. We waited for perhaps ten minutes in the silent lifeless room.

Finally, my visitor arrived. It was Miss Fanshaw. She marched through the door with her usual upright bearing and forthright manner, her gaze sweeping with disdain over the portraits of the physicians on the wall. When she saw me, her face froze for a split second and her pace faltered, but she recovered her composure. I rose to my feet and put out my hand, but instead of taking it she embraced me warmly, clutching me tight against the great shelf of her bosom for a long moment. Her affection almost overwhelmed me. She sat down at the table, moving the chairs so we could sit face to face, and taking off her gloves and setting them down on the table as she chattered in her usual disconnected way.

At last, she paused, glancing at Mrs Clinch, who was staring out of the window, lost in her own musings. Then, she lowered her voice. 'Now! I had the greatest difficulty getting your parents to reveal your whereabouts. It was only when I told them about the rumours circulating among my young ladies that they finally divulged the secret. I was determined to come as soon as it could be arranged. I might have come sooner, but my own mother has been very unwell and as her only child I had to spend several weeks in London looking after her.'

'I'm very sorry to hear that.'

'Never mind, she's convalescing now. But listen! The fact of the matter is I'm fonder of you than you possibly imagine, my dear. I take a great interest in my young ladies, and my first thought was I must do anything I can to help.'

'How did Mama seem to you when you saw her?'

She considered for a moment. 'Frail, is how I'd put it. She was in a bath chair, apparently too unwell to walk about.'

This didn't altogether surprise me. Mama had taken to the bath chair on previous occasions; it was quite usual for her to lose the use of her limbs during a bout of neurasthenia. 'Did she say anything about me? About what happened? I've had no word from her. If only she would write to me.'

'She said she missed you dreadfully. But listen, you're not to worry yourself about her. It's *you* who I'm concerned with. Listen, my dear, we must speak in confidence.' She called over to Clinch: 'I say, could we have two cups of tea? Would you mind?'

Mrs Clinch got up and lumbered over to a mahogany sideboard at the far side of the room, where she poured tea from a samovar. Miss Fanshaw leant closer to me. 'They haven't had you in leg irons?'

'No! It's not like that nowadays.'

'Oh, thank heavens. The idea's been preying on my mind. Look, we haven't long so I'd better get to the point. The first priority, as you say, is to secure your release from this place. I know you're highly strung, but you are not mad.'

Mrs Clinch arrived and put the two cups of tea on the table. Miss Fanshaw waited for Mrs Clinch to return to her station before continuing.

'When we've got you out of here, we need to make sure you don't fall into the same trap in future. You mustn't mope about waiting for a man to rescue you. That way madness lies, if you'll pardon the expression. We need to get you fixed up with a job and an independent income. That should present little difficulty for a clever girl like you.'

'A job!' I sighed. I imagined myself in a dreary bedsit room, in penury and obscurity.

'Oh, don't look so downcast! We can't expect to enjoy the freedoms and privileges men enjoy if we don't accept the responsibilities that go with them. I have a suspicion about you young women. You say you want rights and liberties but I fancy it's fashionable posturing rather than genuine revolutionary spirit. Your self-respect still depends on the adoration of some fool of a man. As soon as they let you out of here, I want you to come to see me. I insist on it. I won't have you falling into your old ways. It's time you had a proper education in the ways of the world.'

'What I want is to be an artist. But Dr Rastrick won't even let me paint.'

'That's appalling! It's downright cruelty for someone like you. I will write and demand an explanation.'

I leaned closer to her and lowered my voice. 'I've succeeded in getting hold of paper and pencils, and in secret I've managed to produce portraits of some of the patients. I'm quite proud of them. If only there was a way to smuggle them out to you.'

'It's dreadful you have to sneak about like that,' whispered

Miss Fanshaw. 'I'll have a word with this Rastrick fellow and set him to rights.'

'No, please don't. He'll only stop me drawing, and probably punish me too.'

'He'd punish you for that?'

I nodded.

'Good grief!'

'Mr Lilley suggested I could work in an artist's studio and establish myself that way. Perhaps when I'm free of this place, that would be an option.'

'Wilf said that, did he? Well, I hope you're not lured by the idea of becoming a muse to a male artist, and then forgetting all your own ambitions.'

'Not at all. How is Mr Lilley, by the way?'

'You're not languishing here, thinking about him?' she said, looking closely at me.

'Of course not,' I said, looking away to hide my blushes.

'I haven't laid eyes on him recently,' she said. 'He's been working on a new series of paintings for some time and he's being morbidly secretive about it. His friends worry about him, those few who remain loyal, but he's too proud to accept our help. We fear Paris was too much for him, whatever he claims to the contrary. He certainly came back much reduced. And terribly discouraged. And then there was the summer show at the academy. His mermaid, the one he'd been working on for the last couple of years, was rejected by the Hanging Committee. Apparently, there was a glut of sirens this year.'

'How unfair!'

'And then there was that awful news about . . . ' She faltered, then said quietly: 'About Fanny.'

Fanny Kerrich! The woman whose fragile beauty stared out from so many of Mr Lilley's canvases. The woman who had posed for his siren. I felt a stab of jealousy hearing her name. Miss Fanshaw took out a handkerchief and dabbed her eyes.

'Mr Lilley's laundry girl? Has something happened to her?' I asked.

'Of course, you won't have heard,' she said, her gaze cast down. 'She passed away.'

'How shocking!'

'Five more minutes, ladies!' called Mrs Clinch.

'It was a few weeks ago,' said Miss Fanshaw. 'From some curious wasting disease, apparently. My first thought was it must have had something to do with Wilf. Heaven knows what put that frightful idea into my head. There was an obituary. Do they allow you to see *The Times* here? The correspondent said something about Fanny rising up from lowly beginnings and living a bohemian lifestyle, before being married to a titled gentleman. The correspondent was one of the art establishment, someone Wilf fell out with a few years ago. He acknowledged Wilf had been Fanny's mentor, but made it clear that he held her reputation in higher esteem than Wilf's. That will have upset Wilf. My dear, are you quite yourself? You've turned pale as a ghost.'

'Time's up!' shouted Mrs Clinch.

'You must write to me,' said Miss Fanshaw.

'I mightn't be allowed.'

'Really? That's an outrage.'

'Come along now, ma'am, if you don't mind!' cried Mrs Clinch. 'We mustn't let Miss Pring get too tired.'

We rose to our feet. Miss Fanshaw smiled sadly at me as she

put on her gloves. 'I shall make some enquiries on your behalf.'
There were tears in her eyes. She embraced me again, whispering
into my ear, 'My dear, you must be strong. Chin up, now.'

Then she turned, and walked out briskly, but for once with
her head down.

23

One evening, on the way down the stairs to the dining hall for dinner, Eliza Feldwicke, the most crazed of all the women in the secure ward, climbed over the banisters and leapt to her death. Afterwards, fear stalked the ward. A rumour circulated that Eliza had been thrown over the banisters by a spectral figure. Meanwhile, out of sight, the body was removed, the floor mopped. I shuddered as I imagined Dr Rastrick removing Eliza's brain, measuring it and putting it inside one of his labelled jars.

The following evening, Mrs Rastrick appeared in my cell. She closed the door and stood with her back to it. She seemed unsettled. 'I mustn't stay,' she said in a lowered voice. 'I came because I remembered that poor woman was one of those you'd drawn.'

'Eliza's the second woman in just a few weeks.'

'Oh, Miss Pring! Try not to dwell on it. It's in the nature of things here. The numbers this year are no higher than in others. And at least your drawing means there is something left to remember her by. I'd better go. The staff are very much in evidence tonight.' She paused with her hand on the door handle. 'I wanted you to know you have a friend.'

She turned and opened the door, then gasped with shock to find Mrs Tuckwell, the housekeeper, confronting her.

'Mrs Rastrick! I didn't expect to find you here,' said Mrs Tuckwell.

Mrs Rastrick's mouth opened as if she was about to answer, but no words were forthcoming. I had to come to her rescue, but how?

'Mrs Rastrick came to ask if I wanted a prayer book,' I said. 'Some of the ladies are distressed about Eliza passing away, and they might like me to read to them.'

'You must be very busy, Mrs Tuckwell,' said Mrs Rastrick. 'I won't get under your feet. Good evening to you.'

Mrs Tuckwell stepped aside to let her pass. When Ellen was gone, she stepped into the room. The ill-humoured attendant, Miss Nettleship, followed directly after.

'This wasn't Mrs Rastrick's first visit here, was it?' said Mrs Tuckwell.

'No,' I said. 'She often chats to patients. There's a group of unlettered ladies on the ward that I read to and Mrs Rastrick was trying to be helpful.'

'Yes, I'm aware of your little Bible group. Nothing on this ward escapes my attention. The chaplain has organized a perfectly satisfactory literacy class, so I see no need for it.' She looked about my room with her nose in the air. 'I'm constantly on the lookout for any signs that patients are unsettled, and it's especially important at this sad time. Is there anything you wish to tell me?'

I shook my head.

'Then you won't mind if we take a look in your desk drawer?'

'I'm a private patient here. What I keep in the desk is my own affair.'

'Miss Nettleship, open the desk drawer, would you?'

I blocked Miss Nettleship's path. 'There are personal documents in there. Intimate letters to members of my family.'

'We're not interested in your letters. We just want to make sure there's nothing in there that shouldn't be. Now, move out of the way.'

I stood my ground. 'I've drawn some pictures,' I said. 'They're my property.'

'Please, step out of the way,' said Mrs Tuckwell, taking a step towards me.

I relented and sat on the bed, my arms folded. I fought to control my anger as Miss Nettleship took out my pictures, the box of crayons and the pencils. Mrs Tuckwell took the portraits I'd drawn, and glanced at each in turn with distaste, before folding them roughly and putting them in her apron pocket.

Her cheeks were flushed. She was exultant. 'As you well know, you're forbidden to draw or paint. It's for your own good.'

'What proof have you that drawing is doing me harm?'

'I'd have thought it was self-evident,' she said. She turned and walked to the door, with Miss Nettleship following. On the threshold, she looked back. 'Let's see what Dr Rastrick has to say about your drawings, shall we?'

When they were gone, I paced up and down my cell for a long while, beside myself with rage. Mrs Tuckwell was no more than a jealous bully, a cold-hearted, puffed-up devil who resented me for winning the friendship and loyalty of her charges. She had no care if we were happy, no desire to unburden us of anguish or fear or confusion. She only wanted us brought to heel. I keenly felt the humiliation of being at the mercy of this coarse and ignorant termagant. I would never forget the contempt she showed for the portraits I'd made. When she came to the picture of Eliza, she was utterly unmoved, even though we'd lost her only the previous day. And yet Mrs Rastrick had been moved to tears by my work. I paced up and down, plotting my revenge on Mrs Tuckwell, until I was weary. Then I threw myself on the bed and wept bitterly. All was hopeless. I'd been a fool to regard my pictures as a small act of defiance, and to believe I could reclaim the souls of those women by drawing them. I would die and be buried in this place and there would be nothing to show I'd ever existed.

★

During the recreation hour the following afternoon, the patients were told to gather in the ward for an announcement. Mrs Tuckwell stood on a chair and called for our attention.

'Splendid news, everyone!' she said, beaming. It was rare to see her smile – and alarming. 'We have the result of the recent inspection by the Commissioners in Lunacy,' she announced. 'The formal report will not be published for some time, but Dr Rastrick has been given to understand that the standard of care at Hillwood Grange has been judged outstanding for the third year in succession. This could not have been achieved without the cooperation of all of you, working hard to present the hospital in its best light, and assisting the inspectors as they made their rounds. You may all give yourselves a round of applause.' Those patients capable of understanding her clapped in a half-hearted way. 'Dr Rastrick has asked me to inform you that all patients will be invited to a musical recital by the asylum's own orchestra next month, the date to be announced shortly. And, as promised, there will be double helpings of treacle tart for everyone this evening.'

I felt a severe tightness around my skull and had to sit down. Rage consumed me. I imagined myself doing severe violence on Mrs Tuckwell and on Dr Rastrick, lashing out wildly at them with an ill-defined implement, screaming hateful bile as I beat and gouged them. At a certain point I became aware someone was addressing me. It was Mrs Clinch.

'You're to see Dr Rastrick immediately in Mrs Tuckwell's station.'

I got to my feet and stomped towards the little dispensary in the middle of the ward that Mrs Tuckwell used as her office. I was taking deep breaths to control my temper. I reached the office and knocked on the door. From within, Dr Rastrick called, 'Enter.'

Once inside, I couldn't rid myself of the idea I was in a small narrow cabin onboard a ship. The room lurched and I reached for the counter before I could fall. I sat on a stool, and felt precariously high up. Dr Rastrick's case was on the floor, with all his measuring equipment inside it. I imagined removing a blunt instrument and dashing his brains out with it. Dr Binkes was sitting alongside him at the counter and they were looking at a notebook. When Dr Rastrick addressed me, his voice had a hollow ring.

'Miss Pring, good day to you. Dr Binkes is joining us. How are you feeling?'

'What does it matter?' I muttered.

Dr Rastrick gave Dr Binkes a meaningful look, and Dr Binkes

scribbled in his notebook. Dr Rastrick turned his gaze on me and sighed. 'What are we to do with you? You were expressly told not to draw, paint or read, but you've gone behind our backs, showing great cunning. The result is plain to see. Your nervous energy is finite and you've exhausted it, the very thing we wanted to avoid.'

I stood up and walked over to Dr Binkes, seizing the note-book and walking away with it.

'Come along now, give the book back,' said Dr Rastrick.

'Why don't I take the notes for a change?' I asked. 'What a story I could tell. I ought to tear this up.' I held the book as if I was about to rip it in two.

'I warn you in the strongest terms not to do any such thing,' said Dr Rastrick. He took a step towards me. 'Give me the book, please.'

I tried to tear the notebook in two by pulling its spine apart but couldn't, so I tore out several pages and threw them into the air so they floated through the air and scattered about the floor. Dr Rastrick seized my wrist and pulled the book out of my hands. Fearing what I might be capable of, I slid down the wall until I was sitting on the floor, then turned to the wall, resting my head against it and clutching my knees to my chest.

'I'm going to review her treatment,' Dr Rastrick said under his breath. 'This is most disturbing. Be a good fellow and call for assistance.'

When Dr Binkes had gone, Dr Rastrick stood over me, gazing down in a peculiar way. His brow gleamed with sweat and a lock of hair fell over his face. My heart was hammering. I wondered what might provoke him to strike me. And if he did so, would I be removed to another asylum? Would *he*? He pushed his hair out of his eyes, then stooped to pick up the torn sheets of paper from the floor. He put them on the counter, then picked up the notebook and tried to put the pages back in place.

'You've triumphed,' I said. 'Why don't you fetch your camera and take a photograph of me for a souvenir?'

He slammed his hand down on the counter, making me start. 'How dare you!' he shouted, rising to his feet. His face was shaking. I'd never seen him angry before and it shocked me. 'Is it not sufficient for you to have raised a complaint to the commissioners about your treatment? And after all the efforts my staff have made on your behalf. The entire asylum doesn't revolve around you and your needs.'

'But this is what you want, isn't it? What you've wanted all along – to provoke me, to prove me mad.'

He glared at me, his fists clenching and unclenching. He took a step towards me, but, at that moment, Mrs Tuckwell entered with Miss Nettleship behind her, holding a side-arm dress and a pair of fingerless padded gloves. Dr Rastrick scribbled something on a sheet of paper and handed it to Mrs Tuckwell. She unlocked the dispensary cupboard, took out a bottle and put it on the counter, then began to measure out a dose. Miss Nettleship pulled me to my feet, put the gloves on my hands and tied them at the wrist.

'The dry wrap for tonight,' said Dr Rastrick. 'Chloral and quinine, for the next week. I've indicated the dosage.' He lowered his voice. 'I suspect solitary vice. I want you to give her bromide of potassium every evening. I think it best if the night watch looks in on her on the hour.'

'It's for your own good, my dear,' said Mrs Clinch, gazing at me ruefully.

Mrs Clinch and another attendant took me back to the ward. My temper was spent and I was weary, so I stood unmoving as they pulled the strong dress over my head. They pushed my hands and arms into the sleeves which were stitched to the side of the dress, then they tied the strings at the back tightly. They each took an arm and dragged me to the bed, stiff as a board, then they wound the bed sheets around me, pulling them tight over my chest and neck until I thought I might suffocate. Finally, they wrapped a blanket around the entire bed, tucking it under the mattress and clasping me so fast that I couldn't move my limbs. It was still broad daylight.

After that, they left me alone, unable to move from the neck down. It was a long time before the light began to fade. In the depths of the building, I heard dormitory doors slam shut and keys turn in locks. The sedative made my eyelids heavy, and I lost consciousness. I awoke at some point to find it dark as sin, but for a misty brown strip of light around the door and a ghostly luminescence above the small iron grate in the floor. The gas boilers in the basement shuddered for the last time before shutting down for the night. I had never grown used to the utter silence of the countryside and it spooked me, especially now I was unable to move. I fell into another stupor and dreamed of an army of spectral spiders with long spindly legs scuttling over my face in the moonlight. I was awakened by a screech, an owl perhaps, or a woman locked in the strong room down in the basement. In the dorm next door, someone complained about a bed-soiler. The air was cold on my face, and the room smelled damper. Under the tight bedding, I was stifled and sweating. Itches in various places kept me awake for a time, maddening and persistent. Under the covers, I tried to move my hands, my fingers flexing helplessly in the padded fingerless gloves. I struggled with all my might to free myself. I thought of the long night ahead of me and panicked. I was helpless and suffocating. I wouldn't be able to stand this for another hour, let alone until morning. My heart raced. I screamed. An attendant came in and untied me from the side-arm dress and gloves. She opened the little window overhead to its full extent, then pressed a damp flannel to my forehead. Not long after, I drifted into darkness.

24

One morning, about a week later, I lay in bed, trying to rouse myself from the gluey sleep induced by the sleeping draught I'd been plied with the night before. There was a knock on the door and Mrs Tuckwell entered. It was rare to get a visit from her, so I knew it must be something momentous.

'Your father is coming later this morning,' she announced, without preamble. 'Up you get now, ready yourself.'

I sat up in bed, rubbing my eyes. 'Papa coming? That can't be. I was given no warning.'

'It's come as a surprise to me too. Perhaps Dr Rastrick was concerned you'd become overwrought if you had advance notice.'

I looked at the blue silk dress hanging limply on the door hook, its frayed collar and cuffs, its washed-out colour, with creases and signs of repair everywhere.

'Had I known my father was coming, I'd have had a dress laundered and pressed. And my hair . . . '

'Quickly now, there's no time to waste.'

After breakfast, Mrs Clinch helped me rinse my hair. Then she propped a small mirror against the wall on the little desk in my room. I viewed the ravages of so many weeks in the asylum. The outdoor work had coarsened my appearance. My complexion was ruddy. The luxuriant black curls of my hair that once clustered over my brow, now lay flat, dry and brittle. Most harrowing of all was the expression in my eyes.

'We'll soon have you looking like a duchess,' said Mrs Clinch, scraping the brush through my hair.

I tried to collect myself. In spite of all, I must appear composed to Papa. I had to convince him I was in my right mind. I would tell him how I longed to see Mama, that she was never out of my thoughts. That I regretted my behaviour towards Felix. I would persuade him to allow me home, even if only for a few days. By which time, he and Mama would be convinced I was better off staying home permanently. But what did I dare reveal of Dr Rastrick's machinations?

'There, that will do,' said Mrs Clinch. 'You look a picture. You'd cut any girl in England to shivers.'

After that, the bellicose Miss Nettleship took over, escorting me to the Committee Room with her usual ill grace. As we descended the broad central staircase, I was suddenly lightheaded. The steps beneath me billowed and rolled and the staircase plunged into shadow. I gripped the banisters and shut my eyes for a moment, catching my breath and waiting until I could trust myself to descend to the bottom. Nettleship issued a long-suffering sigh. We reached the ground floor and made our way along the broad corridor that led to the main entrance, then we turned a corner and stopped at the committee room where I'd had my encounter with Miss Fanshaw. Miss Nettleship unlocked the door.

Once we were inside, she sat in a chair by the door and I took a seat at the far end of the long table where the Committee of

Visitors and other dignitaries had their meetings. The chamber had the stale, dingy smell of a room that was in use only infrequently. Miss Nettleship took out a book from her apron pocket and began reading, her brow knotted: 'The Handbook for the Instruction of Attendants on the Insane'.

I looked at my hands, which were dark as mahogany from the sun, and covered in little nicks and bramble scratches, the skin dry and flaking, the fingernails worn down to the quick. I had always had quite large hands for a woman, and now after months of toil in the kitchen garden they were like those of a hardy peasant. I hid them in my lap. A glint from an object on top of a cabinet caught my eye. It was a silver ornament in the shape of a cricket bat mounted on a wooden plinth. Engraved on it were the words: 'HAROLD A. RASTRICK, GOLDEN BAT AWARD, 1857, LEWES OLD GRAMMAR SCHOOL'. Just then, I heard Dr Rastrick's voice in the corridor. I couldn't hear what he was saying, but he sounded like the soul of discretion, an exemplar of calm authority and civility. My father, by comparison, sounded subdued, uncertain, more querulous than when I'd last heard him.

Finally, Papa stepped into the room, looking a little lost. He held his bowler in his hands and was turning it in circles absent-mindedly. He was greyer and more drawn than before. When he saw me, his eyes filled with tears. I leapt to my feet and ran into his arms, stifling my sobs against his chest. He stroked my hair, just as he had when I was his little Honeysop, and I had come running to him after one of my tantrums. We went to sit down, far enough from Miss Nettleship to speak with comparative privacy.

'I'd have been here sooner,' said Papa, 'but Dr Rastrick decided the head attendant should give me a tour of the grounds, showing me the gasworks and so on. Then he insisted on presenting me with the latest report on the asylum.'

'Tell me – how is Mama? I think of her constantly.'

'She's more herself as time passes. She sends her love. She misses you too.'

'Did Miss Fanshaw pay you a visit?'

'She did, indeed. The woman's a formidable advocate on your behalf. She encouraged me to press Dr Rastrick to grant me an interview with you and, well, I'm here as you see.'

'Miss Fanshaw said Mama was in a bath chair.'

'Let's not concern ourselves overmuch with Mama for now. I'm here to find out how you are faring.'

'And my brothers – how are they?'

'The two middle boys are well. And little Archie has settled into prep school.'

'And Lance?'

Papa sighed and bowed his head. 'You'll remember he attempted to join the Guards. Well, I'm afraid he hasn't been successful, and he's taken it rather badly.'

'Oh dear.'

Papa glanced at Miss Nettleship. Noting she was preoccupied with her book, he removed something from his jacket pocket and put it in my hand. I glanced at it before quickly slipping it into a pocket of my dress; it was a small cloth purse tied with a drawstring.

Papa leaned towards me and said quietly, 'You might order some books, or some sweets.'

'I doubt Dr Rastrick would allow me to buy books. You spoke to him about my progress?'

He looked away, towards the window, where the wind shook

the bare autumn branches in a kind of dream. 'I understand you've been working in the gardens. You're brown as a berry. It might be the right prescription for you. Perhaps the doctor's right – it's as well not to have your nose in a book all of the time.'

'He allows me children's books and Tennyson. And the Bible, of course. But I'm altogether forbidden to paint.'

Papa looked at me. 'Yes, he said that you'd gone against his wishes and done some drawings. Perhaps it's for the best. I seem to recall you were making all those pictures before . . . well, before.'

'If I could come home, I'd be able to help Mama,' I said. 'Managing the servants, keeping the books. I can support her. Everything will be different. If only she would come to visit me, and we could talk.'

There was a loud snore. I looked over and saw Miss Nettleship had fallen asleep, her chin on her chest and her lower lip protruding, her book still open in her hands.

'Papa, listen to me,' I whispered urgently. 'Things here are not as they seem. Dr Rastrick is a dangerous man with perverse obsessions.'

'Please, don't overexcite yourself, my dear. Rastrick's a pompous windbag, I grant you, but he seems level-headed.'

'He's too cunning to do anything that looks untoward, but he means to drive me mad.'

'My dear, you're not yourself, you don't look yourself. You're likely imagining things. Is there anything in particular that he's done?'

'Look, we haven't time. Arrange for me to come home before it's too late. If I'm not better in a few weeks then you can send me back. I will agree to seeing another consultant if you wish – one unconnected with Dr Rastrick. He has no grounds to keep me here, not really . . . '

'This is his field so we must abide by his judgement. And after all . . . Perhaps you've forgotten why we were obliged to send you here in the first place.'

The room pivoted and I thought I might faint. 'Papa, the longer I remain here, the worse it will be for me. I cannot endure much more, and if you won't help me then who on earth will? You don't know what Dr Rastrick is like. He's persuasive, oh, so very persuasive. But there's a dark side to him you haven't seen. I have good reason to believe he intends to lock me away here for good.'

'Why would you think such a thing?'

'I've overheard him say as much. And he wants to experiment on me and other women.'

Papa shook his head, disbelieving. 'But what has he actually done to you?'

There was a loud sound, and I near jumped out of my skin. I turned and saw it was only Miss Nettleship snoring again. She was sound asleep.

'Listen, Papa. He has me wrapped in sheets at night so tight I can barely breathe. He never listens to a word I say, is forever poking and prodding me, plying me with sleeping draughts to keep me docile, testing my reflexes with a little hammer and . . . he's performed the most intimate examinations. He has a peculiar preoccupation with my most private bodily functions.'

'Isn't that the sort of thing these doctors routinely do? And, for all I know, he's had cause to restrain you. He told me you've shown a tendency to fly off the handle, which came as little surprise to me. He said that recently you seized his case notes and tried to tear them up.'

'Yes, because I'd seen the vile lies he'd written about me. He uses the fact that Grandpapa had several spells in an asylum as evidence against me. He keeps other doctors away from me, except for one junior fellow, a milksop who he can bully into doing whatever he likes. I overheard him talking to some other mad-doctors, and he told them he wanted to lock women with hereditary madness in asylums to stop them having children. That's what he's doing here, I'm sure of it, while he pretends to be running an ordinary asylum. Everybody here calls the women his "darlings". I'm one of them. He has taken photographs of us. He says they're to train doctors to recognize symptoms of insanity, but really it's to prove his theory.'

'He's taken a photograph of you? Good Lord. Suppose people were to see it? Visitors and the like. What use is it being a private patient if he uses no discretion?'

'He regards himself as rational and objective, yet any sane person can see he is doing these things to me, and to other women, for peculiar and unseemly reasons. He has an unhealthy fascination with certain women. I think it's because we offend his notions of how women should be.'

'But listen, my dear – if you lose control of yourself, then what is he to think? You've always had that tendency . . . '

'I know I have a fearful temper. But so too does Lance, and he's far more violent than me, and yet nobody ever questions his sanity.'

He scratched his head, and looked about him, bewildered. 'What am I to do? I've never liked Rastrick. But your mother sees him as the fount of all wisdom.'

At that moment there was a loud thump on the other side of the room. Miss Nettleship groaned, then roused herself and looked about her in a daze. She pushed herself up to standing, and picked her book up from the floor. Then she took out her watch and peered at it.

'Heavens above, we've run over by five minutes. Mr Pring, I'm afraid Dr Rastrick's orders are that we're not to tire out your daughter, so I must ask you to say your farewells.'

Papa rose to his feet. He walked over to Miss Nettleship with a determined stride.

'Fetch Dr Rastrick for me, would you?'

Miss Nettleship puffed out her chest. 'I beg your pardon?'

'I'm telling you to fetch Dr Rastrick. I wish to speak with him immediately.'

'But Dr Rastrick's a very busy man. I can't ask him to stop what he's doing, just like that . . . The head attendant, Mr Pockock, might be able to speak with you.'

'In that case, you may tell Dr Rastrick that I am removing my daughter from his care with immediate effect.'

'Wait! You mustn't do that, sir. It's against the regulations. Just give me a moment and I'll get him. Stay right where you are.'

While we waited for her return, Papa stood on the spot, rocking on his heels, his brow knotted and his lips moving although he uttered no sound.

'Papa, we should go now, right away. Let's not wait for Dr Rastrick. He will find a way to keep me here. Where is the carriage?'

'Leave this in my hands.'

Then Dr Rastrick appeared, looking ruffled and annoyed. 'You wished to see me?'

'I'm removing my daughter from here. Without further notice. Send me your bill, and I'll settle it.'

Dr Rastrick shook his head. 'I'm afraid that's not possible.'

'I insist on it, sir,' said Papa.

'Look, shall we sit down and discuss this? Whatever the problem is, I'm sure it can be quickly rectified.' He pulled out a chair for Papa, and sat down himself. But Papa remained standing. 'I think it best that Miss Nettleship takes Violet elsewhere while we discuss this difficulty.'

'I'm not letting my daughter out of my sight.'

'Well, this is irregular. I can't think what's persuaded you to take this line with me.' He glanced at me as he said it. 'Of course, it can be most upsetting to encounter a close family member in these circumstances.'

'I intend to get another physician's opinion on my daughter's condition.'

Dr Rastrick massaged his temples with finger and thumb. 'I think we should consider the implications before doing anything rash.'

'My mind's made up. From now on, I intend to take full responsibility for Violet's care.'

Dr Rastrick deliberated for a moment. 'I must warn you that removing Violet at this delicate stage in her treatment would put her at great risk.'

'You think all your learning gives you an exclusive purchase on the truth, but I beg to differ. I'm taking her home.'

'I'm simply offering my clinical opinion, based on empirical evidence. In our conversation earlier, I alluded to certain worrying tendencies. And I would point out that your daughter is not my sole concern. I have responsibilities to the public as a whole and cannot allow a patient with Miss Pring's history to be released without due consideration. Her admission was fully certified and is legally binding. You were made aware of this at the time. If you abscond with your daughter, she will be sought out and returned to this hospital.'

What 'history'? I wondered, frantically. What was it that had happened in the interval of time that was lost to my memory?

'Are you threatening me, sir?' said Papa.

Dr Rastrick lowered his voice, and adopted a more accommodating manner. 'Please, Mr Pring, there's no need to take that tone. There are certain matters I prefer not to discuss with your daughter present, in particular your wife's condition.'

'Mama's condition?' I cried. 'Is she worse than I thought? Is that why she hasn't come to visit me? I must see her.'

Dr Rastrick sighed. 'Your daughter is becoming increasingly distressed, Mr Pring. I'd be remiss if I didn't intervene.' He rose to his feet and summoned Miss Nettleship, took her to one side and muttered some instructions to her, after which she hurried off.

Papa loured at Dr Rastrick. I had never seen him this way before. 'When you've given Violet her medicine, we'll take our leave of you,' he said.

'For your own sake, Mr Pring, think clearly about the consequences of what you propose. Please, sit down for a moment. I insist.'

Papa and I sat down at the long table. He held my hand, as we listened to Dr Rastrick hold forth.

'If you cast your mind back to the dreadful aftermath of that evening . . . '

I shook with fear. 'What evening? What happened? Will one of you tell me?'

'Don't upset yourself further, my dear,' said Papa. 'We will shortly be away from this place, and we'll discuss this then.'

Dr Rastrick resumed: 'It was not possible for you to manage your daughter at home. Ordinarily, cases like this are in the first instance reported to . . . let us say the relevant authorities. You wanted to avoid that, and I judged your daughter not to be in her right mind, so I offered to admit her to Hillwood Grange. Had I not . . . Well, I need hardly spell out the implications.'

'That's enough!' said Papa. He closed his eyes and lifted his free hand, placing it on his chest. I gripped his other hand more tightly as he took several deep breaths.

Dr Rastrick's response was softer, his tone more conciliatory. 'It was your strong wish that the worst eventuality should be avoided, and I took it upon myself to provide you and your wife with an alternative.'

'Yes, yes, indeed,' said Papa. 'But I would contend that while Violet had lost the balance of her mind at that moment, she has since recovered her senses, and to remain here will only bring her further grief.'

Dr Rastrick's chest rose and fell as he considered for a moment. When he spoke, he assumed an impatient air and his tone was markedly cooler.

'If you remove your daughter today, it will be my duty to report this to my professional body. An investigation will follow, and inevitably your daughter's confinement will become public knowledge, together with the circumstances that led to it. It's out of my hands.'

'I ask you once more,' said Papa. 'Out of compassion and consideration for what is best for Violet, will you allow her to leave with me?'

'I'm afraid that's out of the question – for reasons I've already explained.'

At this moment, Miss Nettleship and Mrs Clinch appeared in the doorway, Mrs Clinch with a medicine bottle in her hand.

Papa rose to his feet, and I with him. A strand of grey hair fell over his brow. He looked older than when he arrived, his gaze inward. He embraced me and spoke into my ear: 'This fellow has us in a bind, my dearest. I have no choice but to leave you behind. Be brave, and endure. But rest assured, I'll enter into correspondence with anyone who might be of any influence. If legal redress is the only solution, then so be it. God damn it, I'll sell my books if it comes to it.' He stepped away, gave my arm one last squeeze, then picked up his hat from the table and walked unsteadily towards the door. The two attendants stepped aside to let him through, and he departed without a backwards glance.

I was at the end of my strength. Mrs Clinch had me drink the sedative and it soon worked its effects, rendering me numb and drowsy. It was all I could do to reach the table and drop into a seat.

At some later hour, I woke up in bed and looked about me. The sun was low in the sky. I had slept through the day. There was a diamond-shape on the wall opposite my bed, shadows of trees quivering like reflections on water. The taste of the sedative I'd been plied with was still on my tongue, and my mind was muzzy. What had happened that morning was indistinct and confused in my memory. I stirred, and saw I was still in my day clothes. Turning onto my side, I felt a lump under my hip. I reached into my pocket and found the purse Papa had given me earlier.

I pulled the drawstring and emptied the contents into my palm: five half sovereigns. Quickly, I rose and put the purse in my desk drawer, telling myself that later I would find a loose panel of wainscotting and slide the coins behind it. Then, sitting on my bed, I wept bitterly. The encounter with Dr Rastrick that morning came back to me, and the horror of it made coherent thought hopeless. I would never escape his clutches. If only I could remember the period just before I arrived at the asylum. Something awful had happened to Mama, and it was clear I was implicated. Yet when I tried to recall that time, I experienced the same sensation as before, a sharp pain deep in my skull, together with nausea and light-headedness.

Not long after that, I was in the dining room, staring down at a scratched tin plate of boiled ham, potatoes and greens floating in a smear of brown grease. The sounds of clattering cutlery and women's muttering voices were muffled and seemed far away. A stale aura hung over the rows of dining tables, while the further reaches of the dining hall were insubstantial as the boundaries of a dream. Amber autumn light from the floor-length windows failed to penetrate the swirling haze. Overhead, cheerless chandelier lamps were suspended in gloom.

Somewhere, a kettle was near boiling, its whine building in intensity. As it reached boiling pitch, I became aware of a continuous knocking sound. I looked down and saw the cause. My hand was banging my mug on the table. A peremptory voice called for the banging to stop. I met the gaze of Wall-Eye across the table, and she picked up her mug and began banging it in time with mine. Her friends, the country ladies who worked with me in the garden, joined in, and some of the imbeciles too, until lots of women around the room were drumming in rhythm. Above the racket, the attendants could barely make their voices heard. I rose to my feet and threw my plate, careless of where it might land, and heard it clatter across the floor. Then I threw my mug, and my bowl of tapioca. Around me plates and tumblers began to fly about and I was deafened by riotous voices bouncing around that cavernous chamber and feet stomping on the wooden floors. Chairs were overturned. There was maniacal laughter. The kitchen staff took cover under the counter. The country women overturned our table while others scrambled for safety. Some took shelter under tables. Lamps fell from the chandeliers and shattered on tabletops. Soon, most of the patients were cowering at the side of the room. Reinforcements arrived, attendants from the other female wards.

I stood in the heart of the melee, tears rolling down my cheeks. Then a powerful force barged into me and threw me headlong. I landed hard on the floor, on a protruding bone in my hip, and a moment later was covered by a hot heavy suffocating weight. Humid breath brushed my cheek, while all around the shouting and shrieking continued. The world was knocked out of kilter, turned on its side. I looked under a table and saw women crouching there, some with their hands over their ears. I turned my head and saw Mrs Tuckwell's red face bearing down on me, her spittle-flecked lips, her grey eyes gazing fiercely into mine. It was she who had tackled me and who now restrained me in a stifling bear hug.

'Let go of me, you monster,' I cried, as I struggled to free myself.

'Calm yourself, madam, or it will be the worse for you.'

She took my wrist and pulled my arm behind my back,

bending it at the elbow. It hurt terribly, especially when I tried to wrest myself free. I heard myself scream.

A moment later, another sturdy woman appeared and she and Mrs Tuckwell held me face down against the floor. For a while, I lay there panting, crushed against the hard floor planks. Then I was roughly lifted to my feet. Mrs Tuckwell looked me over quickly and two assistants dragged me out of the room. I saw they were taking Wall-Eye out too, and several of her friends. Other patients stood by the wall and gawped as I was led away. Mrs Tuckwell and Miss Nettleship took me down the central staircase, keeping a firm grip on me. Down and down we went, all the way to the basement, where they took me into a small treatment room. Miss Nettleship unbuttoned my dress and roughly removed it, throwing it into a basket. Mrs Tuckwell lifted my vest and looked at my bruises, while Nettleship fetched something from a shelf. It was a strong dress, the sleeves sewn into the sides.

Just then, Dr Rastrick entered. Without a word, he approached me and gripped my arm. He raised his other hand, which held a long syringe with a cloudy substance inside and a fearful spike projecting from the end. I looked away and felt a sharp prick in my arm.

'Give her two hours in the strong room,' he said, and marched off.

25

I was given a series of warm baths, the first lasting for an hour and then increasing by an hour a day for five days. Immersion in warm water was supposed to restore nervous equilibrium, or in other words make me docile and tractable. I lay in a torpor of mind and body, cold compresses on my forehead, my vest and drawers ballooning around me. I was drowsy, bored, uncomfortable, life and energy leeching out into the water. Nothing to do but stare for hours at the whorls on my fingertips, the film of murk on the water's surface or the line of scum above the waterline. Now and then an attendant came to pour more hot water in, and dip her thermometer into the water.

Changes were made in the ward. At least three attendants were present at all times. I was forbidden to read to Wall-Eye and her friends in the recreation hour. Sometimes I saw my friend Ada Meggett, sitting on the benches on the lawns, with other convalescing patients. I missed her terribly.

One afternoon Mrs Tuckwell approached me during the recreation hour.

'There's something I'm to tell you,' she said. 'A gentleman is spending some time here at Hillwood, a doctor from France. He has achieved some interesting results using hypnotism . . . '

'Hypnotism?'

'That's correct. Dr Rastrick has agreed he can try it with a select few women patients. The Frenchman has requested that you take part.'

'I don't understand.'

'If you have any questions, you may speak to Dr Rastrick. You're quite free to refuse to take part.'

My only experience of hypnotism had been when I saw Annie De Montford at the Empire Theatre a few years previously. The woman was small in stature but with piercing eyes and a commanding presence. She'd invited young men up onto the stage, put them in a trance and then persuaded them to perform foolish antics to roars of riotous laughter. She'd even persuaded one of them to stab his friend with a feather which she had persuaded him was a knife. A report in the *Brighton Gazette* had said it was all a cheap trick, and the supposed volunteers had been planted by De Montford in the audience.

I wondered whether hypnotism could be more than a music hall stunt, if it could reach into parts of a person's consciousness normally concealed even from themself. The idea made my pulse race. It struck me that I had always felt I must hide a part of myself from the world. I would put on a social mask when with Lottie and the other young ladies, attempting to seem just like the rest, or at least like the more popular girls. And then there was the exhausting ordeal of presenting myself in acceptable fashion to Mama's appalling friends. I had always been most myself when alone with my paint pots. I could give my imagination free rein, lose myself.

The thought of the Frenchman revealing my inner secret self unnerved me. Perhaps it would play into Dr Rastrick's hands.

He would pounce on it as proof of my evil inheritance, the primitive bestial urges that my degenerate nature was unable to subdue. My mind was made up. I would refuse to take part in the hypnotism.

And yet . . . If the Frenchman was to discover the key to my malady, and his diagnosis contradicted Dr Rastrick's, there might be grounds to put me under the care of another mad-doctor, one more disposed to return me to health. And could my circumstances really be any worse than they were already? After Papa's visit and the riot, I had slid into dejection. I'd lost hope of ever freeing myself from Dr Rastrick's snare.

After deliberating at length, I sent word to Mrs Tuckwell that I was prepared to take part in the Frenchman's experiments. That very day my medication was suspended. Mrs Tuckwell told me this was at the request of Dr Serrurier. I had difficulty sleeping for a night or two, but after that I enjoyed the deepest sleep I'd known since my childhood. Every morning I awoke alert, with no trace of the thick grey fug that had hung about me in the previous weeks.

★

When the day came for me to meet Dr Serrurier, I was in a fit of nerves. The therapy took place in a small room with a row of chairs against one wall, a desk at one side and a window opposite showing a patch of colourless sky. I sat in a chair with rounded armrests and a padded seat covered in leather. Dr Serrurier sat at the side of the desk, rather than behind it. He didn't see fit to rise or introduce himself. His legs were crossed and his arms rested on the wooden arms of the chair. His posture suggested a trance-like concentration. I didn't at first notice, but an attendant was sitting in the corner of the room.

There was something of the monk about Dr Serrurier, a detachment, an otherworldly quality. Yet his suit and waistcoat were well-tailored, and his yellow tie was carefully knotted. He was not handsome but his peculiar stillness gave him a certain presence. I tried to restrain myself from fidgeting, and from scratching the rash that had risen on the back on my hands. Dr Serrurier gazed at me through small round metal spectacles. His gaze was soft and unreadable. His beard was full and long, trimmed so that it narrowed towards the bottom, the colour of fox fur. He was in his late twenties, I supposed. I had grown used to the intrusive gaze of men of his class, but I was disarmed by his bearing, his quiet concentration. In stark contrast to Dr Rastrick, Dr Serrurier seemed to have all the time in the world. Above all, I felt the magnetic pull of his will. Was he was waiting for me to speak, or daring me to? There was a notebook on the desk.

'Is that my case history?' I asked.

'Indeed it is.'

'You've read it then?'

He picked up the notebook, frowned at it, then dropped it. 'I have perused it,' he said. 'In general, I prefer to draw my own conclusions. In the first case, I like to observe a patient's comportment.'

I sighed, crossed my arms and looked out of the window. I was weary of men observing my 'comportment'. The minutes passed. I wondered about Dr Serrurier. He spoke English with only the faintest French accent. If anything, it was his grammatical precision that gave him away. The room's stillness closed around me, and all I could hear was the hiss within my eardrums.

'Your English is good,' I said, to break the silence.

'My mother was English. Sadly, she died when I was ten years of age.'

'I'm sorry to hear that.'

'You have had a series of warm baths. That's useful,' said Dr Serrurier.

'You've cured women in Paris with your methods, I suppose?'

He changed the cross of his legs and smoothed out a crease in his trousers with his palm. 'In France, derangement takes a different form. What I see in this institution are very English symptoms. For example, I have not seen one case of *la grande hystérie* which is endemic in *la Salpêtrière*. Instead, I find delusions and anxiety – about identity, and social position, about money and religion. In France you would be treated differently, with a different diagnosis, and perhaps with different results. This is what I've learned during my stay here. But tell me, have you had experience of hypnosis?'

I thought of Annie De Montford at the Empire Theatre, but shook my head. Dr Serrurier's steady gaze discomfited me. I felt as if I was somehow losing my grip on the everyday world, and feared I might slide into a state where I was under his control.

'Before I can hypnotize you, I must first ask for your consent.'

'Very well, you have my consent.' Even as I muttered these words, I regretted them.

He rose to his feet, and approached me, taking something from his jacket pocket. It was a chain, at the end of which dangled a bright golden disc about the size of a sovereign. He stood before me, so that the disc floated a few inches in front of me and above my head.

'First, I must verify that you can be hypnotized. Please, will

254

you hold both your arms out before you – like this?' He showed me what he meant, his arm held out straight before him, fist clenched. I complied. 'Now keep your gaze upon the disc.'

The disc revolved slowly on its chain, glinting as it caught the light.

'Think of nothing but sleep,' he said, repeating the words quietly from time to time as the moments slowly passed. My arms gradually grew heavier. 'You are feeling very tired . . . You long for sleep.' His voice was low, lulling. 'Your eyelids are heavy, your eyes moist. Do not close them. Continue to gaze at the disc.'

I swayed back and forth, on the brink of a descent into oblivion. My pulse raced in my temple. I longed to lower my arms, but at the same time I had a floating sensation as if I was becoming weightless.

'You are beginning to blink. The world about you is becoming faint. You are falling . . . falling . . . Please, all your concentration must be on the disc. Think of nothing but sleep. You cannot see distinctly. You are losing feeling in your limbs.'

My eyelids closed and I felt myself sinking by degrees into a dark bog, my limbs numb and heavy. But then there was a rush of heat to my head and my heart began to thump frantically. I opened my eyes to see a shape looming over me, dark against the light, a cobra fascinating its prey. I was transfixed, unable to move. I gasped for air, and it was some time before I could breathe evenly.

When I had recovered, Dr Serrurier took my pulse, then returned to his chair and put his golden disc back into his jacket pocket.

'We have not succeeded,' said Dr Serrurier. 'A pity. The truth is that not everyone can be hypnotized. For example, refined people, such as yourself, are often not impressionable. Nor are the insane when they refuse to cooperate.' He picked up my case history and began to leaf through it.

'Do you want me to go then?' I asked.

'One moment,' he said, putting the file back on the desktop. He mused for a moment, stroking his fox-red beard. 'I have an idea. Let us talk about your art. I wonder how you would feel if I could arrange for you to make pictures.'

'I'm afraid Dr Rastrick won't allow that.'

'Perhaps he would, if I could prove the therapeutic value.'

'Dr Rastrick would argue it frays my nerves, that I will only overexert myself and it will all be too much for my frail female constitution.'

He looked puzzled, and then smiled. 'Tell me about your painting, your drawing? When you are working, do you ever lose awareness of all else besides?'

I thought of the strange back-to-front mermaid I had painted after Mr Lilley praised my work at the art class, the picture that so impressed him. It was among those burned by Mama. 'There have been times when I forgot myself for a time, yes. And when I saw the results, I was surprised.'

He leaned forward, his gaze lowered. 'I have seen in your case history that you have taken up drawing and painting most intensely at times of crisis – at points when you have suffered with your nerves or you were experiencing a change of life, that is to say a biological change. Perhaps there is a link between your art and your malady. If you were able to paint here in this room perhaps you could reach a state of profound absorption, one where you would be suggestible to hypnotism. With your permission, I will consult with Dr Rastrick.'

'I'm afraid you'll have no luck with that,' I said. 'Dr Rastrick is determined to stop me ever painting again.'

★

The next day I was in the garden on my knees among rows of celery. It was a windy day, but I was sheltered from the gusts by an ancient wall with ripe morello cherries trained to grow against it. Whenever the attendant's back was turned, I popped a cherry into my mouth. I was absorbed in my work, when I heard my name called softly. When I looked up, I found Ellen Rastrick standing at the wall. She had her back to me, and was picking cherries. Her maid stood alongside her, holding a basket to collect the fruit.

'We've been given permission to pick some cherries,' said Ellen. 'It was the only way I could speak to you. Mrs Tuckwell has her staff watching me like a hawk. I heard you'd been restrained. How appalling.'

I glanced up at her. As she talked to me, she directed her gaze at her maid to make it seem as if they were in conversation. How well she must have trusted her.

'You've met Dr Serrurier. I understand he's carrying out experiments on you. He's staying in the house with us for a month. Things got off on the wrong foot the first night when Harold insisted on explaining the rules of cricket. But to the point – last night, Dr Serrurier proposed to Harold that you should be allowed to paint during your encounters with him. Harold refused outright. Then Dr Serrurier got up and went straight out in the drizzle – heaven knows where – and didn't return for an hour. Instead of coming down for breakfast this morning, he went directly to the asylum building.

'The point is, Harold only agreed to Dr Serrurier's visit because he wants to have his papers published on the continent, and Dr Serrurier has powerful friends. At breakfast, I pointed out to Harold that he depended on this man's goodwill, so he should consider letting you paint. Harold surrendered. He sometimes does, you know. Anyway, it means you can have my paint tubes. Perhaps if we show that painting does you no harm, Harold could be persuaded to allow you to paint in future. We'd better go, before anyone gets suspicious.'

26

Several days had passed since my first encounter with Dr Serrurier. I sat in the same upholstered seat as before, but now I was at a large table. To my surprise, instead of finding an attendant sitting in the corner of the room, Dr Binkes was there instead. His notebook was on the desk before him.

For perhaps two hours, I sat painting and drawing. Scattered over the tabletop were abandoned sketches, and objects for still life drawings: a rock, flat on one side with an ancient creature like a giant woodlouse impressed into it, autumn leaves, maple, oak and ash, a pot where mushrooms on long stalks drooped over the sides. I was unable to lose myself in my work, conscious that Dr Serrurier was watching me, waiting to pounce. He was in his usual seat to one side of his desk, reading a book: *De la Suggestion dans l'État Hypnotique et dans l'État de Veille*. I was bored. Still life had never excited me and my efforts were desultory. I preferred to create scenes from my imagination, my own peculiar fancies, or to draw people. Dr Serrurier was a distraction. At one point he took out a penknife from his jacket pocket and peeled an apple, circling it with the blade with great precision so that he produced a spiral of continuous peel which finally fell all of a piece onto a saucer before him. Then he brought the apple to his mouth and bit into it. His teeth crunched into its flesh. When he had finished the apple, he used his knife to clean his fingernails.

I began a preliminary sketch for a new picture. The notion came to me unbidden. I hoped to paint it in oils one day, a big picture, a six-footer. Rather than begin with a definite composition in mind, I felt my way inch by inch across the page, and the results were fragmented and disordered. I worked quickly, knowing I would be interrupted in midstream. What emerged was a sketch of a masked ball in a Venetian palace that had somehow merged with a forest full of strange topiary tangled up with wild overgrowth. The stucco work of the palace was modelled on the ceilings of the asylum. I tried to catch the atmosphere of a fairy picture that made a great impression on me as a young girl: John Anster Fitzgerald's *The Dream*. My only rule was that the picture would have no logic, rules or science, like *Alice in Wonderland*. I wasn't aware of the moment when the brush was removed from my hand.

I was floating in the darkness. I heard Dr Serrurier's hollow tones: *I would like to return to an encounter in your recent life – your visit to the artist Mr Lilley in the weeks before you were to be married. Try to remember that day. What first comes to mind? What do you see when you look about you?*

'I see nothing. It's silent.'

Do not struggle to remember. Simply wait until something appears.

'But there's nothing to see. Mr Lilley and I talked. We drank and smoked. There was a storm and I had to stay at his house that night. I was engaged to be married and I should never have gone there. What use is it imagining those scenes?'

Try! Think about how it was late in the day. Look around you and use your senses. What do you hear? What do you taste? What do you feel?

'I'm lying on my back in a kind of fever, neither fully awake nor asleep. My throat is dry. I taste alcohol. Bile. The smell of the room is very particular. Cigar smoke, furniture polish, mildew. Rain smatters against the window pane, gushes down the drainpipe, without end. I am drifting into sleep, and all I feel is the coming and going of my breath, the rise and fall of my chest. But there! The floorboards creak—'

A cymbal clashed and I opened my eyes. My surroundings, the plain little room, looked strange to me. I had the sense of having been absent for a long period of time. Under my dress, I was clammy. My throat was dry. There was a beaker of water on the table and I sipped from it. Dr Serrurier approached and stood over me. He seemed distracted, intense, quite different to his languid demeanour before.

'Miss Pring, it's necessary for me to examine you.'

I nodded. He bent over me and took my pulse. Then he studied each of my eyes in turn, holding the lids back with a thumb.

'You aren't experiencing any unpleasant sensations, a head-ache for instance? Dizziness?'

'I feel a little strange, but not unwell.'

'Can you describe this strangeness?'

'It's rather difficult. As if I've been in a very deep sleep. And it's hard to fully rouse myself.'

'And what do you remember of the sleep?'

'Only that you were asking me about Mr Lilley – the time I visited him.'

'And then? What happened after that?'

'Well, nothing. The next thing I remember is the clash of the cymbal. And waking up.'

Dr Binkes was still sitting in the corner with his notebook. Dr Serrurier gave him a significant look. Then he paced up and down the room for a moment, apparently lost in thought.

My picture was still on the table. Before submitting to the hypnosis, I had apparently made more progress with it than I realized. Much of what I saw before me was altogether new. As if it had been painted by another hand. Any attempt at lifelike perspective or scale had been abandoned. The sky was rendered in jarring harmonies of intense violet and rose. A peculiar story seemed to unfold on different parts of the paper. Some details reminded me of the folk superstitions of the country ladies. A black dog with eyes like burning coals, ethereal barrow wights, headless white stallions, witches riding hellhounds. Very tall women stood about and made obscure gestures to one another. They wore owls or peacocks for hats, and their gowns slipped from their shoulders exposing alabaster skin. Lower down, their torsos and limbs were covered in fur or feathers in bright pink or turquoise. Colours I had never mixed before. At the bottom of the page were catacombs with broken dolls on shelves, some with missing limbs or heads. The picture began to shimmer, the bird-women winked at me or beckoned me, and I found myself becoming faint and had to look away from the picture. I realized Dr Serrurier was studying me intently.

'Does the picture disturb you?' he asked.

'I can't remember painting it – at least there is a lot that's unfamiliar to me.'

Dr Serrurier sat down at the table opposite me. He took off

his spectacles and polished them with a cloth. His face was rigid with tension and he had acquired a tremor in his right hand.

'Would you mind telling me: who is Eloise?'

'I had a governess of that name when I was a child.'

'Do you ever think about Eloise now?'

'Rarely.'

'What do you remember about her?'

'Mademoiselle Dufort, Eloise that is, sometimes hinted at adventures she'd had in Paris. I was a child at the time. She made a strong impression on me. She was very different to my mother, and I suppose . . . '

'Tell me more about your governess.'

'It was in the days we lived in the grand house in Hurstpierpoint. Mademoiselle Dufort was young, ethereal, French. On Mama's insistence she taught me repetitive pastimes, embroidery, music. But I preferred drawing and painting and so did Mademoiselle Dufort. In time, we became intimate friends. Perhaps the woman was lonely. She let slip tantalizing details of her romantic adventures in Paris. She let me address her by her Christian name: *Eloise*, a name that sounded like a caress. She gave me French lessons. I loved the language for its sensuous quality, and because it allowed me to say things Mama would not understand.

'Then Mademoiselle Dufort was dismissed. We moved to Brighton. Mama took charge of my education. Forced me to accompany her on a dreary round of social calls. Taught me vital skills such as the correct deportment for a lady when alighting from a carriage. Sometimes our route passed the girls' day school and at such moments I was sick with envy to hear the young ladies behind the school walls calling to one another in their cut-glass accents.'

'But Eloise left an impression on you?'

'Yes, now that I think of it. She made me feel a lady might live with a certain licence, a freedom from constraints and duties.'

Dr Serrurier peered at the picture. 'I think . . . I'm *certain*, we have made a discovery. I do not wish to raise false hopes, but I ask you to put your trust in me. We will meet in two days' time, and then I will present my pathological opinion. Until then, I advise that you rest. Have courage.'

27

The date of the next meeting was two days later. It could not have come too soon for me. In the interval I could think of nothing else. I entered the room and found Dr Serrurier alone. First, he took my pulse, listened to my breathing with a stethoscope, inspected my eyes, tapped my kneecap with a little hammer, took my temperature with a thermometer. Then he went and sat as usual in the chair placed at the side of his desk, and crossed his legs.

'I needed to ensure you were well before commencing,' he said. 'Your vital signs are normal. At our last meeting the hypnotism was successful. In fact, my expectations were exceeded. Dr Binkes made a record of what occurred. I would like you to read the transcript. However, I must warn you that some of the findings may disturb, confuse or distress you.' He lifted Binkes's notebook from the table. 'You're under no obligation to read these notes. But I advise you that these discoveries could provide the key to your recovery. However, I ask you to think carefully before deciding.'

'Do you think your discoveries could lead to my discharge from Hillwood Grange?'

'That would be for Dr Rastrick to decide. Alienists are only at the beginning of understanding such phenomena, so we must tread carefully. It is my professional opinion that further hypnotism could lead to your recovery.'

My mind was made up in an instant. 'Show me,' I said. 'Let me read the notes.'

PATIENT NOTES: VIOLET PRING
27th SEPTEMBER 1886
DR G. BINKES

Dr Serrurier: And now – what is happening?
Darkness. A flickering candle. Mr Lilley is sitting on the divan, reading a book by the light of an oil lamp.

Dr Serrurier: And then?
'And then nothing. I fell asleep and woke up the next day very much the worse for wear. I went home and Mama made a scene.'

Dr Serrurier: Wait. Just a little longer. Try to remember what happened next? We are back in Mr Lilley's rooms. Picture the scene. What do you see around you?
Assez, oublie-la! Forget Violet. Her memory cannot be trusted. Listen to me if you want to know the truth.

Dr Serrurier: Listen to whom? Who is speaking now?
Vous pouvez m'appeler Eloise. I'm Violet's better self. She's a coward. I'm without fear. I'm the one who creates her drawings, her paintings – the good ones at least, not the sentimental animal pictures or the fey landscapes she paints to please Mama. I'm

*the one with a fearless imagination, the one who goads her to
capture her waking dreams in paint or charcoal, I'm the one Mr
Lilley sees in Violet, the one he really wants. Yes, he's fascinated
by Violet – so conventional, so unspoilt – but only because he
knows she has another side. He's seen it in her work. He's
intrigued by the contrast between that unworldly creature and the
shocking products of her imagination – or rather my imagination.
Mr Lilley at bottom is like all men. Je sais ce que les messieurs
veulent vraiment.*

<u>Dr Serrurier: Dites-moi ce que nous voulons?</u>
*Très bien, puisque vous insistez. Lottie and I once stole away
after a musical show at the Empire. We went into a public house.
We were wedged against the bar, the din so tumultuous we could
scarcely hear one another. Lottie wanted to gawp at the prostitutes
as they preyed on drunken men. I saw she was bracing herself to
take greater risks. The gin was to give her courage. Soon we were
outside again. It was cold and my head was fuddled. I was a little
unsteady on my feet. Ladies of the night were working the pavement, strutting, elbows out, monstrous caricatures of women with
queer artificial voices, like men's, leaving a poisonous trail of cheap
perfume in their wake. Lottie insisted on following one of them.
The woman was leading a drunken fool across the road and into
the warren of narrow streets near the seafront. Suddenly, the pair
disappeared as if they'd dissolved into the wall. But they'd only
slipped down a dark narrow lane. We pursued them. It was so
dark in the alley we might have stumbled over them had we not
heard them first, the whore's coaxing tones and the man's grunts.
A sordid little scene, the woman on her knees. We turned and
fled, followed by a torrent of appalling language. Back in the safer*

streets, we laughed hysterically. Then Lottie put on her serious face and said: 'Disgusting, isn't it? Shameless.' As if we'd been on a mission to improve the morals of fallen women.

The incident was never mentioned afterwards. Lottie no doubt wanted to put it behind her. As for Violet – she simply had no recollection of what happened after we left the Empire. You see, I have a great advantage over Violet. She is utterly unaware of my existence, but I know her every thought.

A poison entered my bloodstream after that escapade with Lottie. I could never be on New Road after dark without feeling an urge to seek out danger. And it's natural to be curious, isn't it? Especially about what is forbidden. There were several secret forays. On certain evenings when I was with Lottie and the other ladies at a talk or a musical soiree, I feigned illness or made some other excuse to leave. I'd assure my friends I would safely make my way home, but instead I'd disappear into the night. It was about the time Mama was constantly parading Violet before eligible gentleman, when the weight of the family's expectations weighed most heavily upon her. You cannot conceive how deep my loathing for Mama was at that time. I wished her dead. And my excursions into those rank back alleys were to spite her, at least in part.

The most curious thing was that I saw men of my own class in those places, supposedly respectable gentlemen, the very type that Mama presented to me as eligible bachelors. I watched them as they were escorted, somewhat the worse for wear, into seedy boarding houses, even saw them consorting with desperate women in backyards, sometimes with scrawny girls, little more than children, other times with older women who might well have had children at home to feed. If I was seen loitering and challenged, I'd pretend I'd taken a wrong turning and got lost, and I'd hurry away.

It's all rather sordid, but you did ask. And I deserved to have adventures, just as a man does, just as Lance did.

Dr Serrurier: Can we return to the night with Mr Lilley, Eloise?
Wait! Don't you want to know more about me? How will you understand me otherwise? We must begin at the beginning. Violet is fifteen years old. She awakens one morning to find the bed sheets damp and stained deep red. She fears she will bleed to death. Some vital part of her has been dislodged during a furtive nocturnal episode of the sort no respectable English lady can ever speak. The housemaid puts her out of her misery. She explains the great secret of women's biology, the curse all women have borne since Eve first brought sin into the world. She also helpfully provides a rag. Mama has taught Violet many important lessons, such as the correct way to enter a room and that a young lady should never ask questions. But she has neglected to explain the basic facts of life.

This abrupt end to Violet's childhood leaves her fearful. She has an urgent desire to save her tarnished little soul. Seeks answers in Papa's books. Is inspired to seek a higher standard by which to live her life, one aloof from the narrow and self-seeking temper of the times. She turns to God, as cowards often will. She sweeps the floor at St Michael and All Angels. Runs stalls at the church bazaar. Goes from door to door with the collection box so the roof can be repaired. Dear heavens!

Then – an unlooked for romantic infatuation. A young man, altogether unsuitable in Mama's eyes – he is penniless. Timothy Nevott is the choir master and organist at St Michael's. Nervy, with painfully thin legs and a perpetual head cold. But he has fair hair and blue eyes and she decides he has the face of a Renaissance angel. He is devout, his mind on higher things. As he conducts the choir, she watches his long, expressive fingers. He blushes if she catches him gazing at her during choir practice, and if she stands too close to him, he develops a rash on his neck. Under his influence, she grows fervent about the Anglo-Catholic religion and avows that she will become a nun. Isn't it hilarious? She paints a picture of the two of them in medieval costume, kneeling side by side in a chilly old Norman church, a delicate watercolour, a symphony of muted greys in which her scarlet robe stands out. Red for sin. The two penitents, their knees aching on the hard stone flags, their hands held before them in prayer, their gazes raised to where Christ hung on the cross, his marble limbs lit by a slanting beam of light that directs the lovers' gazes towards Him and away from earthly longings. She hides the picture in a drawer and shows it to nobody, least of all Tim.

And then — heaven forfend! — she finds herself alone with Tim in the chancery. They are admiring the stained-glass windows. Oh, pour l'amour de Dieu! I cannot abide another moment of this tortured self-denial. It is time for me to intervene. I look into Tim's eyes and try to convey to him that I'm overcome by the beauty of the moment, that I'm no longer able to control myself. I see he understands. I embrace him. I press myself against him. My lips seek his. He makes a half-hearted attempt to throw me off. You can imagine the scene. Of course, I am only fifteen and as ignorant as Violet about what to do next.

Alas, it transpires that someone is spying on us, another young lady in the choir. Afterwards, the rector accuses Violet of 'hounding the young man to distraction'. Tim is moved to another parish.

The little scandal precipitates Mama's first episode of nervous prostration. And Dr Rastrick makes his first appearance in the house, damn him!

Dr Serrurier: This is all most interesting. You can tell me more another time. But for now, Eloise, could we please return to the night with Mr Lilley? He has left your bedside. Now what?
A long pause.

'Where do you think you're going?' I ask.

'You're awake,' he says. 'I thought you were fast asleep. Please excuse me for taking such liberties. Your breath was laboured and I was concerned. I'll leave you in peace.'

'How disappointing. A man of your reputation!'

'I beg your pardon?'

'I thought you'd at least attempt to seduce me. Perhaps you don't want to.'

A pause, then: 'Have you forgotten you're engaged to be married? Try to get some sleep now.'

'Forget about my engagement. It's of no consequence. I want you to take advantage of me. I insist on it.'

'I'm afraid your engagement will seem of rather more importance in the morning.'

'You plied me with alcohol; you must have known this was a possibility.'

'Look, this has gone far enough. Let's draw a veil over it. Try to rest.'

'Such gallantry! I'm surprised at you. Can't you see I want to be expelled from the ranks of virtuous women? I want you to ruin me. I'll never forgive you if you don't.'

A pause.

'You'll never forgive me if I do.'

'Then what is there to lose?'

'No, and that's an end to it.'

I wait for a moment, then I break into copious weeping. I've learned this generally works with men. Soon he's at my side, stroking my hair.

'Please, don't distress yourself, you're a charming young woman and I've greatly enjoyed your company. If we were better acquainted . . .'

'Could you ever love me?' I look into his eyes.

'Yes, I believe I could.'

We kiss passionately. Vous pouvez deviner ce qui se passe ensuite.

28

As I read the transcript of the hypnotism, I shook my head with disbelief. What was this nonsense? A troubled young woman's reverie, no more. Private thoughts that should never have been overheard. I was angry and distraught. I raged incoherently at Dr Serrurier, sobbing, blaming him for putting such outrageous notions into my head. He sent me away with a note for the attendants. I was confined to my room, with an attendant looking in on me every twenty minutes to ensure I wasn't harming myself.

I paced up and down the narrow cell in circles, my mind seething. Dr Serrurier had clearly conjured the hallucination out of thin air. The voice of 'Eloise' was foreign to me, her knowing insinuating voice altogether unfamiliar. Nor did I have any recollection of the scandalous conduct she described. I was horrified at the notion that Eloise could take command of me and persuade me to do such abhorrent and shameful things, and I had absolutely no memory of the events described.

As for my supposed seduction of Mr Lilley, the idea was preposterous. To suggest I could entirely omit so appalling an occurrence from my memory! Those shocking words could never have come from my lips. Yet, as I thought back, I couldn't deny that after the visit to Mr Lilley's rooms, there was physical evidence of my undoing. I took no notice of it, wholly distracted by the row with Mama. And in any case, I knew little or nothing of my own biology.

And then I recalled Dr Rastrick's physical examination of me when I first arrived at the asylum, his hands prying and probing under a sheet that he had spread over my raised knees for the sake of propriety. I understood now that he would have established that I wasn't intact, and recorded that fact in the records. And Dr Serrurier would no doubt have had access to those notes. So, when he hypnotized me, he had already surmised what had happened. Knowing this official record of my undoing was circulating among these gentlemen shamed me, and angered me. Why was it acceptable that men like Mr Lilley, or Lance for that matter, could ruin young women and not be shunned by polite society, yet the women were cast out into darkness for the same transgression?

If I was to accept that the revelation about Mr Lilley might be true, then the same must apply to the other discoveries that arose under hypnosis, such as the alarming way I threw myself at the choir master. Yet I had always had an inkling that something unseemly had occurred on that occasion, because afterwards Tim had been sent away. Then there were the supposed compulsive forays into Brighton's sordid back streets. Impossible! I couldn't imagine anything less in character. And yet I had a vague recollection of going into the public house with Lottie.

What was I to make of Dr Serrurier? I feared I was no more than an idea to him, a case study to take advantage of to further his professional advancement. Yet in that moment I could think of nobody else in a position to help me. I remembered

Mrs Rastrick telling me that he and Dr Rastrick were at loggerheads. In my desperate situation, I began to wonder if Dr Serrurier's discovery might somehow turn their rivalry to my advantage?

As the hours passed my feelings gradually changed towards Eloise. She was shameless, there was no denying it, but she was also strong, fearless, audacious. She was prepared to say things I feared even to think. And in a perverse way, thanks to Eloise, I could absolve myself of responsibility for my own untoward thoughts and actions. It occurred to me that women were constantly playing different parts, depending on their audience. Lottie, for example, my fragrant friend. She collected admirers wherever she went with her charm, her open good-natured personality, her natural unaffected manner. But I knew another Lottie. Mercenary, proud, scheming and disloyal, yet for all her faults, much more diverting than the vapid creature her male admirers knew.

And who was I, Violet Hester Pring, when all was said and done? My memory could not be depended upon. And what exactly were memories? An exact representation of what had occurred? Certainly not. Memory didn't reveal the past, but some vestige of it, coloured by what happened later and what is happening in the present moment. Memory is at the service of our will. We hide from what it's inconvenient to remember – or unbearable to acknowledge. How else could we live with ourselves?

My thoughts turned to my last days of freedom, the days after that dreadful morning when I returned from Mr Lilley's rooms after spending the night there. Now I knew what had really taken place that night, I saw Mama's suspicions had been well founded. My last memory before waking up for the first time in the asylum, was of her fainting and falling to the floor. But every so often I had a fleeting glimpse, or perhaps a sudden sensory impression, of a party, our annual summer party I presumed. A misty vision of ladies sitting about in a group whispering behind their fans, their fine dresses spread about them. Echoes of excited voices, almost deafening. A smell of lime and then Felix approaching out of the throng, his hair and moustache oiled. Was it possible that Dr Serrurier could help me recover those lost days and hours before I was removed to Hillwood Grange?

Eventually, I wore myself out with these deliberations and fell asleep. I awoke the next morning with an ominous feeling about what the future might hold. It frightened me to know I couldn't trust my own memory. But then, Mama's entire project when raising me had been a training in not seeing what was dangerous or forbidden, in denying what could never be acknowledged.

That evening, Mrs Clinch and Nettleship were working their way through the ward, changing bed linen. My door was ajar and I heard them talking in the little corridor outside my room.

'So, who is this fellow of yours?' asked Mrs Clinch, under her breath.

'He's a Time Man serving out his sentence,' said Miss Nettleship. 'Went mad in Lewes prison, so they took him on here, helping out on the men's wards. We got to know each other at the New Year's Eve Observance.'

'But how do you ever see him, when he's on the male wards?'

'He's filched a key. I meet him in a cupboard off the main corridor.'

'Oh, lor! Think, what'll come of you if you're caught.'

'I don't give it any mind. Even if they send him back to the nick, he'll have served out his sentence in six months, and then we'll be together. I've had enough of working from four in the morning until sunset, day in, day out, and all for a pittance.'

'It's better than working the land though. I don't fancy being a straw trusser again, I can tell you.'

'Nor me. Churning and cheesing twice a week, milking the cows of a morning, feeding the pigs. Five men in the house and me having to boil the linen and make the beds, and my old dad an invalid so I had to empty his chamber pot twice a day, up and down those stairs. But I ain't sticking it in Hellwood, whatever happens. Makes my blood boil, getting looked down on by townies like Mrs Fuckwell. Blast the woman!'

'Oh mercy! Mind she don't hear you saying such things.'

'Let her hear. I'll be hitching off out of here soon enough. Time to call it a day.'

'What's he like, this fellow?'

'He ain't from the Denes like us. He's a foreigner from inland Sussex. Couldn't stick going back to his missus, he says. He's clever, got all sort of plans. He wants me to be the go-between to folk outside. Jack knows people in Brighton, you see. Businessmen, just like him. You've got to grab opportunity by the forelock, for he hasn't got a tail – that's what Jack says.'

'But you won't run off with a crazy gaol-bird, surely?'

'Mayhap, I will. He's only pretending to be mad, see.'

Afterwards, I thought about Miss Nettleship's secret arrangement and wondered if I might ever be able to make use of it.

*

The next day I was at work in the kitchen garden, planting daffodil and tulip bulbs for the following spring. It seemed an eternity away on that bleak October day. The last of the year's dry brown leaves flew around me in spirals. The wind moaned in the trees and rattled the panes of the glasshouse, a harrowing and empty sound. Something caught my eye and I looked up the slope that led to the lawns. A short dumpy figure in a bonnet and a dark coat was making her way down the slope, lifting her skirts so as not to lose her footing. It was my friend Ada Meggett. She was dressed for a journey. Of course – she was leaving for the convalescent home. As she drew nearer, I saw the velvet on her coat collar was worn and a button at the front was hanging by a thread. Her face was flushed and there was a look of panic about her. I wanted to go to her, but hesitated. Since the sordid revelations of the last hypnotism, I had felt myself an impostor. Ada was an honest and respectable woman, and I feared I was not the person she took me for. But any such qualms were forgotten when Ada threw her arms around me and hugged me tightly. We embraced for a long moment, both of us in tears, and it seemed Ada would never let me go.

'You mustn't miss your carriage,' I said, as I released myself from her grasp.

'I'm not going. I can't bear it.'

'I won't hear such talk. Go back now before the carriage leaves without you.'

'I can't keep it up no longer. Pretending I'm ready to go when I'm not. Why don't I just stay here and we can work in the garden together like before. I feel at home here.'

'I won't hear of it. You must go. As soon as you pass through the iron gate, you'll be free of this spell.'

'No, Violet, I'm staying put. My nerves are worn to shreds. I can't stand another minute of trying to pretend I'm right when I'm not.'

I looked over my shoulder. The attendants' backs were turned. I took Ada's arm and led her behind the glasshouse.

'Listen to me, Ada. You're getting on that coach. Everybody has to pretend. You have only to put on an act for the hour it takes to get to Burgess Hill. Once you get there, they'll look after you.'

'They'll see I'm not right and send me back. I saw the archangel Gabriel standing at the end of my bed last night.'

I took hold of her and shook her. 'Stop this now. You saw no such thing. You're frightened, that's all. As soon as you're out of this monstrous place, the voices will stop. We'll write to each other. As soon as I'm free I'll come to see you, I promise. Don't forget to put your address in the letter.'

'I can't go back to Helmont Street. Not after what happened.'

'The corporation will have rebuilt the house. You can make it new. And you'll have your three girls to help you. You want to see them again, don't you?'

'I'm no use to them. They're better off without me.'

'I'll be out of here before long, Ada. You just have to wait a little while and then we can go out on the town and have a gin sling together and sit and chatter to our hearts' content.'

'You won't want to know me when you're back with people of your own sort.'

'Nonsense. I'd be proud to be seen in your company. I've never had a better friend than you. You've helped me more than you'll ever imagine. Don't spoil everything now, when you're so close.'

'I haven't slept these last three nights,' she said, in a wheedling voice. 'My wicked no-good father pawned the silver spoon my grandmother gave me when I was christened, and he spent the lot in the pub—'

I slapped her face. 'Snap out of this, for God's sake!'

She stood there a moment, with her mouth open, touching her cheek with her gloved hand. Then she looked around her. Before I could stop her, she bent down and picked up a brick from the old ruined wall. She hurled it at the glasshouse and it shattered a large pane. I put my hand over my mouth in despair. Mrs Clinch and another attendant came rushing into view.

'What's happened here?' said Mrs Clinch.

'Why should Ada be allowed to go home when I'm kept here?' I cried. 'I won't stand for it.'

'Mrs Meggett, what are you doing here?' said Mrs Clinch. 'Run along now. You'll miss your carriage. Quickly, off you go. You've said your goodbyes.'

Ada was about to speak, but I gave her such a look she thought better of it. She turned and climbed up the slope. Mrs Clinch was eyeing me suspiciously.

'Well, this is a turn-up,' she said. 'I shall have to report you to Mrs Tuckwell. She won't be pleased.'

'Go ahead, report it.'

★

Dear Violet,

It seems an eternity since I last saw you. I've spent most of that time in Bolivia which is probably just as well because I had no appetite for skulking about in Brighton. Too many sad memories, and I didn't want to bump into anyone after what happened. My pride's taken a hell of a pasting. But it wouldn't be right to end things on such a sour note after all those years, so I thought I should put pen to paper.

I think it's fair to say I've returned from Bolivia a changed man. It gets a chap thinking, when he spends weeks watching an army of men blast and dig a tunnel two miles long through a mountainside. The sheer scale of it is overwhelming. We lost dozens of men to injury and disease. Labour's cheap here and so are men's lives. I'm glad I saw it at first hand — a man should know where his money has come from. But there were times when I wondered if what we were doing was worthwhile, given the scale of the destruction. Such musings aren't in my nature, as you know, so they must have been prompted by my general mood. My heart was broken, after all. And then I came down with jaundice, and for a few long weeks it was touch-and-go. Fever and diarrhoea took their toll and I'm literally half the man I used to be. I doubt you'd recognize me if we passed in the street. I shan't pretend that in my darkest hours I didn't think about you. On the positive side, my investments in the silver mines are paying off handsomely.

I can't deny being angry with you these last few months. And it wasn't easy to forgive you after you disgraced me in front of my parents and friends. But I take my share of the blame. I see now that I rather pushed you into the whole sorry mess. And I realize that you weren't the robust creature I took you for. Believe me, I would never have pursued you so relentlessly had I admitted to myself how fragile you were. Recently, I paid a visit to your home to ask after you, and your mother told me where you are. Thank heavens you're now being looked after. I'm sure you're in the best place, all things considered.

I've since had ample time to ponder the situation between us, and I see how pig-headed I was. You were right – we were never meant to be together. We're like chalk and cheese. So perhaps some good will come of this. When you get better, you'll be able to find a chap with whom you have more in common. He'll be a lucky man.

Yours,
Felix

P.S. Hope you've had leisure to paint some pictures.

I cried when I received Felix's letter. I was moved by the strength of his feeling for me, and saddened that he was saying goodbye after so many years. At the same time, I was appalled by his project in Bolivia, the deaths of so many men, and to what end? But the line that had the most potent impact on me was the reference to me disgracing him in front of his parents and friends. Here, at last, was a clue to what might have happened in the lost days before I arrived in the asylum.

Dear Felix,

Your letter touched me more than you can imagine. Your words reminded me of how good and loyal a friend you were over so many years. Memories of happier times flooded back to me.

Your adventures in Bolivia are a testament to your courage, determination and persistence. You've always had those qualities, and I should have appreciated them more than I did. How you must have suffered during your fever and how lightly you dismiss it. I'm glad you're now reaping the rewards.

I won't say too much about my treatment here. Whether it's the best place for me, I cannot say. I have made some friends among the patients, ladies with none of the advantages I've had, and it has opened my mind to other women's lives and problems. Perhaps my experience here is comparable to your adventure in its own way. I too am crossing new frontiers. But of course, unlike you, I didn't choose my fate.

Papa came to visit recently. He may have intimated to you something of my present circumstances. I wonder if I can ask you a favour? I will perfectly understand if you feel it is unfitting, but perhaps you would consider speaking to my mother again and urging her to visit me here. I miss Mama greatly. I fear there are misunderstandings between us and as long as they remain unresolved I'll never be happy.

Yours, with the greatest affection,
Violet

★

The day after receiving Felix's letter, I returned to the room where the hypnotism took place. Dr Binkes sat in the corner, his notebook in his lap, as before. The paints, crayons and brushes were set out on the table. Dr Serrurier sat in his usual place to the side of his desk. I was more wary of him than before, still painfully aware of what had been exposed to him in our previous encounter. His own demeanour was a little different than previously. He seemed nervy, alert.

'Tell me, how have you been since the last hypnotic trance?' he asked, his spectacles glinting.

I paused to collect my thoughts. I too was nervous. 'I cannot deny I was distraught to begin with,' I said. 'I suspected you had somehow tricked me into putting on that performance. But the more I thought about it, the more I was prepared to entertain the possibility Eloise might truly be a part of me. But how could that be?'

'We are at the frontiers of a new science of the mind,' said Dr Serrurier. 'In England nothing is known about the recent discoveries. I will explain as best I can.' He began to expound his theory. Most of it was barely comprehensible, but certain phrases lodged in my memory. 'The waking or normal personality has no memory of the hypnotized state. There is a lower level of consciousness which arises from sleep. It can give birth to doubles, or alternative selves, aberrations of memory. It can reveal dreams and secret desires that are not allowed to surface in the waking consciousness. Among the alienists in my circle, this is known as "doublement".'

I was reminded of sensational newspaper stories about multiple personalities and the crimes they committed when their bestial selves were given free rein.

When he was finished, I asked: 'Will you be able to recover my memory of whatever happened before I was incarcerated here, the events that led to my confinement?'

'That is precisely what I hope to discover,' he said.

'And if you succeed, might I be released from Hillwood Grange?'

'That is a decision only the superintendent can make. But I will certainly discuss your case with him.'

A few minutes later, I was at the drawing table again. It was difficult to lose myself in my work. I was frightened of what might come to light under hypnotism. I began many compositions, only to abandon them. It was more than an hour before I became absorbed. I was working on a picture of a clockwork automaton of the sort one sees in certain shop windows. Mine was female. I used grey crayons and white highlights for the glint on the metal, and put bolts in the joints of her moving parts. Over her heart, I drew a keyhole. Whoever found the key would be able to learn her secret, to operate her and make her dance to his tune. Or perhaps not? Perhaps he would only find another keyhole waiting for him. How was I to show this in the painting? I would paint different moments of time in different parts of the paper. The picture was for Dr Serrurier. A provocation. He was intent on finding the key to unlock the secret of my madness and discover who I really was, but he might need as many keys as Mrs Tuckwell carried on her belt.

The moment arrived when the brush was removed from my hand and I entered the trance.

★

Dr Serrurier: Look about you; listen, what do see, hear?
Colourful moving smears, impressions. A window. Grand ladies
in shot silk dresses of shimmering taupe or silver, being handed
down from carriages. Hats with ostrich feathers. Glossy horses in
handsome trappings. Smiling faces, a crush of guests in the hallway
proceeding towards the drawing room. Clamorous voices bouncing
off the walls. Sly gazes, nervous glances.

Dr Serrurier: How do you feel?
Painfully alert, every nerve thrilling. So many gazes are on me.

*Dr Serrurier: What is on your mind? What do you fear? What
do you wish for?*
To avoid Felix. That's why I've taken a post at the doorway into
the drawing room, so I can greet guests as they arrive. Smiling,
smiling, my jaws aching from smiling. Servants drifting in and
out with trays of iced sherbets, cakes and wafers. Brightly coloured
glass jars and fine china dishes. Too fragile. Something priceless
will get broken, surely. That vase, see, over there, is a souvenir
brought back from Venice after my parents' honeymoon. But it's
all fading now . . . It's becoming dark.

*Dr Serrurier: Please try to relax. Breathe deeply. Now, tell me
what sounds you can hear?*
Piano music. Singing. A syrupy rendition of 'Come into the
Garden, Maud'. Mama's voice. I see her now, over there. She

looks strained. Polite applause. A Chopin waltz. One-two-three, one-two-three. Chatter, laughter. Ladies sitting about in a group, like wallflowers at a ball, fine dresses spread about them. And there they are: Mr Skipp-Borlase and his preening desiccated wife. I know I should make conversation with them. But I can't, I simply can't.

Damn Mrs Skipp-Borlase! Look at her holding forth in that stilted way, always on her dignity. J'ai besoin de plus de champagne.

<u>Dr Serrurier: Eloise, c'est vous qui parlez?</u>
Peut-être. Pourquoi devrais-je vous le dire? I don't trust you, Frenchman. And don't interrupt. Mama told me to move among the guests. Nobody should feel left out, she said. So, that's what I'll jolly well do. Papa looms before me, standing with several men of about his age, a wary little smile on his lips. One or two of his ghastly chums nod at me.

A florid old fellow is in full flow: 'A blatant attempt by Gladstone to keep the Tories out of office till the end of days. The very idea that men in the lower orders without a scrap of education should be allowed to elect the government . . . '

'Beggars belief,' says another fellow, gruffly.

'What was that, old chap?' says another fool. He's at least a thousand years old. He turns his ear towards the speaker.

'We're talking about Gladstone's Bill, sir,' the florid one shouts.

'Ah, indeed,' says the ancient. 'Country's going to the dogs.'

A portly man catches my eye and smiles in an avuncular way. 'I do beg your pardon, ma'am. We've allowed ourselves to get rather carried away.' He rocks on his feet. 'And I don't believe I've offered my congratulations to you.'

The florid man is still opining. 'It will be women next, if we're not careful,' he says, glancing at me. 'Pardoning your good self, ma'am.'

My face is hot. I hear my voice, strident: 'Would you mind explaining your objections to extending the franchise to women?' I'm too loud. People are looking at me. Good, let them. Champagne slops out of my glass onto the floor.

'Is that a serious question? I'd have thought it was obvious,' says the fool.

'Not to me, I'm afraid. Perhaps you could enlighten me.'

Papa says, 'Violet, my dear—'

The florid man cuts him off. 'It's hardly a topic one can discuss with a lady. Let's just say it involves female biology and leave it at that.'

'Well, we wouldn't want to offend the gentlemen's delicate sensibilities, would we?' I say. More heads turn in my direction.

Mama appears at my side. 'Come along, gentlemen, no politics,' she says. 'Now, if you'll excuse us . . . ' She has my elbow. I'm being led away.

'What on earth are you doing?' she says. 'Have you entirely forgotten yourself?'

'Sorry, Mama, a momentary lapse.'

I slip away, sipping my champagne, spilling some down the front of my dress. I'm unsteady on my feet. A boisterous rendition of 'Three Little Maids' is under way. And there's Felix's voice booming over the general babble.

'Never fear,' he is saying, 'I'll be back down here on a regular basis, helping to organize rifle meetings for the boys and doing the odd bit of fundraising.'

A searing pain in my head, a wave of nausea. He's talking to *a young lady; she nods politely, a fixed smile on her face, her gaze wandering. Her eyes say: 'Help! Save me from this crashing bore.'*

There is no possibility of me spending my life with Felix. I see that very clearly. But here he comes.

'Caught you at last.' His moist lips on my forehead. 'We've hardly talked.' His hair and moustache are oiled and he smells of lime. He gazes into my eyes, his eyelids lowered in a louche way. 'I'm looking forward to the day when I shall have you to myself.'

'Felix! I'm not happy. Not happy at all.'

That puts him off his stride. 'Chin up, my dear. We're on the final furlong now.'

I understand what I must do. I must stop this madness. I must break off the engagement, quickly. Before Felix and Papa make their speeches. But it's too late.

'Look, let's get the public announcements over and done with so we can both relax,' says Felix. The instant the music stops, he taps his glass with a silver spoon. The talk subsides. The room becomes ominously silent.

'Ladies and gentlemen, thank you for your attention,' says Felix. 'I'm overjoyed to see so many friends, old and new, here tonight. I'd like to thank our hosts, Mr and Mrs Pring, for organizing such a wonderful party.' Applause. 'Now, I hope you all have a champagne glass to hand—'

'Stop! Stop it, Felix.' I hear my own voice echo around the room. It sounds strange. The party guests exclaim, express their shock. 'I can't let this go any further,' I say. Deathly silence now. 'I appreciate it is awfully . . . unforgivably inappropriate, especially when . . . '

Felix grips my elbow firmly. He murmurs: 'Darling, you've

overdone it.' He turns to the guests and raises his voice: 'All this excitement is enough to try anyone's nerves,' he says, with a false laugh. 'Now, will you please raise your gla—'

'No, let me finish,' I say, breaking away from him. 'I'm letting everyone down, I know. I should have spoken up long before now. I did try. But, oh Lord . . . I can't go through with it. I simply can't.'

Mama steps forward, grips my arm. 'I assure you things aren't as they seem,' she says to the guests, that fixed smile still on her face. 'Now, darling, let Felix finish the toast.'

'No, Mama — stop it!' I say, jostling her. 'Let go of me.'

Papa approaches. 'That's enough, Violet.' His face is puce, his jowls shaking. 'My dear friends, I sincerely apologize on behalf of my daughter. Forgive her — she is suffering from an acute nervous illness. The excitement of the big occasion has overwhelmed her. I think it best if we take her to her room . . . And I offer my most sincere apologies to Felix and to Mr and Mrs Skipp-Borlase. Come with me, Violet.'

I try to wrest myself free of Papa's grasp and bump into a table. There is a crash and the sound of breaking glass. Shattered blue shards are scattered around my feet. Mama's honeymoon vase. I push through the guests to reach the door, tripping on the hems of dresses.

Out on the street, in the darkness, I realize just how inebriated I am. I wander blindly. For how long I don't know. But then I find myself hobbling about on the beach near the West Pier, a shoe in one hand. The heel has snapped off. A cold breeze races in off the sea. I must sit down. So weary. The shingle is hard and lumpy under me. I clutch my knees to my chest, shaking uncontrollably. Far out I see the water and wonder how cold it is, how it would feel to be engulfed by it, to choke and feel one's lungs fill with water.

Now the bloated red sun sinks into the horizon, dissolving into red streaks in the water, as a pink blush bleeds slowly over the heavens, turning stray pale clouds into burning coals. It grows darker and the sky becomes violet, the sea too. It's a very low tide, and where the shingle ends there is a vast glassy plain where the sand is exposed. People walk up and down, dogs too, their elongated silhouettes mirrored beneath them. A coal brig is anchored some way out, sitting on the horizon. All is transfigured. The world is proving itself to be more beautiful than I've ever known it. It is miraculous, proof that everyday life is an illusion. My elation is almost unendurable, the rush of sensations overpowering, the hairs on my arms tingling with the cold breeze rushing off the water. I know I must live and live fully from this moment on. Nature has revealed herself to me so I will have the courage to paint, to capture her essence and make others look, really look, at the world as it is. I will paint with all my senses. I am filled with immense courage and faith and an intense love of life, love of the world and everyone in it, for my brothers, for Papa.

And Mama. I must tell her. I must show her the truth. If she loves me, she will listen. I see with utter clarity that I must hurry back home and explain it all to her, now, quickly, while the miraculous vision is still fresh in my mind.

On my return, I step into the house and find it still and silent and reproachful. A strong odour of alcohol and stale perfume assails me. In the hall mirror a woman stops to stare at me, unkempt and dark-haired with a wild stare, her eye-black running over her cheeks. I walk into the drawing room to find a dreamlike scene where everybody has been spirited away. Champagne glasses have been left everywhere, on the mantelpiece, the floor, the top of the piano, some half-full, others empty, others turned on their sides or smashed into pieces. Pieces of wafer and smears of cake are trodden into the rug.

And there is Mama. Erect and perfectly still on the settee, her gaze vacant, her eyes glittering. She is grey and lined in the dappled light of the chandelier. I perch myself on the armrest of a chair, clutching myself tightly, looking down at my laddered stocking, my big toe poking through the silk, the black grime under my toenail. My shoe is still in my hand.

'Mama, I want you to listen to me. I know the situation seems irredeemable at the moment. I see how dreadfully upset you are, but I demand that you hear me out. You see, the truth is that everything is going to be all right. I promise you. It's all for the best in the long run. I know it's hard to believe now, but in time you'll see I was right to do as I did. I've just had the most remarkable experience. I went to the beach and there was a sunset so beautiful, so wondrous, it was as if God had shown his face to the world, and I saw our lives as they could be rather than as they are. And as I sat there, I suddenly saw everything clearly. It's impossible to describe.'

Mama's expression is still rigid, her gaze fixed on the floor a few feet before her. But I won't be thrown by her stony silence. 'We must peel away all pretence and fear, peel it away. I was never meant to marry Felix. What I'm trying to say is, what happened earlier . . . I'm sorry that I hurt you, that I've embarrassed you and Papa. But I should have put my foot down long ago. I know you have only ever wanted what was best for me, at least according to your own beliefs and principles. But I would never have been happy with Felix. I don't need wealth and status. I want to make art and I don't see why I shouldn't, simply because I'm considered to be the wrong sex. I would rather be a poor artist living on thin air than to spend my life in regret—'

Mama breaks in, her tone venomous: 'Felix would have let you paint, you stupid girl. You talk as if that pastime was a suitable vocation for an adult woman.' She is shaking with anger, still refusing to direct her gaze at me.

'But I'd rather marry a penniless man out of love than to marry Felix. I tried to explain this to Felix, but he's impossible. And with all the money that was tied up in it, I felt compromised. I never meant to hurt you, believe me. I know it seems catastrophic to you, but I'll write to apologize to Felix, and explain why it was necessary. Of course, he'll be angry at first, but if he really loves me then he will come to accept the life he offered wasn't suited to me.'

Finally, she raises her gaze and looks me in the eye. 'That's enough of your raving. Not another word. Look at you. This is worse than I could ever have imagined.' Her voice is hoarse. 'Now, you will be quiet and listen. How dare you come home drunk and in this rapturous state of delusion after what you did tonight, and then tell me that everything is going to be all right. How dare you! Felix and his family left shortly after your appalling display. You will never be married now. Do you know what that means? You'll die a lonely old spinster. And I'll never be able to show my face among my friends. What have I done to deserve such a daughter? You're nothing but a faithless egoist who's never thought of anyone but herself.'

She rises stiffly to her feet and walks out of the room. I pursue her as she stomps up the stairs, hauling myself up by the banister rail. When she reaches the top, she turns, and wheels around and we face each other.

'Stop it,' I cry. 'You won't run away this time. This is your fault as much as mine.'

'How on earth is it my fault?'

'You don't love me. You never have.'

'I've made every sacrifice to prevent you ruining your life. What more could I have done?'

Papa staggers out of his room and onto the landing, grey and haggard. 'That's enough, for God's sake,' he says. 'Go to your room, Violet, before the constabulary appears on our doorstep. These dramatics won't help matters.'

Mama looks at him coldly. 'It's too late for you to put your foot down.'

'Mama, it needn't be like this. Please . . . ' I plead.

'You're not right. You never were,' she says, giving me a hateful look. 'You're not my daughter; I don't know who you are.'

'Stop this, immediately, both of you!' shouts Papa.

'The marriage was for you, not for me,' I yell at Mama. 'To save the family's standing, to rescue you from penury.'

There is a tearful cry from my youngest brother, Archie: 'What's happening, Mama? Why are you all shouting?'

'Look what you're doing to this family,' Mama says, venomously.

'Let's stop this, Mama, please.' I try to embrace her. She pushes me away, but I grasp her arms tightly. We are teetering at the top of the staircase. I'm shaking her vigorously, or she's shaking me, I cannot tell which. We stumble back and forth. She tries to wrest herself from me, but I won't let go of her.

'What does any of this matter now?' she says. 'It's over. I disown you.'

Papa appears and takes my arm, attempting to pull me away, but I cling on and Mama and I lurch back and forth. A red mist descends. The same I'd known as a child in moments of rage. I'm shaking Mama, oblivious to everything else in the world, shaking her violently. Then I let go. With horror, I see her falter, then lose her footing and fall backwards down the stairs, her limbs entangled in her skirts, her arms flailing, until at last she lies, perfectly still and silent, at the bottom of the staircase.

29

My dearest Mama,

I have discovered the reason I'm here, and it is almost more than I can bear. Believe me when I say that until two days ago I had no memory of what happened that night after the summer party. If I had, I would have written to you long before now. I had no intention of hurting you, not even in that wild state, and what happened was an accident that came about in the confusion of the moment.

These last two days have been the worst of my life. Once I knew what had passed between us, I became delirious, nauseous, clammy and breathless for several hours. I was incapable of reflection. Crushing fatigue followed – I slept for a day and a night, tormented by hideous nightmares. It is only today, weak and clammy, that I've gained the strength to write to you. It has been desperately hard to find words to express how I feel. I've made several attempts at this letter only to discard them.

I expect Dr Rastrick has kept the truth from me because he feared I would collapse under the strain of knowing. Perhaps he was right. Just imagine how I feel now I know I was responsible for the injuries that have kept you wheelchair-bound all this time.

It appals me that while we've been apart I have brooded angrily on the injustice of my confinement, and yet I have given little thought to how you must have been suffering. I even blamed you for my confinement here.

Through hypnotism, I've learned that I'm not the person I thought I was. A light has been shone into the darkest corners of my memory. Perhaps the demands placed on me throughout my life, the constant chafing against my natural inclinations, made me hide from myself any deed that violated the world's presumptions about me.

Oh Mama, I imagine you at home in the bath chair and I'm filled with sorrow. I should have felt compassion for you before, out of the natural sympathy of a child for her mother. Does this make me a monster? The problem was I doubted your love for me. I believed you had put the family's good name before my happiness, and that your desire to keep up appearances trumped all my hopes. Felix has written to me recently. His letter moved me. I realized I do have feelings for him, but those of a sister for a brother. If I'd married him, it would not have gone well. I know you did everything with my interest in mind, but my marriage to Felix was never to be.

Before now, my sole wish has been to escape this place, and of course I still hope to leave here, given time. But it's now more important for me to win your trust again. I may not be able to marry well, but I believe I can give you other reasons to be proud of me. Miss Fanshaw, my art teacher, was kind enough to visit me here and she suggested I might take up a job when I leave and earn an independent income. One day I might even do some good in the world.

Please consider coming to visit me. I know how arduous the

journey will be, given your condition. But with Papa's help, it's not so very far, an hour or two at most. You might make part of the journey by train to Haywards Heath. I would love to see your face again. I know things cannot ever be quite as they were, and that we will never have the future you had hoped for, but there might be compensations. I could be a help to the boys, once they have children of their own, a strict governess. How are my brothers? None of them have written to me. Am I such a pariah that I don't deserve so much as a letter? I am alone here, separated from those I love and who love me. I have a terrible fear that I might never see you again.

With all my love,
Violet

After my letter was sent, I spent every moment anticipating its response. I was crushed when each morning arrived and no missive came from Mama. Then on the third day, I received her reply. As I tore open the envelope, my heart filled with hope.

My dear Violet,

I'm pleased you finally found it in your heart to write to me. It must have been a terrible shock for you to have learned what happened the night of the summer party. Needless to say, there will be no summer parties in future. You mustn't blame yourself too much for what happened. You ask me to forgive you, but really there's no need. I know you weren't yourself at the time. But I'll never forget the look in your eyes. I'll carry the memory to my grave. I may not have always been the mother you wished for, but did I really deserve that?

Felix, that dear boy, came to visit me for a second time — despite having every reason to shun the Pring family. I hardly recognized him. He's a shadow of his former self, but I suppose he'll recover in time. He said you'd exchanged letters. Despite what happened at the summer party, he came to petition me on your behalf, asking me to visit you, just as you did in your letter.

My dear, it is simply not possible for me to visit you, or for you to return home. We cannot accommodate you here, not even for a short time. The entire house has been reorganized, at some expense. I'm very much house-bound. I am restricted to the ground floor and I have to be helped down the steps onto the streets. Reaching the seafront is an expedition, and I have to be wheeled up the hill afterwards by a grudging maid. So, you see, a trip to Hillwood Grange is out of the question. I receive few visitors at home. After the party, many of the better sort dropped me, and paying visits myself is not an option.

Believe me when I say that I always did what I believed was right with regards to yourself. I did all in my power to prevent you becoming an old maid. You were always feather-brained, with your head in the clouds, even as a child. I tried to instil in you the feminine virtues.

You often complained about me not sending you to the girls' day school, but I had very good reasons. When your uncle Jonathan fell into a dissolute existence, squandering his estate on fast company and gambling, our own fortunes went into decline. This was the reason we were forced to leave the big house in Hurstpierpoint and move to insalubrious Brighton. It was why your father's financial expectations were not realized when Uncle

Jonathan passed away. And why Lance was the only one of the boys who was able to go to Eton College. Now can you better understand my dedication to ensuring you married well, and my determination to ensure the defects of your character were concealed until you reached the altar? I scraped together the funds for your art classes, your theatre tickets and the membership fees of select sport clubs. It was all so that you would gain an entrée to high society. And we scrimped and saved to pay Dr Rastrick's fees, so that your mania could be kept at bay. It is hardly surprising I developed neurasthenia.

As you grew up, I lived in fear of you showing those tendencies again. Every time you had one of your vibrant spells, I feared it would boil over into something worse, something irrevocable. So you can imagine my horror when I saw those disturbing pictures of yours. Art should be morally uplifting and improve our taste and judgement. It should civilize us, not return us to the primeval swamp. Art has a social mission. If we're to sleep safely in our beds at night, we must show a good example to those less fortunate souls huddled in insanitary slums under railway bridges. But you know my views on these matters.

I saw in Felix a young man capable of managing the excesses of your nature, but after your affair with that louche artist this was never to be. To think my own daughter was ruined, only weeks before she was to be married. Everything I'd tried to achieve, all the sacrifices I'd made for you, come to naught. You were always too fragile to survive among that sort, too sensitive, too idealistic, too foolish. Perhaps this is what ultimately turned your mind. My greatest fear had always been that my father's illness would be passed down to one of my children, so it was devastating to have it confirmed by a man of Dr Rastrick's *reputation. I have put my trust in him and I depend upon his discretion.*

You enquired about your brothers in your letter. Lance grows more dissolute by the day. It breaks my heart to see it. The younger boys, thank heavens, are applying themselves to their studies. Your father has been forced to part with most of his precious books to pay for my treatment and for yours — and I won't deny I'm glad to see the back of those volumes that poisoned your mind to common sense and virtue.

Well, my dear child, you are out of my hands now. It is not for me to say if it's safe for you to leave the hospital; it is Dr Rastrick's decision. When that might be, I cannot tell. I should inform you that against my wishes your father made enquiries about the possibility of your removal to another hospital, but I'm afraid his influence has waned in recent years.

Do not think I've withdrawn my love for you. I pray for you every night and ask that you will make a recovery in time and that you will one day resume your life outside that institution. It's quite sensible for you to lower your expectations of life in the way you suggest. Perhaps, before too long, we can have tea together.

Sincerely,
Your loving Mama

My hands shook as I read Mama's letter. Her tone shocked me. She claimed she had forgiven me when it was clear in all she said that she hadn't. She refused to countenance the very idea I might ever return to the house. In her letter, she had saved her cruellest remark for the final line, proposing that we might one day have tea together, as if I was no more to her than that dreadful gossip Mrs Runniforde.

I wept, and finally came to accept what I had always denied to myself: that my mother had never been able to bring herself to love me, even when I was a child. Reading between the lines of her letter, I sensed her abiding anger, her disappointment, her distaste and disapproval, and the satisfaction she now felt, knowing I was paying the price for letting her down so dreadfully.

But what light did her words shine on my madness: the great holes in my memory, the eruptions of violence, the transgressive thoughts and deeds, the *doublement* where another self, Eloise, took possession of me? Surely, my mind must have been turned by a catastrophic event or series of events? But I searched my past in vain to find a cause. I was never locked in a cupboard, or in a Red Room for that matter, or punished for one of my brothers' deeds. My favourite doll was never taken from me, there was no fairy-tale ogre, no weeping on the hearth like Cinderella, no cruel beatings with a rod, no chilly boarding school where I was bullied by mistresses and classmates alike and fed watery gruel.

The only explanation for my derangement was the persistent war of nerves between Mama and myself. For days on end, sometimes weeks, she refused to see me, she withdrew her love. She reminded me constantly that her love must be earned. She let it be known I was the cause of her unhappiness, her neurasthenia, and even the family's ill fortune. But I could redeem myself. All she asked of me was that I make a good marriage.

★

After receiving Mama's letter, I was oppressed by a heaviness of spirit. I gazed out at the world as if through gauze. This was not an ideal mood for an encounter with Dr Rastrick, but as luck would have it, he chose that moment to make one of his rare appearances in the ward. Instead of passing me by, as was his usual habit, he came directly over to where I was sitting, alone by the window.

'Miss Pring,' he said, 'I think you should know Dr Serrurier has returned to France.'

'Returned to France? Surely not. Did he not speak to you before he went?'

'It was necessary for him to part without delay. I'm afraid I was misled about his intentions here. I let him use hypnotism on the understanding it was to correct physical problems, to redirect dormant impulses in the nervous system. My expectations were based on Dr Charcot's work on hysteria in Paris, where hypnotism has proved effective.'

'But wait! Dr Serrurier's hypnotism *was* effective. He found that I have another identity, one I hadn't been aware of before. He told me he'd made an important discovery, and suggested it would be worth seeking another medical opinion on his findings. Didn't he mention any of this to you?'

'Yes, he said something along those lines, but look here, I'm familiar with these dissociation theories. It's all metaphysical bunkum fit for sensational novels, not for serious medicine. When Dr Serrurier requested that he visit this hospital, he omitted to mention that he had turned coats and joined the new psychological school in Nancy. He was a Trojan Horse here. But I'm confident he's done no permanent harm.'

'His hypnotism helped me remember things – incidents I had completely forgotten . . .'

'The tricks of a spiritualist medium, not a neurologist. His methods are akin to primitive exorcism, witchcraft. They revealed nothing he hadn't already read in your case notes.'

'But under hypnotism I recovered my memories. And I was allowed to draw and paint while Dr Serrurier was here. Will I be permitted to continue now he has gone? I'm certain it helped my nerves.' Even as I spoke, I heard the nervous strain in my voice.

'That wouldn't be advisable, I'm afraid. However, be assured your paintings are of interest. Indeed, they may well serve some useful therapeutic purpose. Now, if you'll excuse me.'

Later that day, Mrs Tuckwell informed me that I would be put back on the sedatives I had been on before Dr Serrurier's arrival.

*

The next morning, I was queuing with the other women outside the dining hall at breakfast time. Miss Nettleship came rushing up the stairs, flushed with excitement. She rushed over to Mrs Clinch. They were just close enough for me to catch the gist of what they were saying.

'A patient has turned her toes up!' she whispered, breathlessly. 'I saw her on the trolley; they pushed her right past me. Lying there flat as a herring, she was. They were taking the body down to His Lordship's lab when I passed them. Post-mortem next, I suppose.'

Mrs Clinch wrinkled her nose in distaste. 'Never wastes much time, does he? Who was it though?'

'It was that Miss Pugh.'

'Miss Pugh? Well, that doesn't altogether surprise me.'

So Edna May Pugh had finally succeeded in starving herself to death. My efforts to make her eat her meals had failed. My attempts to talk her out of her romantic infatuation with a gentleman who had long forgotten her had made no impression. How many patients had died since I arrived in the secure ward? Three? Four? The crazed Eliza Feldwicke had thrown herself down the stairwell within the last month. And not long before that, Peggy Paynter had taken her own life. How could I ignore the circumstance that all three women were numbered among Dr Rastrick's 'darlings'? But I had been closer to Edna May. It affected me more profoundly. And what was this about taking the body down to His Lordship's lab?

★

I am running down a dimly lit corridor. I arrive at doubled doors over which there is a sign: NEUROANATOMICAL LABORATORY. I hammer on the doors until they are opened. I see a wasted corpse lying on a raised table under a sheet. It is Edna May. There is a neat incision around her forehead. Her brain is displayed on another table, sliced into neatly labelled segments. Near the table I see a bone saw with bloody teeth and a claw hammer. Dr Rastrick is standing in a blood-stained apron before a large weighing scales. On one scale lies Edna May's heart. I hear a familiar voice.

★

'Wake up, wake up, Miss Pring!' I opened my eyes and saw Mrs Clinch, the attendant, looking down at me, her face flushed.

I was damp with perspiration in spite of the cold nip in the air. My heart was palpitating and I shook violently.

'You must have been having a nightmare, the way you were carrying on,' said Mrs Clinch. She had moved to the table by the door and stood with her back to me.

I had been dreaming, but the dream seemed all too real. I remembered, the evening before, seeing Mrs Clinch put her keys down for a moment. I recalled thinking of snatching them and . . . But I could remember no more. My mind was clouded by the sedation.

Mrs Clinch came to the bedside. I felt a cold flannel on my brow. 'Here, this'll soothe you,' she said. 'Oh, you were in a bad way yesterday. But you needn't fret. Nothing's going to happen to you, Dr Rastrick's made sure of that. He's issued a caution ticket to stop you coming to harm. It means you'll be on constant watch. An attendant will always be on hand to help you dress and undress. Your clothes will be put away overnight, so you don't come to any harm. The night watch will look in on you every fifteen minutes. You'll be searched morning and night in case you've got something on your person you could harm yourself with. So, you see, even if you can't take care of yourself, you'll be well looked after by us.'

Mrs Clinch began gathering my day clothes, presumably to prevent me trying to strangle myself with them. Outside the room I heard two voices: those of Mrs Tuckwell and Dr Rastrick.

'Continue with the nightly doses of paraldehyde,' said Dr Rastrick. 'And I'm prescribing quinine daily until further notice to reinvigorate her shattered nerves and mercurous chloride to purge her nervous system.'

'She's delirious at present,' said Mrs Tuckwell. 'Should we consider delaying the quinine until she's more herself?'

'That won't be necessary. Start the dose this morning.'

30

About that time, a large bill poster had been pinned to a notice board in the ward:

HILLWOOD GRANGE LUNATIC ASYLUM,
ANNUAL FANCY DRESS BALL, ALL
SOULS' DAY, FRIDAY 2ND NOVEMBER

As a reward for this year's outstanding report from the Commissioners in Lunacy, all patients were invited to the ball. Volunteers were called for to help with preparations. The Visitors' Committee, Poor Law officers and various other representatives of the great and the good would be in attendance. Guests would enjoy a supper of roast beef and beer. Following the success of the one-act farce at the New Year's Eve Observance, there would be another short humorous play directed by the chaplain, followed by a dance. All proceeds would go towards the upkeep of the hospital. In small print at the bottom, it was advised that all patients were invited, excepting epileptics, imbeciles, those currently in the infirmary and those with dementia or severe infirmity. There was a picture of the revellers at a mad masque. These wore costumes from history, fairy tales, nursery rhymes and so on. Male patients leaped about, doing high kicks or turning circles with their elbows linked. At the bottom it advised that carriages would arrive at 9 o'clock to take guests home.

★

Nettleship came to my cell one evening. Her hair was dripping, the shoulders of her dress soaked, the blue ribbon in her cap undone and dangling. Her countenance was even sourer than usual.

'Mucky weather out there,' she said. 'Enough to choke a Spaniard. Get yourself changed, so I can get on.' She fell heavily onto the chair by the desk and began undoing the laces of one of her boots. She touched the sole of her foot and winced. 'These rotten corns! Been rushed off my feet all day. I'd sling my hook if I could. Paid a pittance we are, us attendants, and yet we do all the work. First on duty and last to eat. Expected to come in every day fresh as a daisy. I trained for my certificate but where does that get you? Make one mistake and you get bawled out by Mrs Tuckwell – who has her favourites, by the way, so no chance of advancement for the likes of me. Running out of patience, I am. Been bit, kicked, spat at, had more than one chamber pot thrown over my head in my time. Puts a tidy old strain on the nerves, that does. Then you're expected to be the eyes and ears of the doctors, when all they do is swan around like emperors, scribbling in their case books and fiddle-farting with their stethoscopes to no end I can see. Dr Rastrick gave me some ointment for my corns. For all the use it was, I might as well have found a bramble that's growing into the ground at both ends and crawled under it – a sovereign remedy for corns that is.'

309

I threw my day dress on the bed and slipped my nightdress over my head. I was drowsy with the sedative I'd been dosed with a few minutes earlier. But I had been waiting for a moment alone with Miss Nettleship. I hadn't forgotten the conversation I'd overheard between her and Mrs Clinch a few weeks back when I was in the bath.

'How I put up with it, I'll never know,' Miss Nettleship was saying. 'No choice, I suppose. I'm not going back to the slop-shop to work eighteen hours a day making ball dresses for the likes of you, my lady. Never a penny left of my pay. I'll set up a boarding house in Brighton. That's my dream.'

Miss Nettleship stopped moaning while she put her boot back on and tugged on the laces. In the silence I remembered what I'd heard her say that time. About a convict, a man who feigned madness to get himself sent to Hellwood. Nettleship had a name for him. A 'Time Man', wasn't it? I took a deep breath.

'Aren't you planning to run away with your Time Man?' I asked, before I could stop myself.

For a long moment, my words hung in the air. Miss Nettleship sat there, bent over her foot. Finally, she sat upright and looked at me. 'What was that you said, just then?'

'One time you were chatting outside my room, and I heard you telling Mrs Clinch about your man. You needn't worry, I shan't say anything about it.'

'You'd better not, miss, or you'll regret it.'

'It's just that I was looking for someone who might be kind enough to post a letter for me.'

Miss Nettleship glared at me, her mouth agape and her lower lip jutting. 'Blow me down,' she muttered. 'Not quite as addled as you look, are you?'

'I only ask a small favour. You can trust me absolutely.'

'You crafty devil. Now, let me get this straight: if I won't post your letter, then you'll snitch on me – is that it?'

'Nothing of the sort! Although I might need you to send more than one letter.'

'You can go sling your hook. I've a mind to report you for this.'

'I have the means to pay. Would a half sovereign be sufficient?'

Miss Nettleship's gaze shot to the little desk, then to the floorboards and under the bed. Then she got to her feet and went to the door. She paused, holding the handle. Without turning to look at me, she said: 'You better learn something about people hereabouts. You may push and you may shove us, but we're damned if we'll be drove.'

★

Dear Mr Lilley,

I wonder if you remember me? I paid you a visit with your friend Miss Fanshaw over the summer and you were kind enough to look at some pictures I'd made, and to give me some encouragement to continue in my artistic ambitions. Indeed, we even talked about the possibility of my becoming a professional artist. On a second occasion, I arrived at your house uninvited, and you let me in. There was a ferocious storm and you allowed me to stay in your rooms overnight. I will never forget our passionate <u>discourse</u> that night, how we defied convention and propriety. I have no regrets about what happened.

Since then, I've suffered a change of fortune. You may recall that I was engaged to be married to a gentleman and that I was unhappy about the arrangement. I complained of being forced into a marriage of convenience, when I have always wanted to marry someone of my own choice. Suffice it to say, the engagement was broken after an incident at a party in my parents' house. I have a shocking disclosure to make, and feel reluctant to do so, but how will you understand my situation otherwise? The fact is I have been confined to a lunatic asylum. I am at present buried in the depths of the Sussex countryside in an institution which you may have heard of, Hillwood Grange. It would be perfectly forgivable if you chose to discard this letter now, on the assumption you are being pursued by a woman who is out of her wits. That is not the case, I assure you. There has simply been an unfortunate misunderstanding. Which I will tell you all about, if you wish to hear.

Since I've been here, I've suffered privations too numerous to recount, but there is one which will surely arouse your sympathy: the doctor I mentioned above has refused to allow me to draw or paint. Perhaps you can think of a way he could be persuaded to lift this prohibition.

You'll be wondering what I hope to achieve through this appeal to you — especially when we are barely acquainted. I write because, in the few hours we spent together, I felt a deep connection with you which I have never felt with another, and I hope you might have felt a little of the same. Being able to paint again would make me feel closer to you.

I apologize if this letter is unwelcome or unbefitting. But if you feel inclined to respond, I would love to be brought up to date with your affairs. Or even to begin a correspondence, albeit a secret one.

*In case it's at all relevant, I must add that I have been permit-
ted very few visitors, and only <u>those sanctioned by my parents</u>.*

Yours sincerely,
Violet Pring

★

I had a nervous time of it over the next day or so. I knew Miss
Nettleship was untrustworthy. And she wasn't stupid. She was
perfectly capable of calculating that if she refused to send the
letter and I informed on her regarding her clandestine meetings with the Time Man, then the two of them could simply
deny there was any truth in it. The Time Man was an adept
confidence trickster, and Miss Nettleship a born liar. It was their
word against the ravings of a mad woman. I had to rely on Miss
Nettleship being greedy enough to want to keep the money,
knowing that there was more to be had later.

Violet!

*Of course, I remember you. Your letter is neither unwelcome nor
unbefitting. How could I forget those few short hours we had
together? To hell with convention and propriety. I often think
of those remarkable pictures of yours. I'm astounded to learn of
your ordeal.*
*After hearing nothing from you after your visit on that day,
I wondered what had happened to you. I was concerned I might
have got you into difficulties by permitting you to stay overnight,
and then sending you home by cab in the morning in some disarray*

– especially given your circumstances. Afterwards, I called on Gwen – Miss Fanshaw, that is – on several occasions, meaning to ask her if you were well, but she wasn't home. I even went to Gwen's Wednesday afternoon class hoping to see you there, only to find it was cancelled until further notice.

Gwen had been nursing her sick mother, as it turned out, and when we finally met, she told me your wedding had been called off and that you had been sent away. I was troubled by this disclosure, and concerned lest my influence might have played some part in ending your engagement, and causing the breakdown of relations within your family. I was anxious to find out where you were. But short of hiring a private detective, what was I to do?

And now I have discovered your circumstances, I fear I may have said careless things that day that made you feel dissatisfied with your life, without any concern for the possible consequences. If so, I'm anxious to make amends. It distresses me that a person with a talent so profound, and at the same time so fragile, as yours should be banished to such a place. And this doctor has no right to forbid you to paint.

As for myself, I have been hard at work, but it's mostly employment of an artisan nature to keep the wolf from the door. I won't bore you with the details. And I will say nothing of my career, as there is little worth relating. Ho-hum. It was ever thus for we artists.

I often think of your courageous visit to me that day. You made a profound impression on me. You gave me hope, at a time when I was overwhelmed and despairing. I beg you not to give up hope for yourself.

I want to get this letter to you quickly, so forgive me if it seems rushed and careless. If there is anything, anything at all, I can do

to help, then let me know immediately. I infer from your letter
that an official visit is not a possibility. Let me think. There may
be a way around that.

And, yes, I too felt the connection you spoke of in your letter.

Yours, with the greatest respect and affection,
Wilf Lilley

★

I think it was a Sunday morning in mid-October, shortly
after I had received Mr Lilley's letter. My awareness of time
had become vague, with each day like every other. I was among
the patients filing towards the chapel for the Sunday Divine
Service, a line of wretches huddled against eternal drizzle. I was
one of the 'watched' ladies towards the rear, so the attendant
kept close by me. We marched in silence to the rhythm of
tramping boots on the gravel path. Rooks issued their stark calls
in the surrounding mist. We proceeded into the chapel, closely
shepherded by the attendants. I took my place in the rear benches
where the women were obliged to sit, out of sight of the men so
we wouldn't inspire lewd thoughts. There was the usual musty
chill, and scents of incense mingled with polished wood and
cut flowers in the chancel, and another odour I couldn't quite
place. Then I saw the watery golden and green light trickling
down from the high arched stained-glass windows. The dreary
sound of a creaking harmonium seeped out from somewhere
near the altar. Rain drummed on the roof.

At the altar, the chaplain stood in his vestments, his back
turned as he arranged the instruments of his office. There were

perhaps forty worshippers. The chaplain turned and intoned: 'Blessed be God the Father, God the Son and God the Holy Spirit.' His voice droned through the order of service. I mumbled the responses, taking my cue from my neighbours, and tried not to fall asleep. My only prayer was that the moment should arrive soon when I would be permitted to sit down and take the weight off my feet. On the men's benches, a man cried out, 'Behold, Jesus Christ Our Saviour!' His arms stretched out before him, and he swayed in religious ecstasy as if the Good Lord stood right in front of him. I saw from his features he was of the type Dr Rastrick referred to as congenital idiots. The chaplain continued regardless, intoning the words of the service in a flat drone. At my side, a woman took a dead field mouse out of her pocket and held it in her hand, stroking it.

I became aware of that scent again, the one I'd noticed when I first entered. It was sharp, penetrating and definitely familiar. It seemed to be coming from the male benches in front of me. I raised my gaze, and looked at the backs of the men. At that moment, a man several feet away turned his head and looked about him. He had raven-black hair and a full beard and wore a dark coat. I recognized his fine profile. Of course, the smell I'd noticed was Mr Lilley's distinctive French cologne. I had to support myself on the bench. His hair was a little more flecked with grey than I remembered, but it was most certainly him. After taking several deep breaths, I looked up from my prayer book once more. Mr Lilley was facing the altar, looking up at Christ on the cross. I closed my eyes and sent my thoughts through the cold air: *Turn, turn your head and look at me.* As the congregation sang the first verse of 'Father, hear the prayer we offer', Mr Lilley glanced over his shoulder and our gazes met.

He nodded almost imperceptibly, before turning away and lowering his gaze. The voices of the worshippers were raised in song. I loved the hymn they were singing, more now than ever, even when sung by a choir of wavering, faltering voices. I added my voice to the chorus and sang with heartfelt sincerity.

> Be our strength in hours of weakness,
> In our wanderings be our guide;
> Through endeavour, failure, danger,
> Father, be thou at our side.

Later that day, Miss Nettleship passed on a second letter, addressed to her in Mr Lilley's hand.

Dear Violet,

I must apologize for my unexpected appearance in the chapel – it must have given you quite a turn. I have a great deal to tell you. After our correspondence, I was determined to do whatever I could to see you. My first scheme was to write to Rastrick, offering my services as a portrait painter at a very good rate, informing him of my early successes. Like all the best salesmen, I warned him to take up the offer quickly as I had already agreed to take on a number of commissions and my diary was rapidly filling up. The idea was that once I got into Rastrick's house, I'd be able to discover the workings of the asylum, and hopefully gain entrance to it and somehow meet with you, perhaps even spirit you away. Far-fetched, perhaps, but thousands of people disappear every year and take up new identities elsewhere, in new cities or even overseas.

Rastrick didn't take the bait. However, in his reply he asked if I could recommend a good copper-plate engraver. It so happens that much of my income has come from engraving in recent years. I wrote back to offer my services, and as a result I am currently lodged at the Jolly Poacher Inn in the village just outside Hillwood Grange. I will be here for a month. The alehouse serves decent beer, there's no shortage of contraband brandy and the landlady cooks a hearty breakfast. Rastrick sends a dog cart from the asylum to collect me every morning. My first discovery is that every cart that comes and goes is given a thorough sniff by a fearful-looking mastiff at the gatehouse.

I will be in the hospital every day until November working on engravings of what Rastrick calls 'female patients of special scientific interest'. He wanted me to work solely from some ghastly photographs he's taken, but I persuaded him to also allow me to draw the patients from life. I argued that drawing would allow me to modify the portraits to better portray the symptoms he wished to bring to prominence, before reproducing them in copper plate.

I must tell you what I've gleaned about Rastrick. On the day of my arrival, I spent the night in his house in the grounds of the asylum. The place, incidentally, is woefully furnished and hung with appalling pictures in the worst taste. I had the dubious honour of having dinner with him and his wife. Rastrick has a decent wine cellar, by the way. After dinner, I had to endure a game of whist, Rastrick and I playing against his wife and the maid. We lost, as my attention was elsewhere. I was watching Rastrick carefully. He is distant from his wife, and seems to treat her like a private secretary. I observed the demeanour of Mrs Rastrick and her maid and — as one familiar with the Sapphic tendency — I drew my own conclusions.

After the ladies had retired, Rastrick and I sat up drink-ing for an hour. He brought out a very good bottle of whisky, half-full, and between us we polished it off. I believe I got the measure of him that evening. I asked him more about the purpose of the engravings. He banged on at length about taxonomy and diagnostics. He seemed happy to have a chance to sound off. I understood him reasonably well, despite his attempts to bamboozle me with scientific language. His intention is to make an example of the women, to turn his poor benighted patients into symbols or general types, representatives of different forms of moral malaise, like characters in a genre painting.

I asked him to tell me more about the individual women in his research group. I suggested it might help me to capture their particular types of morbidity. He rambled on about the group as a whole, then he singled out one individual who he found particularly confounding. He got rather excitable and red in the face and couldn't rein himself in, as if he'd been waiting for an opportunity to unburden himself. He'd been sipping steadily at the Scotch and was pretty tight by this stage. The patient in question was dark and well proportioned, with a compelling gaze. An alienist had to be on his guard against her sort. I pressed him on this, and he said he believed this mysterious personage was manipulative, volatile, dangerous. He confided his concern that he might be detaining her more on account of his fascination with her case than for her own good. For this reason, he had scrupulously kept his contact with her to a minimum.

Afterwards, he blithered on in more general terms, some hogwash about how insanity was a bodily disease, rather than a psychological one. This contempt for psychology possibly explains his blindness to his own hidden desires. I'm convinced he desires you, Violet, even if he won't acknowledge it to himself. He knows he can never possess you and he's punishing you for it. Rastrick is a mind doctor who doesn't know his own mind. He conflates moral philosophy with natural science. He sees his role as fixing his patients, like a railway engineer repairing engines so they can be put back onto the right tracks. And he doesn't want his mission to end at the asylum gates. He wants to weed out all the degenerate breeding stock in England and build a super race of perfect people. In other words, people like himself. God forbid he should ever succeed.

The longer he reflected, the more pessimistic he became, or 'melancholic', to use his terminology. I surmised that he has no true friendships, only professional relationships. His preoccupation with women's moral insanity, as he calls it, struck me as obsessive, a symptom of what he'd probably call 'monomania'. I'm convinced there is something unsavoury about the man. He seemed to have little sympathy for his female patients, other than pitying condescension.

My dealings with Rastrick have given me a new sense of determination. I'm not sure where we go from here, but I will do everything in my power to ensure that you and I meet again soon, even if in less than ideal circumstances.

Do not ever give up hope.

Yours,
Wilf

31

So, Mr Lilley had answered my summons. From that moment, every evening, as soon as I was left alone in my room, I put my fingers down my throat and brought up the foul sedatives I'd been dosed with. My mind had to be alert. Fearfully so. I slept little and lost all appetite for food.

Just two days after Mr Lilley's appearance in the chapel, I was told that my portrait was to be drawn. This was surely what Mr Lilley had referred to in his letter. I was almost beside myself with anticipation. I busied myself doing what little I could to repair the ravages the months at Hillwood had made to my appearance. Two more of my dresses had been sent after Papa's visit, and I put one of them on. It hung rather loosely on my diminished frame. But then I was told Dr Rastrick had stipulated patients must wear the official striped uniform for the portraits so I had to change. I washed my hair and appraised my appearance in a mirror provided by an attendant. My skin was sallow, my face gaunt. My hands were pink and blotchy, reminding me of the large red hands of the mermaid in Mr Lilley's picture, posed for by Fanny Kerrich, his laundry girl, lately deceased.

At the allotted time, Mrs Clinch brought me to the room. She took a seat near the door and we waited in silence. After a short time, I heard brisk masculine footsteps, and smelled that distinctive cologne, and a moment later Mr Lilley was there, actually there before me, removing his coat in one fluid movement and hanging it on a hook on the door, with that feline, almost feminine, grace I'd noticed in him before. I dared not look him in the face. Mr Lilley, on the other hand, made a consummate show of indifference to my presence as he busied himself arranging his things and positioning his chair. And then I heard that deep and sonorous voice once more.

'Let me see now,' he said, looking at a paper form he was holding. 'Miss Pring, is that correct?' He placed a chair a few feet from his own. 'Please, sit here. Now, try to be at your ease. Direct your gaze over there into the corner, if you wouldn't mind. It will all be quite painless and over before you know it.'

He sat, and rummaged in a leather case. Then, he put a pad of paper in his lap and began to study my face, changing the angle of his head as he scrutinized me closely. He held his pencil out before him, erect, to measure perspective. Then he crossed his legs and began.

For some time, we sat, in silence, apart from the scratching of Mr Lilley's pencils on the paper. Every so often, he asked me to change my posture and the angle of my gaze, to look up or down or left or right. It was strange to sit there passively, as he constantly alternated between peering at my features and trying to capture them on paper. There was an intense energy in his movements. What were his feelings as he drew? Was it all simply a perfunctory mechanical operation, his mind accurately rendering the angles and hollows and textures of my face? Or were his aesthetic faculties aroused? I snatched glances at him. Those same fine features, his hazel eyes, his face more careworn and lined, with some broken blood vessels on his magnificent long nose. He had the heavy unruly beard of a satyr. I was aroused, by the heat in the room, by Mr Lilley's constant gaze roaming over every part of me. I began to imagine how it might have been that night we lay together and felt faint. I had to fight to steady my breath.

Perhaps he noticed. 'Are you comfortable?' he asked, without any particular emphasis.

'Yes, thank you.'

'Good.'

'May I ask what Dr Rastrick intends to do with this picture?'

'They'll be used for a book he's planning to train doctors in accurate diagnosis.'

'But why doesn't he use his photographs for the book?'

'Photographs don't reproduce well. My sketches will be made into engravings which better suit the purpose. Apart from that, I can make certain changes, as instructed by Dr Rastrick, to give emphasis or add details. Yesterday, for example, I drew a patient with religious monomania and he asked me to portray her with her palms pressed together in prayer.'

After this brief exchange, Mr Lilley continued to draw in silence for several minutes. Mrs Clinch yawned and slumped in her chair. She had her usual high colour and mawkish expression. I noticed her eyelids drooping, but whenever she was about to doze off, she managed to jolt herself awake.

Mr Lilley murmured something: '*Nous devons nous débarasser de cette femme.*' He kept his gaze on his drawing, shaking his head as if he was talking to himself.

His deep voice and the caressing music of the French language threw me, confused my thoughts. I knew he was covertly addressing me, but what was his meaning? I repeated Mr Lilley's words slowly in my mind, my lips miming them. *Débarasser?* I couldn't recall the verb from the French grammar I'd been studying. I caught his eye and tried to convey to him that I didn't understand. He rolled his eyes in the direction of Mrs Clinch, and I saw what he was suggesting.

'*Oui, mais comment?*' I said, softly.

'*Je suggère, peut-être . . . Vous pourriez faire semblant d'avoir une crise?*'

'What's that you're saying, there?' said Clinch. 'What talk is that?'

'*C'est Français,*' he said. 'French, *madame.* I spent some time in Paris, and sometimes I forget I ever left.'

'Well, I'll thank you to keep to the Queen's English today, if you don't mind.'

'*Bien sûr.* Understood.'

I racked my brains. *Une crise?* A crisis? Then it came to me what he wanted me to do.

Mr Lilley interrupted my thoughts: 'Please continue to direct your gaze into that corner, if you wouldn't mind, Miss . . . ?'

'Miss Pring,' I said, complying with his instructions.

Several more minutes passed. I caught Mr Lilley's eye, and he nodded. I knew I must act. My nerves were so fraught, my body so pent up with tension, that the sudden onset of breathlessness that overwhelmed me was quite genuine. I really did choke with each frantic gasp, the room really did reel about me. I got to my feet unsteadily, put my hand on my chest and felt my heart jitter frantically under my palm. I felt myself close to swooning, and dropped to my knees, taking deep breaths.

Mr Lilley cried, 'Don't just stand there, woman – fetch a doctor, for God's sake. Your patient's having a seizure.'

Mrs Clinch looked this way and that for a moment in a quandary, then dashed out of the room. Mr Lilley crouched down beside me, and put his hand on my shoulder. I was on hands and knees, my breath laboured, my body trembling violently.

'We've little time,' he whispered. 'Can we depend on this Nettleship woman?'

I could hardly speak for breathlessness. 'For now. But I'm at risk here.'

'Are you sure? How?'

'From *him*.'

'From whom? Not from Rastrick, surely? Heaven help us. He hasn't . . . Has his conduct been unbecoming?'

'Not as such, but . . . It's too involved to explain now.'

He glanced towards the open doorway, then got down on his knees so that we faced each other. He stroked my hair, my face. 'What's to become of you, my living breathing Ophelia?'

'Will you save me?' I asked.

'Difficult. I'm not a free agent here. Could we persuade your friend Nettleship to help us?'

'I'm not sure. She's fraternizing with a male patient. She meets him secretly. A convict. We could threaten to inform Dr Rastrick.'

'A convict? What on earth?'

'He pretended to be mad to get out of prison.'

'I see. He might be useful. Do you know his name?'

'Jack, I think.'

'Damn it. There'll be a hundred Jacks.'

'Hold me tighter!'

He frowned, and glanced towards the doorway, but he

embraced me tightly. We kissed and our hands roamed over one another.

'Now, quickly!' I said. I lay on my back and lifted my skirts. I hardly knew myself in that moment.

'This is utter madness,' he said. But I pulled him down on top of me and he offered no resistance. I felt his warm weight, his hunger as we kissed. We grappled wildly, breathlessly, and the night we spent together in his bed returned vividly, through my skin, my senses, my nerves, my memory. I became Eloise. But this time, on that hard floor, our mutual fear and desire was raised to such a pitch it was all over in a few wild thrusts. I was unable to suppress a long sob of pleasure at the final shuddering stroke.

That very moment, advancing steps sounded out in the corridor. I covered my limbs and rolled onto my side and Mr Lilley quickly made himself decent, just before Mrs Clinch hurried into the room, with Dr Binkes behind her, looking bewildered.

'Thank the Lord you're here!' said Mr Lilley, rising to his feet and dusting off his trousers with his hands. 'As you can see, this lady needs your urgent attention. I'm afraid I was of no use at all.'

As he spoke, I writhed on the floor moaning, my passion still unspent.

'Never mind, leave her with me,' said Dr Binkes.

Mr Lilley picked up his things.

'You had enough time, did you?' Mrs Clinch asked him.

'Just about,' said Mr Lilley, as he left the room.

I was changed in those few snatched moments of bliss. I'd tasted something and now I would always yearn for more. Was I mad to dream of escape and freedom with Mr Lilley?

32

That afternoon, staff and patients gathered in the Great Hall to prepare for the All Souls' Day fancy dress ball, the night when dead saints would walk the earth. The cavernous hall bustled with noise, colour and industry, resembling a church bazaar or a medieval castle. Tables were set out in rows and covered with different coloured odds and ends of fabric and old frocks, hats, paste jewellery, cheap hairclips, charitable donations from the well-to-do of the parish. The attendants sat alongside their charges wielding scissors, and those patients who could be entrusted with a needle and thread were stitching costumes. On the perimeter of the room, the sturdiest of the attendants stood guard. I was in a corner with the other women from the secure ward, cordoned off by a rope. Miss Nettleship was rummaging through a pile of clothing on a table. She pulled out a black garment and carried it over to me, folded over her arm. She held the garment up for me to see.

'This will do,' she said.

It was a moth-eaten black taffeta ball gown with lace trimming on the collar and cuffs. She showed me a black veil. 'Just the thing, isn't it? Now, slip your dress off so we can see how it fits.'

'Not here, over there – behind the counter,' I said, crossing my arms over my chest defensively.

'Oh, we are a modest thing, aren't we?'

When we were behind the counter, where we couldn't be seen or overheard, I unbuttoned my dress, and said: 'I want to see Mr Lilley alone.'

'So that's your game, is it? Well, there'll be no more help from me. I'd never have sent those letters if I'd known that man would ever show his face here. I've taken no end of risks as it is, so let's hear no more of this nonsense.'

I took off my dress and put it on the counter, then she slipped the black gown over my head.

'There's a lot of slack in the bodice and the skirt's too short,' she said. 'Wait now.'

While she went to fetch a sewing box, I racked my brains. I still had two half sovereigns hidden behind the wainscot behind my bed. The others I'd used to bribe Nettleship to send the letters back and forth between Mr Lilley and myself. She returned, and pulled the bodice tight around my ribcage, gathering the spare material in her stubby little fingers. 'It needs taking in. I'll put the pins in first. I tell you what we'll do with all this extra cloth. We'll make ruffles with it and sew them to the bottom of the skirt so it's long enough. We'll put a square of stiff paper under the veil to raise it over your head and then you'll be perfect. A Spanish maiden. With black cloth, it's always that or a nun. To top it off, I'll give you some card and you can make a paper fan.'

'Listen! I'll pay you if you help me to meet with Mr Lilley. *Ouch!*' A pin had pierced my flesh.

'I told you I won't. Now, that's enough out of you. And keep still, we want your costume tight around the bodice.'

When she'd finished pinning, she took up a needle and did some stitching, working quickly. When she was done, she removed the pins and I took off the dress.

'I'll take it over and get them to finish it off,' she said. 'You can go back and sit with the others.'

'I'll give you another half sovereign,' I said.

'Will you never stop? I'll search your room when I get the chance and find out where you've hidden those coins and take them off you.'

'I wouldn't do that if I were you. Not unless you want me to tell Mrs Tuckwell about you and Jack.'

'Why, you sly devil! After all I've done for you.'

With that, she turned, and walked away with the black dress on her arm.

After some thought, I hatched a plan for my escape. On the night of the fancy dress ball, with all that noise and everybody's back turned and the corridors and wards deserted, Mr Lilley and I would slip away in the darkness and confusion. Miss Nettleship would leave the door unlocked that led out into the stable block. Mr Lilley and I would climb into a carriage and drive out through the great iron gate which would be wide open on that night.

I said nothing of this to Miss Nettleship. I was waiting until after she had cleared the way for my next encounter with Mr Lilley. I saw what I had to do in the meantime; I must follow Jack the Time Man's example. He had got out of prison by pretending to be mad. Now, I must appear too feeble-minded to arouse any suspicion. It helped that I'd been cooped up with lunatics all those months, and had plenty of time to observe genuine madwomen at close quarters. And at any rate, my grip on the everyday world was loosening. What would 'Eloise' have done in such circumstances? She would have thrown herself into the part. So I wandered through my days like a somnambulant. When I worked in the garden, I spoke to nobody. I muttered to myself, or sang old snatches of nursery rhyme. I kept my mind empty, as thick as the white mist that draped itself like cotton wool over the morning fields. I put blooms in my buttonholes, and flower chains in my hair, as if I'd become the ghost of poor dead Edna May. I trudged about, picking apples by the cartload, and pushed the wheelbarrow back and forth to the winter store until I grew callouses on my thumbs and my knee joints were as creaky as the barrow's wheels. If I saw the other women looking at me, or overheard remarks, I affected not to notice. Each day, darkness fell a little sooner than the day before.

I couldn't risk carrying a candle in case it was seen, so I waited for Mr Lilley in pitch darkness amidst the brooms, mops and buckets. There was barely room to move. Outside I heard footsteps, somebody treading softly, and a moment later I smelt Mr Lilley's cologne and made room for him in the darkness. There was a loud clatter as something fell from a shelf and we held our breath for a long moment. In the silence I heard the rapid thump of my heart. When a minute or two had passed, I felt Mr Lilley's arms encircle me.

'Wait,' I said. 'We've haven't long. Will you help me escape from here?'

'Yes, of course I shall,' he said, kissing me. I turned away, took hold of his wrists and forced him from me.

'Listen! There's a ball here in just over a week. Everyone will be in disguise. We can get away then. The attendant I bribed to be our go-between will help us, and the patient I told you about on the male wards. I'll see to it. A door will be left unlocked – but if I walk out of here on my own, I'm sure to be noticed. I need you to be with me.'

'But if you run away, they'll come looking for you.'

This wasn't what I'd hoped for. I thought he'd willingly elope with me. But all he wanted was to grope me in the dark. My mind raced. I was frantic.

'I won't survive the winter in this place,' I said. 'I couldn't bear it. And Dr Rastrick – you don't know what he's capable of.'

'Don't you think you're letting your imagination run away with you?'

'Three women have died in as many months – all in his research group.'

He took hold of my arms. 'You're shaking. Here, take a drop of this.' He handed me a flask and I smelled strong liquor. I took a good swig from it. It warmed me, and soothed my nerves a little. I handed it back to Mr Lilley and heard him glugging. He stroked my hair.

'There must be another way to get you out of here.'

'There isn't, believe me. You're wondering why you should risk everything for someone you hardly know. Yet when I first heard you speak, you said we should put ourselves in the service of higher forces. We mustn't become, what was it you called it – "fanners of the soul's sleep". Such fine and noble sentiments.'

'*Fanners of the soul's sleep* . . . I'm afraid those weren't even my own words; they were Ruskin's. And I was talking about art, not life, which is an entirely different proposition. It was all flannel, in any case. Designed to provoke, to make an impression on my audience.'

'I see. Then you're not the man I took you for,' I cried. 'This is only another adventure for you. You like the idea of me being insane. Ophelia, you called me, that time. You'd better leave. I need to get back before I'm caught.'

He took me in his arms, kissing me and holding me tightly. When he withdrew, he was breathless. 'I'll help you,' he said, his voice thick. 'We'll elope to France. I still have a few old confederates in Paris. We can sail from Newhaven. Now, tell me about this idea of yours. But quickly.'

So, Mr Lilley would come to my rescue. Freedom was tantalizingly close. So why did a slight doubt mar my hopes? Hadn't he hesitated for a moment? I dismissed such misgivings as my own trepidation about the dangers ahead.

33

I encountered Miss Nettleship the very next day and reminded her that I was fully prepared to betray her to Dr Rastrick if she refused to do my bidding. She had every reason to wish to see the back of me, knowing that as long as I was in Hellwood I could give her away at any moment. To seal the bargain, I gave her my last half sovereign.

Later that day, I was working in the garden, clearing the spent potato crops with the rake and making a pile for composting. My mind could find no rest. I dared not think about the fearful trials ahead of me; even less imagine a future in Paris with Mr Lilley. It was a delirious dream.

I heard voices and turned to see two women approaching me, Mrs Clinch and another attendant, a big strapping girl. They were advancing with some intent.

'You're to come with us, miss,' said Mrs Clinch. She wouldn't look me in the eye.

'Is there something wrong?'

'Just come along now,'

The younger woman took a firm hold of my arm.

'Let go, will you? I'm coming,' I cried, but she only tightened her grip.

The women working the plots turned and watched as I was marched away. I wasn't taken to the ward, but led along the path that was usually barred to patients, the one that led to the front of the building. We reached the entrance, under the imposing row of sturdy fluted columns, the paint faded and flaking. Then we climbed the steps up to the portico and entered the building. Once inside, they took me into the administrative offices where, to my knowledge, patients were never admitted under ordinary circumstances. I was taken into a long window-less room with a narrow table in the centre, the varnish very scratched and ink-stained. There was a tin jug on the table, with a beaker. Both sides of the room were lined to ceiling height with shelves packed with row upon row of brown envelopes filed in rows.

'You're to wait here. You may sit down,' said Mrs Clinch. She went to the door, pausing before leaving. 'Oh, Miss Pring!' she said, with a shake of her head.

The other attendant remained in the room, standing sentry at the door. I tried to steady my breathing. I felt trapped in the poky windowless room. I got to my feet, meaning to pace about to calm my nerves, but she ordered me to sit down again. It was an eternity before Mrs Tuckwell returned and took a seat opposite me. The attendant stood behind her, blocking the route to the door. Her beefy arms were folded and her heavy features set in a scowl.

Mrs Tuckwell took an item from her apron pocket and set it down on the desk: the half sovereign I'd given to Miss Nettleship. My thoughts were thrown into disarray.

'Can you explain this?' said Mrs Tuckwell. 'Take your time. This must be quite a shock.'

My mind raced. What else had they discovered?

'My father gave me the coin when he came to visit. So I could buy things for myself.'

'You know the rules. Why didn't you inform a member of staff? All money is kept in our safe. Orders for purchases must be signed off. How much money did your father give to you?'

Should I lie or tell the truth? I decided on the latter. 'Five half sovereigns.'

'Have you ever given away any of this money?'

I stared down at the table, in panic. It was a trap, I was sure.

'This is important, Miss Pring.' She poured some water into the beaker. 'Perhaps your throat is dry. Have a drink.'

I took a sip.

'So, let's try again. Have you ever given any of the money away?'

'Yes, I have.'

'To whom?'

'I don't wish to say.'

'Did you give the money willingly, or were you coerced in any way?'

'I gave it willingly. What will happen to me now?'

'Miss Pring, our chief concern is to stop you coming to any further harm. We need to establish the reason why such a large amount of money changed hands. This is a very serious breach of the rules and action is required. Will you please inform us who it was you gave the money to?'

'Perhaps you already know?'

'We need to hear it from your lips.'

I took a deep breath. 'It was Miss Nettleship.'

'Did Miss Nettleship threaten you in any way, or try to take the money from you forcibly?'

I shook my head.

'In that case, what possessed you to give the money to her? What could you possibly want that would cost so much?'

I was panicking and couldn't think.

'Well?'

'Cosmetics. I wanted cosmetics.'

The two women exchanged a look. The attendant's scowl shaded into a smirk.

'We needed to be sure of the circumstances before deciding what action to take,' said Mrs Tuckwell. 'Dr Rastrick will want to speak to you later today. You can wait here in the meantime. Miss Gravett will look after you.'

Then another interminable wait. I sat there, patient files surrounding me on either side, hundreds and hundreds of official histories, souls trapped in Dr Rastrick's web. Across the table, Miss Gravett slumped in her chair, sucking her teeth, arms folded, her legs stretched out before her. My mind was frantic, disordered. How to proceed with Dr Rastrick? It was obvious I'd lied about the cosmetics, but had Nettleship mentioned the bribes? The letters I exchanged with Mr Lilley? Would she have told them about my plan for the All Souls' Day Ball? She would have said anything to save herself, readily admitted she had exchanged the letters and facilitated my encounter with Mr Lilley if it helped her cause. My only hope was that she'd said nothing, out of fear she'd get herself into even deeper water. But perhaps they had discovered she had a fancy man on the male wards. Then she'd have nothing to lose. Out of desperation, or mere spite, she might have told them everything.

I was in a state of nervous exhaustion by the time I was led from that room and into Dr Rastrick's office. He didn't look up as I entered, but sat behind a large desk with his head down, signing some documents. I sat in a straight-backed wooden chair and waited. The walls were lined with books, back issues of medical journals by the shelf-load, medical treatises in tan leather, the titles embossed with gold on the spines. There was a leather armchair to one side, under the shelves, lit by a standard lamp with a fringed lampshade. The diffuse light illuminated a manuscript that lay on the chair. The title was in large enough type to be legible from where I sat: 'The Role of the Lunatic Asylum in the Recording and Classification of Data for the Expansion of the Nosology and Aetiology of Insanity, by Dr Harold A. Rastrick, Physician Superintendent, Hillwood Grange Lunatic Asylum'. The paragraphs underneath the title were covered in spidery revisions made with a fountain pen, with many lines crossed through. I turned my gaze to the desk. A brass table lamp illuminated a chessboard with ornately carved ivory chess pieces on it. The chessmen were positioned as if a game had been abandoned inconclusively, perhaps in stalemate.

At last, Dr Rastrick looked up from his paperwork and frowned as he focused his attention on me.

'Let me appraise you of our discoveries, Miss Pring. In recent weeks, my head attendant Mr Pockock's suspicions were aroused concerning a patient on the male wards. He put him under surveillance, alerting Mrs Tuckwell at the same time. It transpired that this fellow, a convict as it so happens, had been liaising with a female member of our staff, Miss Nettleship. When Mrs Tuckwell confronted Miss Nettleship earlier today, a substantial amount of money was found on her person. She has been suspended from her duties, pending further enquiries. She named you as the person who gave her the money. I've written to your parents to explain the situation.'

He paused, gazing sternly at me, his hands on the table before him, fingers interlinked. His entire performance was an attempt to unnerve me, to wear me down, I was sure.

He took a deep breath. 'I have another concern in relation to Miss Nettleship's misconduct, a very grave concern. You recently encountered Mr Lilley, the draughtsman who has been doing some illustrations for me. Were you by any chance acquainted with this man before you were confined here?'

For, a second, my consciousness flickered as if it would sputter out, but somehow I kept my grip. 'Why do you ask me such a thing?'

'Because Miss Nettleship says you offered her money to exchange letters between yourself and this man. She claims that you threatened to inform on her unless she arranged a backstairs encounter with him, and that a meeting took place the night before last in a broom cupboard. Is this true?'

I could neither think nor meet his gaze.

After an interval, he said: 'This is a serious matter. If this man took advantage of you, then I should involve the police.'

'Nobody took advantage of me.'

'I see.' He sighed. 'Whatever the case, Mr Lilley was relieved of his duties with immediate effect this afternoon, and escorted from the premises. I would never have allowed him to set foot in Hillwood had I the least suspicion he was an unprincipled adventurer. Only a man of base character would exploit a vulnerable woman like yourself.'

'He's not base. He has other ideals than the ones you hold to.'

'Has he, indeed? I assume these were the ideals that led him to lure you to his rooms when you were engaged to be married to another man?'

'I went to his rooms willingly,' I cried. 'I'd go again, given the chance. You could never understand a man like Mr Lilley, nor a woman like me. You know nothing of the imaginative life of the artist.'

He sneered at this. 'I understand that art is a dangerous stimulant for somebody like you. I saw the pictures you produced for Dr Serrurier. The obsessive repetition, the conundrums, the breakdown of any coherent meaning, the symbols that make no sense to anyone other than yourself, the lack of form, scale or balance. You have over-taxed your intellect and this is the result. Your pictures are fit for nothing but to show the workings of a diseased mind, and that's what I intend to use them for.'

'If you're so confident in your opinion, then why did you send Dr Serrurier away? Was it because he took another view, because you feared he might challenge your diagnosis?'

'I sent Dr Serrurier away because he misled me. As for his fanciful theory, this vogue for split personalities and other nonsense, where does it leave us in practical terms? Would you expect me to release you into society on the assumption that the saner of your two personalities had taken control of your will? Suppose another psychotic personality were to regain control once you were discharged? These theories would be dangerous, were they not so risible. At any rate, I suspect Dr Serrurier planted these supposed personalities in your mind through suggestion.'

'At least Dr Serrurier sees that character and experience matter. He believes memories and feelings are important. But to you we are no more than messy defective bodies that need regulating like machinery. What is this desire to correct and control women? What is the reason for all this endless gazing at us? What gratification do you derive from it?'

'That's quite enough.'

'Tell me, in all truth, what do you really know about women? You barely speak to your wife. She occupies one half of your house and you the other. Your own life is at best a half-truth, is it not?'

'I said enough!'

'No, I won't let you tell me who I am. You shore up your idea of yourself with your endless lists of symptoms and hierarchies, putting us all in ranking order with yourself at the top. It's all you care about. You've lost all fellow feeling, if you ever had any. You have no compassion for the women here. Edna May . . . When she needed help . . . ' Thinking of Edna May, I was suddenly overwhelmed. When my tears subsided, I sat slumped, trembling, staring absently across the room.

When Dr Rastrick spoke, it was slowly and deliberately, with a quaver in his voice. 'I utterly refute the charge that I would allow any of my patients to come to harm. Any alienist worth his salt who had witnessed the last ten minutes would recognize this as an exemplary case study on how moral causes wreak physical changes in women's bodies. Your mother first requested that I take you on as a patient some years ago, and I have kept detailed notes on your pathology ever since. Your childhood episodes of derangement might have been dismissed as momentary losses of control, but what has subsequently emerged is a consistent pattern of recurring psychosis, sexual lability and other wilful transgressive behaviour. For your safety and that of others, I have no choice but to confine you to this asylum, most likely until the end of your days.'

34

The night of the All Souls' Day Ball had arrived. Lurid spectres loomed out of the darkness: a mandarin with drooping moustaches, a marquis with a powdered wig, an old fool in an army uniform carrying a pince-nez, a Zouave hand in hand with Miss Muffet, who had a woollen spider dangling over her head on a wire covered with a stocking. I peered through the veil of my black mantilla, through a laudanum fog, hot and stifled in my deceased old lady's clinging dress. High overhead, flags dangled from poles, the Union Flag and what I supposed were the flags of the nations of the empire. I was surrounded by women. The men were on the other side of the hall, across a wide aisle. Only officials and guests of honour were permitted to gather in mixed company. They stood about in evening dress, enjoying the spectacle. What did it matter what such people thought? Papa would have dismissed them as vulgar county types. Staff lurked amidst the patients, keeping a watchful eye.

There were intermittent bursts of laughter. Something was happening on a stage that blazed with light in the surrounding darkness. Under the proscenium arch, the chaplain capered about in a blue riding coat and fancy waistcoat. He kept turning to deliver asides to the audience, speaking in a forced artificial voice. The head attendant Mr Pockock was his sidekick, Captain Tempest. He stuttered and faltered and had to be prompted from the wings. The audience played along, uttering choruses of droll groans. A woman in a white dress with a crimson sash was trying to force her daughter into a bad marriage. And all for money. The daughter had already secretly wed another man against Mama's wishes. At last, the stale old farce came to an end. The cast took their bows to tumultuous applause.

There was general chitter-chatter as the stage was cleared. The invited worthies formed impenetrable circles. Footsteps scuffed across the parquet, the hems of dresses swept by in a swell of disembodied voices, peculiar frequencies. Insinuating whispers reached my ears from all around the room, gossip and backbiting. I recalled holding Papa's hand in the whispering gallery in St Paul's cathedral. Feeling faint, I went to lean against the wall.

An announcement: 'Ladies and gentlemen, please choose your partners for the first waltz which will be led by King Henry VIII and his wife – or at least she's his wife for the time being . . . ' More droll laughter at this! 'Queen Anne Boleyn.' Henry VIII stepped out, hand in hand with his Queen. It was Dr Rastrick and his wife. He was wearing a hat with a large feather, a fur-trimmed coat, doublet and white hose with garters, a costume that showed his well-turned calves to good advantage. The orchestra of timpani, violin, cello, French horn, clarinet and piano launched into 'Greensleeves', played in waltz tempo, the tuning suspect. Several other couples took to the floor and soon it was filled.

A voice behind me. 'May I have this dance, *señorita*?' That unmistakable deep, velvety baritone. I turned and saw Ali Baba or perhaps Sinbad, a man with brown greasepaint on his face and a heavy beard, a cutlass at his side. It was *him*, his wild hair covered by a red silk turban, his eyes glinting. He wore wide billowing blue silk trousers, tied at the waist with a broad gold sash, pointed harem shoes on his feet. 'If you skulk about like this, you'll only attract attention to yourself,' he said, drawing me to where the waltzing couples were circling. We danced. He danced well, sinuous and light on his feet. We brushed past a Highlander and Little Bo Peep, a Roman empress and a court jester, the bells jangling on his hat. We swerved perilously close to Dr Rastrick and his wife. Mrs Rastrick turned in my direction, and for a split second our gazes met. Did she recognize me behind my black mantilla? Then, the waltz over, Mr Lilley swept me away, back into the shadows.

'When they're all sufficiently drunk, I'll give you the signal to come out,' he said. And abruptly he was gone. I trembled violently. So it was really about to happen. He was going to help me escape. The orchestra was playing quadrilles. The Pied Piper of Hamelin whirled up and down with Little Bo Peep, Jack Sprat flung his wife about, both of whom appeared to be men. Then a wild polka ensued. Sweaty madmen joined hands and swirled around in circles, gathering speed as the tempo of the music increased. They leapt about in a frantic jig, seeing who could kick the highest. One fool pulled my mantilla from my head as he passed me and ran off with it. I was exposed to view.

After this, the pianist played a sedate waltz. I glanced at the clock hanging over the entrance to the hall and saw it was nine-forty-five. Carriages had been due to arrive at nine. The doors of the hall had been thrown open to reveal the brightly lit hallway and the stewards with their orange armbands. The sight made me faint. Some of the more elderly guests were already departing. I felt a tap on my shoulder, and turned to see a man in a scarlet turban walking towards the exit. A moment later, I followed, heart racing. As I crossed the hall, the madness intensified to an insane pitch. I didn't dare raise my gaze. I felt completely exposed without the mantilla as I walked out into the bright light of the entrance hallway, expecting at any moment to be accosted by a steward. My Spanish maiden costume appeared tatty under the bright lights, and I was sure everyone would know instantly I was one of the patients. I found Mr Lilley in his red turban, talking to a woman wearing a cat mask over the top part of her face. He asked politely to be excused, and, as they parted, she miaowed at him, before turning and walking unsteadily back to the hall, a cat's tail poking out of her bustle and swaying with every step. My arm was seized, and Mr Lilley swept me away from the entrance and down a corridor. I covered my face with the fan. Something made me glance over my shoulder and to my horror I saw Dr Rastrick about ten paces away. In fright, I dropped my fan. Mr Lilley tugged at my arm, but I was frozen to the spot. Dr Rastrick began to turn his head in my direction, but at that moment Mrs Rastrick appeared. Her gaze met mine for an instant as she took Dr Rastrick's arm and guided him away.

Mr Lilley led me to a door, opening it with a key from his shirt pocket.

'Wait,' I said. 'Wait just a moment.'

'What's wrong?'

After four long months of incarceration, I had a sudden horror about what might be in store for me outside the asylum walls, and I became unsteady on my feet.

'Trust me, we're almost there,' he said, supporting me with his arm about my waist.

We entered another corridor, narrow and pitch dark, and when we reached the end of it, I heard him turn the key again. Suddenly, we were outside in steady drizzle. I felt the cold clean night air, and smelled odours of straw and horse dung. We walked over cobbles, past the ghostly shape of an unharnessed coach across the courtyard. A thump inside the stable made me jump. A horse whinnied. The arched coach entrance was ahead and beyond that a soft shimmering light in which splinters of rain were falling. We stepped under the arch. I took a deep breath as Mr Lilley peered around the corner to make sure the coast was clear. Then we stepped out, and my eyes were dazzled by a long row of coach lamps that followed the curve of the drive.

There was a creaking sound, and then feet landing on the gravel. The figure of a coachman appeared on the path. Mr Lilley took my arm and led me over the gravel, as the coachman opened the carriage door and unfolded the steps. Once I was inside the cabin, the carriage door slammed shut, sealing me in silence and darkness. Mr Lilley sat with his back to the horse and I sat opposite. I smelled liquor on him, mingling with his cologne. I picked up a folded blanket from the seat and put it over my legs. The carriage lurched and then fell into a steady rocking movement, the harness rattling and the horse's hooves scrunching on the gravel. Every moment, we moved further away from the asylum. I could scarcely breathe. I wondered if I would ever feel safe again. Outside, a grey ghostly wall appeared in the halo of the coach's lantern. The wall grew taller and more distinct, until it towered over the carriage and sturdy iron gates lay open on either side. A moment later the coach had left Hillwood Grange and was absorbed into a fathomless black void.

'It seemed a miracle we could just walk out like that,' I said.

'Locked doors aren't what keep people behind bars,' he answered.

The motion of the carriage changed; I was bumped about, thrown from side to side. We progressed in fits and starts, and then the carriage came to a grinding halt and I was almost thrown into Mr Lilley's lap. A moment later, I heard the coachman shouting, 'Move on there! Gid up!', and the dull thud of the whip on the horse's hide. The carriage jerked violently forward, but then it rolled back again. Minutes passed. Having got through the gates of the asylum, it would be unbearable if we were caught now. I could hear the driver outside. There was a grating sound and I thought he must be shovelling earth. The carriage door opened and cold air poured inside. The driver stood below, rain dripping from his hat. 'We've got a wheel stuck in a mud hole,' he says. 'I can't get the limbers to turn in this sludge. I'll try digging us out with the shovel. Weeks of rain, you see. It'll be better once we get through the turnpike – if we ever get that far. I've put a plank under the wheel. I'm just going to the front to pull the horse.' He slammed the door shut. A moment later, I heard him yell: 'All right, let's go. Heave, now!' The horse snorted and whinnied and the cabin ground and rattled as if it might shake itself free of the bolts that held it together. The carriage juddered forward, only to roll back again. The driver tried twice more. On the third attempt the coach lurched forward. We were back in motion.

'I'm at my wit's end,' I said.

'You're exhausted, poor thing,' said Mr Lilley. 'Take a sip of this and try to get some sleep.' I took the flask and had a good swig of his whisky. It was rough, but it soothed me, and the jogging motion of the carriage lulled me, until my eyes closed and I drifted off to sleep.

I opened my eyes and looked out the window into darkness. The ghostly white form of Lewes Crescent emerged out of the night. A row of lamps lined the seafront road, each with its own ghostly copper halo. Beyond, the sea and sky were one and the same, black and impenetrable. Mr Lilley sat opposite me, dozing, his flask in his hand. There were pale patches on his face where the brown greasepaint had rubbed off. His turban had been removed and his wild hair fell over his face. The carriage turned into Sussex Square and soon it shuddered to a halt on the cobbles at the entrance to the mews near Mr Lilley's rooms. He handed me down and dealt with the cabman. A crack of the whip, and the vehicle pulled away.

Mr Lilley took my arm and led me to the house. He thrust the door open and led me up the narrow staircase. There was a sour smell, deeply unwholesome, a mixture of cigarette smoke, condensation mould, decay and a pervasive putrid stink that seemed to come from the very fabric of the building. Strips of wallpaper hung from the wall under the dado rail. We entered his rooms, and I heard the hollow echo of our footsteps. His portmanteau was packed and waiting by the door. Mr Lilley lit a lamp as I wearily dropped onto the divan. The seat was cold and sticky to the touch. I was weary and hardly knew if I was awake or dreaming. The oil lamp revealed the dingy room in a cold and unforgiving light. What had seemed romantic before now looked jaded, threadbare, seedy. The empty cold hearth was shrouded in cobwebs, the floorboards riddled with woodworm. Out of the corner of my eye, something shot along the skirting board and disappeared into a hole.

On the table before me was an overfull ashtray, and a plate with a thin strip of fish skin on it, brown and curling, possibly a herring from a street stall that had been lying there for several days. Against the wall there was an unfamiliar piece of furniture, a work bench, on top of which was a wooden block with a round leather bag on top of it, and clutter all around, an eye-glass stand, a glass globe filled with water, rows of carving knives and burins of different sizes, bottles and piles of copper plates.

After a lot of splashing of water in the closet, Mr Lilley appeared, rubbing his hair, face and beard with a towel which looked none too clean. He went into his kitchen and came out with two glasses which he put on the table along with a bottle of absinthe. He sat in a chair opposite me, uncorking it.

'Let's celebrate,' he said.

'I shouldn't. Not tonight. I'm exhausted. Let's wait until we get to Paris. I've only now realized that I've nothing to wear tomorrow.'

'Never mind, some of Fanny's old clothes are still in the wardrobe. She's a tall broad-shouldered wench like you. Or she *was*, I should say. When we get to Paris, we'll have you measured for new dresses.'

I said nothing. The last thing I wanted was to put on one of Fanny's dresses. And the offhand way he described her made me shiver. He passed me a tumbler with a murky green liquid in it, like something from the bottom of a pond, but with a misleadingly wholesome aroma. I took a sip.

'You've never told me what Fanny was like,' I said.

'You and she couldn't be more different. She was languid, whereas you are nervy and fervent.'

'Forgive me, I'm on edge.'

'You're entitled to be after such an ordeal.' His voice was thick. He stood up, a little unsteadily, then got down on his knees before me. He put his arms around me and kissed me, his breath reeking of liquor. 'I like you this way,' he murmured into my ear, then kissed me again. I couldn't surrender to him, not the way I had in the asylum. He looked into my eyes, frowning. His eyelids drooped, and I wondered how drunk he was. But I tried to shake off my sudden antipathy towards him: he had done so much for me, taken a great risk. I told myself he was more apprehensive than he seemed, and was drinking to calm his nerves. He sat back in his chair, crossing his legs. I looked at him properly for the first time. He lit a cigarette, holding out the open packet towards me, but I refused. He gestured towards the workbench, his arm flailing.

'You've seen the engraving tools,' he said, blowing a wreath of smoke from his lips. 'This is what I'm reduced to: prostituting myself. Making reproductions of popular pictures I despise. I even copied one or two of my own works, thinking it might advance my reputation, but to no avail. So, you see what it is to be an artist in these times.'

'It's a great injustice. You're not as well established as you deserve to be.'

He swilled his glass, looking into it. 'Everyone in London abandoned me,' he said. 'Then the leading lights in the academy conspired to destroy me. It's three years since they accepted one of my paintings. They hung it over a door, where nobody would see it. Then, last year, virtually nobody called at my lodgings on Picture Sunday to see my treatment of Ulysses and the sirens. And this year the Hanging Committee rejected my mermaid out of hand.'

His morose mood disturbed me. Surely this was not the way he should be speaking when we were embarking on something new and wondrous?

'I was in London last month, Fitzroy Square,' he continued. 'I couldn't sell a watercolour even for ten shillings. I fear my work has become an anomaly. A note of originality is of no use unless it strikes a chord with the times.' He sighed. 'There are occasions, more frequent as time passes, when I feel I no longer have the strength to take up the mantle.'

'But don't you have friends in Paris who will help you?'

'Friends!' He laughed, ruefully. 'We shall see. But you're right. Once we get to Paris, I'll rally, never fear. I have to get out of here. If I stayed another week in this cheap preening backwater, I'd shrivel up and die. Do you still want to be an artist after hearing this?'

I felt a growing coldness towards him, and something else – a tinge of fear. I told myself this was because of all I'd suffered at Dr Rastrick's hands, and because I was shaken after the nerve-racking escape. Now, I found myself wondering about Mr Lilley. He made it sound as though he might not have any true friends in Paris at all. And yet he'd told me we were dependent on their support. To avoid meeting his gaze I looked around the room, where paintings were propped against the wall. From everywhere, Fanny's face stared out from the gloom.

'You still put Fanny in all your pictures, don't you?'

He sipped his absinthe. 'They're old pictures. I intend to sell them, but I'm not good at parting with things. After she left me,

I wanted to have a picture of her in every gallery and drawing room in the land, so she could never escape me. Strange to think, isn't it? But now I have you.'

'I'll be able to paint too, when we get to Paris, won't I?'

'Yes, why not?'

'I did some work in the asylum. Pictures of the women patients. It was a departure for me. I wish I could show them to you.' He sat there in silence, staring sullenly into space. 'You haven't lost faith in my talent, I hope?'

'Oh, you have talent. Of course you do. I'll never forget that picture of yours. The unicorn.'

'But I've never painted a unicorn.'

'Certainly, you have. Perhaps you're forgetting.'

'No, I'm absolutely sure. Could you possibly be thinking of one of Fanny's pictures?'

'Perhaps I am. Oh well, what does it matter?'

I was horrified at this dismissive attitude. Such a contrast with how he'd responded to my art before. And to confuse my pictures with Fanny's! Perhaps he had no memory of my work at all.

'We may need more funds at some point,' he mused. 'I wonder if it might be possible for you to write to your family in a few months. Didn't you say you were close to your father?'

I stared at him in disbelief. How could he think that would be a possibility in my circumstances?

'Never mind, for now,' he said. 'We'd better get some sleep. Long journey ahead and all that.'

He lumbered across the room and lay on his back on the bed, still wearing his Arabian Nights costume. A moment later, he began to snore.

35

I couldn't bring myself to follow Mr Lilley to bed, so I lay on the divan, still wearing the old lady's black dress. It was cold so I put Mr Lilley's coat over me. Frightful thoughts ran through my mind. I had strange half-dreams, at times believing myself back in my bed at Hillwood Grange. Once or twice during the night, Mr Lilley cried out in his sleep, bestial wails. What demons were tormenting him? His enquiry about my parents' finances disturbed me, not least because it suggested his own funds were limited. I began to doubt whether our plan to live in Paris was feasible. And I began to doubt Mr Lilley. He was not the man he seemed before. But he was my only hope.

When it was almost light, I succeeded in drifting off to sleep, but I was soon awakened by his feet on the floorboards. A door closed. I heard water splashing. When he reappeared, I pretended to be asleep at first, watching him dress himself in a clean shirt, cuffs and collar. He put on a sombre black waistcoat and a purple necktie. He looked handsome and dapper. Once dressed, he made tea and put a cup down for me on the occasional table. I sat up, and put the coat over my shoulders. The room was freezing. I sipped my tea, cradling the cup in my hands to warm them, while Mr Lilley took papers and documents out of drawers. He packed them in the open portmanteau. Then he went to the hearth, threw some logs into the grate and lit the fire, pumping a bellows to coax the kindling into flame.

'You must be cold,' he said, looking over his shoulder as he warmed his hands before the blaze. He said it kindly. 'Just stay exactly where you are and rest. I'll take care of everything. Do exactly as I say, and tomorrow morning we'll *déjeuner* on the Boulevard Saint-Germain. With luck, we'll meet some artists of my acquaintance and then . . . Well, we'll see.'

This was the Mr Lilley I'd known before. The one who'd encouraged me in my ambitions, and who risked his reputation to rescue me from Dr Rastrick. Yes, he had been morose the previous evening. He had every right to be. He had been unfairly overlooked as an artist. It was a travesty that someone of his talent should be reduced to making a living as a copper-plate engraver. If he was bitter at times, it wasn't surprising. In my exhaustion, I had reacted disproportionately to his sour mood. He had always treated me with respect. I reminded myself that it was I who had seduced him. Considering all he was doing for me, how could I not trust him?

He came and sat in the chair opposite me, gazing at me across the low table. 'I'm going to have to leave you alone here for a short while,' he said. 'I need to arrange for a cab to pick us up from Sussex Square at midday. If there's a knock on the door, ignore it.'

He took his hat from the stand, and was about to leave.

'Before you go, there's something I ought to tell you,' I said. 'Last night you asked if I might be able to get money from my family. That won't be possible. There's something you don't know. I've had no chance to explain.'

'I'm sure it can wait.'

'No, I'd rather tell you now.' My heart was beating rapidly. I took a deep breath. 'I'll be brief. Before I was confined to the asylum, my mother and I clashed. It was because I refused to marry Felix. I created a scene at a party in our house. I'll tell you all about it one day. The point is that Mama and I had a dreadful argument, and she chased me up the stairs. I was frightened. She was so hateful. And I wasn't myself that night. There was a struggle between us at the top of the stairs. And somehow, I don't really know how, but she tumbled down, and since then she hasn't been able to walk. She's crippled. Mama blames me for it. I'm sure she thinks I belong in the asylum and if she ever discovers my whereabouts, she'll tell Dr Rastrick. I'll be locked away forever. I thought you should know this before we leave for Paris. We should know all there is to know about each other.'

He gazed blankly ahead of him, an eyebrow raised, his mouth set in an expression of astonishment, or perhaps anger. After a long pause, he said: 'Well, my mysterious dark lady, what else have you kept from me?'

I rushed over and embraced him. We held each other tight.

'Nothing, I've kept nothing from you,' I cried, looking into his face. 'Everything will be all right, won't it?'

'Yes, of course it will,' he said, brushing a tear from my cheek with his thumb. 'You've been through a great deal, but it will all be different from now on.'

Then he was gone. I heard his footsteps on the stairs and a moment later the front door slammed. The silence of the room gathered about me, like a physical presence, unnerving me. I sat down, but got up again after a brief moment, restless and preoccupied, and paced about. My stomach was churning, but I had no appetite. I couldn't imagine ever being in Paris. It seemed wholly unreal. I could only think of the coming hours, the exhausting and frightening ordeal of travelling, official documents, a foreign city where danger might lurk around any corner. But most terrifying of all was the possibility of being apprehended at the last moment and sent back to Hellwood – and to Dr Rastrick.

I went to the large window and opened the curtains. The window pane hadn't been cleaned for months. Down below there were tangled overgrown shrubs and rampant nettles. Further back, I saw the drab rear elevations of the grand buildings in the square. I turned back to the room. My gaze fell on a curtain of a tired grey colour. I remembered it concealed the doorway to the stairs that led to Mr Lilley's attic studio. I recalled Mr Lilley coming down from there and putting a key in a drawer in the cabinet at the side of the room. He was always insistent that nobody should see his work in progress. But if he trusted me, if we were to elope to Paris together in sensational fashion, shouldn't I know everything about him? After all, he knew everything about me. I went to the cabinet. The drawer was unlocked. I fumbled about among his papers until I found the key. Then I ascended the staircase and stopped at the door at the top. I turned and looked down again and felt faint. I had reason to fear staircases. But I mastered myself and turned the key in the lock. The door was wedged shut and needed a good push to get it open. A stale masculine odour was released from the room.

I moved slowly into the queer half-light of the room and it seemed to close around me a little more with each step. I hardly dared turn to look about me, let alone turn my head to look back towards the door. I was sure there was a presence in the room. The air was so stale and cloying, I could barely breathe. The studio was a large high-ceilinged space, open to the rafters which were covered in a mesh of ancient cobweb. A shaft of murky light filtered through a large rooflight near the centre of the room, the glass splattered with gull droppings. The iron casement was closed, and several small flies circled wearily underneath it. The room was like a rag and bone yard, and I had to weave my way through broken chairs, ceremonial swords, strange naval instruments and other junk. The only clear space was in front of a large fireplace on one side. Behind the fender stood a black coal scuttle, a dustpan and brush and an ornate iron poker with a serpent wrapped around its handle. The hearthrug seethed with silverfish and its coloured threads had been all but devoured.

There was a stepladder in one corner, splashed with paint of every colour. In the centre of the room, directly underneath the rooflight, was a threadbare velvet drape hung from a square iron frame suspended from the rafters. I dared not draw this back, not yet. For the time being, I glanced about me at tall heaps of rolled-up discarded cloth, stained with different coloured paint. Books were propped against the wall in disorderly fashion, *The Apocrypha*, *The Talmud*, and others.

My gaze was drawn to paintings chaotically stacked against the wall in the shadows under the eaves. The reclining or sleeping damsels depicted on the canvas to the fore would have seemed decorous at another time, beautiful girls in gauzy clinging dresses, a breast revealed here, an outstretched arm there. But now I saw them as corpses. There was a bluish tint to their pale white skin. They lay about, silent, passive, immobile, helpless. Mr Lilley had attributed symbolic values to the women in gold lettering over their heads: Hope, Reason, Truth, Repose, Wisdom. I was reminded of Dr Rastrick's taxonomies of women's symptoms.

The longer I looked, the stronger the hypnotic effect, as if I was becoming entranced, falling under Mr Lilley's dark power, just as I had fallen under Dr Serrurier's. Was there a sinister explanation for the obsessive latticed patterns that recurred over and over in his pictures, the trellises, the barred shadows and stifling rooms in which the women were confined behind locked doors? All this beauty and decay seemed obsessive, a symptom of a monomaniac's *idée fixe*. Did the pictures hint at an obscure compulsion, a secret weakness, a morbid or immoral tendency? It wearied me to think of the obsessive hours of labour needed to apply layer upon layer of paint, disguising technique behind photographic verisimilitude. What private meanings did these pictures have for Mr Lilley? To me, on that morning, in that cramped and stifling room, his pictures all hinted at ensnarement.

Then I came upon a picture of Fanny Kerrich on her death-bed. So here, then, was the ghost that haunted the room. On the wall behind Fanny's bed the shadow of a man was just discernible. Was Mr Lilley haunting her even in death? Was he responsible for her demise in some mysterious way, as Miss Fanshaw had seemed to imply? Or was the shadow an actual shadow – because Mr Lilley had entered the room and was standing behind me at that very moment? I turned to look, but found I was alone. On the floor near the picture was a crumpled preliminary sketch, and I surmised that Mr Lilley must have cold-bloodedly sketched Fanny as she died. Had he been with her at the end? Could he have drawn her at the moment of her death? Or just after?

More images lay about on the floor. Photographs of nude female figures in artificial poses, the sort sold as artists' aids. The young women looked sedated, their expressions blank, and again I was reminded of the women in Dr Rastrick's photographs at the asylum. Among the photographs were sketches in pencil, charcoal, chalk, each executed hurriedly, wildly, many of them crumpled or torn. They seemed to depict writhing figures in frenzied unequal struggles, unspeakable ravishing.

So far, I had held back from discovering what lurked behind the worn black velvet drape that boxed off the centre of the room. Now, I approached. The curtain resisted me and I had to tug hard to make it jerk along the rail. Then I stepped through the gap and into the innermost recess of Mr Lilley's mind. What I saw was an oval picture on an easel. The picture depicted a woman reclining on her back, in a diaphanous white garment which closely moulded her form. She lay on a coffin-shaped stone slab and appeared from her pallor and her prone posture to be dead. Her body seemed to be tilted towards me and I imagined the corpse sliding towards me and out of the canvas. I stood at her feet, and saw her splayed soles were raw and soiled from her journey to meet her fate. Her white garment was grass-stained. Her hands were in her lap, and her knuckles bore similar scars and scratches to my own hands from working in the kitchen garden at Hellwood. She clutched a bouquet of violets, signifying modesty and faithfulness. Some of the petals were crushed and their pigment stained the white gown she was wearing. Around her neck was a slender silver necklace with a Celtic cross. Behind her was a hawthorn bush with virginal white flowers and behind that the sky, where dark threatening clouds were massing. There was no explicit clue as to how she had met her end, but the atmosphere and symbolism strongly suggested an execution or blood sacrifice. Then I looked more closely at her face and gasped. It was *my* face. It was *me*. Her eyes were open, staring unseeing out of the picture – staring at me. Her mouth was slightly open. It was then I noticed something on the grass nearby: a broken bow. Was this Mr Lilley's retort to my self-portrait of myself as an archer, the first of my pictures he'd seen? The garment I wore in his picture resembled the one in mine. But my wild black mane had been shorn, and the electrical aura around my head was gone.

I noticed that scattered over the floor were several portraits, preliminary sketches of my face. I was wearing the striped asylum uniform. With a start, I realized Mr Lilley must have made these drawings when he visited me in the asylum. He had drawn my head from several angles, including the one in the painting. A cold bead of sweat ran from my hairline and down my cheek. He must have had this picture in mind as he drew my likeness that day. My face must have been the last part of the painting he executed. The handling, the polished finish of the rest of the picture, could only have been attained by months of intense work. The result was a stultifying deadness, with something disturbing beneath.

I thought about Mr Lilley's deathbed portrait of Fanny Kerrich. Hadn't Miss Fanshaw said something about an obituary? Fanny had outdone Mr Lilley artistically. She had found a husband who supported her ambitions. But Mr Lilley had pursued her relentlessly and would never let her go, not even in death. Was it possible he had even taken her life? Or willed her to death perhaps? Or put a pillow over her face? Or fatally infected her with his own neurosis? Or even literally infected her with a disease he'd caught in the brothels of Paris?

After all, what did I really know about Mr Lilley? Perhaps he'd once been a revolutionary, but long ago he'd turned his back on the world, become a prisoner of his own technical mastery, doomed forever to correct and improve every last inch of the perfect surfaces of his canvases. Alone in his attic, unseen, he was ensnared by his own morbid repetitive obsessions. He reminded me of Dr Rastrick. Both men sought an obscure gratification from defining women, labelling us, controlling us. After all, a woman must know her place. If a man erred, he brought catastrophe on himself. But when women strayed from the virtuous path, the whole edifice of society was undermined. And there was always a gossip like Mrs Runniforde to spread one's disgrace far and wide.

What sort of man was Mr Lilley? What was his purpose in absconding with me? Was this a rescue or an abduction? Should I have ever trusted him? Was he disturbed, in the grip of a morbid obsession? I had feared for my own sanity, now I feared for his. Pressure had built in my eardrums to a deafening pitch, so that I didn't at first hear his footsteps pounding on the stairs.

'Violet!' he cried. His voice was urgent. 'Where in God's name are you?'

36

Reeling with fear, I gripped the easel. An artist's mahlstick that had been propped against it fell and clattered loudly on the floor. A moment of silence followed, then I heard feet pounding towards the attic. I stepped out from behind the black curtain and stood there, frozen to the spot. Mr Lilley appeared at the door, breathless. His hair was dishevelled and there was a sheen of sweat on his face.

'What the devil are you doing in here?' he bellowed.

I was scarcely able to speak. 'I'm sorry,' I stammered. 'I didn't think you'd mind – not when we're about to share everything.'

'Nobody enters my studio. Nobody at all.'

'Forgive me. I shouldn't have.'

'This is a vile betrayal.'

'But I thought after sharing my history with you . . . '

He looked at me, baffled.

'I mean what happened with my mother.'

'I should have handed you over to the police there and then.'

He looked around the room, then his gaze fixed on the open black curtain.

'Damn you!' he said, under his breath. 'Why did I leave a madwoman alone in my rooms?'

'Perhaps it's just as well I looked behind the curtain,' I cried. 'Your picture – why didn't you tell me you were painting me? And such a morbid subject. Why hide it from view like that? And the picture of Fanny—'

'Be quiet. Not another word. Did you think a strumpet like you could ever replace her? That you could ever be a match for Fanny? Never! I was with her at the end. I saw her draw her last breath. I never loved her more than in that moment. Now, come here and let's have no more of this.'

He stepped towards me, holding out his hand as you might to a naughty child. I took several steps backwards, then my heel struck something. I turned and saw the steel fender around the fireplace was blocking my way. The black poker with the ornate serpentine handle was propped against the marble surround. I turned to face him. I hardly recognized my own voice: 'Don't come any closer, I'm warning you.'

'That's enough. You're going back to the madhouse where you belong.' He stood there for a moment, glaring at me, his chest heaving. Then he lunged towards me. I reached behind me, seized the poker and swung it at him with all my might. My eyes were shut, but I felt the vibration in my forearm as the poker struck home. When I opened my eyes again, I saw him swaying, dazed, but still on his feet, his head lowered as he breathed heavily.

'I should have killed you when I had the chance,' he gasped. He made a gagging sound in his throat, and blood spurted out of a nostril and over his black suit jacket, streaking it with crimson. Then, he lurched forward and spat out a great purple clot which splattered over the floor. He looked down at it for a moment with a puzzled expression, then dropped heavily onto his knees, and finally fell onto his front. He lay there, his head turned to one side at an unnatural angle, an arm twisted under his torso. Blood and spit bubbled out of his lips and a crimson puddle began to form around his head. I turned away, and put the poker where I had found it. After this, I was frozen to the spot, staring into the grate, incapable of rational thought. Eventually, I turned and knelt beside Mr Lilley. Taking hold of his wrist, I felt for his pulse in the way Dr Rastrick had done to me so many times. I shuddered to find his skin already cold. No life throbbed under my fingertips. Overwhelmed by nausea, I got up, my hand over my mouth, and fled the room, shutting the door behind me. I rushed downstairs and into the closet where I retched violently. When I had recovered, I looked at myself in Mr Lilley's mirror. A face frowned back at me with an expression of pure derangement. The skin was mottled and weathered, but sickly pale, the brow furrowed with a deep groove between the eyes. I shut my eyes, and breathed slowly and deeply for several moments.

I dropped down on the divan, trembling and light-headed, trying to think. Here, then, was the final proof of my psychosis. I had killed a man. Dr Rastrick could not have engineered things better had he planned the whole thing for himself. All that was left was to gather the strength to go to the constabulary and make my confession.

Who was I, when all was said and done? Who was Violet Pring? An idealist deluded by her own romantic dreams? A vain woman who longed to be gazed upon and admired? A muse to inspire men to greatness? A labile creature prone to violence and sensual abandon? A murderess? An artist? Or perhaps all of these things.

All my life I had been trained to have only publicly acceptable thoughts and perform publicly acceptable deeds. When I erred, I hid any memory of it deep in the darkest recesses of my mind. How, otherwise, would I have been able to present an acceptable front to polite society? But then Dr Serrurier's hypnotism opened the cage and my devil came out roaring. Should I now accept my culpability, my dreadful guilt? I raged against the prospect. Wasn't Dr Rastrick a murderer too? Hadn't his darlings died because of him, in the service of his ambition? It was unthinkable that I should go back to the asylum now. I must go forward, I must go on. I wasn't like Mr Lilley, incapable of choosing the direction to take with his art. I would embrace change, whatever the challenge. I was free, now, of all the constraints that my family had placed on me – this was my chance to break free altogether. A man could spend a day working on a square of canvas the size of a tuppence piece and take years to finish a painting. For a woman that was impossible, unless she happened to be an heiress. But I could do this. I could make my life anew. And make my money somehow.

A thought struck me, and I felt a jolt of hope. Nobody but Mrs Rastrick had seen me escape from the ball with Mr Lilley. I was certain I could trust her. And nobody would have recognized Mr Lilley on that night, not in his disguise. I noticed his portmanteau over by the door, and searched its compartments. There was his toothbrush, nail polishers, cologne, cigarette holders, pocket handkerchiefs, starched collars, silk socks, gloves, shirts and waistcoats, a frock coat. Everything he needed to present a good appearance.

The will to survive is the keenest force in nature. It shocked me into life again as if electricity coursed through my veins.

When Mr Lilley was discovered in his attic, there would be nothing to connect his demise to me. He might easily have fallen heavily while inebriated. Or he might have come home to find an intruder in the house and then been fatally attacked. I went to the window and closed the curtains. I took off the black moth-eaten dress and threw it down, then removed my petticoats, vest and stockings. Then I took a scarf from a shelf in the wardrobe and bound it tightly around my chest until my bosom was flattened. I found Mr Lilley's freshly laundered full-length flannel drawers and a vest with long sleeves and put them on. I chose a simple white shirt and buttoned it up, attaching the collar and cuffs. I decided on a blue tartan waistcoat and a black lounge suit. The jacket was a little roomy around the shoulders, but otherwise fitted me well. The trousers were quite loose around the waist, but the braces held them up. I put on a pair of Mr Lilley's shoes. My feet didn't fill them, so I put on two pairs of socks. I opened the wardrobe door so I could look at myself in the full-length mirror. It wouldn't quite do, not yet. I found some nail scissors and, looking at myself in the mirror on the inside of the wardrobe door, I carefully snipped at my hair until it was collar-length. Then I swept up the hair from the floor with a dustpan and brush and threw it on the fire that Mr Lilley had lit earlier that morning. It was still smouldering. I put more kindling on the hearth and an extra log, then threw my discarded black dress, vest and drawers onto the flames. Finally, I threw my underskirts onto the hissing logs and watched the fire consume them. There were plumes of black smoke, and the room filled with an acrid smell.

Next, I went back to the wardrobe and took a Derby-style hat from a shelf and put it on. I opened the curtains to let in more light and better see how I appeared, and paced up and down before the wardrobe mirror. The freedom of movement afforded by a pair of trousers was revelatory. I adjusted my carriage, adopting what I hoped was a convincing masculine posture and bearing. Chin up. Shoulders back. Practice would make perfect. It occurred to me it was fortunate I had a low voice. I began to believe that if I lost myself in my performance, I could become Mr Wilfred Lilley, at least for as long as required, the time it took to get to France. The less I thought about it, the better. Now I'd become a man, I would act decisively and leave someone else to clear up the mess.

I looked through the compartment in the portmanteau where Mr Lilley had put his documents. There was his bank-book, a copy of a letter of credit to a bank with a Paris address which conveniently included a sample of his signature, a wallet with forty pounds in bank notes and two or three pounds in change. And, of course, there were two tickets for the ferry from Newhaven to Dieppe.

By that point my euphoric mood was subsiding. Was I really prepared to never again see Papa, Mama or my brothers? It wasn't that I owed my family a debt of gratitude. My well-meaning but irresponsible papa, my cold scheming mama – both in their different ways were to blame for my having been locked away. But how would they feel when I disappeared out of their lives altogether? Mama would be tormented by remorse, or perhaps not. Papa might suffer qualms – ironic given his life had been dedicated to ducking every difficulty and responsibility. As for my brothers, they would soon get used to the idea. I thought of all those paintings of genteel, well-regulated families, where everyone observed the proprieties of family life. In my family portrait there would be an empty space where I had once stood. The thought moved me to tears.

As my confidence ebbed, I grew fearful. Would I be able to hold my nerve when the moment came to present my travel documents? Would I panic when I stepped into a Parisian bank a day later to withdraw a sum of money sufficient to survive for the first few perilous weeks? What life would be open to me in the months and years to come? Would I find myself sitting to artists in draughty studios, and earning a few extra centimes for cleaning their brushes or perhaps by providing more demeaning services? Would I one day write an account of a young woman who escaped one night from a lunatic asylum in England and was never seen again? It was all too frightening to contemplate. But then I remembered Dr Rastrick, and recovered my resolve. If I stayed in England, I would be his prisoner for life. Either that, or they would hang me. And it would give me some satisfaction to know I had finally outwitted him.

The cab was almost due. My heart hammering, I picked up Mr Lilley's coat from the divan and put it on. I saw his scarf lay underneath it, so I wrapped it around my neck, up to my chin and ears. Just before I left, I dabbed a spot of his distinctive cologne under each ear. Then I picked up the portmanteau, and went down the narrow stairs to the front door. Without a backwards glance, I stepped out into a bright cold morning, and heard the door slam behind me. I walked through the mews and a moment later Lewes Crescent opened out giddily around me. Ahead was the severe line of the horizon, dividing white sky from gunmetal grey water. All that separated me from France was that narrow channel. To the east, where my cab was bound, the sun throbbed, its blinding white light diffusing into writing cloud that seemed soiled as the discharge of a factory chimney. I saw where the cab was waiting and walked stiffly towards it, almost out of my mind with terror. As I drew near, I heard a gruff call: 'Cab for Newhaven, mister?' I didn't respond, thinking the cab was for a gentleman rather than for me. 'Cab for Mr Lilley?' the driver cried.

I nodded and climbed in, pulling down the blind. A moment later, the cab shuddered forward, carrying me towards an unknown future.

Historical Note

Wilfred Lilley is correct to say that Violet Pring's painting of a reversed mermaid was something new in all of European art; it anticipates René Magritte's surrealist painting *The Collective Invention* by almost half a century. Violet's work also shares characteristics with that of her contemporary asylum patient, Richard Dadd, whose pictures featured doppelgangers, paradoxes and irresolvable contradictions. Her compositions further resemble the work of twentieth-century surrealist artist Leonora Carrington, who also wrote an account of her time in an asylum.

When it comes to diagnosing Violet's illness, various split personality and dissociation theories have been advanced since her time. But perhaps we should apply the view of Dutch psychiatrist Dr G. Kraus on the madness of Vincent van Gogh. He rejected various hypotheses and concluded that Van Gogh 'was an individual in his illness, as well as in his art'. Maybe we can say the same of Violet.

Acknowledgements

The road to publication for this novel took in a pandemic, a complicated house move and various other challenges along the way. I would like to thank all the talented people at HarperCollins HQ who made the journey possible. It proved more difficult to voice a female character than I first anticipated, and I relied on two editors, Kate Mills and Rebecca Jamieson, to steer me in the right direction. On the home front my wife Sally and daughter Georgia also offered valuable insights – and my son Declan gave moral support. Thanks also to my agent David Headley, for setting the wheels in motion.

Captivated by *The Darlings of the Asylum*?

Read *Wrecker*, Noel O'Reilly's powerful debut exploring the dark side of Cornwall – the wrecking and drowned sailors – where poverty drove villagers to dark deeds . . .

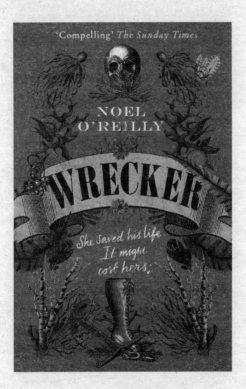

Available now.

ONE PLACE. MANY STORIES

Bold, innovative and
empowering publishing.

FOLLOW US ON:

@HQStories